Color

CHINESE LITERATURE TODAY BOOK SERIES

COLORATURA

Li Er

Translated by Jeremy Tiang

UNIVERSITY OF OKLAHOMA PRESS : NORMAN

This book is published with the generous assistance of
China's National Office for Teaching Chinese as a Foreign Language,
Beijing Normal University's College of Chinese Language and Literature,
the University of Oklahoma's College of Arts and Sciences,
and *World Literature Today* magazine.

Library of Congress Cataloging-in-Publication Data
Names: Li, Er, 1966– author. | Tiang, Jeremy, translator.
Title: Coloratura / Li Er ; translated by Jeremy Tiang.
Other titles: Hua qiang. English
Description: Norman : University of Oklahoma Press, [2019] | Series: Chinese
    literature today book series ; volume 8
Identifiers: LCCN 2018033190 | ISBN 978-0-8061-4423-8 (pbk. : alk. paper)
Classification: LCC PL2946.E72 H8313 2019 | DDC 895.13/52—dc 23
LC record available at https://lccn.loc.gov/2018033190

Coloratura is Volume 8 in the Chinese Literature Today Book Series.

Translator's Note

Coloratura doesn't so much have a narrator as a compiler—one so eager to keep herself out of the limelight that we never find out her name, only that she is the daughter of a character named "Broad Bean," whom we only ever meet as a child. It seems fitting to have an anonymous figure as our guide through a novel whose central question—who was Ge Ren, and what was his fate?—is never fully answered, and perhaps never could be. No human being is fully knowable, and all we ever see of each other is glimpses of the truth.

For the most part, the story unfolds by means of collage: the compiler assembles information and places it in front of us, leaving us to draw our own conclusions. Three narrators give their accounts of what happened in the months and years leading up to Ge Ren's death, one in the immediate aftermath (in 1943) and the other two at a remove in time (in 1970 and 2000). Interspersed with these strands are other voices—quotes from people and books, some real and some fictitious. Their accounts don't always agree with each other, yet no one is lying to us. These are just the stories they have told themselves about the world.

Exacerbating the confusion, these events take place during a particularly chaotic period in China's history. Following the end of dynastic rule in 1911 and the May Fourth Movement of 1919, the country's destiny was very much up for grabs, with the Communists and Nationalists fighting for control. Ge Ren was swept up in this sense of revolution and possibility, taking part in the Long March of 1934–35 that helped bring Mao to power, though unlike most of the other characters, he wouldn't live long enough to witness the outcome, let alone to grow cynical about it.

While the events of this novel re-examine China's revolutionary history, the epic mode is not the only one in which Li Er is capable of working; his great strength is versatility. In contrast to the historically and geographically sweeping *Coloratura*, for instance, Li's 2004 novel *Cherries on the Pomegranate Tree* takes a much smaller canvas. Here he paints the political scene in a tiny village, as the hapless village head fights to win re-election despite the many comic mishaps standing in her way. The difference in scale aside, the ambitions of *Cherries on the Pomegranate Tree* are just as vast, as it takes on issues such as China's one-child policy. Through his varied body of work, Li maintains one constant: a bone-dry sense of humor and quirky sensibility that never fails to surprise. An example: one of his short stories is narrated by a fetus.

This ability to shift between different perspectives is one of the joys of Li Er's writing. In *Coloratura*, we see through many pairs of eyes as we accumulate facts and opinions, but ultimately we end up not much wiser as to what actually happened. As the compiler reminds us, "'Truth' is the core of the onion. You peel away layer after layer, only to discover nothing at all."

List of Characters

Names in regular type are fictional characters; those in boldface are real people.

Ah Qing — see Zhao Yaoqing

Bai Ling — granddaughter of Bai Shengtao

Bai Shengtao — a doctor in the Communist Army; a scatologist; narrator of the first section

Reverend Samuel Beal — a missionary in China; coauthor of *The Mystery of the Orient*

Bingying — see Hu Bingying

Broad Bean — daughter of Bingying and Zong Bu

Cai Tingkai (1892–1968) — **first a Kuomintang general, later a Communist general**

Cai Yuanpei (1868–1940) — **president of Peking University; Esperantist**

Chen Duxiu (1879–1942) — **cofounded the Chinese Communist Party with Li Dazhao in 1921**

Dabao — a bandit; real name Guo Baoquan

Dai Li (1897–1946) — **chief of the Kuomintang Secret Service; husband of Butterfly Wu**

Ding Kui — aide to Fan Jihuai

Ding Ling (1904–1986) — **a Chinese writer**

Dou Niancheng — Ge Cundao's killer

Dou Sizhong — Tian Han's subordinate; antique shop owner

Reverend Ellis — coauthor of *The Mystery of the Orient* with Reverend Beal

Fan Jihuai — a lieutenant-general in the Communist Army; later a noted legal scholar; narrator of the third section

Jacques Ferrand   a French journalist

"Fresh Flower Tune"   Yang Fengliang's mistress

Ge Cundao   father of Ge Ren

Ge Ren (1899–1943)   poet, scholar, translator, revolutionary

Ge Zhengxin   nephew of Ge Ren, the son of his twin sister

Guo Ping   grandson of Guo Baoquan (Dabao); secretary-general of Baibei municipal government

Claire Hollingsworth (1911–2017)   **British journalist; author of** *Mao and the Men against Him* **(London: Jonathan Cape, 1984)**

Hu An   father of Hu Bingying

Hu Bingying   well-known actress in the 1930s and '40s; wife of Ge Ren

Hu Shih (1891–1962)   **a scholar; later a Taiwanese diplomat to the United States**

Hu Zikun   paternal grandfather of Hu Bingying

Hu Zongnan (1896–1962)   **general in the Nationalist Army**

Huang Jishi   cofounder of the *Shanghai Harbor Daily*

Huang Yan   a fellow passenger on Ge Ren's passage to Japan; later an émigré to America and the author of *Dreaming Back a Hundred Years*

Kang Youwei (1858–1927)   **a Nationalist who wanted a constitutional monarchy**

Kawai   Japanese; brother of Kawata and Noriko; a businessman

Kawata   Japanese; Ge Ren's tutor at the Beijing Medical Academy

Kong Fantai   Ge Ren's cellmate; a descendant of Confucius

Li Dazhao (1888–1927)   **cofounded the Chinese Communist Party with Chen Duxiu in 1921**

Li Youyuan (1903–1955)   **composer of "The East Is Red"**

Lin Huiyin (1904–1955)	also known as Phyllis Lin; an architect and writer who designed the National Emblem of the People's Republic of China; aunt of Maya Lin
Lin Xinyi	Ge Cundao's lover
Little Red Woman	actual name Hong Yan; Peking opera performer, and Bai Shengtao's companion on the train to Hankou
Little Woman Red	granddaughter of Little Red Woman; also a Peking opera performer
Liu Faqing	grandson of Liu Shaoqi; a monk
Liu Shaoqi (1898–1969)	an influential Communist, later purged
Mei Su	a famous opera performer; a friend of Bingying
Meng Dequan	father-in-law of Bai Shengtao
Noriko	Japanese; sister of Kawai and Kawata
Qiu Aihua	adoptive son of Fan Jiuhuai
John Leighton Stuart (1876–1962)	a missionary; later U.S. ambassador to China
Su Xiaoxiao	a fifth-century courtesan (died in 501 at the age of nineteen)
Tan Sitong (1865–1898)	one of the "Six Gentlemen Martyrs" of the Hundred Days' Reform
Tang Enbo (1898–1954)	a Kuomintang general
Anthony Thwaite	the British author of *Beauty in a Time of Chaos*
Tian Han	raised in the same orphanage as Ge Ren; later an officer in the Communist Army, deputy chief of the Border Anti-Traitor Division
Wang Shiwei (1906–1947)	a Chinese journalist/writer, executed by Mao
Butterfly Wu/Hu Die (1908–1989)	a famous Chinese actress in the 1920s and '30s

Wu Yishi	Bai Shengtao's driver on the way to Baibei
Xu Yusheng	editor of *Scattered Scriptures* and a friend of Ge Cundao
Xu Xilin (1873–1907)	**a revolutionary; executed by firing squad**
Xu Zhimo (1897–1931)	**a poet; romantically involved with Lin Huiyin at one point**
Yang Fengliang	a Communist general; Ge Ren's jailer at Bare Mountain
Yang Min/Minghui	grandson of Yang Fengliang; later a monk
Yin Jifu	an editor; drowns himself during Ge Ren's passage to Japan
Yu Fenggao	head of the investigation team at Zhao Yaoqing's detention camp
Yu Liren	son of Yu Fenggao; founder of the Huawei Consumer Alliance, a Ponzi scheme involving Alaskan seal oil
Zhang Xiruo (1889–1973)	**a Chinese politician who took part in the 1911 Revolution**
Zhang Zhankun	head of surgery at Yan'an
Zhao Yaoqing (Ah Qing)	a revolutionary, later detained; a friend of Ge Ren and Bingying; narrator of the second section
Zhao Zhongxiang (b. 1942)	**a TV presenter of *Animal World*, among other programs**
Zhu Xudong	ghostwriter of Tian Han's autobiography
Zong Bu	cofounder of the *Shanghai Harbor Daily*; author of *Half a Lifetime*; Bingying's lover, and the father of her child
Zou Rong (1885–1905)	**a Nationalist revolutionary; died in prison**

Coloratura

Foreword

I realized yesterday, to my shock, that this book has accompanied me for a full decade now. Still, if my efforts lead to a greater understanding of Ge Ren's story, then I would have no regrets about those ten years.

This book was not a solo effort, but rather was pieced together with the words of many other people. First of all, I have to thank Dr. Bai Shengtao, the convict Zhao Yaoqing, and the noted legal scholar Fan Jihuai, who bore witness to Ge Ren's life and participated in the creation of history, and narrated it here. The reader will soon see that the stories they tell have all the power of the best detective fiction. Their accounts constitute the main part of this book. I am also grateful to Miss Bingying, Mr. Zong Bu, Mr. Huang Yan, and Mr. Kong Fantai, as well as our overseas friends Mr. Anthony Thwaite, Reverend Ellis, Reverend Beal, M. Ferrand, and Mr. Kawai. In the supplementary portions of this work, their written and spoken words contextualize and explain the main narratives. Where necessary, I have added interpolations in square brackets to clarify and provide additional information.

You may read this book in any order you choose: as printed; starting with the second or the third section; or by following only the main narratives and leaving the supplementary portions till later. You could even alternate reading the third section with parts of the first. In order to help you distinguish them, the main parts of the narrative are in this font, and supplementary material in this one. The sections are not numbered, to remind you that you may use your own understanding of the story to reorder the book. I do this not to be unnecessarily mysterious, but because Ge Ren's story does indeed play out in this way.

Some say that Ge Ren's life and death is every one of our lives and deaths. Others believe that Ge Ren had a tail—a peculiarity that both enhanced and damaged his reputation—and that if you were not careful, he would hit your nerve endings with it. Yesterday morning, I turned on my computer and saw an email from a friend insisting that Ge Ren was a magic carpet who could send you soaring up above the clouds, but also plummeting into the abyss. As for whether these viewpoints are right or wrong, perhaps the reader will be able to decide after reading.

The last thing I have to say is that, although I am Ge Ren's last surviving relative, the quotations in this book remain the opinions of their respective authors, and I have selected them impartially. I urge you all to remember that time has passed between these events and their telling, and the narrators themselves have inevitably changed during this interval. Such differences might account for some of the misguided viewpoints. I trust readers to approach these mistakes in the right spirit, and so have not made too many amendments. All I have done is gather these words, correcting obvious errors and filling in omissions. Naturally, as Ge Ren was a family member, and I love him more with each passing day, it has been hard for me to maintain neutrality and detachment during the ten years I spent on this book. While editing, I often found it impossible not to laugh out loud, or burst out sobbing, or shiver in silence . . .

PART ONE

To Tell the Truth

Time: March 1943
Place: En route from Baibei to Hong Kong
Speaker: Dr. Bai Shengtao
Listener: Lieutenant-General Fan Jihuai
Transcriber: Fan Jihuai's aide, Ding Kui

News

General, to tell the truth, it was Tian Han who brought me the news. I was still in Back Ditch then. In your line of work, of course you've heard of Back Ditch at Date Garden. Right, there was a northwestern public school there, and a detention center. I was in the detention center, naturally. Coming up on two months there. That night, when Tian Han came to see me in Back Ditch, I thought for sure he was coming to send off a hometown fellow. It was the end of the road for me. Really, after studying medicine and being on the battlefield, I had seen my share of corpses. I shouldn't have been scared. Yet as soon as I saw him and smelled the reek of alcohol coming off his body, my gallbladder shrank, like I'd plunged into ice. But the news he brought was unexpected.

He led me out. I saw his bodyguards in the courtyard a dozen paces away, hunched over like moving shrubs. There were also sentries and guard patrols, all holding those red-tasseled spears, though the tassels looked black [in the dark]. At that moment the north wind rose, and snow began to fall. A bodyguard walked over and gave Tian Han a twill shirt, like something a hospital patient might wear, but softer than you'd get off a country loom. Only the top brass and those scholars who'd just arrived in Yan'an wore stuff like that. I won't lie to you: when Tian Han draped it over my shoulders, my tears started flowing, and snot followed. Tian Han looked at me as if he wanted to say something, but he kept quiet. My brain was all jumbled up. After we'd been standing outside a while, he said, It's cold here, let's go back to Back Ditch. Instead of leading me back to the detention center, he took me to a nice, warm cave house. I took in the pictures of Lenin and the classroom charts on the wall, and realized we were in one of the offices of the northwestern public school. He took off his shoes, pulled out the insoles, and held them over the brazier with tongs. A guard came in and tried to take them from him, but he waved the guy away—told him to stand outside and not let anyone in. Soon the cave was stinking from his roasting shoes, and with the smoke from the coal fire, my eyes could barely stay open. You'll laugh at me, but the smell actually seemed pleasant at the time. Intimate. He undid his pants and tossed a flea into the flames. I heard it go pop. He caught a few more after that, but those he didn't burn; he squashed them with his fingernail.

The alcohol fumes coming off him were intoxicating. He rooted around in his clothes a bit and produced a wine gourd. He handed it to me, and then he pulled out two cups, which he quickly wiped clean with his thumb. He poured himself a drink, then one for me too. "Drink up. What? Do I need to serve you?" This was the first time in two months that someone had offered me a drink. Tears filled my eyes. When he rummaged around in his shirt and came up with a couple of pig trotters, I had to bite my lip to stop drooling. Tian Han asked how my drink was, and I said, Fine, it's great. And that's when I got the news. I had just taken my first bite of trotter when he said, "There's something I need to tell you: Ge Ren's still alive." I was so startled I jumped to my feet, as if the flames had scorched my ass.

To tell the truth, I could hardly believe my ears. Last winter, in Year 31 of the Republic [i.e., 1942], I got back to Yan'an from the front line, and Tian Han tearfully told me that Ge Ren was dead. His eyes and nose were streaming as he said how, in the summer of 31, Ge Ren had led a unit on a mission one evening to a place called Two Li Mound, and out of nowhere they had encountered some Japanese soldiers. Two Li Mound has a Guan Yu temple, and Ge Ren's troops fought the enemy all around the temple for hours, before finally sacrificing themselves for the nation, becoming heroes of the People. He mentioned that some people were privately comparing Ge Ren to Guan Yu himself, and the local populace was calling for a tablet to be raised to him in the temple. When Tian Han told me this, I wept and didn't know what to say. For the next long while, I dreamed of Ge Ren every night, and each time I'd wake up sobbing. Who'd have thought, after all that, that Ge Ren would still be alive?

Having made his announcement, Tian Han slapped his thigh hard and yelled, "Fuck a donkey, I'm so glad, so glad. Comrade Ge Ren survived the worst—he's sure to be rewarded. So many sleepless nights I've had." Then he immediately warned me not to tell a soul. It'd be disastrous if word got out; the Japanese and the Nationalist rebels would surely bring forward their attack, and if that happened, Comrade Ge Ren's life wouldn't be worth very much.

There you go, sir, you know what's what. You're right: Tian Han had something else on his mind, and that's why he braved the snow to come see me. I'd thought of that too, but he wasn't bringing it up, and I didn't dare broach it. As I gnawed the last bit of flesh off one trotter, he finally said he was ordering me to go on a trip south, to bring Ge Ren back. Hang on, let me think what he actually said. Ah, that's right: "Comrade Ge Ren's had a hard time down south. He was feeble enough to start with, and his lungs are bad. This will have been hard on him. Go fetch him back, and let him rest up a few days in Yan'an. You're a doctor, you're the best person for the job. What do you think? If you do this for me, I will talk to the leadership afterward about fixing your problem. Even if you aren't ashamed to be labeled a Trotskyite, I'm ashamed for you. Who asked us to be from the same village? But let's be upfront about this. If you mess this up, don't blame me for punishing you, like when Zhuge Liang tearfully beheaded Ma Su in *Romance of the Three Kingdoms*."

He kept things vague. Only said south, no mention of Bare Mountain, and even less of Baibei Town. I answered, Well, I'm just a lowly scholar, and I've already made a grave error going down the wrong path. I don't know if I can do this. He said, It doesn't matter if a cat is black or white, as long as it catches mice. So I wish you all the best on your mission. I asked if the leadership had already made up their minds. His face sank, and he held up the red-hot tongs. "You, oh you, you're like a dog that won't stop eating its own shit. I need you to remember something: If it's not your question to ask, then keep your mouth shut, and definitely don't go writing about it in your diary. If you didn't say anything, no one would take you for a mute. And if you don't write in your diary, no one will think you're illiterate." I jumped to my feet and said, I tramped across the county to get to Yan'an because I wanted to make a sacrifice for the Revolution. Now that my chance has come, I'll bleed or get beheaded if I have to, but I won't lose sight of the lesson you've taught me.

Tian Han's orders were for me to stay in Back Ditch that night. He even told the guard to let me have a cave to myself. I didn't sleep a wink, and kept getting up to pee. Each time that I shook myself off, I would bow to the bust of Lenin. Because of the snow, both heaven and earth were the sort of gray that made it look like sunrise was imminent. The rooster must have been bewitched by the snow, because it kept crowing in the middle of the night. On every crow, I scrambled out of bed and stood there, involuntarily lifting my leg. After a few times, my right leg started twitching, and I began to worry that the inflamed veins in my right calf would get worse, which would force me to delay my departure. Since entering the detention center, I had gotten kicked quite a few times on that spot, and it was very sensitive.

People need to say how they feel—that's a kind of happiness. Yes, when I thought about how Ge Ren and I would be able to pour our hearts out to each other, I felt this would be a good trip. When Ge Ren laid eyes on me, he was sure to turn bright red. He was a bashful fellow, and would blush at the slightest kindness. You're right, sir, that's not in keeping with his status as a revolutionary. Once he found out I had traveled thousands of miles to fetch him, I would be staggered if he didn't flush red. That's what I was thinking as I drifted off to sleep, while the rooster crowed on. No sooner had I dozed off than there was an enormous crash, and someone started shouting, Alert! Alert! while others wept and cursed. I thought the enemy must have arrived, so I picked up a large stone, thinking I could at least make a last stand. Then I listened more closely to the screaming, and realized that one of the caves that made up the detention center had collapsed, crushing several prisoners. Good question, General Fan. How could a cave collapse just like that? Could it be that these convicts had been so bold as to dig an escape tunnel? If even I could think of that, then naturally the Back Ditch interrogation team would too. My scalp went a little numb, and I imagined seeing the bullets enter right between their eyebrows.

I was lost in thought when a figure darted in, grabbed my arm, and dragged me out. I said, "How can I help you, comrade?" He told me to shut up and follow him. In the courtyard, there was enough blurry light reflected off the snow for me to see that he was one of Tian Han's bodyguards. The little bastard was chatty; he told me that his boss had sent him to see if I was injured. After a while, we got to a livestock pen, and there was Tian Han. His hands were tucked into the sleeves of his sheepskin coat, and a cigarette dangled from his mouth. He told me to leave Yan'an at once. I was to rush to Zhangjiakou with all possible speed, where I would meet Dou Sizhong, and only then would I travel south to fetch Ge Ren. No, sir, he still hadn't mentioned Baibei. As for my actual task, he said that Dou Sizhong would explain in person. And who was Dou Sizhong? One of Tian Han's subordinates. They'd been through thick and thin together, and Dou was fiercely loyal. More about him later. When he [Tian Han] mentioned Zhangjiakou, I immediately thought of my father-in-law. That's where he lived. I worried I'd get him into some kind of trouble, through association with me. But Tian Han's so clever, you see, nothing escapes him. He could tell from my momentary hesitation what was troubling me. "This has nothing to do with your wife's old man. It's all about Comrade Ge Ren. Comrade Dou Sizhong will tell you where to find him." I asked if Bingying was still with Ge Ren, and if I should bring her back too. Tian Han frowned and said, Just carry out your mission, and don't ask any more questions. It was cold, so I asked if I could go get some extra clothes. He tugged me back. "It's all prepared for you, even your underpants. The letter for Dou Sizhong is sewn into those underpants." And he gave me special instructions not to mention Ge Ren's name along the way. "Remember this: his code name is Zero, meaning he's round and full. I hope you fulfill your mission roundly and fully." He pointed into a gully. Down below, I could just make out a donkey and a man at the bottom.

Tian Han left. Feeling momentarily dazed, I stood in the snow for a while. The blizzard grew heavier. I waited for Tian Han's figure to vanish completely in the direction of the mound before I set off into the gully. Wind swept off the bald mound, slicing against my face like knives. But when I thought about how I would soon be with Ge Ren, none of that mattered anymore. The fence around the livestock enclosure rattled violently, and would later be wrenched up entirely by the wind. Some birds were startled into the air—I don't know if they were crows or magpies. Magpies have a grudge against me, because I once treated a constipation case with stewed magpie. What is it they say, two for joy? They're supposed to welcome guests, but here they were, jabbering and trying to drive me away. General, at the time, I could not have expected that I'd never return, like a melon taken off its vine. What? When was this? Uh, I truly can't recall. After two months locked up in Back Ditch, my brain wasn't working very well.

Common Knowledge about the Battle of Two Li Mound

According to *World War Two: China*, on May 1, 1942, the commander-in-chief of the Northern China Area Army, General Yasuji Okamura, led three brigades and two divisions, fifty thousand troops in eight hundred motorcars, tanks, and airplanes, utilizing the military tactics of "crisscrossing nets," "clearing across diagonals," and "repeated joint attacks," plus the strategy of "three alls." Thus began a two-month-long sweep of the Jizhong Plain anti-Japanese forces, as the general attempted to encircle and wipe out the Eighth Route Army, which was, in Okamura's own words, "as slippery as an eel, impossible to lay hands on." From May 16 to June 20, the Japanese Army carried out a sweep within the triangle bounded by Hutuo River to the south, Deshi Road to the north, and the Fuyang River to the west. That's when the Battle of Two Li Mound took place. Later on, the Japanese publication *A History of the Great East Asian War* would call this "a typical skirmish in the May 'mopping up' campaign."

The Battle of Two Li Mound was first mentioned on October 11, 1942, in a *Border War Report* essay titled "A River of Iron behind Enemy Lines." The author was Huang Yan, who back in the day set sail on the same ship to Japan for his studies as Ge Ren and the third narrator of this book, Fan Jihuai. In the third paragraph of "A River of Iron behind Enemy Lines," Fan Jihuai writes:

> Many fine young Chinese men and women were nobly sacrificed in this anti-purge campaign, giving up their lives for their nation. . . . During the flax field battle, my deputy chief of staff, Comrade Zuo Quan, ordered his troops to repeatedly charge at the enemy, attacking the Japanese with everything they had, leading to huge numbers of casualties on the other side, until they were unable to carry on. At midnight they retreated into the flax field, with Deputy Chief of Staff Zuo selflessly leading the pursuit with no regard for his safety. Unfortunately, he was struck by a bullet and became a martyr on Crucifix Peak. In the Taihang foothills, the female fighter Huang Junjue found herself surrounded, and although she struggled valiantly against the enemy's strafing, she was finally cornered and chose to end her life by jumping off a cliff, a fine example of womanhood. During the Battle of Two Li Mound, the cultural instructor Comrade Ge Ren encountered the Japanese while carrying out his duties, and he fearlessly took his attackers down with him, winning glory even in death. . . . The People lost a hero, and the resistance lost an able foot soldier. The army mourned him with one voice, swearing that this blood debt would be repaid whatever the cost . . .

The mention of Ge Ren as a "cultural instructor" was a little at odds with reality. His actual status at the time was translator for the Marxist-Leninist Institute's Compilation and Translation Unit. Many years later, when Huang Yan brought up the matter again, he took the opportunity to correct this error. This was in his memoir *Dreaming Back a Hundred Years*, which he wrote after migrating to America.

> This was when Ge Ren was working at the Compilation and Translation Unit of the Marxist-Leninist Institute, where he specialized in freely rendered translations, as well as researching the romanization of the Chinese language. You could say he was well-off, because in addition to his wages, he also received fees for his writing work. Because I was his classmate in Japan, he often invited me over, along with two others from his hometown—Tian Han, the deputy chief of the Border Anti-Traitor Division, and border doctor Bai Shengtao—to enjoy some delicious peasant food. . . . On one of our expeditions, I discovered that he enjoyed picking the goji berries that grow in between tombstones, which he called "dead children's prayer beads." Ah, how time slips away. It's been more than half

a century since the Battle of Two Li Mound. If Ge Ren's tombstone is still standing, it must be covered in dead children's prayer beads by now. He used to say that Chinese farmers had always been reluctant to slaughter cows, which were essential to their livelihood, so he'd once had a notion to replace the mentions of "roast beef and potatoes" in Trotsky's writing with "goji berries and dog meat."

Huang Yan's work also made one thing clear: even half a century later, people continue to believe that Ge Ren died at the Battle of Two Li Mound. It would seem this has passed into common knowledge. In the recently published *Prominent Individuals of Modern China*, Ge Ren's date of death is still given as 1942.

In the spring of 1998, I visited Two Li Mound, and stopped by the Guan Yu Temple, which was said to be where Ge Ren was martyred. The temple on that spot now was reconstructed after the Cultural Revolution. In front of it was a stone tablet commemorating how the local government had raised funds to rebuild the temple in order to develop the tourist economy. Just inside the front entrance was another tablet, this one a relic from the old building. The ticket seller told me that the stone tablet was retrieved from his son-in-law's donkey pen. It was from the twenty-third year of Emperor Kangxi's reign, and told the colorful story of Guan Yu's life: "Guan Yu, the Marquis of Hanshou Village, was not under Cao C—'s command, but worked with all his might for the Han imperial court. Was he not a t— to the dynasty? Putting down the Yellow Turban peasant uprising, routing large numbers of e— troops: was he not a savior of the common folk? Seeking his brother over thousands of miles, being personally responsible for an army section, finally dying for a good cause, did he not burnish and d— his reputation?"

The tour guide explained to me that the missing words on the stone tablet had either been blasted away by rifle fire or kicked away by donkeys. He also said that a TV crew for the game show *Happy Camp* had shown up to film the tablet for a quiz. I saw a clip of the recording—the question was about the reason for the missing words. The official answer was, "These marks were left during the fighting between the Eighth Route Army and the Japanese." The special guests—film, TV, and pop stars—were repeatedly nudged toward this response by the host, like blind cats that eventually catch a dead mouse, and were able to claim their prize: a box of Alaskan seal blubber oil. In order to prove the profundity of his understanding, the host added an explanation: "That question was an easy one, because this is common knowledge. On June 1, 1942, the famous translator, poet, and linguist Ge Ren encountered the Japanese at close quarters, and a fight to the death ensued. If any of our viewers still can't recall who Ge Ren is, it'll surely come to your mind as soon as I mention Bingying. Yes, that's right, smart alecks. Bingying was a well-known actress of the 1930s and '40s. Even if you haven't heard of David Beckham, you will definitely know who Victoria is. Right, Ge Ren was Bingying's husband. No, no, no, Ge Ren is dead—he sacrificed his life for his country. That's common knowledge."

Dear readers, you might make fun of me for this. As Ge Ren's descendant, even I accepted the common knowledge of his death in 1942 at Two Li Mound until I saw Bai Shengtao's memoir. As for the details left out by that common knowledge, such as what Ge Ren was doing at Two Li Mound in the first place or what mission he was carrying out, those things seemed insignificant. When we're dealing with common knowledge, it seems that our only choices are to accept and go along with the known facts, or else ignore them completely.

Donkeysky

To tell the truth, Tian Han wasn't bluffing. The donkey cart really did have everything—food, drink, clothes. Even booze. Remember the wine gourd from earlier? That was there too. The order fell on me like a mountain, and I left in such a hurry that I didn't have many clothes, but Tian Han left me a padded jacket and thermal trousers, and even underpants. As I got changed there on the cart, I picked up those underpants and kissed them, as if they were my own family.

General, have you been to Shaanbei? Right, don't ask questions, just talk. I'll start with the donkey. You won't find better workers than those sweethearts. Plowing, turning millstones, hauling coal—you need them for all kinds of things. Folks around here say "donkey" for everything. When you're swearing at someone, you call them a donkey. If you mess something up and you're angry at yourself? Then you're the donkey. Don't laugh—I'm just telling the truth. If you're in a good mood, you say "donkey" too, soft and tender, like you're sweet-talking a girl. When I first got to Yan'an, revolution fever was high, and we threw ourselves into our work. One time we heard that Hu Zongnan's troops were coming our way, so we had to scram. There weren't enough vehicles, so I carried an injured patient on my back, over hill and dale, a whole two li. That's when they gave me the nickname "Little Donkey." That made me really happy, like a laurel wreath on my head. I'd wake up smiling at the thought. Then I became a Trotskyite, and people started calling me "Donkeysky" instead.

The villager driving the cart knew about my nickname. He told me that by the time I found Trotskyism, he was way ahead of me. He used to be Kang Sheng's landlord. You know Kang Sheng? He headed the Central Department of Social Affairs. The villager told me he'd seen Chairman Mao many times, and Wang Ming too. The guy was an alkie, and while

I was taking a piss, he stashed my wine gourd in his jacket. After a drink, he started talking more, rambling from one thing to another. He said that Wang Ming's Lenin jacket was always spotless, like a lady's. He took another gulp, turned around, and said, "As for you, they call you Donkey, but there's not a single hair on your face." With that, he started guffawing. He had a weird way of laughing—his neck shrank back and didn't stick out again until he was done, as if he were laughing with his neck. I told him, My real name isn't Donkey, it's Bai, and I do so have hair on my face, but I shaved it off for the long journey. He said he knew, he was aware of all of that, but it was so miserable going outside in the snow, he was just teasing to cheer me up.

What's that, General? You want to know how I became a Trotskyist? Ah, now, that tale starts with a donkey too. Or more accurately, donkey dung. It's cause and effect—more donkeys mean more dung. With all that dung, you need a campaign to get rid of it. And when you have a campaign, someone's in for bad luck. Let's see, it all started with us doctors suggesting a dung pickup. This was after a fighter tried to call a meeting one night, but as soon as he stepped out the door, his foot landed right on a donkey pat. It was like stepping on ice; he screeched and slid all the way into a tree trunk. His leg was already injured, and he wasn't supposed to put weight on it. Now the bone snapped clean in two. When a commander came to visit him in the hospital, the doctors suggested calling on the local villagers and asking them to hang diapers off their animals' rumps. That would collect fertilizer, keep the roads clean, and prevent these sorts of accidents. The commander was delighted—he rubbed his hands and declared, "Fuck a donkey, that's a fine idea." But then he brought up a practical difficulty: the locals were happy to send their own kids out in fatigues to die for the Revolution, but getting them to give up some cloth for a dung diaper was harder than pulling teeth from a tiger's mouth. Still, he said he'd think about this idea. We waited a long time, but never heard anything back. Then out of the blue, the higher-ups said that American journalists were visiting Yan'an, and we had to make a good impression. The organization decided that before the Americans arrived, we'd have a big old dung-clearing campaign.

Public opinion is at the forefront of revolution. A slogan went up on the hospital wall: Serve the war effort, sweep dung back to the fields. The propaganda teams at the newspapers and student organizations even came up with a planting song to spread the word. And the lyrics to Xian Xiang-hai and Sai Ke's "Production Cantata" got changed to "February brings springtime along / Every family's busy picking dung / Hope the harvest this year is good / More crops to feed our troops." To get more attention, Yan'an even put together a concert. The two lead singers, who came from the provisional capital of Chongqing and the isolated island of Shanghai, were both now in the choir here. The Shanghainese one came to see me as a patient once. She told me she had spent time in Germany, where she learned to sing coloratura. "Coloratura? Doesn't that just mean colorful language, talking nonsense? What did you need to go to Germany for? We have plenty of that here in China," I said. She pinched me and said I was a bumpkin who had wasted his time in Russia. Then she pointed at her jade-like throat, gesturing at various spots, to explain that coloratura was an ornamental vocal technique that took a minimum of several years to learn. She made it sound so divine that I asked her to show me. Ha, to my ears, it might as well have been a donkey braying, all breathy and quivering. She sent the choir conductor a pamphlet explaining how Americans like this sort of thing, but he said that when the Americans arrived, we should introduce them to our "February Brings."

On the night of the concert, they sang "February Brings" with its altered lyrics, and that performance served as a rehearsal for the Americans' visit. The Chongqing singer was in high spirits. As soon as she got on stage, she yelled in English, "Are you ready?" We shouted that we were, and only then did she begin singing. She liked to thrust her mic toward the audience and ask us to sing along. Even though no one did, she still said, "Lovely singing, lovely. Let's do it again, shall we?" Then she went on, "Let's see which side of the hall can sing louder. Yes! Let's have some applause. Show some support." At her urging, we raised the dung baskets we'd brought above our heads, following her and swaying to the beat.

That's the good thing about these campaigns: you see results right away. Men and women, young and old, everyone carried these baskets woven from willow branches, and as soon as we saw a piece of dung, we'd scoop it up. The streets were spotless, like Shanghai's Huaihai Road [N.B. formerly known as Avenue Joffre]. But then one morning, when I was coming back from the hospital after a night shift, I saw goats and cows grazing outside. And of course, no matter the hour, there'd be donkeys too. The donkeys were led through the streets in outlandish costumes: padded blankets around their middles and bits in their mouths, plus collars—as if they were on their way to a banquet and had to wear neckties. [The donkeys] rolled around, sending dirt flying everywhere. Yan'an opposed liberalism, but those dumb beasts didn't go along with that. They were already liberated, shitting everywhere. So what was going on? I thought this must be some kind of cattle market. Later on, I found out the reason we had livestock roaming the streets was so that there would be enough dung for the people to pick up, to raise the dung-collecting campaign to a whole new level. At that moment, as I stood there confused, I heard the whine of a suona horn, and when I turned to look, there was a marching band and lion dancers. Amid this merriment, people were picking up dung. My mistake was to notice a few pellets in the middle of the road, just lying there invitingly like gold nuggets. Swaying to the beat of the folk dance, I shimmied my way over, but no sooner had I grabbed the first piece than someone confiscated my dung scoop. It was our head of surgery, Zhang Zhankun. He was also in charge of the hospital's dung-collection team, and he had spent time in Russia too. We normally got along, and had once shared a cave. I said to Leader Zhang, "As you can see, I'm taking part in the dung-collecting campaign." He said, "This dung was placed here for the commanders, not for you. If you pick it up, then what will they collect?" I joked, "The donkey will shit again." With that, I tossed the pellets into my basket. Zhang Zhankun flew into a rage and kicked my basket over. "That'll teach you to pick up dung! That'll teach you to disobey orders!" He even shoved my shoulder blade, so that I nearly fell to the ground like the unfortunate injured soldier. Zhang Zhankun was usually a mild-mannered man who treated me with respect, and I couldn't wrap my brain around his sudden violence. When he kicked me again, I drove my elbow into his belly. I didn't use much force, and he didn't fall over. He simply smiled: "Oh my, the donkey has quite a temper." I smiled too, and thought that would be the end of it. Instead, Zhang Zhankun stole my journal from under my pillow the next day and turned it in to the Party. That's when the trouble started.

To tell the truth, the page of that diary that got me in trouble recorded a conversation I'd had with Ge Ren, Tian Han, and Huang Yan. Now that I think of it, I only had that journal in the first place because of something Ge Ren said. He told me that keeping a diary would enrich my inner life, and that not having an inner life was like not having a shadow, like a room without doors or windows. He probably never imagined that I would put everything down in my journal. What? You know Huang Yan too? That's right, he's a journalist and an editor. That time, a bunch of us were sitting in our cave talking, and as we chatted away, we got around to Trotsky. Ge Ren told an anecdote: The year that Trotsky was exiled by Stalin to Alma-Ata [N.B. currently the capital of Kazakhstan], mass campaigns stirred up a massive peasant revolt. Trotsky thought the Soviet regime he and Lenin had built was in imminent danger of being destroyed by Stalin's despotism and dangerous behavior. But rather than return to Moscow and take advantage of the instability, Trotsky decided to write letters to his friends, persuading them to consider the big picture, to find common ground and not bear grudges, and to help Stalin get through this difficult period. I wrote this all down in my diary. Luckily, I didn't mention that I'd heard it in Tian Han's cave, nor that this story came from Ge Ren's lips; otherwise they'd have been in hot soup too. I get scared when I think about it, even now, because I nearly wrote down something else Ge Ren said: If Lenin's successor had been Trotsky, then Trotsky would have done exactly what Stalin did, and gone after his former comrades-in-arms. Wine is wine in the bottle, and it's still wine if you put it in a gourd. Later I thought, if I'd written this down too, even if I'd had a hundred acres of heads, they'd have lopped off every single one.

After the diary was handed in, I was taken for questioning. Even now I still shake when I think about the interrogators. They walked in and immediately smacked their guns down on the table, so loud it scared the wits right out of me. You have to understand, this wasn't like a gavel—these were Type 38 rifles they had liberated from the Japanese. When I was taken in, someone was in the middle of a session. He was an intellectual, and was being condemned as a Trotskyite for his loose lips. On his way back from hearing the latest report being read out in the square, he was walking by the river when he said to someone else, "That Madame Mao, hitching up her trousers and pretending it's to catch a flea, when really she just wanted the soldiers to gawk at her legs. Shameless." His words reached the authorities, and he was taken in. Wang Shiwei happened to have recently said something similar, so the anti-traitor team decided they must be fellow conspirators. After some digging, they discovered he'd been at Peking University with Wang Shiwei. To start with, he was stubborn, refusing to admit he was a Trotskyite, which led to his being detained and hung from a roof beam. In the time it took to smoke a pipe, he had admitted to Trotskyism. I heard an interrogator say, "Good, you've come out with it. We'll be lenient if you tell the truth, strict if you resist. If you do as you're told and own up to being a Trotskyite, you will get to eat a bowl of egg noodles." The fellow must have been starving to death. After he had finished the first bowl, he wiped his mouth and said he had something else to confess: he was a spy. For that, he got another bowl of egg noodles. Dabbing his lips, he said he wanted to thank the Party, because he had just had an egg with a double yolk. Then he said there was something else. This time he bragged that Chiang Kai-shek was his nephew and Soong Mei-ling was his niece. What about Soong Tzu-wen? Also a nephew. He was crazy, completely crazy, even claiming that Hu Zongnan and Yan Xishan were his godsons. No egg noodles for him this time around. All he got were a few lashes of the cane. He killed himself the same day. Used what he'd learned, and hanged himself from the same roof beam. He didn't use a rope, but his own belt. His last words were "Philosophers say no man can hoist himself off this planet, but I've done it."

What? You want to know if I [was] hanged? Yes, of course I was. That's right, I got to eat two bowls of delicious egg noodles too. The second bowl was because I told my interrogators that everything I wrote in that journal came from Zhang Zhankun. I didn't want to crap on him, because pushing the blame onto others isn't my style. Leave me alone, and I'll leave you alone; come after me, and I'll come after you. He was locked up in Back Ditch too. While I was there, I would hear him howling like a mad dog in the middle of the night, cursing my ancestors eight generations back. To start with, I was still angry. If I'd been a dog, I would definitely have lunged at him and torn the son of a bitch to pieces. But I'm human, and the head on my neck is there for thinking. I thought there was no need to sink as low as him. How can I explain this? In the beginning, I felt a bit remorseful and thought I'd been too hard on Zhang Zhankun, but then my regrets evaporated for the same reason, namely that I'm a person, not a dog, and I can think. I thought what I'd done was to learn from the past and avoid future mistakes, treating the illness to save the patient. And with that, I felt a lot better. I covered my ears and said, Go ahead, donkeyfucker, curse all you want. I'll pretend my ears are full of donkey fur and I can't hear a thing.

To tell the truth, in Back Ditch, I didn't wait for someone else to come along and think for me, I did my own thinking. I looked into my heart and admitted I'd made mistakes. Everything else aside, just look at how I picked up that dung. When I said, "The donkey will shit again," I committed an unforgivable fault. After being educated by the Party for so many years, I should have known how to consider the problem from the donkey's perspective: these donkeys' rations had been reduced again and again, but to serve the Revolution, they had continued turning millstones, hauling coal, plowing. Their bellies must have been empty, but they had responded to the dung-collecting campaign, shitting if they could, finding a way to shit even if they couldn't. It couldn't have been easy! Yet I, an educated intellectual, hadn't shown any empathy for these creatures, just expected them to keep shitting, keep shitting. That's as serious a mistake as clichéd propaganda, as sectarianism, as subjectivity. Where's your class solidarity, has it been eaten by dogs? Can it be that you're less enlightened than a donkey?

Remember I said earlier that when I was hanged from the beam, the cart driver was there too? He was all haughty, saying the rope they used was an offering from him. It was no ordinary straw or hemp rope, but reins left to him by his ancestors. For sacrificing such a fine rope, he and his son got a bowl of egg noodles each. He told me that at the time, he was anxious about the rope breaking, because it was his family's most prized possession after their donkey. He used it to bundle hay, to herd livestock, and to tie people up. His son's brains weren't too good, so his daughter-in-law would run off to her parents' home at the drop of a hat. They lived in Jialu Town [formerly Chia Lu Town] in Jia County [formerly Chia County], far enough from the sacred place that it was a pain to have to go get her and bring her back, a journey of a day and a night, not to mention that he'd have to sweet-talk the in-laws. In the end, the best thing was to tie her to the bed. He told me with utmost sincerity, "Donkeysky, to tell the truth, when this sort of crap happens to you, if you don't have a length of rope handy, there's really no way around it."

Shooting the Breeze with Tian Han

Tian Han lived a long life. When he succumbed to a stroke on June 5, 1991, he was ninety years old, which you might say is all a person could wish for. In the years before his passing, a man named Zhu Xudong was constantly by his side. Zhu was the credited editor and true author of *Tian Han: An Autobiography*. After Tian Han's death, Zhu began releasing transcriptions of their conversations. During one of these, Tian Han revealed for the first time that it was he who suggested to the Party that Ge Ren should be sent to the front line. In this conversation, he also mentioned a Japanese man named Kawata:

> At this time, Ge Ren was translating Lenin. Someone asked him if old Trot [i.e., Trotsky] was a bastard. So ride or get off the donkey—just say he's a bastard, and that'd be that. But no, my old pal never saw a pot he didn't like to stir, so instead he said Trot was Lenin's friend. Now, that was the truth, but at this particular point in history, the truth was a misrepresentation. Who could believe that Lenin would be friends with a bastard? Based on these words, it would have been perfectly fair to label him a Trotskyite. Ah, the poetic temperament. As I understand it, that's like the donkey's temperament: stubborn! He couldn't control his own tongue. Afterward I had a word with some people, and one way or another, I managed to get the matter hushed up. To be frank, I should admit that I did this partly for selfish reasons. If I hadn't, they'd have hauled me off too, because we were from the same hometown, Qinggeng. As far as other people were concerned, we were close enough to wear the same trousers.
>
> Subsequently, another problem arose. One day we received a letter

written [mailed] from Shanghai. As soon as I saw the handwriting on the envelope, I knew it was from Bingying. Because of my duty to Ge Ren, I opened it instead of showing it to him. As soon as I ripped it open, a problem came spewing out. Not a little problem, either, more like a scorpion's sting. The letter said she'd been thinking about returning to France, and asked if Ge Ren wanted to come with her. If he didn't, and if he hadn't found another woman, then she'd come join him in Yan'an. It also said that if he kept refusing to reply, then she would stop writing him, she really would stop this time. It sounded like there had been quite a few letters before this one. My whole scalp went numb. Bingying was an artiste with a complicated background, and she encountered people from all walks of life. I happened to know that she'd had dealings with an American [actually, he was British] named Anthony. A woman like that is as dangerous as a time bomb. If she came to Yan'an—well, that was unimaginable. One thing was certain: if that happened, Ge Ren and I would both be out of luck, completely out of luck, even dead out of luck.

Paper can't hide a fire. Sure enough, just a few days later, someone summoned me to the banks of the Yan River for a chat, and asked if Ge Ren was still in touch with Bingying. What could I do except pretend ignorance and ask, Oh, is he? My face was so full of sincerity that he had to believe me. This person said that to learn from the past and avoid future mistakes, treating the illness to save the patient, he would investigate till he knew the truth. There was no point in getting anxious—already there was a cold sore on my lip. I couldn't just watch as he slid toward the pit, so I went straight to the Marxist-Leninist Institute to find Ge Ren, intending to ask what was going on. When I got there, I saw a whole group of people having a shouting match—utter chaos. Apparently a dish had no sooner arrived at the table than Wang Shiwei's chopsticks zoomed in on a piece of fatty meat, and he stuffed it right into his mouth. At the time, fatty meat was far more precious than lean. As you know, Wang Shiwei was later revealed to be a big Trotskyite. His problems were already showing themselves. A horde of people were screaming for Wang Shiwei to get beaten up, even lunging at him, but as for Ge Ren, he was trying to stop the fight. At that moment I thought, ah, old pal, you might stop this problem, but a bigger one is on its way. And with that, I sank into gloom.

A few days later, we got our hands on an important report. Yasuji Okamura's favorite officer, Major-General Sakamoto, then commander of the Hebei-Bohai Special Zone, had recently led a Japanese delegation to a place called Song Village to study military matters. We also found out that this delegation included a man named Kawata. We had to get this information to the Eighth Route Army south of Hutuo River, so they could make all the necessary preparations to seize one or two members of the delegation if the conditions were right. The intelligence team asked for my views on who would be best to dispatch. So I thought, why not send Ge Ren on this little jaunt? They asked if he could be trusted, and I said yes. They said he was a bookish weakling, so what would happen if he encountered enemy soldiers? I told them that he and Kawata from the delegation were old acquaintances, and if he really did run into the Japanese, he would find a way to escape, and he'd probably persuade Kawata to come with him. If that happened, we'd be able to prize Kawata's mouth open, and get even more valuable information. My thinking was very simple: to use this opportunity to send Ge Ren away for a while, till the danger died down. This was around the time the Rectification Purges were just getting underway. Of course, I had also considered the worst-case scenario: Ge Ren might die. As far as that went, my calculation was that it would still be better for him to die at the hands of the Japanese than to get done in by his own side. You know, that's just what I thought at the time; I had no idea it would actually turn out that way. Bad luck, that was truly bad luck.

And that's how Ge Ren ended up going to Song Village. Yes, Song Village is known as Chaoyang Hill these days—that happened during the land reforms. Later on, there was an opera called *Chaoyang Hill* that was about this place. Ge Ren left Yan'an at the end of May. The problem was, before he even got to Chaoyang Hill [Song Village], he encountered the Japanese at Two Li Mound. They can be cunning devils, and they had sent a recce ahead of the delegation to lay out defenses and sweep for mines. That's who Ge Ren and the others ran into. The Japanese were pursuing a scorched earth "three alls" policy—when they encountered any Chinese, they would kill all, burn all, loot all. Anyway, all our troops were killed. Ge Ren too. That was a Monday, the first day of June. An easy date to remember, Children's Day. Of course, the blood debt had to be paid; we couldn't let our comrades bleed in vain. On June 20, as the enemy was pulling back, we laid an ambush at Chaoyang Hill [Song Village], and it came off beautifully. They weren't able to run away in time, so they were left howling and cursing their parents for not giving them another pair of legs. After sweeping the battlefield, we captured a major. That's right, it was Kawata! He was jabbering away, spouting some nonsense about being in China to do research for the Greater East Asian Cultural Co-Prosperity Sphere, saying that he'd studied under Mr. Fujino together with Lu Xun. What? You think you can hide behind Lu Xun and we'll just let you off? I smacked him across the face. A while later, he killed himself by taking poison when we weren't paying attention. No, he didn't commit seppuku, because he didn't have a knife!

Later on, I often thought how Ge Ren had died too soon, but also at the right moment. As you know, not long after that, Wang Shiwei, his colleague at the Marxist-Leninist Institute, was labeled a Trotskyite, hacked to death, and thrown down an abandoned well. But Ge Ren, thanks to my excellent arrangement, escaped this disaster. I can put my hand on my heart and assure you that if he hadn't died, he wouldn't have stopped at calling Wang a Trotskyite. We'd have labeled him a spy too, and the shame of that would have clung to him for ten thousand years. Comrade Zhu, you tell me, if that isn't a timely death, what is? So when I heard he'd been killed, I was proud to say we came from the same hometown. It's true, I shed some tears. But! There are tears, and then there are tears. Let's put it this way: my left eye shed tears of pain, while my right eye was weeping with pride.

This conversation took place in the spring of 1990. Mr. Zhu Xudong later told me that Comrade Tian Han said to him over and over, "We're just shooting the breeze, and shooting the breeze is always the truth. This is all under the table; there's no need to report it, no need to write about it in any books." Which is why you won't find this passage in the official publication *Tian Han: An Autobiography*. It was released separately, under the title *Shooting the Breeze with Tian Han*. By the way, both Chaoyang Hill and Kawata, whom Tian Han mentioned, will show up again many times in this book.

The Premature Child

Sitting in the donkey cart, I thought about how sharp Tian Han had been. I was indeed the most suitable person for this job. Firstly, I came from the same hometown as Tian Han and Ge Ren, and secondly, I was a doctor. You couldn't have entrusted such an important, difficult task to anyone else. When you need to fight a tiger, it's your own brother you send, and although Ge Ren and I weren't actually related, we were as close as brothers. I saw him before he was born—of course, I mean his mother's swollen belly. Ge Ren's mother could write poetry and draw pictures, and Ge Ren would later enjoy doing those things too, probably influenced by her. Now that I think about it, Ge Ren's and Bingying's mothers looked a little like each other: the same forehead, the same eyes, and especially the same smile lines around their mouths. At a quick glance, they could have been the same person. To tell the truth, it must be fate that Bingying and Ge Ren had so much love and hatred between them, an entanglement so powerful that they could never extricate themselves.

Fine, we won't talk about that. Let's go back to Ge Ren. I remember he was born at the time of the demonstrations in the Yihai Year [i.e., 1899], a premature baby. My fifth aunt was the midwife. What demonstrations? It was the first anniversary of the six gentlemen martyrs of the Hundred Days' Reform being laid in the ground, and we were supposed to be celebrating. The rumor at the time was that Ge Ren's father had had dealings with the "six gentlemen." In order to shut other people's mouths, the entire Ge family took to the streets. Just as the procession arrived at Kylin Bridge, his mother suddenly collapsed onto the railing. They quickly got her home, and she immediately went into labor. She had a double birth [i.e.. twins]. Ge Ren was first, followed by a girl, who came out with the umbilical cord around her neck. She died soon afterward. Much later, in the Soviet Union, Ge Ren once said to me that the moment he was born, the god of death was already his companion. That's what he meant. According to my fifth aunt, Ge Ren's afterbirth was very light. The people of Qinggeng Town call this a "straw birth," and say a child born like that will surely do well in life. Medical professionals take a different view, though. We would simply say that his afterbirth was smaller because he was born prematurely. I believe that's also why he later developed lung disease. The medical text-books tell us that premature children have insufficiently developed lungs, with fewer pulmonary alveoli than blood vessels, which makes internal bleeding more likely. General, do you know what Ge Ren's childhood nickname was? That's right, Duo. I guess you do know him well. Allegedly it was for the two whorls he had on his head, though Ge Ren later said that his mother must have been thinking about his late sister, the girl baby who died. I believe, though, that she might have had yet another reason: her terrible loneliness, seeing everyone around her happily married—so many loving couples, while she was all alone. And so she called him Duo because she missed her man, and was hoping Ge Ren's father would come home soon, so the pair of them could be reunited.

At the time, Ge Ren's father was still on the run in Japan. Whenever Ge Ren got home from school, he'd want to help his mother with the house-work, but she would only allow him to do one thing: go out and buy some western fire [i.e., matches]. In a smoking household, you could do without anything but matches. It was Ge Ren's grandfather who smoked—he was an opium fiend. I remember his pipe from when I was little. It had a jade mouthpiece and an engraved silver pattern on the stem. When he reclined to smoke, because the couch wasn't long enough, he'd have a small stool for his feet. Ge Ren's mother would scoop a little opium from its porcelain bowl with a metal spatula, then light it from the opium lamp. The glow of this lamp winked bright, then dim, like the sulfurous flames of hell. As the saying goes, one household smokes and three smell it. The peculiar aroma seeped through the walls, and everyone around who'd ever tried opium would stop what they were doing and sniff the air vigorously, like dogs. Ge Ren's mother urged him to smoke less, but he just spouted some cock-eyed theory about their ancestor Ge Hong, who tried to concoct pills of immortality—because he didn't have opium, said the old man. If he'd had opium to smoke, what would he have wanted with immortality? Whenever Ge Ren returned with the matches, his mother would pull a couple from the bundle, then carefully scrape the red phosphorus off with a little knife, into an empty matchbox. She was clever about this, never taking any more, so the grandfather never noticed. She once said to Ge Ren, "Duo, by the time this box is full, your father will have come home." Sometimes Ge Ren would secretly add matchstick heads to the box, imagining that this would make his dad return sooner. In the end, though, when the matchbox filled up, what happened was that his mother died.

She washed it down with tiger bone wine. There was something in that liquor that made the red phosphorus even more poisonous. Even so, at noon the next day, she still hadn't breathed her last. The local doctor came to call, and said to Ge Ren's grandfather, "I've smoked a few pipes of your opium, so I'll tell you the truth: if she does happen to live, she'll be left a vegetable. It's up to you whether or not I should try to save her." Ge Ren's uncle was still at home then, and he said of course they should try to save her. The doctor said, "All right, go to the outhouse and bring back a few scoops of shit. Listen, only the runny stuff, no clumps." To the people who'd gathered to watch the fuss, he said this would treat poison with poison, and also force her to vomit up the red phosphorus left undigested in her belly. Ge Ren's mother was still lucid, and she kept her mouth shut tight to refuse any treatment. By the time Ge Ren got home from school, the doctor was covered in crap. Ge Ren spat out blood and collapsed by his mother's side. Oh, now that I think about it, that was probably the first time in his life that he vomited blood.

I was present when Ge Ren coughed up that blood. A while later, my fifth aunt and I carried him to our home. We gave him food and drink, and slowly talked him around. I stayed with him for the next several days, never leaving his side, terrified he would try to end his life. After a few days, his mood seemed to improve. When the matter came up again, he said, "Brother Bai, I will make it up to you all in the future." He wasn't just blowing hot air—he actually kept his word, and sure enough, I would receive many favors from him in the time ahead.

Ge Ren's Family Tree

As Bai Shengtao has mentioned Ge Ren's ancestor Ge Hong, I will add some more facts here. According to the Ge family tree, Ge Hong of the Eastern Jin Dynasty was indeed their distant forebear. The entire Ge clan from around Qinggeng Town all come from Boluo County on the northern shore of the East River in Guangdong. Mount Luofu lies within the borders of Boluo. According to the historical record, Ge Hong cultivated spiritual teachings in himself as a young man, then later studied under Zheng Yin, learning how to make the pills of immortality. Later on, he brought his son and nephew to Guangdong. He settled down on Mount Luofu on the northern shore of the East River, where he created those pills and also wrote *Baopuzi*, a collection of his essays, consisting of seventy chapters: an "inner" twenty that talk about the immortals' secrets for controlling energy and warding off disaster, and an "outer" fifty that discuss gain and loss in the mortal realm and good and evil in our world. Ge Hong died at an advanced age, and was buried on Mount Luofu.

Probing further on, further out, according to the family tree, Ge Hong's great-grandfather was Ge Xuan, who was in turn a descendant of Yu the Great. In *The Book of History: The Classic of Yao*, it says that at the time, "floods of water sliced the land, surrounding the hills and valleys"—hence the need for Yu the Great to push back the waves. While Ge Ren was in Shanghai, he had some dealings with Mr. Lu Xun. The Japanese man we mentioned before, Kawata, wrote in his early work *Recollecting an Encounter with Lu Xun* that on October 11, 1932, Ge Ren was having a long conversation with Mr. Lu Xun when it came up that Ge Hong was his ancestor. Ge Ren said he was writing an autobiographical story called *The Walking Shadow*, which would mention his predecessor Ge Hong at the beginning. "But isn't it against the law to write about Ge Hong?" asked Lu Xun. He continued:

> You could be cunning about this. When Gonggong challenged Emperor Zhuan Xu for the throne, he attacked Mount Buzhou in his rage. That's what I want to write about, Mount Buzhou and the origin of the rule of law. I'll do this with cunning, and I'm going to tweak the nose of that solemn, lofty mask. I've heard that Yu the Great was your ancestor, so why not write about him? I've even come up with a title for you—how about "Curbing the Flood"?

As everyone knows, it was Lu Xun and not Ge Ren who ultimately wrote "Curbing the Flood," finishing the manuscript in November 1935. A few months later,

Lu Xun fell ill and died in Shanghai. Ge Ren sent a condolence telegram: "Such is life, floods of tears; a world of sorrow, surrounding the hills." Those phrases "floods of tears" and "surrounding the hills" were an echo from *The Book of History: The Classic of Yao*, the same words quoted by Lu Xun in the opening sentence of "Curbing the Flood."

Moving closer to our time, the Ge clan in Qinggeng Town had twenty generations of name prefixes picked out: "Gong Yi Ding Tian Jing, Rong Hua Ju Yong Qing, Fu Wei Chuan Gao Gui, Xin De Cun Xing Zheng"—meaning "Righteous is the word of heaven, glory in the eternal Qing. May our good fortune bring nobility, and our hearts follow the right path." Therefore, Ge Ren's great-grandfather was Ge Xintang, his grandfather was Ge Dechen, and his father was Ge Cundao—Xin, De, and Cun. Ge Ren's generation should have had names starting with "Xing," but his father wasn't around when he was a child, and his grandfather didn't care about family tradition, so he never got his rightful prefix.

The female infant Bai Shengtao mentioned, the one who was strangled by her umbilical cord, was of course also of the "Xing" generation. On August 7—Ge Ren's birthday—the family noticed that this baby was silent, and her face had turned dark purple, so they put her in a reed basket and flung her into the Ji River. At this point, I should reveal that the girl didn't actually die—miraculously, she survived her ordeal. This was my great-aunt. As for my mother, Ge Ren's daughter, she should have been of the "Zheng" generation.

I've visited Ge Ren's birthplace Qinggeng Town twice now. The town gets its name from Mount Qinggeng, which is just behind it. It still looks exactly as it did in old pictures, with every inch the same. In the winter, Mount Qinggeng is decorated with puffs of white clouds. In the spring, when the snow melts, the creek that flows through the hills swells into a river that flows through Qinggeng Town, beneath the Kylin Bridge, where Ge Ren was born. Ge Ren's nephew still lives there today. In terms of seniority, I should have called him "uncle." His name was Ge Zhengxin. Like everyone else, he thought Ge Ren had died at Two Li Mound in 1942. He told me a bit about the circumstances of Ge Ren's birth, as well as the story about how my great-aunt was given up for dead as a baby. Needless to say, he had heard all of this from the older folks. His version was more or less the same as Bai Shengtao's account:

> I heard that my uncle [i.e., Ge Ren] was born during a march. That was his destiny. That fellow later ran around everywhere, off to Japan one minute, to the Soviet Union the next. Oh, that's right, it's just called the Russian Commonwealth now. Anyway, he was never still, and in the end he died far away, somewhere called Two Li Mound. You have to follow your destiny.
>
> The old folks all say that he was born at high noon, when your shadow

is shorter than your fingertip. Right after he came out, another baby followed, a girl this time. But her fate was bad, and she died right away. Around these parts, children don't drink milk right after they're born; they are given the "five flavors" instead. What five flavors? Vinegar, bitter goldthreads, salt, hook-vines, and sugar. Anyone who gets through five measures of vinegar is prime minister material. After the vinegar comes the goldthreads. Babies don't have teeth, so these are cooked into a broth with the salt and hook-vines. You hold their noses and force it down. Then brown sugar water right at the end—as the saying goes, sweet after bitter. When they came to give her the five flavors, the old folks realized that the girl's cord was strangling her, wrapped so tightly around her neck that her face had turned purple. She wouldn't drink the vinegar, and she refused the sugar too. What child in the world doesn't like sugar? Only a dead or simple-minded one. My great-granddad put the girl in a basket, covered her with hook-vine leaves, and left her by the river outside the town limits.

The old people say my great-great-aunt [i.e., Ge Ren's mother] wouldn't stay put during her confinement month, but kept sneaking off to the riverside. She never saw the dead baby. How could she have? It had long since been snatched away by wolves. But her mind couldn't turn the corner. They'd come and find her, my bluestocking great-great-aunt, screaming and sobbing hysterically. For a while, it was like there was something wrong with her brain. Sometimes she'd say out of the blue that she could hear a child crying, so hard its eyes were swollen to the size of red dates. She made it sound like it was right there in the flesh, down to its facial feature—a terrifying image. Luckily this didn't happen often, so the family managed to ignore her. The old people say she would light incense and talk to her dead daughter. She finally walked down the road of despair [i.e., committed suicide], probably because she'd been so tormented by these peculiar notions. That's just my guess, of course. None of the old folks could give me a clear account of this business, so of course I can't give one either.

I should mention here that the girl baby, my great-aunt, was rescued by a foreign missionary. I will have more to say about that later. This was the Reverend Samuel Beal, who was at the time spreading the word of God around Qinggeng District. The day Ge Ren was born, he took a picture of the march. That photograph was later published in *The Majesty of the Orient*, the book he coauthored with Reverend Ellis. When my great-aunt was still alive, she had the image copied and enlarged. Although I wasn't able to make out Ge Ren's mother in the crowd, I still felt like I'd received a treasure, and I kept it safely in my desk.

The Magic Trick with the Hat

To tell the truth, I had a trying journey to fetch Ge Ren from Baibei. I didn't want the villager to suffer along with me, so when we got to Chahar [N.B. a former province, later absorbed into Inner Mongolia, Hebei, and Shanxi], I urged him to go back. He said no, he didn't want to leave me on my own, the road ahead was too turbulent. I said, Well, then, how should I thank you? He threw his head back and chuckled, then said he'd be fine as long as there was alcohol. It was getting dark by then, and we happened to be passing by a town. All around us were mounds of earth lightly scattered with vegetation. As we chatted, a madwoman suddenly ran out from behind one of those hillocks, disheveled and squawking non-stop. Chasing her was an old man in a short coat, wielding a wooden stick that he was using to hit her. I tried to speak to him, but he ignored me. Seeing how pale and scrawny he was, I thrust a flatbread at him. He took a bite and yelled at the woman's back, "Good dogs don't die at home." I later discovered that the woman was his daughter. The devils had defiled her, so he thought she'd brought shame upon their house, and he was chasing her out. The Japanese are terrible people. When I was in Shanghai, a friend told me they're all perverts because Japan's an island nation and they eat a lot of shrimp and fish—seafood is full of phosphorus, a stimulant, so they can't help themselves around women or alcohol. The same friend also said that Japan wanting to conquer China was like a snake wanting to swallow an elephant, and snakes were the most despicable creatures. That friend of mine had a good line in wordplay. He quipped that they'd even nippon themselves, let alone other people. All right, enough of that. I didn't mean anything by that; I'm just telling you how dangerous the journey to Baibei was. If we had been unlucky, we might have run into the Japanese.

The town was called Dexing. As we entered, I spotted a tavern flag fluttering by the side of the road. I treated the driver to a round of meat dumplings and some drinks. The booze was brewed from sweet potatoes, so strong it was like swallowing fire. He guzzled the stuff like nobody's business. Before long, he was reeling and babbling about his son, saying how smart that silly boy was. Tapping his chopsticks on his thigh, he said, "That kid of mine, easy as holding a stick, he could ride a horsey, just like an opera performer. You're supposed to study opera with a master, but he didn't have one. He learned to ride on his own." He was smiling as he talked, but his words made my heart twinge. There was a guesthouse right behind the canteen. Thanks to the booze, I fell asleep very quickly, but I was awakened a short while after that. My hometown acquaintance was bragging to the guesthouse manager. The way he was talking, Tian Han was practically a god made flesh. Strictly speaking, he shouldn't have been spouting off like that, because this was all top secret. That's when I came to my senses and saw what was going on: the manager was an old friend of the driver's. We didn't just happen to be passing by this town; he had arranged the whole thing.

I had heard about the incident he was describing. Here's how it happened: When Tian Han's troops first got to Yan'an as the advance party, he summoned all the villagers to the river bank for a meeting. There he showed them magic tricks. He asked if they kept chickens, and they said, We don't keep a fart. Hu Zongnan seized all of them, and now we don't even remember what the hell chickens look like, not even how many legs or eyes they have. Tian Han said, In that case, I will get a chicken for you to raise. He took off his hat and held it upside down so they could see that it was empty. Holding it with one hand, he scrabbled around inside with the other. A moment later, he ran his hand down his sleeve and tapped the brim, and out of the hat popped a little chick. Next, Tian Han asked the crowd if they wanted to raise pigeons. They were all mesmerized by this point, and said yes. He tapped the brim again, and produced a fluffy bird. They watched awestruck as it soared up into the blue sky. Tian Han told them pigeons made bad pets—they were all traitors and liked to abscond with other people's pigeons, so forget it. With that, he whipped out his gun and shot the bird dead. Tian Han said that on such a cold day, they must be freezing their ears off, and none of them had hats. He reached into his own hat and produced one hat, two hats, three hats—so many hats they flew out like magpies. The villagers were overjoyed, and Tian Han said, This is what Communism is. And just like that, in the time it took to smoke a pouch of tobacco, the villagers were convinced.

When I woke up, my driver was describing the trick with the hat, adding lots of his own embellishments. According to him, the first reaction came from the dogs. They thought the hats flying through the air were flatbreads, so they lunged at them. The wind made the hats flip over and over, and so the dogs followed suit, turning somersaults too. He even mimicked the dogs as he spoke, twisting his neck this way and his ass that way, and as he contorted he said further that the dogs found they couldn't chew their way through the hats, so they held them in their mouths and took them to their owners. When someone hollered for a donkey, Tian Han said that as long as they all worked hard, he promised chickens and donkeys for every household. And here the driver put one hand on his waist, pointed out the window, and said in a fair imitation of Tian Han's voice, "There'll be donkeys, there'll be women, there'll be everything."

Seeing the manager's eyes almost bulge out of his head, I couldn't help laughing. My driver, seeing me awake, not only didn't shut up, he pointed at me and said, "Ask him if you don't believe me." So as not to spoil their fun, I nodded. I remembered him telling me on the way that he'd gotten a wife for his son by swapping a chicken for her, so I joked, "You know, manager, his daughter-in-law came out of Tian Han's hat too."

"There were pretty girls in there too?" The manager's eyes widened again. I nodded once more. Ha, with that, my driver grew even more animated. He made the trick with the chicken and the hat sound like the most incredible thing—some nonsense about squatting at the very front of the crowd on the day of the meeting, and being so sharp-eyed and swift-footed that he grabbed the first chicken and the first hat to emerge, a hat that his son was still wearing to that day. As for the chicken, when he went matchmaking for his son, he sealed the deal by handing it over as a gift to his in-laws in Jialu. He made sure to stress that this was a hen that laid eggs in all four seasons, and mentioned that many people in Jialu Town had examined the bird. He paused here to ask if I knew Li Youyuan. I said, Yes, wasn't he that farmer who sang "Flying with the Wind"? He said, Yes, Li Youyuan was a man with brains. He was great at singing and planting things, and when he was in the city for a market, he even made a special trip to see the driver's hen, which he said was more resplendent than a phoenix. Following his lead, I blurted out some nonsense about Li Youyuan bellowing out a couple of lines on that day—"The East is red, the rooster crows, a phoenix has landed in Jialu Town." No sooner had I spoken than the driver said, "Oh, you know about that too?" He even asked if I'd been in Jialu at the time. I wanted to laugh, but didn't dare. Then he took my tall tale further, bragging that Li Youyuan was able to sing "The East Is Red" because of that hen of his.

The driver told the manager to look him up if he was ever in Yan'an—he would take him to meet Tian Han, and Kang Sheng too. The manager was so blown away, his jaw dropped wide open. Having done enough swaggering, the driver lay down. Shaanbei people like to be bare-assed [when they sleep], but he didn't want to take his shorts off. "I have a paper ball, and that's how we were able to meet all our contacts on this trip." It was in a little pocket at the front of his shorts. He started rummaging around down there vulgarly, even disgustingly, to fish out the wad of paper, wave it in front of me, and stuff it back in. As for why it was there, he said he only felt safe with his cock pressed against it. He had no idea what was written on it, because you could take a dipperful of words and he'd only recognize one in ten of them. I knew he was lying. Along the way, when we'd passed by a place called Yanzhuang Village, there had been a notice at the entrance, and he had gone over to have a look, shaking his head and tutting as if he understood what it said. I asked if I could have a look at the paper. He hemmed and hawed, claiming "the Party" wouldn't let him show it to anyone else. I wanted to tell him that I also had balls in my shorts, and a party in there too.

Later that night, when I went outside to take a piss, I saw a man leading a camel through the rear courtyard. He looked like a salt merchant. I wondered, could he be a contact too? Our donkey seemed to get along well with his camel; they were licking and sniffing at each other. It was all quite Communist, the way they were shoving hay at each other with their snouts. Back inside, I peered out through a crack in the window, and saw the cool gleam of the moon on the camel's hump. When the donkey lay down and started rolling on the ground, the camel began to bellow, as if cheering it on. The moon was at its highest point, showing its delicate features like a maiden's face. I stared at it for a very long time. Even the toad's palace on the surface was clearly visible. I imagined this radiance pouring down on distant trees and ditches, and also on Ge Ren, whom I would soon see again. Did he know I was coming for him? Was he, like me, also staring at the moon? I felt even more grateful to Tian Han. If he hadn't pulled some strings on my behalf, I'd still be locked up in that cave in Back Ditch, where of course I never got to see a moon like this. You're right, at the time you could have beaten me to death, and I'd never have guessed they were sending me to Bare Mountain for this. Just like I'd never have imagined that the following morning, when the red sun rose in the east, our breakfast would be camel meat. As for the salt merchant, he'd been hacked to death and thrown down a dry well. The manager told me and the driver that he was a wealthy guy. It wasn't his finery; he even had a gun in his back pocket. In those troubled times, who still went around in fancy clothes? No matter how you sliced it, he wasn't a good person—probably a traitor or deserter. Best to chop up someone like that.

The manager passed us the camel meat and asked us to relay a message to the Party, to let them know he'd killed a traitor. He even said ingratiatingly to the driver, "I don't want to take all the glory. It was nice to meet you; let's say we did it together." And with that, he performed his own magic trick, pulling out a couple of tied-together objects from his sleeve. If I weren't a doctor, I wouldn't have been able to make out what his treasures were. Ears! The salt merchant's ears. They had been sliced off neatly and washed clean. Evidence that he had killed a traitor. I was so shocked I broke out in a cold sweat, and my own ears started humming. My god, if

I hadn't had the driver with me, would I have ended up like the merchant, down that abandoned well? With my ears chopped off too, so even in hell, I wouldn't be able to hear a thing.

Li Youyuan's Son

Following the clues left by Bai Shengtao, I was able to find out more about the driver. His surname was Wu, and he was born in the Year of the Dog. His nickname was Dog's Bollocks, but his real name was Wu Yishi. The first clue was those reins, the ones used to string up Bai Shengtao and bind his daughter-in-law. The second was his feebleminded son. Halfwits have their own kind of good fortune, and this fellow later had four children of his own, two boys and two girls, a perfect set. His youngest son was called Dog's Bollocks too—he used his dad's name for his son, and there was nothing anyone could do about it. Luckily, Little Dog's Bollocks wasn't born until after his namesake had passed, so there was no confusion. Putting these two hints together led me to Dog's Bollocks himself. He died in 1944, so I don't have a lot to say about him.

As for Mr. Li Youyuan, I will add a little information. He composed "The East Is Red," and has a connection to this book's second narrator, Ah Qing. During my visit to Shaanbei in the fall of 1996, I spent a night in the Jia County capital. A worker at the hotel told me that we were just a stone's throw from Jialu Town, where Li Youyuan used to live. I hurried there that night. Only when I got there did I learn that Mr. Li was actually from Zhangjiakou, a little distance from the town. The hotel security guard I'd paid to accompany me said he would rather give me a refund than follow me there, even if I offered him more money. His reason was that the area was unsafe, and he wasn't willing to lose his life for a paltry sum of money. The next day, when the red sun rose in the east again, I went to Zhangjiakou on my own. There I met Li Youyuan's son, who was basking in the sun outside his cave house. He was in his seventies, and he had a white towel over his head. Seeing someone approach, he started weeping like a child, saying, "I can't see [the] sun anymore. My heart is all dark inside, my heart is dark." But he actually wasn't blind; his eyes looked perfectly fine.

Inside the cave was a picture of a middle-aged Li Youyuan. Dabbing at his tears, his son said his father had died of "swelling disease." As for what that actually meant, he couldn't explain. All he said was, "He kept swelling and swelling, until finally he'd swelled right up [i.e., to death]." Looking out his front door, I saw a courtyard full of red dates drying in the sun, with a few chickens strutting around them, and I suddenly remembered that Wu Yishi had given his in-laws a hen—assuming he was telling the truth—which might well have been some sort of blood relation to these birds. Farther in the distance was the bald earth mound (known locally as Earth Plateau), deathly still. A few decades ago, Mr. Li

Youyuan stood on this mound, facing the sun or the glittering constellations, singing, "The East is red, the sun will rise, and from China comes our Chairman Mao. . . . Oh my, aiyoh, he is the People's great savior." All the old folks in the village remembered that during Li Youyuan's time, this village was full of song. They told me, "Everyone could belt out a few notes, whether they sounded good or not." I asked the younger villagers if they knew any folk songs. One guy hesitated, then abruptly held his head up and said he could sing "The Story of Spring," "Descendants of the Dragon," and "So Happy Today." He went on, "Most people over forty can sing, especially during the New Year. Those of us under forty don't know how. That's the honest truth."

Before departing, I went to say goodbye to Li Youyuan's son. The old man repeated, "I can't see [the] sun anymore, my heart is all dark inside." And again he wept like a child, tears and snot streaming down his face.

Zhangjiakou

Have you ever eaten camel, General? Don't worry, you haven't missed anything—the meat is fibrous, like the rough hemp they make ropes from, and it has a sort of grassy odor. At the time, though, I found it absolutely delicious. In Marxist terms, its use-value was higher than its price.

The guesthouse manager had planned ahead—he had already pressed some camel meat overnight till it was as dense as a tea brick, ready for us to take along. I tried to bite off a piece as we left. Huh, it was tougher than the sole of my shoe. You had to chew on it a bit, moistening it with your saliva, till it softened enough for you to gnaw some off. Outside the town, I said to the driver, That camel rider died quite horribly. The driver said, Who asked him to be a rich man? You really can't tell a book by its cover. Only now that I knew him a bit better did I realize his belly was full of these ideas. He said, The Revolution means we'll have to get rid of the few people who have money. Then we'll have to give the money to the many people who don't have any. When we reach that point, we won't be far from Communism. I asked if he was planning to bring back the story of the manager's heroic deed, and he said, "Like hell! If he gets sent away and they get a new person in, will we still get to eat meat next time around?"

He was afraid I didn't know how useful he was, so he kept showing off in front of me, claiming that if I hadn't been with him, that same knife would have plunged into me, and I'd be a ghost now. That was true. Just as I was about to thank him, he abruptly stuck out his tongue, pretending to be a ghost. His tongue had a thick yellow coating, as if he had tuberculosis. As the saying goes, mouth like chicken liver, from this long illness you won't recover. I thought the poor bugger would have a short life. What's that? You want me to look at your tongue? Of course, General. To tell the truth, it's good—not just your tongue, but your lips and teeth are excellent too; you're sure to live past a century. Lips are the king, teeth are the ministers. Or the lips are the walls around the city of the mouth, the gateway to the tongue. Open or closed, the honorable lips keep the mouth secure. To tell the truth, none of that coloratura stuff, your lips are apricot pink, which means abundance will come without your having to seek it out. You should come and have a look too. [N.B. Here he is speaking to Fan Jihuai's aide Ding Kui, who was taking down his words.] See, when General Fan's lips are closed, they make a long, straight line. What does this tell us? That the General considers every issue thoroughly, and he deals with every task in an orderly manner. What's more, the General's tongue is long and thick, which means the path ahead will be smooth for him, and he's on his way to great fortune and success. I'm not trying to flatter you, General. If one word of this is untrue, you can shoot me dead right now.

All right, I'll continue. We went on walking for a long time, and at noon some days later, we finally got to Zhangjiakou. Dou Sizhong lived on Fourth Street in this village. His official status was owner of the Longyu Shop, which sold furs and antiques. This was a branch of a business that had its headquarters on Gaoyibo Hutong in Beiping [now Beijing]. Fourth Street had a few brothels too, one of which, Jade Flower, shared a courtyard wall with Longyu. You [meaning Ding Kui] don't need to take this down. There's no point, anyway; the cunning rabbit has three burrows, and by the time you people get there, Dou Sizhong will be long gone. At the time, I wasn't able to see him right away. An old shop attendant welcomed us with great ceremony. He offered us a couple of bowls of noodles, then went to get some hot water so we could wash our feet and rest. The driver refused the water—he said getting your feet wet made it easy to catch a cold. He asked where the boss was. The attendant said he'd gone to Dihua [N.B. now Ürümqi], and he wasn't sure when he'd be back. He handed us over to a younger attendant, who I could see was another old acquaintance of the driver's. Right away they started calling each other donkeyfuckers. The young attendant was twenty-five or twenty-six, with well-formed features and good manners. Later I learned that he'd graduated from Nankai High School. I don't know his real name, so I'll just call him Nankai. As he said "donkeyfucker," his shoulders drooped, and there was hesitation in his voice—as if he were only saying the word to prove he could fit in with the revolutionaries.

Sure enough, the driver knew this place well. Without waiting for Nankai to lead the way, he took me straight to a room in the back courtyard.

No sooner had I lain down than Nankai came in. He sat cross-legged on the heated bed and asked about my troubles, then started chatting. "I heard your father-in-law lives in Meng Village. That's not far from town. While you're here, why not take the opportunity to visit him?" His words set off a buzzing in my head, as if a nest of hornets had taken up residence there. To tell the truth, my ballsack shrank at that moment. It's true, I had hoped no one would find out about this. Ever since I'd become Donkeysky, I had worried that the old man would get into trouble. Turns out scandal moves faster than the wind. It looked like they had long since seen right through me. I murmured that I didn't think I would, because I wouldn't want my private affairs to interfere with revolutionary work. To tell the truth, General, I really didn't want to go. My wife died early on, and my son was sent to Meng Village not long after he was born—I hadn't seen him since. If I showed up out of the blue, what would my son think of me? Would he appreciate the gesture? If he sent me away, that would be shameful. The more I thought about it, the less I wanted to go. But Nankai kept insisting, as if I'd be making him look bad if I didn't go. I said I hadn't brought a present, and there was no time to get one. I could hardly go empty-handed—maybe another time?

"You could leave anything till another time, but not this," said Comrade Nankai. "Respecting the old and adoring the young is a traditional Chinese virtue." I wanted to laugh at him. Did he really think that other nationalities don't take care of their elderly or love their children? But I didn't say a word. He went on, "Anyway, I've already got a gift ready for you, a fine specimen of a sheepskin coat." Just as I was feeling beleaguered, the driver decided to chime in with "Stop pretending. Don't you still have a piece of camel meat left? Just give that to your dad-in-law. Unless you want to keep it for yourself?" I was in a rage, but I didn't dare lose my temper, so I just stood there staring blankly. A moment later, Nankai was leading a horse over. A fine one too, dark gray with white markings, its mane and tail clipped short. Nankai informed me that it was Comrade Dou Sizhong's, captured from the devils. Then he tugged at the bridle and invited me to mount. "This is a good animal. Many others want to ride it but will never have the chance!" Something about his tone told me he'd take offense if I kept refusing his offer. General, there were some things I only understood later. They were so insistent on my going to Meng Village because they wanted me to know that my father-in-law's life was in their hands. If I was dishonest with them, or even a tiny bit negligent in my duties, he'd be the one to suffer for it.

I went. Of course I went. Would I dare not to? Comrade Nankai escorted me. Meng Village, my father-in-law's home, was five or six li from Zhangjiakou. According to legend, Lady Meng Jiang—the one whose tears tore down the Great Wall—was born there. As I trotted along on the horse, I started smiling. Nankai asked me what was so funny, and I said I was thinking of my father-in-law—how he could endure suffering, and knew how to get on in life. If he were to go to Yan'an, he would surely end up as a model worker like Zhang Side. He always kept his head down as he walked, and if he saw a fallen branch, he would pick it up for firewood. His eyes glowed at the sight of a metal wire—he could turn it into nails. My wife once told me that when she was a child, he restricted them to two meals a day after Eighth Month, and made them go to bed early on the grounds that an early night prevented hunger and saved on lamp oil. In the summer, other people complained about the heat and stopped working early, but he always refused to go home. His back was tanned so dark and shiny that he was nicknamed Blackfish. When there wasn't anything to do on the farm, he ran an occasional business. What kind of business? Trapping wild larks in the woods and bringing them into town to sell. Now that I was chatting freely, I told Nankai a story about my father-in-law and meat. One year the family chicken died, so they ate it. Everyone else tossed out the bones and feet they'd gnawed clean, but not my father-in-law. He saved a chicken foot, and dropped it in his soup at every meal, so blobs of grease would float to the surface. My brother-in-law's mouth watered at the sight, and he spent all his time scheming to steal that chicken foot so he could steep it in his own bowl. That was precisely what my father-in-law wanted. One day he summoned the entire family, held up the foot, and asked, "What's this?" His son replied, "A chicken foot." My father-in-law said: "Open your damn eyes wider, and look closely." My brother-in-law, drooling now: "A delicious, fragrant chicken foot." My father-in-law lost his temper and smacked him across the face. "Son, this is family property. You have to be born into plenty, and also die in peace, if you want to hang on to it. Whoever can endure the longest will have the most to leave behind." I said to Nankai, You ought to hang on to that sheepskin jacket, my dear comrade—the camel meat will be more than enough for him. Think about it: if a chicken foot can be family property, then such a big piece of camel meat might well be the whole countryside to him.

I started chuckling again. Nankai was paying close attention, but he didn't so much as crack a smile the whole time. His lips twitched when I got to my father-in-law's answer, but he clamped down on them. As he did so, his jaw muscles jutted out, as if he were experiencing a bout of constipation. When he finally did laugh, it wasn't at my words, it was because of a dog. As we approached the village, a lame dog ran out to welcome me, the prodigal son-in-law. He ran straight up to us, then started circling. I pulled the horse to a halt and eyed the dog, wondering which way to go. That's when he suddenly raised his crippled leg, twisted his body, and let loose a stream of pee onto the horse's shank. By the time I'd turned around, he was done. Could he have been so dazed by hunger that he'd mistaken the horse's leg for a tree trunk? Nankai could no longer suppress his laughter, and dissolved into giggles. I understood that he was able to laugh now because the dog was a lower-order animal. There were, of course, the pathetic running dogs of the capitalists, but that wasn't a significant difference. You could mock them or yell at them and still be in the right. It was different with people. Human beings had class differences, and you had to keep a safe distance rather than simply expressing your feelings, even mirth.

To tell the truth, all the way there, I'd been hoping that my father-in-law would be out. But when I got to his door, there he was—as if to make things difficult for me. Confusingly, he was asleep in bed, whereas normally he was never still. The full bedpan suggested that he hadn't been up for some time. Was he ill? Dying? Those were my immediate thoughts, mixed with a certain amount of relief. He had always been skinny, but human-shaped. Now he looked more like a bird. One of his legs was sticking out from the covers, the ankle gleaming gray. As a doctor, I could see the shadow of death in that gray. He seemed to mistake me for someone else. "Hey, what are you doing here?" he asked. When I told him my name, he slid bare-assed out of bed and yelped, "I knew it: the magpies were cawing in the trees first thing this morning. Aren't you in Yan'an?" Then he confessed that he'd thought I was his grand-nephew, my son. I asked how my son was, and he said, "Oh, didn't you hear? He's fighting alongside Peng Dehuai." That's when I learned that my son was a revolutionary too. I asked why he wasn't working on the land, and he said there was no need to, because there wasn't any land left. I lit a fire and sat him in front of the pit. He hung his head and told me he'd been labeled a landlord, so they had taken his land away and redistributed it. My heart thudded. To tell the truth, that moment was like spring rain on the withered stems of my familial feeling, which now sprouted fresh shoots. I decided that after I'd taken Ge Ren back to Yan'an, I would definitely come visit my son, and convince him to cut off this member of the landowning classes. Otherwise his life would be over.

My father-in-law had seen Bingying once, and he'd kept saying how beautiful she was, like a fairy come to earth or the reincarnation of Lady Meng Jiang. He didn't know the truth, so he thought I was secretly in love with her. He even said my face was as hot as a wildfire, leaving me torn between laughter and tears. I had told him we were talking about Ge Ren's wife, and Ge Ren was my brother-in-arms, so no nonsense. Now I was worried he would ask me about Bingying and Ge Ren. If Nankai got suspicious and thought I'd let something slip about Ge Ren, I'd be sunk. And if that happened, I wouldn't be the only one in trouble. But you know, take a landowner like him—you could bump him off with the slightest excuse, as easily as squashing an ant. He had no idea of his own fate, though, and insisted on digging where he shouldn't, which filled me with fear. He said, "Who's that, who's that? He has a pretty wife, like she just stepped out of a painting." Because his daughter was dead, he wasn't bothering to act like an elder around me anymore, but was talking as if we were on the same level. He said a few more things, all pretty horrible. But luckily, thank god, I don't know if he forgot or was being tactful around me, but he didn't mention either Bingying's or Ge Ren's names. I speedily brought the conversation around to him, comforting him for becoming a landlord, advising him to look on the bright side and not carry his worries as a burden.

All in all, Blackfish's words were pretty good. He said he wasn't upset, but in fact overjoyed. By handing over his freshly fertilized fields to the government, he was doing his bit for the Revolution too. I asked how much land he'd had to be labeled a landowner, and he said about 10.74 mu. The dividing line was 10 mu, and anyone with more than that was a landlord. His next words almost made me stop breathing. It was all thanks to me, he said. Back in Beijing, if I hadn't cured his larks, he wouldn't have been able to buy all this land. It was because of the money from that sale that he'd kept catching birds and taking them to sell in Beijing, until he'd put away enough cash for a patch of wasteland by the river. Now I remembered. Many years ago, when I came to Meng Village to get married, I helped him clear the undergrowth from that land, hoping for many good harvests ahead. But no one can predict the future. How could I have known that this piece of earth would inexorably lead to his becoming a landowner?

It was all good, said my father-in-law. Now that his land had been given away, he could nap his life away like everyone else. There were two great pleasures in life: marrying a second wife and having a good sleep. The second wife wasn't going to happen, but he took a good long nap every day. Now that he was warm and his belly was full, his thoughts turned to lust— but he had no money, so he could forget about marrying again. The Party had rescued him, because if he really had taken a second wife, that would have been a betrayal of my late mother-in-law. That's how I found out that my son's grandmother had been dead a few years now. I didn't know what to say, and then I suddenly remembered the hunk of camel meat. If only that could make up for my many failings. When I went out to get it, he crinkled his eyes and muttered, "Fuck your mother, what took you so long? I could smell that as soon as you showed up." He didn't even wait for me to bring it back in; he came running outside, one hand pulling up his trousers, his legs crossed and barefoot, waddling like a clumsy swan. He shut the courtyard gate and drew the bolt. Before he got back to us, Nankai said, "There are two other landowners in Meng Village, and for a place this small, two is enough to fill the quota. The Organization has decided to remove his landlord label. He just doesn't know it yet." My father-in-law said goodbye sincerely—I think he meant it. I hastily told him that the Party's benevolence was as high as the mountains and as bottomless as the sea, and that I'd never forget it, not even when I was old and toothless.

Blackfish took the meat from me, and even offered Nankai some. It was too tough to bite through—it just spun in his hand as if he were holding a hot yam. He picked one corner to attack, and gnawed so hard that his gums started bleeding. I asked Blackfish what he normally ate. With his mouth twisted around, he rolled his eyes and said, "Shit."

Bai Shengtao's Father-in-Law

Bai Shengtao's father-in-law was named Meng Dequan. In 1920, he met both Bai Shengtao and Bingying in Beijing. At the time, Bingying had just returned from France, and had come to Beijing to find Ge Ren. Because Ge Ren was in prison, she returned to France not long after that, and then went on to Britain. All of this is recorded in *Beauty in a Time of Chaos* by Anthony Thwaite, the man Tian Han mentioned to Zhu Xudong. He came to China as a journalist in 1938, and stayed for two years. After the war, he got a job in the Chinese Studies Department of Hull University. Bingying was one of the five subjects of *Beauty*. The other four were Ding Ling, Lin Huiyin, Sun Weishi, and Zhao Yihuo. Apart from Ding Ling, the others were indeed famous beauties. The following passage, containing Bingying's recollections of Bai Shengtao and Meng Dequan, is from that book:

> Memory is a marvelous comb, and also a bar of music whistled through that comb. She had completely forgotten certain incidents that would have seemed important to other people, but she remembered going to the bridge to buy the birds with Bai Shengtao as if it happened yesterday. Bai Shengtao was older than Ge Ren, and had already taken on the role of his protector while Ge Ren was still a child. Now he had come to Beijing to

seek shelter with Ge Ren, in order to find business opportunities. Before this, Bai Shengtao had not known that Ge Ren had taken part in the previous year's May Fourth Movement and was now in the cells at Infantry High Command.

The day Bai Shengtao arrived, she was already planning to visit Beijing Bridge. At the time she was lost in her emotions, uncertain whether to stay or leave. She resolved to see a fortune-teller on the bridge, hoping to get a glimpse into her future. Beijing Bridge was near the Temple of Heaven, where emperors used to pray, an early twentieth-century version of the painting *Along the River during the Qingming Festival*, or maybe Disneyland. Bai Shengtao had once raised pigeons in the church at Qinggeng Town. Having accompanied Bingying to the bridge, he was quickly drawn to the bird market. There he spotted a father and daughter selling larks. Bingying can still recall that the caged larks' wings were drooping, and they appeared listless. The bird seller seemed anxious, and told them he would be willing to let his birds go at a loss. Bingying, who had only wanted to see a fortune-teller, was now being pestered by this bird vendor. His name was Meng, and this was probably Bai Shengtao's first glimpse of Miss Meng. He told the seller that his birds had been sick for quite a while, and would soon die. Before the man became more distraught, Bai said he would be happy to treat the birds, and the seller gave Miss Bingying a few larks by way of thanks. If they could not be cured, he said, then he would sell them off at cost. Bingying claims she was feeling bored, so she followed Bai Shengtao to the bird seller's home. Bai was quite the expert. He fed the birds vinegar mixed with buckwheat flour, and they revived. Then he bought a little opium and steeped it in water to feed the larks, so they would become addicted. Bingying later said this showed how supremely intelligent Bai Shengtao was. Most people who keep birds also smoke, and these drug addict birds would smell the opium and chirp nonstop, making the owners believe they had found the best lark in the woods.

Bingying said that from that day, they started getting to know the bird seller's daughter. At Bingying and Bai Shengtao's urging, she decided not to return to the countryside, but remained in Beijing for her studies. Her father left her the proceeds of his bird sales and returned to Zhangjiakou alone. . . . According to Bingying's recollection, it was after Ge Ren was released from jail that she left Beijing and returned to France. This was firstly because her own daughter was still in France, and she wanted to see her again; and secondly, she had no confidence that her romance with Ge Ren would go anywhere. Before leaving, she put up the funds for Bai Shengtao and the girl to study at the Beijing Academy of Medicine, where

Ge Ren had been before his arrest. She also gave her address to Kawata, asking him to pass it on to Ge Ren. Kawata was a Japanese nihilist, a friend from Ge Ren's time in Japan, now a professor at the academy. He assured her that as soon as Ge Ren got out of prison, he would find some way to bring him to visit her in France. It was his dream to study drama in France.

My god, there was drama still to come—Kawata got drunk and lost the address she had given him. Bingying waited eagerly for Ge Ren in France, but the days passed one after another, and it seemed she would wait forever. A long time later, she finally found out that Ge Ren and Bai Shengtao had made their way to the Soviet Union, and that Bai Shengtao had gotten married before leaving the country, to the girl he had met selling larks on the bridge . . .

I might as well say a little more about Meng Dequan here. About a month after Bai Shengtao's visit, he was declared a tyrannical landlord and sent to the firing squad. Meng Dequan's son, the greedyguts who got smacked by his dad over a chicken foot, was named Meng Weimao. He had fallen ill and died some time before Dr. Bai's visit to Meng Village. Did he die of exhaustion after clearing the land for farming? There is no way for us to know. Bai Shengtao's son took his mother's surname and was called Meng Chuiyu. An elderly man from their village told me that in the spring of 1951, Meng Chuiyu and he were glorious volunteers in the People's Army, and they went into Korea together. In 1953, on the last day of the Panmunjom talks, Meng Chuiyu was retreating when he stepped on a land mine and was thrown up into the sky. Because Zhangjiakou was famous for its larks, who had become a part of its residents' daily lives, it was natural for the old man to make this comparison: "Chuiyu got blown up into chunks of flesh no bigger than a lark." The landowner Meng Dequan now had no descendants. Note my phrasing—it was Meng Dequan's family line that got cut off, not Bai Shengtao's. I might as well tell you now that the third part of this book will be narrated to a woman named Bai Ling. In the summer of 2000, she agreed to accompany Mr. Fan Jihuai to Baibei for an important commemorative event. Miss Bai Ling is the granddaughter of Bai Shengtao and his second wife.

Poetry Recital

We left Meng Village before it got dark. Back in Zhangjiakou, the driver was raring to head back to Shaanbei. He said, You have to beat kids every three days, or they'll get too boisterous. He was worried that his daughter-in-law would be getting into mischief at home. Nankai reminded him to keep an eye on his work. The driver thumped his chest and said, "I know I need to pay attention to improving my thoughts. Donkeyfucker, I've thought this through. Any more nonsense [from her], and I'll rip out her little cunt." And with that, he left. I tell you, if you put two donkeys in the same pen, after a while they'll grow fond of each other. That's even truer of two people. To tell the truth, after the driver left, I felt a little empty.

Now I was in a hurry to see Dou Sizhong. Luckily, I was able to meet him that very night. It was almost dawn, and I was dreaming about my son when there was a click and my door swung open. Nankai was standing in the doorway, holding a lantern. He said, "Comrade Bai, quick, come see who's here." I scrambled out of bed. A figure quickly came over and took my hand. He said not to be so polite, but to get back into bed. His hand was softer than a woman's, as if the bones had been picked out of it. Yes, this was Dou Sizhong. He really did seem like a fur trader, down to the tanner's stink around him. Nankai trimmed the wick and retreated from the room. I immediately thought that Dou Sizhong had never been in Dihua [N.B. now Ürümqi], but must have been in his shop this whole time. And my jaunt to Meng Village was surely his idea too.

I got out my letter. It didn't smell great after being in my shorts for so long, so I blew on it before handing it to him. That was the second time I had brought it to my lips—the first was when I was putting on those underpants, when I had kissed it as if it were family. As Dou Sizhong reached out for it, I swore to him that I hadn't read it, or may lightning strike me down. He smiled and nodded, ripped it open, and glanced at it. Then he said, "I hope you don't mind, that's just the rules. People have to follow the rules. You didn't look at it, so your discipline is strong. You're a good comrade. Here, have a look. It says nice things about you." With that, he handed me the sheet of paper. I said I didn't need to look, but he insisted. It contained a row of English letters, which I quickly deciphered: "Bai is from my and Code Zero's hometown. You can trust him." It was signed "Tian." After I'd read it, he tried to burn it, but his matches were damp, and even after a few attempts, he couldn't get one to light. The stench of red phosphorus gave me a shock. There was now a haze of ash and a faint puff of smoke wafting between me and Dou Sizhong. Nothing is lighter than ash, but when it drifted toward me, I instinctively ducked away.

Dou Sizhong sat cross-legged on the edge of the bed, and asked what the Commander had told me to say. I read him Tian Han's entire message, not leaving out a single word. He didn't show any reaction, as if it were an unimportant matter. Then he turned the conversation around to my father-in-law, and said that before going to Dihua, he had suggested to the Organization that the landlord label should be removed from him. He even asked about my son. I could hold myself up proudly here, and said,

"I'm pleased to let the Commander know that my son is now a soldier, fighting under General Peng Dehuai." He shook my hand and said, "The boy's a hero, just like his father." To tell the truth, although I knew he was just being polite, I still found myself dabbing away tears.

After a moment's pause, I couldn't resist asking how Ge Ren was doing. He said, "Code Zero is in Baibei Town on Bare Mountain. You'll see him very soon." He also mentioned how, like me, he cared a lot about Ge Ren, and had a lot of respect for him. "He went to Yan'an, and was willing to give up his ministerial position to do translation instead, providing an ideological basis for the Revolution. That's really something." He produced a photograph of Ge Ren from his pocket. "Look, I even kept his picture." He held it up and stared at it a while before showing it to me. It was Ge Ren, seen in profile, in front of his cave house. If I remember right, it was taken by an American journalist named Edgar Snow. He also mentioned that he'd had the honor of reading Ge Ren's poem "Who Was Once Me" many years before, and still adored it—did I know it? I said of course I did. Afraid of letting something slip, I didn't say any more than that. He started to declaim the poem. His voice was hoarse, with an occasional sharp tone, like metal scraping on stone. As he recited, he would abruptly thrust his hands out, startling me. I thought, if Ge Ren were here, he'd be confused by this sight, and surely not admit this was his poem. When he got to the word "stream," Dou pronounced it like the Japanese "yoshi." More often, he chopped up lines into little phrases that came out briskly, forcefully, like an assault.

Who Was Once Me

The poem Dou Sizhong brought up was Ge Ren's most famous piece. There are three versions. The first, completed in Japan, was titled "Broad Bean Blossoms." Unfortunately, this manuscript is lost to us. He finished the second in prison, and as Dou Sizhong said, it was called "Who Was Once Me." The final version reverted to "Broad Bean Blossoms"—I will mention this again in the third section, so we'll leave it for now.

In July 1920, Ge Ren's former cellmate Mr. Kong Fantai mentioned "Who Was Once Me" during an interview with the French journalist Jacques Ferrand. Anyone familiar with the May Fourth Movement will probably have come across Mr. Kong. He and Ge Ren were both arrested the day after they took part in the march on June 3. His status was somewhat unusual: firstly, he was a journalist himself, and secondly, he was a seventy-fourth-generation descendant of Confucius. As a result, when they let him out of jail, he was immediately sought after for interviews, by both Chinese and foreign media. When he spoke to Ferrand, not only did he bring up this poem, he also talked about his time in prison with Ge Ren. M. Ferrand delivered both his interview and the poem to *Nouveau Siècle*, a journal that was causing quite a stir at the time. Claiming a "lack of space," they never published the interview, only the poem:

> Who was once me,
> Who was the daytime in my mirror,
> The rippling brook through the hills
> Or the broad bean blossoms by the water?
>
> Who was once me,
> Who was the springtime in my mirror,
> The bees that swarm in the branches
> Or the lovers singing below the trees?
>
> Who was once me,
> Who was the lifetime in my mirror,
> The blue flame flickering in the breeze
> Or the wild rose unfurling in the dark?
>
> Who warns me in the darkness,
> Who walks toward me from the crowd,
> Who breaks my mirror into little shards
> So that I turn into countless selves?

The interview later appeared in M. Ferrand's essay collection *L'Entretien infini* [The Infinite Conversation; the Chinese edition of this book was published by Close to Shore]. The following excerpt is the section pertaining to Ge Ren:

> F: Mr. Kong, I heard you were locked up in the stables. And you were beaten?
>
> K: No, [conditions in] the Infantry High Command stables are excellent, but I didn't get the chance to enjoy them. (*laughter*) I was kept in a room next to the stables, with brown paper pasted over the windows. There were thirty-two of us in there. By the next day, just thirty. Two died. In the middle of the night, we heard the horses snorting. Did we get beaten? That depends on which end they started from. If the stables, we'd definitely suffer. If the armory, they were usually out of energy by the time they got to my end. We were luckier—it smelled so bad on that side, they usually didn't come over.
>
> F: How did you get through that time?
>
> K: Poetry, singing, meditation, dozing, and also getting beaten up. (*laughter*)

F: Poetry? Singing?

K: That's right. There was a good poem—my friend wrote it in there—and everyone can find his own shadow in it. If you want to see it, I can write it out for you.

F: I don't worship any god as much as the Muse. Could you introduce me to this poet?

K: You'll see him. As you know, he was like me, arrested after taking part in a march. Of course you can see him. But not here, in France. His fiancée is in France. He'll probably go there too. He wants to seek treatment in France. Yes, he has lung disease; he was vomiting blood in jail. If it's possible at that time, I can write a letter asking if he will let you interview him. He's shy, so he usually won't agree. Your coffee is excellent—the best I've ever tasted.

F: Thank you. You say he's shy?

K: Yes, that's right.

F: Ah, shyness is a sort of secret. It's the flower of personal secrets. It's a careful protection of the self.

K: No, he's not selfish. The Chinese are never selfish. In fact, he and I were both arrested because we tried to help other people. He's a professor at a medical school [i.e., the Beijing Academy of Medicine], and I'm a journalist. We have jobs of our own; we didn't need to go on the march to earn money.

F: Mr. Kong, what I meant was, he knows how to grin and bear it.

K: Ge Ren? How did you know he's called Ge Ren?

F: I said "grin," not "Ge Ren." (*laughter*) Although, my esteemed Mr. Kong, you have accidentally revealed his name. I know who you're talking about. I even know his fiancée is Miss Bingying, the daughter of Hu An.

To be clear, as we already know, Ge Ren never made it to France. He went to the Soviet Union instead. It was actually Kong Fantai who, with M. Ferrand's help, went to France. There this descendant of Confucius became a devotee of Rousseau. In the spring of 1943, he returned to China, where he had an encounter with Bingying and Mr. Fan Jihuai, this book's third narrator.

Nosebleed

By the time he was done reciting the poem, the sky was bright. Light streamed through the window onto his face, which was pale, although his ears remained dark, like the words he'd just spoken. It was quite cold, but there was a sheen of sweat on the tip of his nose. I noticed his lips trembling from time to time, as if they'd been bitten by a mosquito. And then something happened: blood began to flow from his left nostril.

I quickly got him to lie down. As I was supporting him, Nankai came in. Dou Sizhong seemed lost in the poem still, and wouldn't stop shaking. Now his right nostril began to bleed too. Nankai said, "Commander is great in every way except one: he doesn't know when he needs to rest!" I quickly said that this was nothing at all, no need to worry. Catch some snails and roast them, grind them to a powder, and blow it up his nose; that should stop the bleeding. Nankai scratched his head and asked where I expected him to find snails on such a cold day. I thought a bit, then told him there was one other way. He asked what method, and I hesitated, but told him anyway. "Go gather some donkey shit," I said. Nankai's face changed color. I hastily explained that in Yan'an, I would burn donkey dung and use the ash to treat nosebleeds. Dou Sizhong said, "Do whatever Dr. Bai says." I was grateful for that. I thought the donkey might have returned to Yan'an, but it surely had left some droppings behind.

We soon found some in the courtyard. I dried it over a coal fire, then held a match to it. Nankai knelt to one side, guarding the flaming dung. When it was burned to ash, Nankai got on all fours, sniffing fiercely at it. His actions made me think of Tian Han's guard. When I treated Tian Han for constipation, whatever medicine I prescribed him, his guard would have to taste first. I didn't give him donkey dung, though, but morning glory and peach blossoms. Now Nankai took a pinch of the ash and put it in his mouth. I asked if there was a sharp taste to it. He nodded. And sweet within the sharp? He nodded. And bitter within the sweet? He nodded once more. "Then that's right," I said. He stared at me for an instant before letting me proceed. I got Dou Sizhong to lie with his face to one side, then blew the donkey dung ash into his nostrils. The bleeding soon stopped. Before Dou Sizhong could open his mouth, Nankai jumped in to say he'd like to thank me on behalf of the Commander. I told Nankai that he ought to thank the donkey instead—it was a revolutionary donkey.

To tell the truth, after the bleeding stopped, Dou Sizhong's attitude toward me changed, as if we were now not only comrades, but war buddies too. He treated me to a sumptuous breakfast: flatbreads and a sheep's head, with sheep kidneys on the side. Those half-cooked kidneys were exactly to his taste. As he chewed on them, he said he couldn't imagine why Ge Ren would have run off to such a godforsaken place, and he'd like to hear my views. Although any conclusion you draw about Ge Ren might be a distortion, I still told him what I truly thought: in my professional opinion, Code Zero might be there to recuperate. He had lung disease, and needed the moist air and sunlight of the south. "What else? Go on," said Dou Sizhong. I had to continue, so I said Code Zero was a literary man down to his bones, and perhaps he was on Bare Mountain because he wanted a peaceful place to write. Unexpectedly, Dou Sizhong agreed with me. He said he'd had those thoughts too. When I got to Bare Mountain, he went on, I should make sure I got every scrap of Ge Ren's writing, and not let any of it fall into an outsider's hands, not a single page—this was the wealth of the Revolution. With a solemn face, he said this wasn't his personal view, but an order from the Commander.

Scatology

Frankly speaking, when I first read Dr. Bai's account, I was confused. This person talked about shit at the slightest excuse—was something wrong with him, or was he just vulgar? But then I realized I'd misunderstood. He was a scatologist, so this was simply a professional habit. Yu Chengze, currently a PhD academic advisor at Shanghai Medical University, was classmates with Bai Shengtao. He recalled that Dr. Bai was the most hardworking pupil in class, and a favorite of Kawata. Professor Yu wrote a feature on him for *Prominent Doctors* magazine, and in the May 1993 issue, we find the following passage under "Tales of the Famous":

> Bai Shengtao was a few years older than we were, and he joined the school later. When he enrolled, Professor Kawata happened to be teaching us lowerclassmen. Kawata's own training was at Sendai University, where he was in the same class as Mr. Lu Xun, studying under Mr. Fujino. Kawata's personality was completely different from Lu Xun's, though—he was more like what we would now call a hippie. He was always talking to us about bowel movements, starting with baby excrement and how amazing it was. He would stand on stage with a clump of infant stool in his hand, rolling it in his palms into a ball, dividing it in two. The stuff is pale yellow, so it looked like he was holding two miniature pears. As he spoke, he would toss them in the air and catch them, over and over, like a magician. Once he summoned all of us to the front, both the boys and girls, to pat it, smell it. Alarmingly, he also wanted us to take a bite and taste its flavor and firmness. Some of the girls covered their faces and stepped away from him. That's when Professor Kawata suddenly put some in his own mouth, chewing it like it was gum, even sticking his tongue out to let us see. I remember that of all the students, the first one to step forward was Bai Shengtao. He was already prepared to sacrifice himself for the right cause. Later on, he was also the first of our group to go to the Soviet Union, and the first in Yan'an. He didn't have to go to Yan'an—he already

had a private clinic in Shanghai at the time. Later on, his whereabouts were unknown, perhaps sacrificed [*sic*].

Kawata explained to us that he was not trying to give us a hard time; he simply wanted everyone to be familiar with the most secret aspects of humanity. Feces, urine, pus, phlegm, as well as blood, cerebrospinal fluid, pleural fluid—all of these were normal biochemical substances. Through them, we could understand human bodies and minds. In a person's life, they expel flatus more than a hundred thousand times, and excrete thirty tons of stool. When someone giggled, he said this was nothing to laugh at. A doctor is obligated to understand these things, just as a carpenter must know how to decipher the markings on a piece of wood. In the following days, we learned a great deal from him about fecal matter, as well as some scatological religious knowledge that no Chinese professor would have taught us. He asked if we believed in God, and no one raised their hand, so he pointed at Bai Shengtao and said, Didn't you use to work in a church? That's how we found out that Bai had been a chapel servant. Kawata told us that western doctors believe God placed many miracle cures in excrement, and this has been proved by experiments: horse excrement treats pleurisy, pig excrement stops bleeding, human excrement is good for circulation and cuts, donkey excrement is used for bloody stools, and cow excrement mixed with crushed rose petals can stop epilepsy and convulsions, particularly in children. Under his influence, we started using excrement in all sorts of comparisons. For instance, in talking about how a doctor's emergency response plan ought to have a strict order, we said that if you had excrement for brains, it was best to first dig a toilet in your head.

Looking back at it now, Kawata was instrumental in the development of Chinese medicine. In the field of medical studies alone, I am inclined to group him with figures such as Norman Bethune and Dwarkanath Kotnis. With today's advanced medicine, perhaps we no longer need excrement for treatment; nor do we often diagnose based on observation of stool. Before Liberation, though, when China was still very poor and backward, torn apart by frequent wars, being able to understand, know, and use excrement was a fundamental skill no doctor could be without. And in this area, Dr. Kawata made an unmistakable contribution.

Now we move on to Bai Shengtao. After coming to Yan'an from Shanghai, his main contribution to the Revolution was in the area of treating constipation. During the Yan'an era, many of those who had been through the Long March suffered from it, due to a lack of fruits and vegetables, and to rice being replaced by millet in their diets. The most well-known of these patients was Mao himself.

As Claire Hollingsworth, the British journalist who became famous for being the first to report the outbreak of World War II, wrote in her book *Mao and the Men against Him* (Jonathan Cape, 1984),

> Life in the security of Yenan gradually developed a social and political pattern. . . . Small incidents assumed great importance amongst the members of the isolated community, and Mao's bowel movements were a constant subject of conversation—the change of diet from rice to millet on top of the hardships of the March had caused him and many others to suffer from chronic constipation—so that after a bowel movement people would congratulate him. This may seem laughable, but there can be no doubt that many of the Long Marchers at the opening of the Yenan period suffered . . .

Like Mao, Tian Han happily accepted everyone's congratulations every time he managed to move his bowels. In *Shooting the Breeze with Tian Han*, Zhu Xudong recorded something Tian Han said as he lay on his sickbed. The "doctor" referred to here is Bai Shengtao:

> Back then, whether or not you could take a piss or a dump was, in a way, the key question of the Revolution. Think about it, Comrade Zhu. If your belly was permanently full of piss, how would you fight a war? That's why we said that constipation and urinary problems were our enemy. Now that I mention it, I really have to thank the doctor. There were two times he came through for us. He got me to drink something a bit like black sesame paste, and everything just shot right out of me. The doctor congratulated me. I asked what this miracle was, and he said morning glory seeds. Later on, we couldn't get any more of those, and he switched to fried carrot seeds. One time, the investigators searched a landowner's house. That fellow was a carrot farmer, so his house was full of carrot seeds. Once we got our hands on a supply, we could go into battle without worrying. There was a saying going around at the time: Pee and shit to clear the way, lead the charge and seize the day, revolution must hold sway.

There are several reasons why Tian Han might have sent Bai Shengtao to Baibei, but there's one reason—or we could call it a precondition—that shouldn't be neglected: Tian Han and the others were no longer constipated, so the scatological expert Bai Shengtao had already fulfilled his role in history.

Hearts Like the Buddha

I wanted to go sooner, but Dou Sizhong insisted that I stay for two days. He said it had been such a difficult journey there, and a TB victim like Ge Ren wasn't going to die just like that, so a couple more days wouldn't make any difference. Besides, if he wasn't a good host to me, how could he ever explain himself to my Commander? To tell the truth, it was really surprising to me that a Donkeysky like me could ever enjoy such hospitality.

That evening, we went for a walk. As it grew dark, the north wind rose, and the air held the scent of snow to come, as well as a hint of gunpowder. He asked me how the Commander and Ge Ren got along. I said, "Very well. They have a deep revolutionary friendship." Next he asked if Ge Ren and the Commander got to know each other in Qinggeng Church. I wasn't sure where he was going with that, so I hedged: "At this moment, the Commander is an atheist."

He said this wasn't a Meeting, so I could speak freely instead of being so anxious. I said it was true, they had indeed first met in the orphanage run by the church. He knew about the orphanage too, because his hometown of Changshu also had an orphanage run by westerners. He also knew that the Qinggeng Orphanage had been set up by Reverend Beal. "Sometimes those who spread western religions also do good, even if these good deeds are only meant to throw people off their guard." I've always been grateful to Reverend Beal, but given the circumstances, I had to listen to him spew insults rather than try to explain. He also asked about Ge Ren's mother's death, and his grandfather. I told him that old Mr. Ge had squandered his family's wealth on opium, and it was after his death that Reverend Beal had the orphanage take Ge Ren in. Dou Sizhong said ah, he'd heard Comrade Tian Han mention this before. Dou also knew Tian Sanhu, whom he called the leader of the anti–western religions movement. On this point, he bragged that Tian Han had once praised him for looking a bit like Tian Sanhu. General, you probably don't know who Tian Sanhu is? He was a distant uncle of Tian Han's. Back in the day, he formed a gang of outlaws in the forest, comparing himself to Chao Gai from *The Water Margin*. Still, as they say, a rabbit doesn't eat the grass by his burrow, and Tian Sanhu never harmed the people of Qinggeng. To tell the truth, with him watching over them, the residents were seldom bothered by marauding rebels. The most foolish thing he did was to burn down Qinggeng Church. This guy came to a bad end. During the Northern Expedition, Chiang Kai-shek wanted to recruit him, but he refused. Old Chiang got angry and bumped him off. At the time, though, hearing Dou Sizhong compare himself to Tian Sanhu, I hastened to praise him, insisting he was indeed a second Tian Sanhu.

I was puzzled. Dou Sizhong evidently knew everything there was to know about Ge Ren, so why was he still asking these questions? Was he testing me, to see if I'd try to flatter him, tossing out all this coloratura?

My god, what if there was something wrong with my answers? I couldn't help but tremble at the thought. To prevent Dou Sizhong from seeing what was on my mind, I pretended to be freezing, clapping my hands over my mouth and blowing on them. I even managed a sniffle. Thinking I really was cold, Dou Sizhong took off his jacket and draped it over my shoulders. I tried to refuse, but he said it was an order. If I caught a chill and had to delay my journey, that would be a great loss to the Revolution. It would have been disrespectful not to, so I had no choice but to put on his jacket. I was reminded of when Tian Han had given me that diagonally striped coat, so I mentioned it. "The Commander has a heart like the Buddha," said Dou Sizhong. "He cares for his men like they were his own sons." Now that I think about it, he was really gilding his own reputation, pretending to talk about Tian Han when really he meant himself. Next he moved on to my Donkeysky problem. "You might be a Trotskyite, but not only have we not beaten you to death, we're even giving you a chance to redeem yourself." His words finally brought tears to my eyes. As I wept, he suddenly changed the subject and asked if I'd heard of the Battle of Two Li Mound. I said that I had. In a voice full of emotion, he blurted out, It would have been better for Ge Ren if he had died then.

I'd had my ears boxed a few times in Back Ditch, and hearing Dou Sizhong say this now, I thought at first that my hearing must have been damaged, but his expression told that me that my ears hadn't deceived me. I was so scared, I stopped breathing. Dou Sizhong said, "You, me, Commander Tian, and many other comrades all love Ge Ren deeply. If he'd been martyred then, he would have become a hero of the People. But now he's nothing at all. If he returned to Yan'an, he'd be treated as a traitor. You have to understand that in most people's eyes, in this life-and-death struggle, if someone isn't a hero, then he's a villain. There'll definitely be people who think there's no way he could still be alive unless he was working with the enemy. Of course, you and I know he wouldn't do that, but the way people are, that's what they're going to think. Even if he isn't executed, he'll be labeled a Trotskyite and [get] expelled from the ranks of the Revolution. The Party might be merciful and let him keep his life, but at that point he might as well be dead."

My brain went boom, like a thunderclap in my head. I pricked up my ears, wanting to hear every word, but they refused to cooperate and buzzed furiously instead. After a while, I steadied myself and asked Dou what we ought to do, though I already had an idea what his answer would be. He scratched his head and said this question had caused him a lot of pain. He'd been pondering it day and night, unable to eat or sleep well.

After much pondering, he had finally come up with a solution: Ge Ren had to die quietly, without anyone knowing. My god, that's what I'd been afraid of [hearing]. The more you fear something, the more it's going to come knocking at your door. He went on, "Comrade Bai Shengtao, you're definitely the best person for the job, but if you're finding this difficult, the Party will think of another way." I didn't dare say too much, so I just asked him if there was any other way. "Naturally. He could pretend to die, and stay silent forever." I hastily told him that I would travel through the night to Bare Mountain and order Ge Ren not to say so much as a single word. No matter how sincerely I spoke, he just listened skeptically. Then he said it was too late for that. According to the latest intelligence reports, Ge Ren had recently published something revealing his identity. To tell the truth, General, I was furious to hear that. I thought, how could someone as brilliant as Ge Ren have done something so stupid?

Dou Sizhong went on, "Comrade Bai, we all have hearts like the Buddha, but in order to salvage this revolutionary's reputation, we will have to kill him. That's right, kill him. Comrade Bai, please don't think of him as a person, but as a type of person. This type of person is wise his whole life long, then makes a huge mistake at a crucial moment of the Revolution. If we still love him as much as before, the only thing to do is eliminate him completely. There is no other way, Comrade Bai. Only by looking at the issue in this way can we pull ourselves out of the pit of suffering." The sun had set by that point, and I strained to hear Dou Sizhong's last words in the dark. He said this wasn't his idea alone; it was what everyone who adored Ge Ren wanted. If the only choices were to give him immortal life through death or to leave him alive in a state worse than death, then we had no reason not to choose the former.

His tone was brisk, as if he were giving the order to a firing squad. I thought I could smell animal skin, like the leather holster for a revolver. It was emanating from Dou Sizhong's waist, much stronger than the scent of snow. The snow would eventually melt, but this whiff of leather would linger through time. I knew that if I uttered a single word now, my head would be blown wide open. General, I now understand that human fear doesn't start in the head, it starts in the feet. First your heels turn icy, then the chill spreads up your legs. Your gallbladder shrinks, and then it continues up your spine. Only at the end does your scalp turn numb. When Dou Sizhong asked what I thought, I quickly replied, "Commander, wherever you point, I will shoot in that direction." He stared at me for a second, as if searching for evidence of something untrustworthy in my face. My expression seemed to satisfy him. He pulled my jacket shut, then patted me on the shoulder blade. "Comrade Bai, you won't be the one doing it. The Party has considered your friendship with the man, and also the fact that you're a doctor. We don't want to make things difficult for you. You won't be the one who pulls the trigger."

That was another shock—I was afraid some other difficulty would rear its head. He explained, "The Party's considered this carefully. It's like rehearsing a play. If you've been practicing with a knife, and I suddenly tell you to use a club, how will you cope? Zhao Yaoqing will do it. He's a soldier, and can kill a person without blinking. Your job will be to pass the order to Zhao, and afterward bring back Ge Ren's writing. Count the pages first, don't leave a single one behind." He emphasized once again that these papers were treasures of the Revolution, and didn't belong to Ge Ren alone—the Commander wanted to see just what it was that Ge Ren had been writing.

On our way back to Longyu, I was most worried about missing Ah Qing's call. Now I understand why Dou Sizhong wanted me to delay my departure: so that I could get a message from Ah Qing first. At the time, if he could have contacted Ah Qing himself, he would have given the order directly. In that case, of course, there'd have been no reason to get me to Zhangjiakou alive. It's hard to know what fate has in store for a person. Still, luck must have been on my side, because no ghosts came knocking at my door. Right up to the time I left Zhangjiakou, I still hadn't heard from Ah Qing.

The Majesty of the Orient

Although he was an important figure in the Ge Ren affair, we have very little information about Dou Sizhong. I could only find one picture of him and Tian Han, in Zhu Xudong's *Tian Han: An Autobiography*. Tian Han is on a horse, while Dou stands by its head, clutching the bridle. Perhaps by comparison with the steed, Dou Sizhong's face looks particularly short. His hair is long, and he has whiskers, making him look a little feline. This photograph was taken in Bao'an in 1936. According to Zhu Xudong, when he asked Tian Han who that was standing beside him, Tian Han answered only, "His name is Dou, like Dou E from *Snow in Midsummer.*" That's the only reference. Which is to say, up to this point, all we know from Bai Shengtao is that Dou Sizhong was originally from Changshu in Jiangsu Province. Other than that, there's no other biographical or personal information we can verify.

Dou Sizhong must have gotten to know Reverend Beal through Tian Han. As I mentioned earlier, the reverend was a former missionary in the Qinggeng District, and later wrote a book with Reverend Ellis called *The Majesty of the*

Orient. Reverend Beal was a very learned man—he had researched everything from the sweet pastries described in the ancient Egyptian *Book of the Dead* to the four rivers of Paradise mentioned in the Qur'an. He had dabbled in medicine too. During the Second World War, he and Reverend Ellis volunteered with the International Red Cross. According to my great-aunt's description, "He was tall and skinny, with giant feet. We nicknamed him the Towering Poplar. He was very gentle, with a soft voice that felt like the wind blowing down from the treetops."

The following passage is from *The Majesty of the Orient*, and describes some moments from Ge Ren's and Tian Han's childhood. [N.B. The "Ge Shang-Jên" (or Ge Shangren, in pinyin) mentioned in the text is Ge Ren—that was his name as a child.]

I arrived in China in 1898, or as it was known to the Chinese, the Wu-Hsü Year. Mount Ch'ing-Kêng referred not just to the hill, but also to an area the size of a small European country. It was also in this year that the Ch'ing government released its *Statutes Guiding the Reception of Foreign Clergy by Local Officials*. As a result of that document, I became known among the local populace as a "West man." Prior to my arrival, church affairs were managed by Revd. W. Ellis. Ch'ing-Kêng Church was built during the seventeenth year of the Wan-Li Emperor in the Ming Dynasty. I had a favorable impression of it. I can still recall the brick-paved pathways, the gold-chased engravings atop the pillars, the portraits of Christ on the cross within the chapel, as well as the statue of the Holy Mother on the altar. Unfortunately, these were all subsequently destroyed.

Revd. Ellis and I established an orphanage at Mount Ch'ing-Kêng. The first child we took in was a female infant who'd been abandoned by the side of the Ji River. Only many years later would I learn that she was the twin sister of Ge Shang-Jên. Some time later, Ge Shang-Jên himself arrived at the orphanage. By then he was a young man, filled with intelligence, his eyes as bright as dewdrops. Even his name displayed a certain consciousness of Chinese religions—"jên," or benevolence, is an important Confucian principle, while "shang" often appears in Confucian texts. His mother was a highly intelligent woman who unfortunately died young. Not long after her passing, his grandfather departed too. There is a matter relating to this death that is worth recounting here. His grandfather had a cat named Mimi. He wiped his opium pipe on her fur, and told the time by her eyes—apparently cats' eyes change at different times of the day. For instance, when a cat's pupils become as thin as a mouse's, stretching vertically across the entire eye, the onlooker can tell it is noon. This old man's love for his cat was even greater than that for his grandson. He even allowed her to nap in his sleeves, and it is said that to avoid waking her up, he would cut off his sleeves if need be. Sadly, in China, love inevitably leads to disaster! Mimi the cat became one of his funerary objects. Before he died, he killed Mimi and made her into soup, which he drank. He must have thought this was the best way to show his love for his cat. She had once played the role of his clock, and so we may conclude that Mr. Ge regarded his own death as the end of history.

Ge Shang-Jên's best friend at the orphanage was named T'ien Ts'ung. None of the boys in our charge had living parents, and T'ien Ts'ung was no exception. His uncle, whose name was T'ien San-Hu, had failed in his duty to care for the child. Many years later, the fatherless and motherless T'ien Ts'ung became a general. At this time, his name was changed to T'ien Han—replacing the "Ts'ung" of cleverness with the "Han" of sweat. Although this was merely a change of one character, it indicated that he had penetrated to the heart of Chinese philosophy. The Chinese are against cleverness for its own sake, but they exalt hard work and endurance. My memory of T'ien Ts'ung is that he was intelligent and active, but a trifle bashful. I can recall a time when I was bringing Ge Shang-Jên back from an excursion. As we entered the courtyard, the other children were playing with sand. A girl walked up to Shang-Jên and placed a handful of fine sand on his palm—in the twilight, it was a dazzling golden color. T'ien Ts'ung came over too. Kicking up a cloud of sand, he sprinted down the heap and up to Shang-Jên. But he was unable to stop in time, and he suddenly fell to the ground, raising a bump on his head. When he saw me standing there, he was so embarrassed by his tumble that his face flushed bright red, like a girl's.

When I think about Ge Shang-Jên and T'ien Ts'ung, my memory lingers on a snowy winter's day. I remember they would often pray among the snowdrifts—afraid that their families would be buried deep, and grow even farther from them. I once took both boys to a cemetery in the countryside. In keeping with Chinese custom, they burned hell money, which was supposed to be legal tender in the lower realms. T'ien Ts'ung couldn't find his family's graves, but Ge Shang-Jên found his. He knelt before them, sobbing quietly. Another scene in my memory is from a day when the wind changed direction and we entered the season of melting snow. Once again I accompanied them to the graveyard. Again they prayed that their loved ones would be able to enter the Kingdom of Heaven. A little girl had made the trip with us. As I said before, she was Ge Shang-Jên's twin sister, although neither of them knew it at the time. She was just as sorrow-stricken as Shang-Jên, biting her lip in silence, her eyes as limpid as a stream. This was her first visit to the cemetery, and she found the surroundings strange. I can still recall how damp and murky the place felt. The withered branches, thick with snow, drooped like blackened clusters of fruit. It greatly resembled the illustrations in the Bible I had shown the children. The ancient vines brought to mind Moses's staff, carved with Egyptian markings. I tried to comfort the children by saying this scene looked like the pictures in the Bible, so surely their families must be in heaven.

Mission work in Ch'ing-Kêng was not as easy as some might believe. Revd. Ellis and I were gratified by the growth of the children, but the truth is, many Chinese related to religion much as they did to their family structures, within which a man frequently had multiple wives. Which is to say, worshiping the Lord was often akin to taking a new concubine into the household. As far as many of them were concerned, the Kingdom of Heaven was not to be found in their hearts, but rather in what they saw around them, in the pastries, ale, and cow's milk. It was for this reason that I later stopped spreading the Word altogether, preferring to spend my energies on teaching the children to read and write. I believed that to these adorable children, knowledge could be the bread for their bodies, the clear water down their throats, the fragrant breezes in their nostrils. And I was content with my lot, for I knew this was the true meaning of heaven.

I did not know that as the Kingdom of Heaven was appearing, a difficulty would manifest itself. The accidental loss of a chess piece often leads to the demise of the entire board, and in the same vein, a great tragedy frequently begins with a single detail. When a girl ran through the fine sand in the orphanage courtyard, the grit kicked up by her delicate feet grew into a sandstorm that ultimately compelled me and Revd. Ellis to leave this place.

The "sandstorm" referred to by the reverend is metaphorical—he means the anti–western religions movement that Tian Sanhu was leading. Reverend Beal's description of him as Tian Han's "uncle" wasn't quite accurate. In fact, he was a much more distant relative, outside the five degrees of mourning. The "sandstorm" did indeed have something to do with the girls' feet, because they hadn't been bound and were growing to their natural size. At the time, such feet were known as little boats. There were four or five girls in the orphanage other than my great-aunt. In the summer, they would often walk barefoot through the courtyard, just like the boys. Whenever outsiders saw their natural feet, they would scream, "How ugly, how hideous! Such enormous little boats."

The children in the orphanage may have been parentless, but that didn't mean they had no relatives. The first conflict arose between these family members and the missionaries. They may not have been willing to raise the girls themselves, but that didn't mean they condoned their having natural feet. They wanted Beal and Ellis to pay compensation—those big feet would ruin the girls' futures, so the West men should make up for that, and consider themselves lucky to get off so lightly. Or if they didn't want to pay up, then they ought to let the families take the girls away and make up for lost time by slowly training them back onto the right path. When I went to Mount Qinggeng, I heard quite a few stories about the anti–western religions movement. The families' plan was to have these girls come home and do manual labor for a few years before marrying them off. When the question came up of how easy it would be to find husbands for them, they had to devise an alternative strategy as a backup option, which was to sell them to the brothels instead. After all, these establishments were frequented by vulgar types who were only fit to sleep with big-footed girls.

So people were banging on the door, while the West men refused to let any-one out. The situation grew tenser by the minute. At the crucial moment, it was Tian Sanhu who arrived to uphold justice. The most recent amended edition of *Chronicles of Qinggeng* (1995) mentions this incident, with text drawn from *The Red Flag Unfurls in the Western Wind* (1968 edition):

> During the noble Anti–Western Religions Patriotic Movement, Tian Sanhu was a pillar of strength. Under his brilliant leadership, the wall of the church courtyard was knocked over, the stained glass windows of the building were smashed with stones, and all the food within the premises was taken away. As for the imperialist missionaries, they fled with their tails between their legs.

We should elaborate on this last sentence, because it wasn't just the "imperialist missionaries" who "fled," but also the future general Tian Han, the People's hero Ge Ren, and Donkeysky Bai Shengtao. My great-aunt left Qinggeng too. In fact, apart from two girls who were dragged back to their families, everyone else in the orphanage ran away.

Travel Companions

The next day, we finally departed from Zhangjiakou. Before leaving, Dou Sizhong spoke to me again, and gave me a letter to pass to Ah Qing. I knew it contained his orders. I immediately proclaimed that, as Comrade Lenin said, I would protect it as I did my own eyes. Dou Sizhong praised me for this, and said if all comrades were as good as me, the National-ists would have fallen long ago, and the Japanese devils would have been driven away. As for my future, Dou Sizhong talked about that too. After completing my task, I was to hurry back overnight, because the People needed a doctor like me. He would send me a companion so I'd have someone to take care of me along the way. General, I honestly had no idea that it would turn out to be a woman. At the time, all I knew was her name: Little Red. Dou Sizhong said she was on her way to Hankou, which happened to be in my direction. To keep things simple, he suggested that we pretend to be father and daughter, or else husband and wife. Father and daughter, I insisted, father and daughter. Dou Sizhong grinned. "Best not be too rigid, or you'll fall into the trap of subjectivity. Getting the job done is most important, so do whatever it takes." I said it was just that I was somewhat older, so father and daughter would be better.

As we left Longyu Shop, I let out a long sigh of relief. To tell the truth, I'd been worried that Dou Sizhong would change his mind at the last minute and send someone else. My nerves were so on edge that when a shaft of light fell from a window of Jade Flower, I swung my head around, convinced that someone was coming after us. There was no one there, just my own shadow, which the beam of light was projecting onto a wall, looking massive, a huge rock tumbling to the ground. Then it was gone. A moment later, another beam of light shot out from another point above—I couldn't tell if it was a battlement or a gun turret on the city wall. The sky was clear, but the moon had not yet risen. Above the high walls, the Milky Way spilled out over thousands of miles. All of a sudden, I thought of Ge Ren. Was he looking up at the stars too? Did he know about my mission? And if he did, how did he feel about it? I cautioned myself to say as few words to Little Red as possible. We both dozed on the way up to the Chahar border—me pretending, her actually asleep—and didn't open our eyes till we got to Beiping. It seemed she was a frequent visitor there—she knew people, and could find her way around. She led me here and there through the city, and then onto a passenger train. There weren't many people in the carriage, and most of the space was taken up by emergency rations. I don't have to tell you what they were for—the Henan famine. Ever since the Nationalists had blown up the dikes and caused the Yellow River to flood, things had been rough for the people of Henan. Naturally, many people believed this was a good thing, because a poorer population would be more revolutionary. Right, let's not talk about that. It was only because of Little Red that we were able to get on that train. She knew the officers who'd requisitioned it well—if she wanted to smoke, a soldier would light her cigarette; if she wanted a drink, a cup of water would arrive. She told me that the soldier's lighter was a gift from her, genuine American goods. I never found out that man's name, so let's call him American Goods. He went off to play cards, got as far as the space between carriages, and turned back. Smiling meaningfully at me, he said, "Are you two a couple, or what?" Before I could answer, Little Red was stroking American Goods' face and murmuring, "Is the soldier boy jealous?" Without having to say so, she was signaling to everyone that they were more than just friends. This was a killer move. While American Goods fetched and carried for us, the other passengers could only stare helplessly. The only person who looked bad was me—a carriage full of people assumed either that I was unable to control my daughter or that my wife was cuckolding me to my face. This was precisely the result Little Red wanted. When she sat on my knee, you could have said this was a daughter behaving childishly with her dad, or equally a wife putting out the fires of jealousy in her husband. Two birds with one stone. I wanted them to know I wasn't just put upon, that I was still a red-blooded man, so I came up with a plan: damn it, if anyone asked me again if we were a couple, I'd say, Sure we are; she's the concubine I've just married. But all the way to Xinxiang County, no one asked me the question.

There were a lot of incidents on the Beiping-to-Hankou route, so the lights in the carriage went out early. American Goods came over with a lantern to ask why we weren't asleep. Little Red said she wasn't tired. He replied, "Have you gotten your days turned around—wide awake at night?" It was a normal thing to say, but Little Red got annoyed. "Hey, you're the one who's turned around. You walk with your head on the ground!" Seeing them about to start quarreling, I quickly tried to calm things down. American Goods claimed he wasn't angry, but then he started an oblique attack with a rant about his niece Tie Mei, who had a hair-trigger temper—she would attack anyone who said the wrong thing. That did it, I thought. Little Red was going to let him have it now. Unexpectedly, though, not only did she keep her temper, she even broke into a smile. Then she said to American Goods, "Look at you: your whole face is sallow from dissipation. I'm sure you've been up to no good. In a minute you'll turn into Jia Rui from *Dream of the Red Chamber*." He answered, "Right, your ladyship. People like you have dragged me down."

There was a hint within those words. Had Little Red perhaps come from Jade Flower, next to Longyu Shop? A short while later, she told me herself that yes, she had worked at a brothel. "You'll find out sooner or later anyway, so I'll just tell you. It's no big deal." She was originally from Hankou, and had gone to Beiping to study with an opera troupe. After her training, she became a good enough performer that many important men in the audience wanted to marry her, but she couldn't be bothered to so much as look at them. She was young and ignorant, and besides, she had become infatuated with a wastrel who owned a foreign car dealership. She ended up as his second wife. When the guy was in love with her, he'd say she was first in his heart, but once he got tired of her, he'd scream that she was just a mistress, and shove her hard into the wall. "When will these bad times end?" she lamented. Not long after that, his business folded, and she thought that was her chance to get away, but instead the bastard sold her to a brothel in Tianjin. Beautiful women always suffer in life, she said, her eyes moist. "But it all worked out—I met my Prince Charming, and escaped from the pit." Her Prince Charming was Nankai—he was the one who had rescued her. He had also worked to correct her thinking, telling her that no one in the world hasn't taken a wrong turn—but while the road behind was twisty, the future was bright and clear, and she had to look ahead. Then the Party cured her illness; otherwise she might have become a crushed blossom long ago. Sometime after that, she came to Zhangjiakou, where she worked in a shop. I asked if she knew the people in Jade Flower. She thought about it and said yes, she felt very sorry for those girls, and when she had time, she would teach them to sing opera. It's always good to learn a skill, and this way they might have a better life in the future.

It was clear to me, General, that her words couldn't be trusted. I was suspicious from the start that she had another mission. I tried to get at the truth by asking why she was going to Hankou. Her reasoning sounded impeccable—she hadn't been back home in many years, so this visit was overdue. I asked who was left at home, and she started weeping. Her parents had long since died, she said, and she was going to see a woman she had trained with. It was this woman who had brought her to Beiping, and she had been another father and mother to her. Not only was she beautiful, she sang wonderfully, and wrote poetry too. Apart from her fate, she was good in every way. She'd heard that her friend had gotten divorced, and she had wanted to visit her for some time, but the Party said the journey would be dangerous, and wouldn't let her go. So she cried in front of them, and crying children are the ones who get the milk—the Organization told her that if anyone was heading south and happened to pass by Hankou, she could go with them. Did this mean that I was her bodyguard? Then she said something that sounded very nice: that the Party had told her to wait in Hankou for me to return, and then she would travel back to Zhangjiakou with me. Afterward, she said, she'd like to come to Yan'an too. She'd heard that Jiang Qing, who had been an actress under the stage name Lan Ping, had taken to Yan'an like a fish to water. She also wanted to bring this friend of hers along, so they could go to Yan'an together.

I'd suspected that this friend [of hers] might be Bingying, and that she was going to find her to explain the situation. Having heard her full story, I changed my mind. Besides, Bingying was from Hangzhou, not Hankou, so they couldn't have studied together.

Little Red seemed tired from having talked so much, and she leaned against me for a while. She was wearing some sort of cold cream that smelled delightful. I asked what brand it was—the ice was broken now, and she was talking to me quite openly. After all, she was a theater person. She said, "Ah, you seemed quite westernized; who'd have thought you were just a bumpkin." It wasn't cold cream, she said, but Feisheng Cheese Cream. Whatever the movie star Butterfly Wu rubbed on her face, she would rub on her own. Don't you believe me, General? I'm just telling the truth. She also told me this cream was manufactured by the Swiss company Siber, Hegner & Co., and if I wanted a girl to like me, I'd just have to give her some of it, and all resistance would vanish. All she had to do was put on a little of the stuff, and no matter where she went, no matter how far away, she'd have men circling her. "Even Yan'an?" I asked. She paused a moment, then said, "Yes, why not? At least at night. Who doesn't want a nice-smelling woman between his sheets?" As for that, I had nothing to say. All the time I was in Yan'an, I never had a nice-smelling woman between my sheets. She went on, "Never mind Yan'an, it even works in the Soviet Union. I've heard those big western mares also use this cream."

A Goose Footprint in Muddy Snow

Little Red's real name was Hong Yan, as in goose—though she went by the stage name Little Red Woman. That's right, she later became the famous Peking opera artiste Little Red Woman. In 1998, she published a book called *A Goose Footprint in Muddy Snow*, a collection of her lectures at the drama academy and various arts conferences. I read the book all the way through, and finally found a speech titled "An Artist's Courage" in which she mentions that trip to Hankou. Although her words are elliptical, we can catch a glimpse of the truth:

> . . . As I said earlier, quite a few comrades have told me that everyone is gaining a great deal from our three days together. It's always better to gain something than not—congratulations, all of you. (*applause*) As a veteran on the front line of culture, when I look back at the past, I find myself filled with emotion. Many comrades already know that we have to be both anti-leftist and anti-rightist, but primarily anti-leftist. Comrades, the path to leftism kills, and at any time could cause death. (*applause*) Before Liberation, I too almost committed a "leftist" error. They asked me

to accompany a comrade to the south, to eliminate another comrade who they said had done something wrong. At the time, I thought this comrade seemed perfectly fine. Early on, in order to find the true ideology of saving his country and his People, he traveled to the Soviet Union—I mean the former Soviet Union. Later he took part in the Long March. Why would such a person be put to death? I didn't trust Wang Ming and the others to bare [bear] good intentions. So I didn't go. Of course, I had to be tactful about it, I didn't just blert [blurt] out the truth. What I told the Organization was, "My dear leaders, it's not that I don't want to go, but I'm worried I won't be able to accomplish this task. You have to be attentive to your female comrades' strengths, and send them to do the things they're good at." This comrade might have come under the wrong influence of Wang Ming's plan, but he was still a good comrade who showed excellent sense. In the end, he didn't make me go, but sent me to Wuhan on another mission. In Wuhan I almost made another mistake. Fortunately I came to my senses in time, or else I would have regretted it my whole life. As for what that was—everyone's time is too valuable for me to go into it here. In any case, it's always worth looking back at your experience, and taking what lessons you can from it . . .

I especially chose this passage, with its rhetorical confusion and, misspellings, in order to show one fact: Little Red Woman knew very well why Bai Shengtao was traveling to Bare Mountain. Why, then, was she going to Wuhan?

The Last Long Journey

Are women in the Soviet Union all big western mares? That made me want to laugh. As for whether those mares use cheese cream, I wouldn't know. I was completely chaste during my time there, and never bothered any of them. Still, when she mentioned the Soviet Union, my heart thudded. You see what a good actress she was. When we first met, she pretended not to know anything about me. But now the truth was slipping out. I thought she must surely know that I'd been to the Soviet Union, and that my nickname was Donkeysky.

She talked for a long time, took a nap, then went off to find American Goods. I sat there alone, thinking how history toys with us, like a whore who knows how to tease her besotted admirers. On my first long journey, I had left with Ge Ren. And now I was going toward him. Only that time we were heading north, and now I was traveling south. The previous time was to help him, and this trip was to kill him. Yes, the other time I'm alluding to is our journey to the Soviet Union. After Ge Ren got out of prison, he wanted to look up Bingying in France. The problem was, he didn't know her address. The man she'd left it with [i.e., Kawata] was a drunkard. He drank too much one night and got into a fight. The other guy ripped his shirt off—and he lost the note, which had been in a pocket. This posed a problem for Ge Ren. He even made a trip to Hangzhou, hoping to get the address from Bingying's father, but the old man had gone off on a long vacation, so there was nothing to be gained there. What then, go back to Beijing and practice medicine? He considered that, but it was impossible. He'd just been released from prison, and the school would surely want him to stay away—they'd be far too frightened to offer him a job.

General, you must know that after the Russian Revolution, many intellectuals looked in that direction and started learning Russian. I won't lie to you, I did too. Yes, from Ge Ren. When he was teaching at the Beijing Academy of Medicine, he would go in his spare time to 10 Dongzongbu Hutong [N.B. The building is currently no. 23 on that street], to the Russian Language Institute there. He wanted to learn the language not just because of their revolution, but also because of their literature. He'd read Qu Qiubai's translations of Tolstoy, and adored them. He also liked Pushkin, whose poetry he said made him think of his mother's early paintings—radiant landscapes, exquisitely pure. At the time, though, he hadn't considered the idea of actually going to Russia himself. Let me put it this way, General: if that man named Huang Jishi hadn't kept coming to visit, Ge Ren would never have gone to Russia. Yes, you're right, the Huang Jishi who founded the *Shanghai Harbor Daily*. One day he came to find Ge Ren, saying he'd seen one of his poems in *Nouveau Siècle* and liked it so much he wanted to work with him. Ge Ren thought this was a writing commission, and said he only wrote verses for himself, which he wasn't ready to publish yet. After talking a while longer, Huang Jishi got up to leave, looking a little displeased. We thought he wouldn't be back, but a few days later, there he was. This time he told Ge Ren that the *Shanghai Harbor Daily* wanted to send a young man with a poetic sensibility to Russia, in order to write an article about the conditions of the Bolsheviki [i.e., the Bolsheviks] after the Revolution, which they would then publish. Huang seemed to understand what would motivate Ge Ren. He said, "If you don't go into the tiger's den, you'll never catch a tiger. Don't you love Russian literature? You'll see its true beauty if you go to Russia." Even then, Ge Ren refused to give in. He just said, "When I eat an egg, I only care if it tastes good. It doesn't matter what the hen looked like." But then Huang Jishi tried another line of attack that hit the bull's-eye. He took out a wad of cash and said, "Doesn't the gentleman want to find Bingying in France? How will you get all that way without some money in the bank? The *Shanghai Harbor Daily*'s fees are very respectable. With this, you'll be able to go look for Bingying." And so Ge Ren agreed.

To tell the truth, at that point, neither Ge Ren nor I knew that Huang Jishi was Zong Bu's friend, nor that Zong Bu was running the *Shanghai Harbor Daily* behind the scenes. It was Zong Bu's idea to send Ge Ren to Russia. He was a mysterious figure, like the mythical dragon whose head and tail you never saw at the same time. Love doesn't come out of nowhere, and neither does hate. Why was he giving us money—what was his real purpose? I couldn't figure it out. Many years later, when I learned about his affair with Bingying, I began to suspect that Zong Bu's motivation might have been to prevent Ge Ren from ever looking her up in France. Is that why he sent Huang Jishi to dispatch Ge Ren to the icy wastes of Russia?

Huang Jishi told Ge Ren that the newspaper would pay for him to bring an assistant along, so he asked if I would like to accompany him—I'd be able to continue my studies there. I said I would talk it over with my fiancée. She asked if I would have enough to eat there, and when I said I would, she exclaimed, "That's manna from heaven—of course you should go!" As soon as she said that, she burst into tears. With all that distance between us, she was worried that I would break things off with her. I said, "What kind of person do you take me for? You think I'm that heartless?" In order to prove that I did have a conscience, I married her before leaving the country. I guess Dou Sizhong had it right—revolutionaries have to talk about faith, not conscience, because only the bourgeoisie and the Japanese care about conscience. They talk about so-and-so having "a bad conscience" at the drop of a hat. There was nothing weighing on my conscience, and that's why my wife died so young. If I'd been heartless and kicked her aside, she would have lived a much longer life. It was because of me that she died. But let's not talk about that.

On the way to the Soviet Union, Ge Ren and I first took the train to Mukden [N.B. present-day Shenyang]. As the train approached the Shanhai Pass, we could see the ocean in the distance. That was my first glimpse of a beach. It was all white, covered in snow. The morning sun was rising from the water, a giant ball of fire. A ship passed by close to shore, letting out a puff of black smoke. Ge Ren said to me in a poetic voice, "Can you smell it—the scent of the sea, the scent of salt, the scent of freedom." He was intensely moved. It was evening by the time we got to the Mukden station. The platform was full of Japanese people like dwarf tigers, and not a Chinese porter in sight. It felt as if Manchuria had already been carved off and given to Japan. Luckily Ge Ren could speak Japanese. He summoned one of them, so we were able to get our luggage out of the station. We were in Mukden because Ge Ren wanted to see Kawata, our teacher from the Beijing Academy of Medicine, who had just come home. You're interested in Kawata? All right, I will say a bit more about him. We followed the map to Kawata's address, and met him on his way home. He was leaning against a woman, who was wearing men's trousers with the fly unbuttoned. Kawata himself was in a dress. He was too drunk to walk properly, and stumbled as if his legs were submerged in water to the knees. When he recognized us, he said to Ge Ren, "I'm so happy, as happy as a donkey." What did you say? Kawata didn't know what a donkey was? I guess I remembered wrong. Maybe he said as happy as a beast of burden. But how could Kawata not know what a donkey was? Aren't there donkeys in Japan? Besides, he had spent so much time in China, I'd be surprised if he really was ignorant of these creatures.

All right, I'll go on. To tell the truth, the next day Kawata insisted on accompanying us to Hsinking [N.B. now Changchun]. Every time the train went around a bend, he would stick his head out the window, saying he liked the screech of metal on metal. While Mukden was the territory of dwarfish tigers, Hsinking belonged to big western mares. There were Russians everywhere, even the carriage drivers. Kawata was mesmerized by the Orthodox icons they carried around, and by the drivers' thick leather hats. He bought himself one, and when snowflakes landed on it, he suddenly broke into a smile. At the Beijing Academy, he'd get drunk all the time—it seemed he was unwilling to ever pull himself out of his stupor. Now he was clamoring to come to Moscow with us. Ge Ren had to tell him that when we were settled down, we would send him a telegram and he could join us in the Red Capital [i.e., Moscow]. But as it turned out, we never had any further contact with him.

Little Red came back from seeing American Goods with a steamed bun and a bowl of vegetable broth for me. As I sipped it, I deliberately said, "This is excellent soup, a bit like borscht. Ah, now if I only had some buckwheat kasha to go with it." As I spoke, I watched closely for her reaction—and sure enough, she smiled a little. More proof that she knew the truth about me. "Kasha" and "borscht" were keywords. When I first got to Yan'an, many people looked down on intellectuals, so I hit back with my trip to Russia, letting everyone know I had spent time in Moscow, the heart of the Revolution. When others complained that the congee was too watery, I informed them that the kasha and borscht I'd eaten in Moscow were even more watery—you could see the moon reflected in your bowl. Those words silenced them. And because Ge Ren was famous, I was able to shelter beneath his flag—every time I mentioned kasha and borscht, I would bring up his name too. Stirring my food with chopsticks, I'd say, "Ge Ren lived on borscht and kasha while he translated Lenin's *The State and Revolution*. You get millet porridge and pumpkin soup too, but I haven't seen you produce anything." Everyone was furious with me, but there was nothing they could do. One day a patient came to see me, but she kept stuttering and wouldn't tell me anything. Finally I figured out what she was trying to say: she was suffering from vaginal discharge. She was an intellectual too, and had studied in France—but France wasn't the heart of the Revolution then, so she was angry and envious of my Russian experience. She'd arrived at Yan'an a year before I did, and she often stood on her status as an older revolutionary. Now I said, "If you'd only spent time in Russia, you'd have eaten a lot of kasha. It cools the body and clears the intestines, gets rid of gonorrhea and leukorrhea." She blushed and said, "There's buckwheat in China too." She was right, but I couldn't be bothered to argue with her. Later on, after I became Donkeysky, "kasha and borscht" became a punch line—the guards loved tormenting me with it during my time in Back Ditch. There were times when I was eating my millet porridge and they'd tap on my bowl like it was a dog's dish: "Hey, Bai, what's that you're eating? You seem to like it." If I said millet porridge, they'd get annoyed. But if I answered buckwheat kasha, they'd grin and slap each other on the back. "Look at this Donkeysky—he doesn't even know what millet is. I could die laughing." No, by then I was no longer angry. Ge Ren once said to me that other people's misfortune was my misfortune too. Once I got to Back Ditch, I no longer believed that. Instead, I learned another theory: your bad luck is someone else's happiness; for one group of people to live well, another group must suffer.

Since Little Red understood what I was saying, I decided to explain a little more. During my time in Russia, I ate a fair bit of buckwheat kasha and borscht. No particular reason; it's just that they were cheap and filling. If I was still hungry, soup would fill me up. As I spoke, I recalled Ge Ren writing late into the night. During this period, Ge Ren would often stay up writing or translating till dawn. When he got hungry in the middle of the night, he would gnaw on some black bread and have a bowl of kasha. He wasn't writing poetry, but rather reports on various subjects. Or else he'd be working on his project to romanize the Chinese language. He was also translating various things. Yes, by that time his Russian was almost native. He even had a Russian name: Melancholsky. Along with the novels of Tolstoy and Pushkin, he also translated many of Trotsky's and Lenin's speeches. Of course, what I most liked to read was his own writing, principally his travelogues—because I'd been to all the places he was writing about. Let me put it like this, General: reading his words made you feel as if you were in the cool of night, enjoying the quiet stillness of nature. So peaceful you could hear the turtledoves grooming their feathers. He liked to examine an issue starting with the details. He once said that other people preferred to take a broad view, looking at things from the top down, whereas he started with the tiniest particulars, working from the bottom up. Others saw the flames leaping from the hearth, but he preferred to watch the sparks leaping free. He wanted to write about small matters, about landscapes. Such as the leaves of a tree rousing themselves in the morning dew, then dozing off again in the heat of noon, and finally growing solemn with the last rays of the setting sun. No, no, none of that is mine, I'm not that talented. It's all Ge Ren's words. Patriarch's Pond in Moscow—it's called Pioneers' Pond now—looks a lot like a lake we often visited in the foothills of Mount Qinggeng, where our hometown was. He wrote an essay titled "Patriarch's Pond" in which he described the ripples across the surface of the lake as so gentle they seemed not like ripples, but rather like strands of the Holy Mother's hair. Because we spent part of our childhoods in a church, we liked visiting churches here—they reminded us of our childhood. They were all exquisitely structured, as if they were made of lace. When you walked in, it took your breath away. In "Patriarch's Pond," Ge Ren mentions horse-drawn carts speeding past outside the church. When we left Yan'an, even as I rode in that donkey cart, I was thinking about a scene that Ge Ren described: A wealthy woman was sitting in her horse carriage, her shoulders bare. She exuded luxury, but there was something inelegant about her posture, as if her coquettish poses weren't practiced enough. I remember Ge Ren saying she was quite possibly some Bolshevik official's wife recently arrived in Moscow from a small town in Georgia or the Ukraine—time would turn her into a real lady. Of course, it was hard to be sure this would happen. Firstly, her position might be usurped at any time by the official's lover; secondly, the official was very likely to be taken out and shot, at which point she'd just be a lowly prisoner.

To tell the truth, ever since Dou Sizhong had mentioned that Ge Ren might be labeled a Trotskyite, I'd been thinking nonstop about Ge Ren's early dealings with Trotsky. I thought that if they really did hang that label around his neck, he might not be able to defend himself, even if he didn't see eye to eye with old Trot. I remember that as a journalist, he had private talks with Trotsky. In fact, I know more clearly than anyone else that even though he eventually came to believe that Trotsky was a mensch who thought carefully about every inch of the big picture, he didn't initially have a good impression of the man. He once told me that old Trot was a nutcase, and that the fleshy bits of his face wobbled even when he wasn't speaking, as if hornets had made a nest beneath the skin. Old Trot had a thick mustache that looked like a shoe brush, particularly when his face was quivering. In another essay, Ge Ren wrote about hearing Lenin speak. This was in St. Andrew's Hall at the Kremlin. Lenin delivered his speech bombastically, switching between German, French, and Russian. Ge Ren wrote that the electric lights shone directly on Lenin's body, projecting a shadow onto the back wall between the words "Workers of the world, unite!" that rose even higher than Pagoda Hill in Yan'an. [N.B. At this point, Ge Ren hadn't yet been to Yan'an, so this is probably Bai Shengtao's own comparison.] It was precisely because of his interactions with Lenin that Ge Ren was seen later as an expert on Marxism-Leninism. There's a saying in Shaanbei: "Even if you haven't eaten pork, you've still seen a pig run." But in the border zone, apart from a few individuals like Wang Ming, most people hadn't been to the Soviet Union, let alone personally set eyes on Lenin. In this regard, Ge Ren stood above the crowd: not only had he seen the pig, he had eaten its flesh too.

No, I wouldn't be that stupid. Aside from mentioning buckwheat kasha and borscht, I didn't breathe a word about Ge Ren on that train, nor about Lenin and Trotsky, either. Loose lips sink ships, and I definitely didn't want to get into trouble again for saying the wrong thing. Little Red encouraged me to keep talking, and I thought the minx was surely trying to lure the snake out of its hole. I could go on, but I'd need to tread very carefully. As they say, there's no honor among opera singers and whores, and if she ever decided to sell me out, I'd end up suffering again. The thought not only scared me, it made me sad as well. Ge Ren chose a good Russian name for himself. Given the way I was feeling, I'd become Melancholsky too.

Melancholsky

Bai Shengtao said that Ge Ren's essays about Trotsky were mailed back to the *Shanghai Harbor Daily*. To this date, however, I haven't found any trace of those texts. Perhaps, like Ge Ren's other writings, they have been destroyed? The fate of the man is also the fate of his words.

Apart from Bai Shengtao's testimony, we also know about Ge Ren's life in the Soviet Union from Kong Fantai's records. Ferrand's essay collection *L'Entretien infini* [The Infinite Conversation] contains an essay by Kong titled "A Winter's Day in Russia." There he gives a full account of Ge Ren's life at the time. This text also proves that Ge Ren did have a Russian name, Malachowsky, which was sometimes written as Melancholsky.

Not long after arriving in France, I received a letter from Mr. Ge Ren, asking if I had Bingying's address. In the same letter, Mr. Ge Ren invited me to join him in Russia. I had wanted to go for a long time, responding to the call of the Russian Revolution. You have to pass through Berlin to get from France to Russia. All by my lonesome, I took the train, and then a motorcar, all the way to Berlin. There were two possible routes from Berlin to the Red Capital. One was overland, via Poland and Lithuania. The other was by water, taking a boat from Rostock to Petrograd, then a train the rest of the way. It was winter, and the River Spree was frozen over. After the icebreaker passed through, chunks of ice would crash into each other, often leaping into the air, white waves spewing toward the sky, and occasionally birds would alight on them. I thought I could see myself and Ge Ren in those creatures. We too had not a branch to perch on, and could only travel on the vast ice floes. In order to see Mr. Ge Ren sooner, I chose to travel overland.

. . . When I first got to the Red Capital, I took up residence at the Communist University of the Toilers of the East. The Chinese students there told me they hadn't seen Ge Ren in quite some time. They thought he was living at High Mountain Sanatorium in Moscow, and that Bai Shengtao, who had arrived with him, was there too, taking care of him while studying medicine. The next day, just as I was setting off for the sanatorium, Ge Ren himself turned up. He was dressed completely like a Russian, in felt boots and a round-brimmed hat, with a pince-nez clamped shakily to his nose. He must have rushed over, because one end of his scarf was trailing on the ground. I didn't recognize him at first. In order to continue the joke, he spoke in Russian and said he was there to see Confumov. He was covered in snow, like an emissary from the gods sailing through the clouds. Only when he took off his hat did I recognize this man as Ge Ren, whom I hadn't seen in so long. Confumov was a gift to celebrate our reunion, a Russian name. Many of the Chinese in Russia had Russian names. Chen Yannian went by Suhanov, while his younger brother was Krassin. Zhao Shiyan's name was the simplest: Radin. Ge Ren's friend Bai Shengtao had a Russian name too: Galormik. Ge Ren's name was one he came up with himself, Malachowsky or Melancholsky. He explained how he thought of it: he was sad every day, and feeling uncertain. This name reminded him to cheer up and stop hesitating—what we would call a motto in China. As for my Russian name, he said it was because no matter where I went, I would always be a descendant of Confucius.

While I was in Russia, I sometimes called him Melancholsky, or sometimes just Melancholy. He knew a lot of people in Russia, but he had few friends. He was closest to a cripple named Alexandrovich, whom we all called Alexander. A former Bolshevik and a scholar of the Orient, he could write Chinese but spoke it badly. What astonished me was that he knew Esperanto. The first time we met, he asked, "Cu vi parolas esperanto?" [Do you speak Esperanto?] Alexander lost his leg in battle. According to him, he met Melancholsky on the day of the Mid-Autumn Festival, and Melancholsky gave him a taste of the mooncakes he had previously only read about. Alexander urged us to go visit Sparrow Hills to the west of Moscow—he said it would be a shame not to visit, because it was from there that Napoleon observed the great fire of Moscow. On that day, because Melancholy had a fever, Galormik [that is, Bai Shengtao] didn't want us to go. A few days later, Alexander got a troika and said he would take us to Tolstoy's birthplace of Yasnaya Polyana. He packed ample supplies of black bread and fried buckwheat noodles. Surprisingly, he also managed to get hold of some bonbons and a bottle of vodka. His little sister came along with him. She was called Nadya, and kept correcting Ge Ren's Russian pronunciation, saying he spoke like a Lithuanian. She was a bright, captivating girl who enjoyed singing and reciting Pushkin's poetry. Galormik said that in the summer, she had brought over a watermelon and said it was from her brother. When he and Ge Ren asked her to have a slice, she blushed and said she'd just had some. But the way she ate the fruit told them that she'd never tried it before. She took delicate little nibbles of the flesh, like a cat. Later on, they found out that the girl was in love with Ge Ren. The excursion to Yasnaya Polyana had been her idea, with me as the excuse. She said to Ge Ren, "Since your friend is here, you ought to bring him around sometimes."

. . . We set out before dawn and arrived at Tula around noon. Nadya told us that the original meaning of Tula is "roadblock." A long time ago, when the Tatars invaded Moscow, the Russians piled up firewood there, and built a wall of flames to keep them out. In the middle of her story, our horse suddenly balked and refused to move forward, stamping its hooves and releasing a steaming pile of manure. A team of horses suddenly sliced through the rowan and pine trees beside us, throwing the snow-covered pine needles into the air so they fell again like raindrops. Nadya's brother cracked his whip, trying to make our horse turn around, but it refused to move. He quickly told us to get out and stand with our hands by our sides. There were seven or eight of them, dressed in tattered clothes. An older one, who looked like their leader, rode to one side and directed his men to back their horses into us until we were forced together. Then, still on his horse, he made a strange speech, which we weren't at all prepared for. The gist was that the Revolution had succeeded, and all intellectuals and property owners now had to listen to the orders of the People. Just as Ge Ren was about to explain, one of the men leaped off his horse and opened his fly. Like a cannon emerging from the city walls, his penis poked straight out. It was already fully engorged, as hard as a police truncheon. Evidently this kind of roadblock brought it and its owner a high degree of excitement. Nadya hid behind her brother, then fainted dead away. I was shocked too. His organ was enormous, like a horse's member. I wasn't being dramatic when I mentioned a truncheon; he really did use his penis like one, smacking it against our carriage shafts. It sounded like the wooden percussion instruments our Buddhist monks use, bang bang, with a hollow echo. As one man spoke and the other banged his wood, the rest of the gang began performing horseback tricks. First they turned tight circles; then they got their steeds to rear up so their front legs were high in the air. One of them ran up to Nadya and, with a lascivious look on his face, prepared to molest her. Just as we were stricken with terror, the leader blew a whistle, and the man withdrew his hands. They all disappeared back into the rowan grove.

We got back into the carriage. Nadya's brother wasn't angry about what had just happened. He seemed to understand these ruffians. He said, They must have thought we were intellectuals trying to make a run for it. Revolution positions the People against intellectuals. At the beginning of the Revolution, the intellectuals immediately began talking about freedom, democracy, the constitution, and bread, whetting the proletariat's appetite. Up till now, however, there's only been footsteps on the stairs. No one's come down—none of these things have actually materialized, not even a reflection of them. This angered the Bolsheviks, as well as the ordinary people. As we say in China, you choose the softest persimmons to bite into—so the People vented their rage on the intellectual class. And the intellectuals had only one way out, which was to flee. And so, seeing that we all wore spectacles, they assumed we were intellectuals on the run, taking all our valuables with us. Ge Ren asked Nadya's brother which class he belonged to. Nadya's brother said he was neither a Bolshevik nor of the People, and he was now no longer an intellectual either. He was a man who couldn't find his classification.

At Yasnaya Polyana, we were worried that our carriage would be stolen, so Nadya's brother and I didn't go inside Tolstoy's house. Nadya and Melancholsky went through the metal gates, but they soon came back out. Afterward, I asked Mr. Ge Ren what he'd thought. He told me he had seen a book in there, a bilingual English-Chinese edition of Laozi's *Tao Te Ching*. He also said the owner mentioned that Tolstoy referred to the courtyard pathway as a French lane. Ge Ren seemed dazed as he said all this, I believe because Bingying's image was swirling through his mind.

On the way back, we passed by Tula again. This time there was no roadblock. Unexpectedly, Melancholsky insisted that we stop there. Nadya was anxious but pretended to be calm. She'd be chatting away, and then suddenly she'd smack Melancholsky and blush bright red. Melancholy suggested that we spend the night at a nearby village. Without waiting for us to object, Nadya clapped her hands in agreement. So we rode through the rowan forest and arrived at a graveyard outside a village, and there we bumped into the bandits again. They must have thought we'd come with reinforcements, because they immediately jumped back onto their horses. The man who'd shown us his sexual organ now fastened his belt, drawing it tighter and tighter. Ge Ren yelled out that he only wanted to talk to them. In order to show that he was sincere, he got us all to remain behind while he walked over alone.

They spoke for a while, then Ge Ren and the leader came back together, and he invited us to be guests in their village. There we not only tasted kasha, but we also got some kind of meat soup. The broth was black, like something squeezed out of a mattress. Steeped in the liquid were little objects that I would have thought were bugs if he hadn't said it was meat. Don't worry—the way their kids gobbled up the leftover soup, we could tell this really was the best they had to offer, and they weren't just trying to fob us off with garbage. They chatted and apologized, then all of a sudden, the leader's jaw dropped open and he started howling. His face was covered in wrinkles and beard, so the tears kept getting caught, until the whole thing was covered with a glittering watery web. I remember that when we left the village, Melancholy told Nadya's brother that before coming to this country, he and many others had thought that Russia was the "experimental laboratory of Communism," and that the Bolsheviks were chemists who had their own theories of revolution, according to which they put the Russian people into test tubes and shook them around, pouring them out as socialist chemical compounds. Now it seemed that this was not the actual situation.

One morning a few days before we departed from Russia, Nadya came to see us. As soon as she stepped inside, she fainted dead away. Her brother Alexander had died. The night before, he hadn't come home, and when Nadya went searching for him, she found him lying in an alleyway off the Arbat, his body already an icicle, frozen to the ground. The blood oozing from his temples had formed little spheres, which glistened like cherries. He must have bled ferociously, because there were smaller globules all over his face and neck. Those had frozen solid too, like tiny goji berries. Ge Ren said that in his hometown of Qinggeng, people called these berries "dead children's prayer beads." Alexander had fallen outside a restaurant, and the frosted glass shade over one of that establishment's gas lamps had been shattered by bullets. The next day, the police hastily announced the cause of death: suicide due to guilt. As for what he'd been guilty of, they refused to say.

After Alexander's death, Ge Ren fell ill, and I had to delay my own departure too. Bai Shengtao said he often saw Ge Ren silently weeping. His face was so smooth, his tears flowed unimpeded, and when they got to his chin, they hung there like raindrops on the edge of a roof. He seldom spoke anymore. Later on he would say he was cold all over, as if he'd fallen into an ice cavern. He couldn't stop coughing, and complained that there was a strange taste in his mouth. Finally he began to vomit blood. "It's been days now since I brought up any phlegm," he said. Without question, his lung disease was getting worse—but he wouldn't admit it, and insisted that it must be a blood vessel that had burst. He wrote constantly, recording his memories of Alexandrovich, as if only words could help him forget his own illness. But I knew that working through the night would only make things worse, especially writing about the destruction of his dreams. I tried to warn him, but he said that writing was the only thing that made him feel safe and happy, like eating a sweet pastry. Even stranger, as soon as each manuscript was complete, he would burn it. He said he didn't trust his own eyes and ears, but would rather believe that everything he saw and heard was just a nightmare . . .

In the next section of Bai Shengtao's narration, we see how he almost mentioned this "roadblock" incident to Little Red on the train, including the display of the genitals. While Mr. Kong Fantai referred to the penis in question as a "horse's member" and a "police truncheon," Bai Shengtao used the term "donkey dick"—though in the end, he refrained altogether.

Eating Each Other's Children

Unable to resist Little Red's blandishments, I was about to tell her about an encounter of mine in the Soviet Union. This was on the way to visit Tolstoy's old home—we were stopped by bandits on the road, and one of them whipped out a penis like a donkey dick and waved it around, trying to frighten us. But I'm a gentleman, so how could I mention such a thing? Since we'd cleared the air between us, I decided to tell the truth. Human psychology is strange—when faced with a seductive maiden, the more you know you shouldn't say something, the more it wants to leap from your mouth. Luckily, American Goods arrived then and interrupted our conversation; otherwise I'd have struggled not to blurt the story out. American Goods lit a cigarette and smiled: "Mister, you're a real gent." Just as I was wondering what he meant by that, he slapped his knee and said we were almost at Zhengzhou.

At the station, American Goods saw me and Little Red onto our connecting train, then continued on to Kaifeng himself. Now it was just the two of us. Little Red dozed off, but I wasn't sleepy in the least. My brain kept playing truant, running off in Ge Ren's direction, and I wasn't able to stop it. I knew American Goods was there to guard the cargo, but I could also tell he was definitely part of the underground. I thought even if he wasn't doing that but had been an assassin, a far more difficult, dangerous task, I'd still have been happy to swap places with him. To tell the truth, at the time I thought that even if Little Red really had been my daughter, I would happily have given her to him if we could trade places. I'd heard that in times of starvation, people would exchange children to eat. I had dismissed that as nonsense, but now I understood why—it would surely be difficult to eat your own child, but much easier to devour someone else's. If your appetite was good, you might even find it delicious.

Thinking of this, my brain lit up. All the way from Zhangjiakou, I'd been wondering why Tian Han hadn't just given the order himself instead of going through Dou Sizhong. Like scratching an itch with six fingers— why the extra step? But the analogy with eating each other's children made the reason plain. Tian Han hadn't told me directly what my mission was, firstly because he couldn't get the words out, and secondly because if I'd refused, he wouldn't have been able to bring himself to bump me off. We were from the same hometown, after all. But handing the matter over to Dou Sizhong made it much simpler. If I hadn't accepted the order, Dou Sizhong could simply have shot me. It was probably the same reasoning that led them to have Ah Qing kill Ge Ren rather than make me do it personally. These details of the execution were, I thought, surely Tian Han's idea as well. He had anticipated all my difficulties. Looking at it this way, should I be grateful to Tian Han after all?

Eventually I grew drowsy, but I still couldn't get to sleep. I leaned against a burlap sack and thought how lovely it must be not to have to think about anything. There could be nothing better in the world than being a burlap sack. If I were one, I wouldn't have to go anywhere. But those thoughts meant I couldn't be one, because burlap sacks don't think. To tell the truth, there are times when I get sensitive to everything, and my brain grows more and more muddled. Then I'm in trouble. The train was hurtling along a flat plain at that moment, but I felt it must be passing through mountains and valleys, swaying along with their contours, and we must be close to Baibei. The train's motion lulled everyone into dreamland: sweet dreams for others, a daydream for me. All of a sudden, I saw Ge Ren standing before me, large as life, sending a shock right through me.

He hadn't changed at all, not one bit. He was still fragile and bookish, wearing round-framed glasses, his face a little flushed. No, it had nothing to do with his lungs—this wasn't the redness of tuberculosis, but of the soul. To tell the truth, of all the revolutionaries I've ever met, Ge Ren was the only one who blushed when meeting strangers. And not even strangers; he'd even redden at the sight of friends he hadn't seen in a while. His blushes were unique—like a girl's delicate rosiness. He stood there a little while reddening, then pulled his hands from his pockets and lit a cigarette. "Hey, Bai, I know you don't smoke, so I won't offer you one. What are you doing on Bare Mountain? Weren't you doing fine in the border regions, curing all those people of constipation? Why did you come all the way here?" I couldn't say anything—I had no answer to that! All I could do was turn my face away from this hallucination that felt so real. I had no idea then that when I got to Bare Mountain, the actual encounter with Ge Ren would be no different.

I don't know how long my daydream would have continued if Little Red hadn't startled me. I remember it was getting more and more jumbled, no longer making sense. For instance, I'm sure that Ge Ren was wearing padded cotton clothes, but also that his legs were bare. They were thinner than before, like a heron's, due to malnutrition and overwork. As it happened, we were passing by a pond at that moment, and birds were skimming the water's surface. There was gunfire in the distance, and I couldn't be sure which of these was part of the dream and which was just our ongoing journey. To tell the truth, I was genuinely worried that I'd lose my mind before we reached Baibei.

Little Red seemed disoriented too. She was anxious, concerned that her friend would know she'd spent time in a whorehouse, and would surely yell at her for doing such a thing. Even though I was still suspicious of her, I couldn't help feeling sorry for her. Thinking of how many days she'd have to spend in Hankou alone, I started to worry. She might have seen something of the world, but everything was so chaotic, who knows what might happen? No, General, that's not what I meant—how could I have fallen in love with her? That's impossible. As we'd say, this was just sympathy between the classes. If you must know, then yes, there was something. Tie two donkeys together long enough and they'll start to have feelings for each other, let alone a man and a woman. But truly, this wasn't love. I hadn't even held her hand! To tell the truth, I really was grateful to her. Just imagine, all the way from Zhangjiakou to Hankou, if I hadn't had her to talk to, my nerves would have snapped clean in two. Of course, it was possible she was in as much trouble as I was, and just as anxious, in which case my joking around probably helped her too. You're right, General, sometimes a man and a woman can heal each other. I said to her in a voice full of emotion, "Little Red, no man can predict his fate, and I don't know if this journey will go well or not. But if I make it back alive, I will definitely come find you in Hankou."

General, no matter what, she was still a woman, soft-hearted and prone to tears. Her eyes reddened at my words, and it looked like the cheese cream she had spread on her face would soon be washed away. I rushed to comfort her. "Don't be sad, I'll be fine. As for your friend, I'm sure she'll understand, and won't give you a hard time." Women accept lies too easily—those few words were enough to bring a smile to her face. To tell the truth, she was quite nice-looking when she smiled—with a hint of shyness, like a new moon in the sky.

At Hankou, she didn't go to find her friend right away, but said that since this was her hometown, she had to play host and treat me to a meal. And with that, she led me to a restaurant. I can't remember what it was called, but I think it was on Dehua Street. All I remember is that the owner was a short man with a high forehead and receding hairline, and a face a little like Lenin's. He asked if we were locals, and Little Red said she was there for her leather business. The man said, in a genteel voice, "It's a pleasure to have guests from afar—come in, come in." The meal was delicious. I had never had pomfret before, and this fish was so fresh it made my mouth feel dirty. Looking out the window, I saw a bathhouse and a barbershop across the road. After lunch, Little Red asked if I wanted to take a bath. I said I should get back on the road, so no thanks. She said, "Being tired or dirty doesn't bother you—you're made of special stuff, but even special stuff needs a good scrubbing now and then. This will be my treat. I will send you off on your journey as clean as a whistle, and then I'll get on with my own work." I asked what else she was busy with. She smiled and said she couldn't go see her friend empty-handed, so she'd have to go shopping for a gift. She knew her friend's health wasn't good, and wanted to buy her some Mei Su pills. "Mei Su pills? Those are for fever and vomiting. What's wrong with your friend?" I asked. She said her friend had always had bad digestion, and was hooked on the stuff—though she wasn't sure after so many years whether she'd gotten better or worse. I thought that was a suitable gift, because it was true that Mei Su pills could clear the gut. She urged me again to have a bath, but thinking of the letter concealed in my shorts, I said, "Little Red, I'll take one when I get back. That's a promise."

At the time, Wuhan was in chaos—the Japanese were fighting the Nationalists, and the Nationalists were fighting the Collaborationist Army. I really shouldn't have hung around, but Little Red was adamant that I should stay at least one day. Don't laugh, I'm telling the truth—I don't think she had any interest in me. She was just worried; after all, we were in the same foxhole. I said, "The situation is getting worse by the day, and I have an important duty to discharge. I don't dare linger for a second." Seeing that I was insistent, she didn't try to detain me any longer. That evening, she bought us another feast, to see me on my way. Her digestion wasn't good either, and I advised her not to drink too much. She told me not to worry, she'd never gotten drunk before. But just as she said that, her face flushed bright red, like a veil dropping over a bride's head. Her eyes glazed over, and she said she wanted to sing me a farewell song. No, General, not "The Drunken Concubine." She sang "Fortune-Teller." As the proverb goes, true genius doesn't need to call attention to itself. I would never have guessed what a good performer she was, with an excellent singing voice:

Such a lonely world, we cannot compel joy.
When the clouds pass from my eyes, then I'll be free to roam.
Springtime wind and rain, make the flowers fall.
I trust spring will come again, and the sweet smells will come home.

I paid attention to the lyrics, and realized she was singing Qu Qiubai's version—the verses he'd written right before he was killed. I had never met Qu Qiubai, only heard Tian Han talk about him. When they were in the Jiangxi Soviet, he and Ge Ren often sang duets. Not only did the two of them look alike, they'd even had the same childhood nickname: Duo.

I asked Little Red, "These words mix happiness and sadness—they're regarded as a classic of the form. Do you know who this lyric was written for?" Unexpectedly, she put her hands over her face and burst into tears. It was something she'd learned from her friend, she blubbered, and she had no idea who wrote it, only that she felt unmoored in the world, and that's why she'd thought of it. I told her she shouldn't sing this in the border regions. It was still a good song, but it wasn't in keeping with the optimism of the Revolution, so it would get her into trouble. She thanked me for the warning, and repeated that she would wait there for me. When I came back, she would throw a welcome feast to celebrate the success of the Revolution. With that, she raised her glass again. "No rush—you don't need to leave town until the sky's completely dark." I hadn't planned to keep drinking till I passed out, but that's what happened next.

Mei Su Pills/Pal

When Little Red mentioned "Mei Su pills," she was actually alluding to a person—the once-famous Peking opera star Mr. Mei Su. Which is to say, when she mentioned those Mei Su pills, she actually meant her Mei Su pal. Little Red was probably afraid that Bai Shengtao would think something was up, so she turned Mr. Mei Su into her female friend. According to *Annals of the Pear Orchard* (Beihai Publishing, 1994 edition), Mr. Mei Su's biography is as follows:

> Mei Su (1902–1986), born Su Mei, courtesy name Weizhi, born in Hankou, of Sichuan origin. At the age of two, he accompanied his father, Su Minghong, to Hangzhou. Su Minghong was a tea merchant; he and Hu Zikun were two of the so-called four great tea traders of Hangzhou. When Su Mei was a young boy, he often accompanied his father to the Great Theater of China in Shanghai to see Peking opera. He developed a liking for it, becoming particularly mesmerized by the Mei [Lanfang] school. He changed his name to Mei Su, and specialized in playing young female roles, taking on iconic Mei parts in *The Phoenix Returns to Its Nest*, *The Drunken Concubine*, *The Rainbow Pass*, and others, also performing in Wuhan, Changsha, and elsewhere. He contributed greatly to the advancement of Peking opera. Because his dancing style greatly resembled Nihon buyō, he earned the adoration of many Japanese fans. Mei Su was full of patriotic fervor, and during the war of resistance he grew a beard as a symbol of his defiance, refusing to perform for the enemy or the puppet government, hiding away in Jiangling County

instead. In 1946 he traveled to Hong Kong, and from there to Singapore, Malaysia, Indonesia, and other territories, to perform for the Chinese populations there. In his later years he published several memoirs, including *The Celestial Beauty Scatters Flowers on Earth*. He died in Hong Kong in 1986.

According to the introduction to *Beauty in a Time of Chaos*, Mei Su and Bingying first got to know each other in Hangzhou. In 1919, when Bingying returned from France, she met Mei Su again in Beijing. According to Bingying's recollection, in the 1930s and '40s, they saw each other again in Hong Kong and Shanghai. Later on, "we also exchanged letters a few times. His handwriting was elegant, but a little lopsided, like a drunken concubine's." My great-aunt once told me she'd heard that Mr. Mei Su never married because he was secretly in love with Bingying. But in conversation with Anthony Thwaite, Bingying didn't mention a word of this. Interestingly, it's Mr. Mei Su who brings up this point in *The Celestial Beauty Scatters Flowers on Earth*:

After the Pearl Harbor attack, the situation in Hong Kong got worse, and soon it was occupied too. You could describe the situation as "the moon drifting in and out of clouds, drumbeats sounding desolately in the autumn wind." I had no choice but to return to Shanghai. Unexpectedly, I ran into Miss Hu there. I was doing vocal exercises in the courtyard when she showed up. One sight of her, and the passion of my early years sprouted fresh shoots. She was well-versed in opera, and could speak knowledgeably about Mei [Lanfang]'s poise, Cheng [Yanqiu]'s voice, Xun [Huisheng]'s noise, and Shang [Xiaoyun]'s toys. Naturally, whenever I saw her, we'd chat about opera. On this occasion, though, I smiled deliberately and said, "I wondered if you were here in Hong Kong, but I thought you might be with Mr. Zong [Bu], so I didn't dare disturb you." No sooner had the words left my mouth than she pretended to be angry, and she almost picked up a plank to hit me. "No? Then don't tell me you're still thinking of Ge Ren?" A cloud of sadness passed across her face, and for my part, there was a wild clanging in my heart. She told me Ge Ren was in Shaanbei. She had sent him many letters, but she hadn't heard back from him. She'd thought of going far away too, but her fears about Ge Ren and her long-lost daughter made her stay her steps. Alas! As Xiang Yu says in *Records of the Grand Historian*, "The time is not right, and the horse will not move—what is to be done?" That afternoon, I screwed my courage to the sticking place, and spoke of my long-standing admiration for her. But she said she was exhausted body and soul, and wasn't able to think about such things. After she departed that day, I would never see her again.

Not long after that, I returned to Hankou. At the start of the Gui-wei Year [i.e., 1943], I encountered my fellow pupil Hong Yan there. Seeing me still single, she asked if I was still nursing a passion for Miss Hu, then if Miss Hu and Ge Ren remained connected despite their separation, and if they were still writing to each other. I could neither confirm nor deny these things, and she asked no further questions. Many years ago, when Hong Yan and I were studying opera together in the capital, we once performed *Lin Daiyu Buries Flowers*, which contained the lyric "If you say there's no fate, then why did I meet him? But if there is fate, do my feelings mean nothing? . . . Think how many tears are in my eyes: how can I let them fall from autumn till winter, from spring till summer?" As moonlight washed over us, Hong Yan and I sang these lyrics once more, and I couldn't help thinking that my own good fortune was, in the end, no more than the moon in a mirror, flowers reflected in water.

These words obliquely reference the fact that Little Red's journey to Hankou did have to do with Ge Ren. She'd been ordered to investigate whether Ge Ren and Bingying had exchanged any letters after the Battle of Two Li Mound, and if the news had gotten out that Ge Ren had resurfaced on Bare Mountain. As for why it was necessary for Little Red and Bai Shengtao to travel to Hankou together, we would have to look at her other duty: if Dou Sizhong managed to get in touch with Ah Qing during this time, then there would be no further need for Bai Shengtao to travel to Bare Mountain, and Little Red would execute him in Hankou. When Little Red said she would "send you [Bai Shengtao] off on your journey as clean as a whistle" and so on, that's what she was referring to. I have no way of knowing what her motivation was for saying these things, unless she derived particular pleasure from making such utterances in front of a man who would shortly be dead.

Of course, as we already know, Little Red ultimately did not kill Bai Shengtao. A little deduction will tell us that the reason wasn't, as she claims in *A Goose Footprint in Muddy Snow*, that she "came to [her] senses in time," but that she had received a message saying Dou Sizhong hadn't managed to get hold of Ah Qing, so Bai Shengtao had to stay alive in order to pass on Dou's orders. In fact, if we pay closer attention to the travel essay "Yellow Crane Tower" in *A Goose Footprint in Muddy Snow*, we can deduce some of what was going on behind the scenes:

Each time I visit Wuhan, I insist on seeing Yellow Crane Tower. A performer has to understand China's traditional culture. Every minute on stage requires ten years of training. You have to travel more, see more, think more. I remember the first time I climbed this tower, which would have been before Liberation, in the turbolent [turbulent] forties. It was a comrade who worked in a restaurant [N.B. Could this be the man who resembled Lenin?] who accompanied me up Snake Mountain. When yours truly stepped onto that bridge for the very first time, it's hard to express how excited I was. Another local colleague came up the tower with me. [N.B. This is probably her former classmate Mei Su.] We shared our thoughts about art and enjoyed the scenic views. After Liberation, my work on the propaganda front brought me to Wuhan many times. I jokingly told my comrades, They call that the yellow crane going and the wild swan arriving. On my last visit, I even brought my grandchildren along. As everyone knows, my granddaughter is inheriting [sic] my art. As we looked around, I explained to her the connection between traditional culture and Peking opera. I'm sure she gained a lot from that. As for my little grandson, he didn't understand all those lofty ideas, but he was still happily jumping around. Looking at my grandson's innocent face, I thought, let the past fly away on the back of a crane. Let us forget what went before: look to the future, and make a beautiful tomorrow!

On the one hand, she emphasizes the perpetuation of traditional culture; on the other, she wants to forget the past. If Comrade Little Red insists on this, no one can persuade her otherwise. I might as well say here that Little Red's granddaughter is none other than the Peking opera performer Little Woman Red, whom we've all seen perform as part of the New Year's Variety Program. She was acquainted with Mr. Fan Jihuai, and will be mentioned again in the third part of this book.

Shit Treatment

There's not much left to tell, General. By the time I woke up, it was daybreak. Little Red was so funny—she had insisted I stay behind, and now she was the one shooing me on my way. As the east grew red from the rising sun, I walked out of the restaurant. Because of the war, there were no trains running within Hankou, so the restaurant owner gave me a lift in his trishaw. Yes, the baldy who looked like Lenin. The trishaw was meant for transporting food—I spotted some fish scales, glittering like broken glass in the sunlight. This felt like a bad omen. Would I end up like a fish on a chopping block, with no way back, never to see Little Red again?

As soon as we got out of the city, the restaurant owner took off, leaving me by myself. I felt a momentary sense of inexpressible freedom, but that was quickly followed by loneliness. Having a tail felt unnatural, but without it, there was nothing to anchor me. Hopeless, I was so goddamn hopeless. To tell the truth, it didn't cross my mind that I could escape. Here's what I thought instead: the best possible ending would be if I got to Baibei, and Ge Ren had already escaped—the chicken flew the coop! That way, I'd be able to explain myself to the Party while my conscience remained untroubled—the best of both worlds. I laughed at this thought, and wished I could take two steps back for every one forward. But then I thought, if I got there too late, and Ge Ren was captured by the Nationalists first, then his life really would be over, and I'd probably get dragged down too. Now I wished I could quicken my footsteps. I walked to a place called Wulong Springs, where I boarded the train. What I needed now was speed—if you go fast enough, there's no time for nonsense to fill your mind. To tell the truth, all the way from Wulong Springs to Bare Mountain, my head felt like it was filled with glue. Outside the window was mountain ridge after mountain ridge, valley after valley, but I saw none of it. Our fate is determined by the powers that be, and it's best not to think about it. I would regroup after seeing Ah Qing. General, to tell the truth, if not for what happened after that, I'd have gone straight to Ah Qing and handed Dou Sizhong's secret letter to him. Ah, but if it had played out that way, I wouldn't be spending time with you now.

Here's what actually happened: The train chugged along all day, then just as it got dark, a passenger collapsed. As a doctor, I had a duty to do what I could. Barging through the crowd, I pulled out the gourd Tian Han had given me and poured a glug into his mouth, but he remained unconscious. His companion held up a lantern, looked at me tearfully, and asked me to please try again. I said if he was going to make it, a needle in his earlobe would wake him up. Sobbing, the friend said, Where on earth would we get a needle? Luckily, a kind-hearted person handed me a length of metal wire wrenched from a birdcage. There was some white stuff on it, probably bird shit, but this was a matter of life and death, and I had to make do. I jabbed the wire into his earlobe. A drop of blood oozed out, as bright and clear as a goji berry in the lantern's light. I froze for a long moment. Someone screamed, "He's alive! He's alive!" An onlooker came over and gave me a glutinous rice cake as a friendly gesture. He said saving a life was worth even more merit than building a seven-story pagoda, and asked if I was a doctor. I said I was, and got him to tell me how much farther it was to Shang Village—Dou Sizhong had told me to get off there, and Baibei would be not far away. I asked what he did, and he said he sold mushrooms, and also sterroos and hens. I didn't know what a sterroo was. He said, A sterroo is a rooster. I realized he was in the habit of flipping words around, so he'd say kusruc instead of ruckus, and derpow instead of powder. To tell the truth, General, I didn't find out his name till later—it was Dabao.

The sky was completely dark now. I felt exhausted, and as the train rattled on, I dozed off, but I immediately woke back up, covered in sweat, as if I'd just climbed out of a well. I dropped off briefly a few more times, and somehow made it through till morning. If not for Dabao's rice cakes and rice wine, I'd have fainted dead away. I was talking to Dabao when the train stopped at a place called Zhiyin. Dabao said he'd asked about this earlier—it seemed the tracks ahead had been blown up a few days ago and hadn't been fixed yet, so everyone would have to disembark. Later on, when I met Ah Qing, I would find out that it was Dabao and his gang who'd planted the explosives. At the time, though, Dabao played the innocent. He told me that he happened to be heading to Ruijin to take delivery of some imported goods, and since he had to pass through Shang Village, we could travel together. He asked where I was from, and what business I had in Shang Village. I made something up about being from Hubei and visiting a distant relative in Shang Village who'd fallen ill. He said, "Oh, Hubei. They say heaven has nine-headed birds, and earth has Hubei folk. People from Hubei are the most capable."

We got off the train, and I followed him to Zhiyin Town. He took me to a rice noodle shop, where two or three guys were waiting for him, all with horses. After we'd eaten our rice noodles, they took me into the hills, and even had a little pony for me to ride. The sun was high in the sky, casting human and horse shadows on the ground, so it felt like I was in a dream. Once again, I thought that moving along slowly like this might mean that Ge Ren would die of his illness by the time I got to Baibei. If that happened, I'd emerge from this unburdened. We climbed a hill, passing through a grove of trees on the slope. I could smell a medicinal plant, a fragrance like wild roses. We passed through another grove and came to a clearing where the low-lying plants were all flat on the ground, as if a donkey had been rolling around. Then we came to two or three wooden huts by a river. Hearing the horses, a woman came out from one of them. She was holding a ladle of water, and a silver bracelet gleamed around her wrist. First she took a couple of sips herself, and then she held the ladle so the pony could have a drink.

They invited me into one of the huts. There were two paintings on the wooden wall: Buddha on his lotus throne, and red-faced Lord Guan. A man in his forties was slouched in a chair, clutching a jade opium pipe. This felt strangely familiar. That's right, General, it reminded me of Ge Ren's grandfather, the opium addict who bankrupted his family. The man before me, though, was dark-complexioned, but that wasn't caused by opium. It doesn't take an expert long to figure out what's what—one look told me he had suffered a serious injury. He was the ringleader, of course, and everyone who came in, young or old, was extremely deferential to him. First we stood around him and made small talk, and only then did we pay our respects to the Buddha. My mind flashed back momentarily to my last night in Back Ditch, when I'd bowed to the portrait of Lenin on the wall. When in Rome. . . . So I kowtowed to the Buddha picture. The man who'd brought me said, "Sir, he's the one you asked for. An outsider, a nine-headed bird." That's when I understood I was there to treat their commander. At this point, what could I do except go along with it? But when I stepped toward him, one of the thugs reached out and held me back by the forehead.

What do we mean when we say it's good to know as much as possible? To tell the truth, if I wasn't able to heal him, then I wasn't getting out of there alive. The Commander naturally didn't trust me. Pursing his lips, he ordered his men to strip off my clothes. The wine gourd Tian Han had given me tumbled to the ground, and in a flash one of them kicked it away—he must have thought there was a weapon inside. Now I was down to my underpants, and thank god—because there was a woman present, they let me keep those on. As I said earlier, I had a treasure in there. That's right, the secret letter from Dou Sizhong. They had no idea, and assumed the massive bulge was just my big dick, which amused them thoroughly. After he was done laughing, Dabao was all smiles, and he even helped me put my clothes back on. As I got dressed, I said to the Commander, "If the good sir doesn't object, I would be very happy to help cure you."

The injury was on his left flank, near the chest. The area around it was grayish-black, the color of a sweet potato left to molder in a cellar. I told him, "This is a metal wound, meaning it was caused by a sharp metal object." His men promptly started murmuring at my accuracy. As for what the object was, I couldn't immediately say. Later on, I found out that he'd been hit by shrapnel from the exploding bridge. I asked him if it itched, and he said, "Yes, it does. It's painful and itchy." I said the pain wasn't important, it was the itching that mattered—if it neither hurt nor itched, that would be fatal. During my time in the Moscow sanatorium, I had learned a trick from a Russian military doctor for dealing with these sorts of injuries. The only thing was, this trick was a little too tricky—maybe even perverse. Yes, General, you've got it—of course it had to do with shit. No, not donkey shit this time, but goshawk shit. It's cooling and has a mild toxin that's highly effective in treating ulcerated sores. When I said that, he reacted just like Dou Sizhong—skeptical at first, then nodding his head. Dabao led a few men out with their rifles, and they leaped onto their horses. I called them back and told them they were looking for stuff from the peak that had whitened from exposure, and also a male goshawk, a live one.

You might not believe it, but they really were obedient bastards. Before dark, they were back with the goshawk shit. I pinched a bit and tasted it, and it was the real thing, what we call white guano in the medical profession. Dabao also had a live goshawk in his hand, blood dripping from its wings. I said, "Your leader might live yet." I mixed the blood and white guano to the consistency of buckwheat kasha. Before smearing it on the Commander's wound, I indulged in a bit of mysticism: I kowtowed three times to the Buddha, pretending to pray for protection. The Commander asked why it had to be goshawk shit, and I had to pull out some coloratura nonsense: "There are clouds in the sky and men on earth. Good men are earthbound hawks, so of course you need a hawk from the sky to treat your wound." In order to preserve my own life and make sure I'd get out of there in one piece, I added, "Metal injuries are connected to the heart. For the next ten days, it's vital that you not have any violent thoughts; otherwise the wound will reopen." No, I didn't say "criminal thoughts"—I was already afraid I wasn't being respectful enough; how would I have dared utter the words? Naturally, I also compared him to the picture of Lord Guan, saying, "After Lord Guan had the bone-deep poison cut out of his body, he followed the instructions of his doctor, Hua Tuo, and didn't use his sword for many days." With that, I kowtowed again to Buddha and Lord Guan.

Spring comes early in the south. Around midnight, thunder rolled overhead, and then it began to rain. The hut Dabao and I were in had a leaky roof, so I didn't sleep much that night. The next morning, Dabao took me to see the leader again. His woman was beaming as she said the Commander['s injury] was better—he could move his arm again, and he had regained the feeling in his fingers. She blushed as she spoke. I told her everything she'd need to pay attention to in the days ahead, then burst into tears in front of her, saying I had a relative who was desperately ill, and if I delayed any longer, I might not see him in time. Her heart softened, and she said she would intercede with the leader on my behalf. He said sure, but he wanted me to stay another night. Then his conscience must have gotten the better of him, because he changed his mind and said they would send me on my way that night. He told Dabao to let me know that his word could be trusted, and everything he said would happen. I thought to myself that the stuff I'd made up must really have frightened him. Otherwise they'd never have let me off so easily.

Dabao

Dabao's full name was Guo Baoquan, and he was Hakka. When Bai Shengtao mentions him turning "rooster" into "sterroo" and so on, that's a regular Hakka speech pattern.

Dabao's grandson Mr. Guo Ping later became the secretary-general of Baibei's municipal government. He directed me to *Records of Famous Hakkas* (Flying Dragon Publishing, 1998). Guo Baoquan's name was listed there along with such ancient notables as Guo Ziyi, Zhang Jiuling, Zhu Xi, Ouyang Xiu, and Wen Tianxiang, as well as, from more recent times, Shi Dakai, Hong Xiuquan, Sun Yat-sen, and Liao Zhongkai, and contemporary Hakkas such as Lee Kuan Yew and Lee Teng-hui. Guo Baoquan's section goes:

> Guo Baoquan, male, from Liancheng County in Fujian, born 1912. In 1939, he joined the militia of rural leader Zhu Yuting [N.B. the commander Bai Shengtao refers to in the previous section] to break down the walls separating farming territories, and to blow up roads and bridges. Later on, he took part in anti-bandit activities, making a great contribution to maintaining law and order in the region around Bare Mountain. In his many years working for the Revolution, he exemplified the Hakka battle motto: "Work hard and have a fighting spirit, to achieve glory in the future." On October 11, 1958, at the age of 46, Comrade Guo Baoquan collapsed and died of exhaustion while building a steel furnace.

Every person profiled in this book—apart from Lee Teng-hui, who was pushing for Taiwanese independence—had an essay after their biographical paragraph, describing one of their heroic deeds. Dabao's was about him blowing up a bridge. The original is rather long; here is an excerpt:

> On that night, the sky was filled with stars twinkling down at earth. Guo Baoquan led his comrades to one side of White Cloud Bridge. Before the explosion, he checked their surroundings one last time. The railroad bridge nestled peacefully in the valley above White Cloud River. How foolish it was, not knowing the destruction that was about to unfold before its

eyes. A comrade named Little Tiger said, "Let's strike, the other comrades are getting impatient." Comrade Guo Baoquan held up a silencing finger. The twin slashes of his eyebrows gleamed in the radiant moonlight, rendering him extraordinarily handsome. Little Tiger's brother, Big Tiger, now came to plead for action. Seeing how filled they were with the spirit of battle, Guo Baoquan felt his heart swell with joy. With a heavy spirit and weighty words, he said to them, "I am aware of the comrades' feelings. But we must consider effectiveness in all we do. Have you any idea what it means to be more efficient? Were we to blow up the bridge with a train on it, that would double our achievement. The train's headlamps will be our command. When you hear me shout, and you see the headlamps glaring, it is then that we will strike." Just at that moment, they heard a train approach, its lights slicing through the darkness. The comrades were filled with excitement, rubbing their hands and uttering wild cries. Comrade Guo Baoquan raised his sword-like brows, rolled up his sleeves, and issued his call to arms: "Comrades, it is the moment for action. Light the fuse!" And with that, at the very instant the train rolled onto the bridge, an enormous bang shook the sky. The railway bridge tumbled into the center of the river. Unable to brake in time, like a wild horse slipping its reins, the train plunged headlong into the inky depths, raising an almighty wave. They immediately heard screams of terror like the croaking of frogs. Those frantic cries raised such joy in the comrades, they could feel their hearts blossoming like flowers . . .

The strange thing was, then-commander Zhu Yuting's name doesn't appear anywhere in the text. When I asked Guo Ping about this, the secretary-general said, "Someone else wrote that. If they didn't mention him, I could hardly grab their wrist and force them to." Not long thereafter, the book's editor informed me that the piece was in fact written by Guo Ping himself. He went on: "Mr. Guo's initial draft was all right, but he's not suited to writing this sort of thing at all—it's far too dry. I had to help him add in lots of color." The editor also revealed that Dabao's raising his "sword-like brows" and rolling up his sleeves as he gave the order were actually details he had stolen from the character of Li Xiangyang in the movie *Guerrillas on the Plain*.

Leave No Witnesses

Bandits' words are worth about as much as their farts. They kept me there till dawn the next day, then let me go. Dabao said their leader was afraid I'd be exhausted from my labors, and he wanted me to have a day of rest. No, I don't hate them. I count myself lucky that I got out of there unscathed. Before letting me go, they produced a stack of silver dollars, which they smilingly offered to me. I said to the leader, "Your graciousness reaches to the heavens—truly, you are Lord Guan come again. For me to treat an illustrious leader is no more than my duty. I would be ashamed to take silver in recompense." Dabao kept pressing them on me, saying that several of his men had stayed up all night for this. It turned out that money doesn't grow on trees, and they'd ridden downhill through the storm the night before to raid a few nearby households. I refused again, adding that the ancient doctor Hua Tuo cured Lord Guan absolutely gratis, and I was determined to model my life upon his. You know what, they actually believed that nonsense.

Dabao sent me on my way. He blindfolded me with some red cloth, the way Shaanbei villagers cover donkeys' eyes to make them pull millstones. No, General, I still don't hate them. They didn't kill me, and I'm very grateful for that. A few hours later, the rain was getting heavier. We got to a slope, and he pulled away the blindfold to ask if we should find a place to shelter. I quickly said, "I don't want to cause you any more bother. Why don't you go back, and I'll find my own way." Dabao's eyes rolled upward as he thought about this. Then he smacked a tree trunk with his horsewhip and said, "Well met and well parted. Mind your way, sir." He said I should follow the river to a place called Phoenix Valley, which would lead me to Baibei Town. I later learned that this was White Cloud River, which flowed through Baibei. Dabao didn't know that's where I was headed, so he added, "Keep heading northeast from Baibei, and you'll get to Shang Village." He gave me his own bamboo hat, although he insisted on calling it a "boobam" hat. For a second I thought he was saying "boom," like I would be blown up. My legs grew weak, and I almost fell to the ground.

Since then, I've found myself thinking many times that if I hadn't run into Dabao, if it hadn't been raining that day, I'd have died without knowing the contents of the secret letter. At the time, listening to Dabao's hoofbeats fade away, I ducked beneath a tree to hide from the rain. It was very quiet, except for a magpie singing nearby, as if it were happy for me. It noticed me watching, shook out its feathers, and flew away with a cry. I thought it must be going to report to Ge Ren. Feeling frustrated, I stood beneath that tree for a long while, completely losing track of time. It wasn't till a thunderclap rolled across the sky that I realized I had somehow stumbled into a bramble patch. Like a dog chasing its tail, I spun in circles in the rain. Another thunderclap roused me completely. I suddenly remembered Dou Sizhong's letter, and my legs started sprinting, carrying me with them, looking for another place to hide from the rain. But it was too late, too late; it was surely drenched by now. Squeezing beneath an overhanging rock, I hastily pulled it from its hiding place. The stamped ink had already started to run. Donkeyfucker, it was like puffs of sunset clouds. I got dizzy looking at it. After a while, I had to quietly chuckle, having suddenly noticed that my dick was dyed red too, like a clown's nose in some foreign film. The envelope had been soaked open. I don't know where the impulse came from, but I couldn't stop myself. Trembling, I slid my fingers in, muttering all the while, "I'm not doing this on purpose, not at all on purpose." To tell the truth, I was begging the Party's forgiveness the whole time. The message was a string of English letters. I sounded them out, and caught my breath:

"Code Zero is to get a speedy death. Destroy his writing. Sort out details later. Leave no witnesses."

Code Zero was Ge Ren, of course. Yes, Tian Han and Dou Sizhong had both said this, zero to represent Ge Ren, a full circle. But what did "leave no witnesses" mean? Even if I had been a stupid donkey, I'd have understood—and I'm not a stupid donkey. In the misty rain, I thought I could see the leather revolver case clipped to Ah Qing's belt, smell the animal skin it was made of.

What, escape? No, General, to tell the truth, I'd had that thought before, but I wasn't willing to do it. I'd heard my comrades saying earlier that if a person doesn't have firm convictions, he might be clear-headed in the morning, but that doesn't mean he won't be confused again come nightfall. As for me, it was precisely my firm convictions that made me believe we were doing this to preserve Ge Ren's reputation, which is why I was trekking all the way to Bare Mountain. Baibei was only a stone's throw away—why would I run away now? Wouldn't it be a shame to have come all this way only to fall at the last hurdle? Holding that secret message, crouched against the giant rock, I finally sorted out my thoughts. Scriptures are scriptures, but each monk chants them in his own way. What if I looked at this differently, and interpreted "leave no witnesses" as an instruction from the Party for me to bump off Ah Qing? Wouldn't that work? If Dou Sizhong hadn't gotten hold of Ah Qing yet, then I could happily hand him the letter and say, "Do as you see fit." He might even be grateful for the warning and feel he owed me a favor. And if Ah Qing's conscience told him to let Ge Ren off, or better still, take Ge Ren away with him, that would have nothing to do with me. As soon as they were gone, I'd be able to tell the Party that I arrived at Bare Mountain only to find that Comrade Zhao Yaoqing had already moved Ge Ren to another location. What if Ah Qing tried to kill me? Well, if Ah Qing saw through my ruse and understood that Dou Sizhong was calling for my execution, I would just have to accept my fate. I certainly wouldn't resist. If my death could restore Ge Ren's reputation, and bring peace to my son and father-in-law, then wouldn't the passing of one Dr. Bai be a worthwhile sacrifice?

That afternoon, I arrived in Baibei Town. You're right, General, I got there three days before you. All right, I'll continue. There's a saying in Shaanbei: spring rain stops at Li Gorge. You often see raindrops pattering down on one side of the gorge while the other remains as dry as a bone. Following White Cloud River, I passed through Phoenix Valley, climbed a hill, and suddenly found myself facing the red disc of the sun. My shadow stretched out behind me, longer than the revolutionary road I'd walked down. Ahead of me were occasional goji trees, their branches tangled with kudzu and rattan vines or bramble bushes. It was too early in spring for flowers, so their limbs were bare and dark. Even so, I imagined I could see, in the fading daylight, goji berries. They were so bright, like tiny lanterns. You're right, at that moment I felt like I was back in Qinggeng. In my and Ge Ren's hometown, goji trees are everywhere by the river, thick clusters of them all around the church. And now, through the goji branches, I could see the town, with smoke from cooking fires rising above it. Baibei—this was Baibei Town. I sprinted toward it, but a second later was sprawled on the ground. The hell with it—I sat there gasping for breath, somehow looking down on myself from above, panting like a dog.

I don't need to tell you what happened next, General—you know. Yes, I didn't carry out Dou Sizhong's orders to go straight to Ah Qing. First I wanted to see for myself whether Ge Ren actually was in Baibei. I saw an old man in the town and questioned him until he told me where Ge Ren was being held. Yes, in the elementary school. I had passed by it earlier. There had been a couple of people pacing outside the school gates, not in uniform, but not dressed like locals, either. I quickly figured out that Dou Sizhong and Ah Qing couldn't have been in contact yet, so Ah Qing was still waiting for me to show up. You're right, General—as I walked toward the school, I could feel someone staring at me from behind. Yes, Ah Qing's underlings. Later, Ah Qing told me they were tailing me because something about me didn't seem quite right. Well, you can see why. I had planned all this out, of course, but thinking that I really was about to come face to face with Ge Ren again, I couldn't help but get flustered, and my legs weren't quite obeying me. No, I didn't manage to see Ge Ren in the end. Before I even got near the school gates, a rifle barrel came down hard on my spine. Then they blew a whistle, and summoned help to drag me back into town. Damn it, all my careful plans were torn to pieces. Never mind. Before I even saw Ah Qing, they tormented me almost to death: they hung me from the rafters and alternately whipped me and drenched me with freezing water. More suffering.

When Ah Qing finally showed himself, I was still spinning in midair. He's quite the actor—first he looked all stern and scolded [his subordinates], then he personally untied me. As soon as my toes touched the floor, he wrapped his arms around me and, practically nibbling my earlobe, said my name. Another shock—I thought he must have already received Dou Sizhong's orders. To tell the truth, as he loosened my bonds, from the way he was smiling, I gave up hope completely, and thought my next stop would be heaven . . .

Bai Shengtao's Ending

Bai Shengtao's narration ends abruptly here. I've seen the original transcript in the archives of the Ge Ren Research Center, and the last word is indeed "heaven." In his early years, Mr. Ding Kui must surely have come across many ancient tablets and bamboo scrolls, because all the materials he prepared look exactly like Han Dynasty records. As to how Bai Shengtao passed the instructions on to Ah Qing, readers will have to wait for the next section to find out.

I might as well finish Dr. Bai's story here. He later settled in Hong Kong and married a Guangdong woman named He Lianhui. Three years after their wedding, he passed away. His son, Mr. Bai Yangu, had two sons and a daughter—Bai Ling, whom I mentioned earlier. Bai Ling had heard about her grandfather's epic journey to Bare Mountain, but she didn't know the details. Her grandmother said her grandfather was "a sealed gourd" who hardly spoke to anyone. After Bai Ling saw copies of these documents, her impression of her grandfather changed completely—she realized how eloquent he could be. She was also filled with admiration for his exploits, exclaiming, "How thrilling! Like a James Bond film!"

In the summer of 2000, after much pleading and enticement, Miss Bai Ling agreed to accompany Fan Jihuai to Bare Mountain. Along the way, Fan recounted his previous journey there. And so history came full circle: back in the day, Bai Shengtao told his story to Fan Jihuai, and now it was Fan Jihuai giving his account to Bai Shengtao's granddaughter. The regrettable thing is, we have no way of knowing what Bai Shengtao would have thought of all this, looking down from his perch in heaven.

PART TWO

Magpies Cawing in the Branches

Time: May 3, 1970
Place: Xin Village Re-Education Tea Plantation,
Xinyang
Speaker: Detainee Zhao Qingyao [Zhao Yaoqing]
Listener: Investigation Team
Transcriber: Comrade Yu Fenggao

Magpies Cawing in the Branches

I knew someone was coming. As soon as I woke up, I heard magpies cawing in the branches, and I thought to myself, someone's coming. I swear to
Chairman Mao, no one gave me a heads-up. Comrades, if I have one good
point, it's that I don't go in for that coloratura nonsense. I really did hear it
from the magpies.

The previous team left me with a volume of Mao's *Three Essays.* Yes,
this one here. It's given me wisdom and courage. I study it every day, and
draw untold strength from it. So what did you bring this time? You want
to know what I need most? Rat poison! No, not for me, for the rats. As
Chairman Mao said, rats are [the worst] among the Four Pests. The rats
are running wild here. I committed a wrong act, but I don't want to die.
When I think of the countless revolutionary martyrs, our forebears who
nobly sacrificed themselves for the good of the People, I don't want to die.

I also need sleeping pills. Chairman Mao talks about "recalling the past,
that towering time." But when I think about that towering time, my food
has no taste and I sleep badly. Revolutionary martyrs flash before my eyes,
and even wave at me. They pour me a drink, hand me a cigarette, stroke
my head, pat my shoulder. All very intimate. No, I wasn't asking for a
cigarette. Well, if you insist. What are these? Phoenix? Motherfucker, it's
been so long since I've had a smoke, let alone a Phoenix. I get emotional
about this brand. I spent time in Phoenix Valley at Bare Mountain, and
seeing this brings it all flooding back.

I'm sorry, there's no water here to make you tea. Water is the lifeblood
of farming. Every mouthful you drink is one less for watering the fields,
so I don't usually drink water. I've practically become a tortoise. They can
live without water. Comrades, have you seen a mountain tortoise? My
god, they just have to breathe a little air, and that's enough to live on. No

lie, I've seen one, trapped beneath a stone tablet. I don't know how long it had been stuck there, but it seemed fine. Its head would stick out, then retract. The power of example is infinite. I want to learn about saving water from that tortoise.

All right, I won't babble on. Go on, then, tell me what you want me to say. Ge Ren again? I knew it. Those two who came the last time, they were asking about Ge Ren too. One of them also had a notebook, and whatever I said, he would write down. If I coughed, he would write "cough." How do I know? Ha! Because the soldier taking notes couldn't remember how to spell "cough." Seeing him get flustered, I said if he didn't know it, he could just sound it out. He seemed to find this strange, and asked if I knew phonetic spelling. Silly! How could I not know it? It was Ge Ren who taught me. Not just that, I know English too. Of course, I only learned it in order to better criticize capitalism, to see the hideous face of capitalism more clearly. If you could be a little generous, and report back that old Zhao is both red and dedicated, I certainly wouldn't deny it.

Start from the beginning? Well, of course, that goes without saying—I swear to Chairman Mao that every word I say is the truth. Ge Ren said long ago that Comrade Ah Qing is an honest man. I can't remember when he said that, but anyway it was more than once. Sometimes when Comrade Ge Ren was talking to me, he would tap me on the shoulder and say, Ah Qing's a good comrade, Ah Qing's an honest man. Humility pulls you forward, arrogance pushes you back. So I hardly ever tell anyone what he said.

What's that? You want a drink of water? All right, I'll go get some. Send someone to come with me? No need, I can carry a pot of water myself.

Re-Education through Labor

In 1969, Ah Qing was detained and sent to the Xin Village Re-Education Tea Plantation in Xinyang District, Henan, to be re-educated through labor. This conversation took place at the plantation. On April 5, 1997, I met Comrade Yu Fenggao, the then-head of the Investigation Team, in Zhengzhou. He revealed that at the plantation, Ah Qing went by the name Zhao Qingyao.

I was given orders to go to the labor farm [plantation]. Before I left, a leader comrade came to talk to me. He wanted me to interrogate a guy called Zhao Qingyao. Zhao Qing like Zhaoqing City in Guangdong. He said the leader of the farm [plantation] had reported to the higher-ups that this Zhao had a complicated history. He wasn't a regular detainee. Now we've finally cleared that up. His actual name was Zhao Yaoqing, and he was from Zhejiang. He was once in the underground, but then he betrayed the Revolution, and for many years his whereabouts were unknown. But nothing slips through the net of heaven, and even though he changed his name and hid for so many years, eventually he did show himself. Now we know that in the spring of 1943, he fled to Zhumadian City, first pretending to be a beggar, then marrying and moving in with his new wife's family. A leopard can't change its spots, though, and this sort of person is always at odds with the People. He was denounced for being against the policy of Educated Youth going up in the hills and down to the countryside. Fuck, he dared to say that Educated Youth in the rural villages were just stealing chickens, having their way with respectable girls, and not doing anything proper. Then the Educated Youth denounced him, and he was sent to be re-educated at the farm [plantation]. At the time, the Commander said to me, It's a good thing the Captain was alert; otherwise this class enemy who'd stayed hidden for so many years might have gotten through two years of re-education, and then slipped away again.

I immediately said that it was nothing, and the Commander needn't worry about a thing. I'd go fetch him back, and that would be it. Comrade Commander smiled and said the main task at hand was to investigate Ge Ren through Ah Qing. Ge Ren hadn't died at Two Li Mound. He had lied to the People and lied to the Party, making it look like he was dead when he was actually fleeing to Bare Mountain. Comrade Commander was far-sighted enough to tell me not to let Zhao know that Ge Ren had been labeled a traitor. Let him speak freely, let him fart his fill. If he asked, I was to tell him that Ge Ren was still a hero of the People. I said I wouldn't dare. He said that I'd just be following orders and no one would give me a hard time about it, so I shouldn't worry. At Xin Village, the first time I saw Zhao Yaoqing, I didn't like him. He stank to high heaven—I'd never seen such a filthy person, as if he hadn't bathed for a century. No, longer, at least ten thousand years. He talked about this and that, pulling the conversation here and there. You'd ask him something, and he'd have eight answers ready for you, all pure bullshit. He played the fool a lot. Sometimes when I'd be listening to him talk, his nose would suddenly twitch, and he'd have to mop up some snot. One time he pretended to tap my shoulder and almost dripped mucus onto my collar. He smoked like a madman, getting through each cigarette in two or three puffs. What fuckery was that? A pack of cigarettes cost more than several pounds of tofu. Wasn't he squandering our country's wealth by messing around like that? We were very efficient. We worked from morning till dawn the next day, and learned a lot. He was from Zhejiang, and picked up the Henan dialect later on. His accent was strange, but I could understand him. I heard that he kicked the bucket soon after we left. Some said it was liver disease, others that he jumped down a well. Anyway, he died. I was angry when I heard. Imagine someone so evil he could have liver disease and not even tell us about it. Ready to croak, and still letting us drink from his cups. How could he? You can't defend that! Just sat there watching us touch our mouths to them. If he didn't want to spread the disease [to us], then what was that about? I heard he studied medicine for a while. If he'd studied medicine, wouldn't he know not to do that? Think about it, what could he have been planning? Heartless scum. Pah!

Comrade Yu Fenggao was really angry. He used too much force on the word "pah," and his false teeth slipped out. At dinnertime, he warmly invited me to continue the conversation at a restaurant across the road. Of course, he did all the ordering, and I paid the bill. I hosted him a few more times after that too. Each time, though, it was me sitting there watching him eat. Interestingly, he had hepatitis B, the same thing Ah Qing suffered from. That's something his son told me, and he never mentioned it himself. All he said was that he had a calcium deficiency, so he had to eat more "animals with shells," meaning seafood. I guess if I'd told him I knew he had hep B, he would have said he must have caught it from Ah Qing, even though almost thirty years had passed since their encounter.

Joyful Song Hill

Fine, you point, and I'll head in that direction. So let's start with Bingying. That would have been in February 1943. That night, I took some buddies out for a bit of fun at the dance hall, and that's where I saw Bingying—Hu Bingying, the most beautiful woman I've ever seen in my life. No, not beautiful, handsome. Calling people beautiful is decadent, but handsome sounds noble and progressive. She looked a bit like Ke Xiang from the model opera *Azalea Mountain*, and that's the honest truth. Comrades, don't get the wrong idea. For an underground worker like myself, having fun is revolutionary. The dance hall was on Joyful Song Hill in Chongqing, one of those fancy joints most people never get to visit. The dancing had already started when I arrived—they were doing the rumba. You know what that is? No, nothing to do with rum.

The rumba is two people dancing. What? Only the Loyalty Dance is considered dancing now? Is that the new directive? Why didn't the leaders arrange for us to study that? All right, I'll continue. Here's how it went—hand me that mug, I'll show you. No, wait, it's too thick—let's use the chopsticks. No, those won't work either—too rigid. Here, one of you come over here, and I'll show you. No one wants to dance with me? No problem, I don't feel like it either. I only love the Loyalty Dance, just like you. Let's put it this way: the rumba is like two caterpillars rearing up and fighting each other: you twist left, I twist right, and then a sudden swerve, so your head spins right around. It was when she turned her head that I recognized her. And it goes without saying, she saw me too. But she didn't stop; she just kept jumping around. She had a hat on, tilted to one side, with a flower stuck aslant in it. A beret—very handsome; you could say she was the most handsome woman in that whole dance hall, and that wouldn't be going too far. And I thought, that's fucking weird. What's she doing in Chongqing?

After that number, I went over to say hi with a glass of wine. She sat there with her legs crossed, and glared at me for a moment. Then she said, "I'm tired, sir. I'm not dancing anymore." I said, "Other people call me 'sir,' not you." She said, "You've had too much to drink, sir. I don't think we know each other." She made me look foolish in front of my buddies. What can I say? If this hadn't been Bingying, I'd have found some way to deal with her and get my revenge. But she was Bingying. For the sake of my dead buddy Ge Ren, I couldn't do anything to her. Besides, I had lived in her home for a long time as a kid. Oh yes, speaking of which, I want to remind you that I was born into a workers' family. Like spawns like. If I'm from a workers' household, then that means I was a revolutionary as soon as I was born.

To continue: She'd made me blush so badly, I wanted to go somewhere else rather than embarrass myself further, but my buddies had found dance partners and weren't ready to leave yet. So I sat on my own, drinking moodily. Then I went to relieve myself. I mean to pee. Oh, you knew what "relieve myself" meant? I never said you didn't understand. I peed, came back out, put a cigarette to my lips, and someone immediately offered me a light. Who else? Bingying, of course. I moved closer, and *phoo*, she blew out the match. She said, Still angry? And she swept the newspaper she was holding over the top of my head. I don't know how she did it, but just like that, all my rage was gone. I was about to ask what she was doing in Chongqing when she leaned over to give me a light and whispered that she needed to talk to me about something: could I come to her place later?

She lived farther down Joyful Song Hill, just a hundred paces from the dance hall. Why's it called Joyful Song Hill? What does it have to do with music and pleasure? Actually, I'm not really sure. Apparently in ancient times, Yu the Great, who stopped the floodwaters, was married there. He threw a big banquet with singing and dancing, and that's where the name comes from. No, Bingying didn't welcome me lavishly in her rooms. She led me to the bank of the Jialing River. Strong winds were blowing off the water, and with the cliffs behind us, it was freezing, but I didn't feel it. Like the song: *Red plum blossoms upon red cliffs, a thousand miles of frost beneath my feet, a month of harsh winter holds no fear, my loyal heart opens toward the sun.* I don't know if she felt the cold. She didn't say a word, just paced back and forth with her arms wrapped around herself, as if she had a lot on her mind. The wind blew her perfume right up my nostrils. One whiff and I was back in Hangzhou. Bingying's home in Hangzhou was full of flowers, though not red plum blossoms, but intoxicating jasmine. When the conversation finally started, it was about flowers. What kind of flowers? Broad bean blossoms. Bingying asked if I'd seen a poem by that name recently. I said I hadn't. She said it was by Ge Ren, a good one, not just good, amazing, and I ought to seek it out. Then she asked if I'd heard anything else about Ge Ren. Right away I started sobbing. I said he'd died such an awful death, and this injury to the nation would be avenged, but the time wasn't right yet. She said, All right, stop that sniveling. And then she muttered quietly, Ah Qing, Ah Qing, if you have any news about Ge Ren, never mind what, come tell me right away. Wait, Ge Ren was dead—what news could there be? I thought she must be talking about his remains. Apparently after he was martyred at Two Li Mound, he ended up in a mass grave because they weren't able to find his body among the other corpses. I imagined she must still have feelings for him and wanted to give him a proper burial. So I said, Don't you worry. Ge Ren's heroic act shook the heavens and earth, and I think of him every moment of the day—as soon as I hear anything, I'll come to you right away.

But it turned out that wasn't what she'd meant. She said she'd been dreaming a lot that Ge Ren hadn't died, that he was still alive. I thought Ge Ren['s death] must have hit her hard. She must be confused, or she wouldn't be talking such nonsense. I was feeling sorry for her when she abruptly said, If he really is still alive, the Nationalists are sure to find out, and they'll kill him. She wanted me to put in a request to go capture him. This put me in such a difficult position, I started crying again. Ge Ren was dead, but even if he wasn't, how could I do such a thing? It would be like slapping my own face. I said, Bingying, listen, I'm human too, not some wild animal. She laughed and said she just wanted me to help Ge Ren, and find some way to move him to a safe place. Even though nothing she said was making any sense, I followed her lead and claimed that I'd dreamed that Ge Ren was alive too, still fighting to liberate the whole of humanity.

Comrades, when I said this, I was already getting suspicious. There was another meaning behind Bingying's words—they no longer sounded like nonsense. Was Ge Ren's death just a false rumor? Where was he, then? Had the Japanese captured him and locked him up in some secret location? If that was the case, I wouldn't be able to save him. At the time, I was a major-general in the Kuomintang, and had to follow orders. You all know the cowardly Nationalists were never going to go against the Japanese. Fuck it, there was only one way out, and that was to tell the news to Dou Sizhong, so he could go rescue Ge Ren. But before I'd verified the facts, just based on that dream of Bingying's, I took the risk of exposing my identity and sent Comrade Dou a wire. By doing so, I committed the "leftist" error of acting rashly.

Broad Bean Blossoms

As I said in the first section, "Broad Bean Blossoms" and "Who Was Once Me" are the same poem, with just a few words changed.

Bingying read "Broad Bean Blossoms" before coming to Chongqing. At the time, she was working as an actress in Shanghai. According to the historical record, her last performance was in a play by Yu Ling, *Long Nights of Travel*, about the tragic lives of three families in the Shanghai International Settlement during the Japanese occupation. After they were forced to stop performing, she and many other actors started spending their nights carousing, trying to drown their sorrows. In *Beauty in a Time of Chaos*, Anthony Thwaite writes:

> Although Bingying was painting the town every night, she felt profoundly alienated from her surroundings. Several times before this, she had considered traveling to Yan'an to be reunited with Ge Ren. The news of Ge Ren's death on the field of war left her rudderless. In her journal she wrote, "The days pass one by one. The window lattice is covered in frost, and I can't see even a speck of hope." It was at this time that Zong Bu reappeared in her life. During the war, he had moved the *Shanghai Harbor Daily* to Hong Kong, but now he was back. Bingying had no idea why he had made this trip. His salt-and-pepper beard and despairing expression showed that he had aged. When he walked in, snowflakes were clinging to his eyelashes, and she thought those had turned white too. He claimed that he was just passing through, but of course she was reluctant to believe that excuse.
>
> He had brought a newspaper with him, the Hong Kong publication *Scattered Scriptures*. While she instructed her servant to fetch him food

and drink, he opened the paper and began reading, as if he had just bought it on the street outside. As he drank his soup, he muttered as if to himself, "Interesting." She asked what was interesting, and he appeared momentarily stunned before looking down to address his meal. She had the impulse to fling the newspaper aside, but fate seemed to intervene, and her fingers found themselves drawn to the paper. As everyone knows, the Greek word "fate" does not mean solemnity, inevitability, or worth, but simply chance, joy, sorrow. When by "chance" she picked up that newspaper, short-lived joy and longer sorrow settled once again on her shoulder.

Her eye was caught by a poem, one with the same title as her daughter's nickname, Broad Bean: it was called "Broad Bean Blossoms," and the author was Melancholy. Now she knew the reason Zong Bu had come all the way from Hong Kong to Shanghai: so she would see this poem. Under her questioning, Zong Bu explained that many years ago, he had seen this poem in *Nouveau Siècle*, though the title was then "Who Was Once Me," and the author was Ge Ren. "His Russian name is Melancholsky, and if I'm not wrong, this is meant for you and your daughter," said Zong Bu. He also told Bingying that he had wanted to publish these lines himself in the *Shanghai Harbor Daily*, but after much thought, he withdrew the piece. "From the contents of the poem, it looks like it was recently altered. Could he have done that just before he was martyred? If not, then it might be someone else's handiwork. Of course, there is one other possibility: that Ge Ren is still alive," said Zong Bu to Bingying. "And if he's still alive, then you two will see each other very soon." In Bingying's recollection of this conversation, Zong Bu's expression was clear—he truly was happy about the possibility that she and Ge Ren might be reunited. At that moment, her anger at Zong Bu melted away like the frost on the lattice . . .

Thwaite continues:

Bingying told me that from that moment on, she suspected every corner of the world of harboring Ge Ren. She decided to fly to Chongqing right away, to see Zhao Yaoqing. Being in the Military Intelligence Department of the Kuomintang, she thought he might already have accurate reports of Ge Ren's whereabouts. Zong Bu wanted to accompany her, but she gracefully declined. On her third day in Chongqing, she finally met him in a bar. [N.B. This is at odds with Ah Qing's own account.] Unexpectedly, Zhao Yaoqing swore on his honor that he knew nothing about it. He was obviously lying. She later heard that not long after their conversation, he traveled to Baibei Town on Bare Mountain. She said that in the days that followed, she recited "Broad Bean Blossoms" over and over on Joyful Song Hill, by the Jialing River, at the Confucian temple, silently weeping . . .

Looking at Ah Qing's narrative, we see that Bingying misunderstood him—when they met, he did indeed "know nothing about this." As for the altered version of "Broad Bean Blossoms," we will come to it again, so enough about that here.

Command

It was uncanny. I could never have imagined that just a few days after that, I really would find out that Ge Ren was still alive. And wouldn't you know it, fuck my luck, the Party was sending me to Bare Mountain. Whether this idea came from Dai Li, I had no idea, and still don't.

You've got it wrong. What kind of dogshit is Dai Li that I would want to defend him? Be serious? I'm very serious! Everyone in the world is scared to be serious, but Communists are the most serious. At the time, I called him Boss Dai. Boss Dai wasn't just Satan incarnate, able to kill a man without blinking, he was also a bronze gourd, sealed tight as a drum. The day before my departure, I saw Dai Li at the White Residence, but he didn't mention this affair. The dogfucker was screaming at everyone. You know what his catchphrase was? He'd shout in English, "Damned fool!" You don't understand English? Here, I'll write it down for you. You're absolutely right! Whatever the enemy opposes, we must embrace. And what the enemy holds dear, we will oppose. But what if the person being yelled at really is a fool, and a damned one to boot? What should we say then? Which is why I never thought that anyone Dai Li shouted at was my friend. It's dog eat dog, and all you get is a mouthful of fur. Yes, Dai Li knew who I was. He knew me because we're from the same town, in Zhejiang—Bao'an [Village] in Jiangshan [County]. There's a hill in Bao'an called Xianxia Peak. He lived there, at Dragon Well Pass, while I was down the hill in Phoenix Village. Speaking of which, are there any more cigarettes? I'll have another. Smoking Phoenix brand makes me think of my hometown, after all. There's a great saying: Elsewhere the hills are pretty and the water clear, and the pretty girls are oh so dear, but there's nowhere like home. All right, back to our subject. I was able to find a perch in Kuomintang Military Intelligence because of this connection. Boss Dai would never have guessed that I was a wolf in sheep's clothing. I was utterly respectful to him on the surface, but in my mind I was constantly thinking about bringing down the entire Chiang dynasty. People at the bottom are the cleverest, those at the top are idiots. Don't think Dai Li is so fucking special; he's stupid in his bones. In his own words, he's the damned fool. If not, how come he couldn't see me for who I really was? Of course, that's hard to separate from my strategy for the enemy. Strategy is the lifeline of the Revolution. For the good of the People, I have a high degree of revolutionary awareness at all times.

Is it all right for me to say that?

It wasn't Dai Li who wanted to talk to me. You just said you understood Comrade Ge Ren's revolutionary life, so you ought to know Fan Jihuai. Yes, he and Ge Ren studied in Japan together, in the old days. Ge Ren studied medicine, and he studied law. As you comrades know, the law is imperialist. It manifests the will of the ruling class, and is a tool of class dictatorship. When I put it like that, you should understand that Fan Jihuai wasn't a good guy. It was probably Dai Li who sent him to see me. He told me he'd had an important report, that Ge Ren was now hiding in Bai-bei Town, Bare Mountain. I kept shaking my head, saying, Not possible, not possible, that must be wrong. He asked why it wasn't possible. I said, People die like lights going out, and he's been dead so long, he's probably stinking up the place by now. How could he show up again? He said, That's just it—when you go, your main task will be to determine whether that person is Ge Ren. If he's not, let him go. If he is, then let's figure out exactly what he's doing there. He also ordered me not to rush into this and scare our target away. Unless I got new instructions, I wasn't to harm a hair on his head.

Stupid! So stupid! Did that really need to be said? Of course I wasn't going to harm a hair on his head. I just thought that, I didn't dare say it out loud, because wouldn't that give the game away? So I asked, Why? He said, Because Ge Ren is a well-known figure, and if we don't handle this now, it'll blacken the name of both the Party and Nation. Fan said one other thing that's stuck in my mind. In *Legend of the Red Lantern*, Jiushan says something similar. He says, That's known as lowering a long line to catch a big fish. Doesn't that sound sly to you? It's the most cunning thing. Later, I thought, motherfucker, I really am the best person for this job. First, I've been to Bare Mountain before, so I know the lay of the land. Second, I understand Ge Ren. Naturally, we could say that's their biggest miscalculation. How could they have known that it was just my body in Cao Cao's camp—that my mind was still with the Han, and my red heart pointed toward Pagoda Hill at all times.

Who was that who just passed by the door? Is he with you? Ask him in. Oh, it's the Captain. He likes my stories, I'm sure he'd like to come in and listen. He sings well, especially "Eternal Life to Chairman Mao," that duet for a man and woman. I heard him do "The East Is Red" as a duet too—he sang "The East is red," and the woman sang "The sun will rise." He said this was an example of men and women teaming up to lighten the load. His woman gave up the ghost last year. Swallowed so much rat poison, it would have killed a water buffalo. Why did she do it? You'd have to ask the Captain. And now he has to sing all by himself, one line in a deep voice, one line at a higher pitch. He comes to see me often, saying he'll sing a passage for me if I speak to him. I like how he sounds when he makes his voice high-pitched for the woman's part. When it's done well, it could transport you up to the Shaanbei Plateau. I'm a man of my word. If he sings one passage, I'll say one thing. No, I've never mentioned Ge Ren to him. In several decades as a revolutionary, I've never said Ge Ren's name to anyone. The Captain's interested in succubi. He can't get enough of the affair between Butterfly Wu and Dai Li. After each bit of gossip, he'll spit and say, Whoa, little she-devil, how shameless. I'm sure he'll expect another story about Dai Li and Butterfly this time.

Where was I? Oh yes, body in Cao Cao's camp, heart with the Han. The Party had inserted me into Kuomintang Military Intelligence as a performer: I was cast in the role of a spy.

A few days ago, there was a film screening at the foot of the hill. The Captain took us there, but we arrived late, so we had to sit in the back. One young man got completely wrapped up in it. He kept muttering, So good to be a spy—meat to eat, wine to drink, and a beautiful woman to warm your bed, lucky dogfucker. If I hadn't been worried about disturbing the audience, I'd have given him a lesson in politics. There's nothing great about being a spy. First, you have to be so thick-skinned, a machine gun couldn't cut through you. Second, you have to be hard-hearted and strike when you need to. If you can't do those two things, and you still want to be a spy, then you're only daydreaming. This guy wasn't looking at both sides of the situation. He just saw someone eating well and boozing it up, but not how much he was suffering behind the scenes. In the beginning, when the Party came to find me to ask if I'd infiltrate the Nationalists, that's exactly what I thought. Later on, when the Revolution exploded deep in my soul and drove out even the thought of selfishness, I finally straightened my thinking. All jobs are equally worthy to the Revolution, so why shouldn't I perform? And I thought I might be prostituting myself, but the Party would raise a memorial to me. Good is rewarded and bad is punished—eventually, if not right away. So? Have I got it right? You came to see me, giving me cigarettes, pouring me tea—are you going to raise a memorial to me?

"The East Is Red"

After this conversation, Ah Qing would finally learn that the reason his identity was exposed and he got investigated by the Party had to do with the Captain. And so the last thing he did before he died was to drag the Captain down with him. Professor Zhang Yongsheng, retired from Jeju National University, was detained at the Xin Village Tea Plantation at the same time—he jokingly calls himself Ah Qing's Re-Education colleague. When I interviewed him, Professor Zhang said:

Ah Qing wasn't lying—the Captain did enjoy singing. His voice was good, so his nickname was "Cicada." There was an old locust tree on the plantation with a speaker fixed to it—filled with bird shit, like a giant bird's nest. You probably don't know that at the time, every speaker in the country was playing "The East Is Red" to start the day, and finishing it with "The Internationale." It was the Captain who put the speaker there.

Before Ah Qing's death, the higher-ups had already started investigating him. They encouraged the agitators among us to bring forward any material evidence and put it in the Captain's hands. What's that? Am I an agitator? Do I look like one? Never mind, we were talking about Ah Qing and the Captain. For a few days, in order to sort through all the evidence, he slept during the day and worked through the night. The problem was that we were all too used to singing "The East Is Red" along with the speaker as soon as we got up. If we didn't sing that tune, we couldn't so much as wash our faces. Out of force of habit, the Captain would sing "The East Is Red" when he got out of bed, even as the speaker was playing "The Internationale." And while "The East Is Red" was blaring, he'd be getting ready for bed, and couldn't stop himself from launching into "The Internationale." If he hadn't, he wouldn't have been able to make himself wash his feet and tuck himself in. Isn't that fucking weird? It might sound weird, but it felt normal to us. One morning, Ah Qing caught him. They were singing "The East Is Red" along with the speaker, and just as they got to "Hooah, haiyo, he is the savior of the People," the Captain was warbling, "No savior from on high delivers, no faith have we in prince or peer." And now Ah Qing had him. He said, "We were singing about the savior of the People, but you were saying there's no savior from on high. Why were you contradicting us? What was your motive? If this isn't a strike against the red flag, then what is?" The Captain's face went green as Ah Qing shot these questions at him.

Thinking about it seriously, damn it, Ah Qing's logic really was impeccable. But at the time, not one of us dared to speak up to support him.

He probably already knew he didn't have much longer to live, and just like a dying pig doesn't fear scalding water, he wanted to take the Captain down with him. Ah Qing's fate was bad, and he died not long thereafter. Shortly after that, the Captain was investigated. Before they could reach a conclusion, he died too. As with Ah Qing, it was suicide. To this day, whenever I hear "The East Is Red," I think of Ah Qing, of the Captain, of speakers. Yes, and bird shit. In the end, Ah Qing was a lucky guy. You see, right before his death, he managed to find a scapegoat. If that's not a lucky man, what is?

Mourning

What? How did I come to know Ge Ren? Well, that's a long story. I met his father first, then got to know him later. His father was named Ge Cundao—he worked at a tea factory in Hangzhou. As for whether he actually was a devotee of Kang Youwei, I haven't looked into that, so I shouldn't say. The owner of the tea factory was Hu Zikun, who'd spent some time in Japan and was friends with Ge Cundao. At this point, Hu Zikun was bedridden and couldn't run the business, but his son Hu An was away, so the burden of revolution came to rest on Ge Cundao. Yes, Hu An was Bingying's father, and Hu Zikun was her grandfather. At the time, my father was working at the factory. My mom died when I was four or five, so he sent for me to join him in Hangzhou. We lived in a leaky house, and it rained all the time, so it wasn't long before my dad died too. Hu Zikun and Ge Cundao didn't kick me out. I stayed in the Hu household for a while and saw Ge Cundao every day. He had a lot weighing on his shoulders, and a strong sense of duty in his heart. Every day, he'd try to increase production for the Revolution, urging everyone to open their eyes wide and keep working till lights out, moving endlessly from victory to victory. He liked me a lot, and kept saying I was clever and sensible, that I might be small but my spirit was huge, and that I came from the same mold as his son. When he was writing, he often let me grind the ink for him. He was a frail, scholarly type, just like Ge Ren would grow up to be. Cleanliness was important to him. He treated everyone politely, and enjoyed brushing his teeth. The first time I saw him doing that, spitting out white froth, I thought he must be a revolutionary ox who'd taken human form.

During that time, there was a woman who often came to see him in Shanghai. She was very handsome, with a scarf around her bobbed hair, like Sister Jiang from the movie. She always brought lots of candy with her, which she would hand out to the workers' kids. What's that, candy-coated bullets? If that's what you want to call them, then the descendants of laborers loved to eat candy-coated bullets. All right, let's not talk about that. Back to Ge Cundao. He was always going to Shanghai too, and whenever he came back, he'd bring me some candy. I kept asking him, When are you going to Shanghai? When is the Shanghai auntie coming here? Whenever I said that, he'd ruffle my hair and tell me I was like his son. I had two whorls on my head, and that's why his son was called Duo. Yes, Duo was Ge Ren's childhood nickname. So I asked, When can I meet Brother Duo? Will he bring me candy too? He said Duo was in Qinggeng, far away from Hangzhou, but the next time he went for a visit, he'd be sure to take me along. Back then, I had no idea that he had never met his son. One time he came back from another trip to Shanghai and gave me some candy as usual, but I didn't take it. I said, Go and see, quick; the old man's in a bad way. Ge Cundao rushed to He Zikun's bedside, but he was gone.

That's how I'm telling the story. Is that all right? Fine, I'll go on.

Ge Cundao wrote to Hu An asking him to come home as soon as he could. Once again, I ground the ink while he wrote. It took a few months for Hu An to get back from France. Well, of course Hu Zikun had been buried by then. When Hu An showed up, I had completely forgotten about Hu Zikun, and it was only when I heard people calling him "young master" that I realized he was there in mourning. He brought his daughter, a girl of seventeen or eighteen in a flowery dress, looking very westernized. Yes, this was Bingying. Mixed-race? No, her mother was an overseas Chinese student. The mother hadn't made the trip, so I never met her. Really, I'm not bluffing. No, Bingying didn't bring me any candy—but she did have a puppy with her. It even had a name, Bastille. I had never heard of a dog having a name before. I quickly became good friends with Bastille. You know the saying, dogs can't stop eating shit. Even now, whenever I take a crap, I think about Bastille. When I told Bingying that Bastille liked eating my poop much more than anything else, she forbade me to ever play with him again. I once heard her say she'd found him on the street outside the Bastille. What do you think, was he a running dog of a late capitalist? I won't lie to you, I've pondered this question before. Hu An told me that even French workers kept dogs. Bastille must have belonged to a laborer, and only got abandoned on the street when his owner could no longer feed him.

Hu An had studied theater in France, and he didn't know anything about the tea business. So just like his father, he put Ge Cundao in charge of the factory, while he was an absentee owner, gadding about with Bingying every day. Like Ge Cundao, he enjoyed making trips to Shanghai, and sometimes Bingying would accompany him. I went along a few times too, and stayed at Sister Jiang's place. Who was Sister Jiang? Didn't I just tell you? The woman who was always visiting Ge Cundao looked just like Sister Jiang. Her name? Her surname was Lin, just like our eternally healthy Vice Premier Lin Biao. Later on, I found out they were planning to establish a library in Shanghai. They had even picked out a location, very close to Sister Jiang's house. Hu An had all the books he'd brought back from France shipped to Shanghai, and was storing them at Sister Jiang's place. I remember this very clearly, how he'd declaim from them in a loud voice. Sometimes tears would stream down his face as he read; other times he'd be laughing. He'd say, This is a comedy, it's by Shakespeare. Who was Shakespeare? He was a westerner, a playwright who wrote foreign revolutionary plays. I didn't enjoy hearing him recite plays, but whenever he asked if he had read well, I would always say yes. When I praised him, he'd take me out for dinner and buy me lots of delicious food. If I said his performance was bad, there'd be no dinner for me; he'd just send me out to fetch some shaomai. What are shaomai? Steamed dumplings with some sort of meat filling. No, no, I'm just telling the truth; that definitely wasn't an indirect request to the Party. When we break for a meal, you guys can have all the meat—I'll be happy with a bowl of soup. If there weren't any shaomai to be had, he'd send me miles away to get bread. At the time, I didn't know what bread was, so it was Bingying who took me there. She told me that in France she ate bread every day. What's that? You think Hu An led a decadent capitalist life? You have to remember, he was in France. What is France? It's where the Paris Commune was. Remember, the Paris Commune came even before the Qiliying People's Collective; it was fucking great. He was in France for such a long time, he must surely have been part of the Paris Commune, gone down to the rural villages, been in a workers' militia, carried a semi-automatic rifle. Bread is capitalist? [N.B. This doesn't seem to make sense, but it's in the transcript.] Hell, you can't say that. Comrade Lenin ate bread too, and he even told the People that there would be bread, there would be everything.

On one of those trips, Ge Cundao stayed in Shanghai an extra-long time. When he returned, he took one look at how filthy the factory was, with flies and rats everywhere, and he got angry. So he led us all in eliminating the Four Pests: kill the flies, kill the rats. Once again we had to keep our eyes wide open, working till lights out. That spring, Ge

Cundao's lights went out permanently. What do I mean? His flame was snuffed out. He died.

How did he die? He got shot. This was on Ge Ridge in Hangzhou. There were plenty of bodhi trees there, and snipers would hide among the branches. Bang, and he was on the ground. That was some coincidence— Ge Ridge really did seem to hold some kind of destiny for the Ge family. Motherfucker, some things just don't make sense. Comrades, you all know that Liu Bei's general Pang Tong was killed by an arrow at Luofeng Hill. I'm not superstitious; I'm against superstition more than anything else. I'm just saying there are some things that really can't be explained. Later on, they found out that Ge Cundao was shot with a revolver. Have you ever seen a revolver? If political power grows out of the barrel of a gun, then it can never be far from the revolver. After so many years in the Revolution, I've had a revolver with me many times when I was tramping here and attacking there. It slips into your pocket, about the size of a pack of Phoenix cigarettes. Yes, I will have another [cigarette]. The revolver's short—shorter than your hard cock. The mouth of the barrel is thin and smooth, like a baby's nostril.

His fate was bad. He got hit by a bullet, but he didn't die right away. When we brought him back, his face was stark white, but he could still talk. I remember he talked about his wife. No, not Sister Jiang, Ge Ren's mother. He said that now he'd get to see her again. But the next day he changed his tune and said he didn't want to meet her, he wanted to be buried in Hangzhou. Hu An said to him, Mr. Ge, don't talk, save your breath. Just shut your eyes if you want to go back to Qinggeng, and leave them open if you want to stay in Hangzhou. His eyes fluttered open, then shut. It was confusing. One morning the doctor changed his dressing, and he suddenly told Hu An that he didn't want to be in either Hangzhou or Qinggeng—that we should bury him in Shanghai, at the spot where the library was going to be. And with that, he said he wanted to see his son. Hu An complained about this, grumbling that he should have said something sooner. But he still sent someone to Qinggeng to fetch Ge Ren.

I remember this so clearly. In order to see his son, Ge Cundao held on for quite a few days. If it was today, we'd say he was struggling on his deathbed. But in the end, he didn't make it. By the time Ge Ren got to Hangzhou, his father was in his coffin, and the coffin was in the Hu family's courtyard, smelling strongly of black paint. When Ge Ren arrived, it was shining in the moonlight, like a marooned rowboat. Hu An led him up to it, and he didn't cry, just stroked it over and over, then bent down to sniff it. He must have thought he was dreaming. It really did feel like a dream. Think about it: this should have been a momentous reunion of father and son, but nothing worked out the way it should have. He'd come all this distance only to find his father's eyes closed forever.

His Father's Death

In 1900, the American engineer John Moses Browning secluded himself in his study and invented the revolver. Photographs show that there was a bodhi tree outside his window. Fourteen years later, a revolver emerged from among the branches of a bodhi tree on Hangzhou's Ge Ridge and shot Ge Cundao dead. At almost the same time, Gaston Calmette, the editor of the French newspaper *Le Figaro*, was killed by a shot from a revolver in a Parisian café. On June 28 that same year, Archduke Franz Ferdinand, the heir to the Austro-Hungarian throne, was shot with a revolver in Bosnia. As everyone knows, Franz Ferdinand's death triggered the First World War. And many years after that, in the spring of 1943, a revolver was aimed once more, this time at Ge Ren's chest. When Browning was creating his invention, did he understand that his inspiration would set off such changes across the world? I have to say a little more about what happened to Ge Cundao after his death. The evidence we have access to makes it clear that in his early days, Ge Cundao was indeed a devotee of Kang Youwei's. After the failure of the Hundred Days' Reform, he fled to Japan. While on the run, he met a Shanghainese woman in Kyoto's Fukurin Library—this was Miss Lin Xinyi, the woman Ah Qing mentioned as looking very much like Sister Jiang. Lin Xinyi knew a young man named Zou Rong who was, like her, from Ba County in Sichuan; with time, Ge Cundao became acquainted with him too. When he found out that Ge Cundao knew Tan Sitong, Zou Rong was in awe of him. In 1903, the three of them took a boat from Japan back to Shanghai. That same year, Zou Rong published his book *The Revolutionary Army* in Shanghai, a call to arms urging the overthrow of the Manchu Qing government. Embarrassed by this, the authorities moved quickly to arrest him, and he had to seek refuge in the British embassy. Ge Cundao was implicated too, and fled to Hangzhou with Lin Xinyi—they had met Hu Zikun a couple of years previously, when he was in Japan to sell his tea leaves. For more information about Ge Cundao's life in Hangzhou, refer to Liu Qinrong's book *Tea Men* (Rapid Press, 1927). In the section about the "Hangzhou tea society," Mr. Liu writes:

> Following the Zou Rong incident, Cundao and his lady friend repaired to Hangzhou. At that time, because I frequently visited my dear friend Zikun's home, I got to know Cundao. On one visit I was in the back garden with Hu and Ge, on a clear moonlit night with light breezes blowing. As

we sat with cups of fragrant tea, the conversation turned to Zou Rong, and Cundao spoke: "Weidan [N.B. Zou Rong's courtesy name] is in the protection of the British. His life is no longer in danger." I was anxious, as westerners have often sacrificed honor for advantage, and suggested we prepare for the eventuality of such a betrayal. Cundao disagreed. "The British, French, and Americans have all pledged their protection to Weidan. Even if the British were to renege, we would still have the French and Americans. Weidan believes that with the philosophy of Rousseau and the morality of Washington, DC, those two countries will not remain bystanders." Brother Zikun commented that when the storm was over, he would personally travel to Shanghai and bring Zou Rong back to Hangzhou. Cundao continued, "Weidan is still a bachelor. I shall do my best to find a match for him, and when he comes to Hangzhou, he can be married." When Zou Rong later died in prison, I understood that even scholars can speak out of ignorance, just as a mushroom doesn't know day from night, and a cicada can't tell spring from autumn . . .

We know from publications at the time that "when Zou Rong was taken in by the embassy, the English were stoic and refused to hand him over, claiming their freedom to protect anyone they chose" (*The Commons*, October 15, 1903), but as the Qing government steadily applied more pressure, "the social elite were clamoring that [they believed] this was an act of violent interference with the Manchu government" (*Gentlemen's Conversation*, no. 13 [1905]). The British folded, and pushed Zou Rong out the embassy's door. He was soon arrested and imprisoned. According to the historical record, when he was first jailed, the intellectuals attempted to set up a campaign to free him. Soon, though, the whole affair was forgotten, and his name no longer appeared in the papers. The next time this youngster came to anyone's mind was two years later, in 1905. That's when Zou Rong, thin as a skeleton, died of illness in prison.

In death, Zou Rong became a holy relic that anyone could take a bite out of. *The Commons* described this, poetically, as "butterfly specimens being far more durable than butterflies themselves." Political factions of all stripes used his passing to promote themselves, and *The Revolutionary Army* was reprinted (or possibly pirated). Sun Yat-sen, known as Cannon Sun, changed its title to *Fighting for Survival* and distributed copies in Singapore, San Francisco, and Japan, which no doubt laid the ideological groundwork for his later ascension to the provisional presidency of the Republic of China.

According to *Tea Men*, after Zou Rong's death, Ge Cundao began collecting various editions of *The Revolutionary Army*. When this book became fashionable, he was happy not just for himself, but also for Zou Rong, saying, "If Weidan can see us from the underworld, he'll surely find this gratifying" (*Tea Men*, p. 49). Some believe that Ge Cundao got the idea of setting up a library while he was collecting editions of this book. As we said before, Ge Cundao met Zou Rong in a library, and perhaps he thought this would be a way to commemorate him. I wasn't able to find out whether Hu Zikun supported this plan. We do have a record of Hu An's feelings, though. Mr. Huang Jishi, who would later establish the *Shanghai Harbor Daily* with Zong Bu, was at the time the editor of *The People's News*. In his memoir *Half a Lifetime* (Flying Horse Publishing, Hong Kong, 1956), he wrote:

> Mr. Cundao's library had the support of a tea merchant who had returned from overseas. No merchant since ancient times has ever been honest, but this man seemed to be an exception. He called himself Vieux-chinois, and when he spoke, he sounded exactly like a westerner. He said, "Building a library is a public project, but building a book collection is a private project." For his part, Mr. Cundao said, "Public libraries and private collections might both contain books, but there's an important distinction. The former is a public enterprise, and the latter is a private endeavor. My friend regards all private endeavors as trash; hence this extraordinary gesture."

Ge Ren planned to build the library on Songlu Road. During the preparatory period, the owner of one of Shanghai's private book collections, Fan Gongming, came to offer his congratulations as a colleague, and even brought along a piece of his own calligraphy: "Books hold a thousand years of knowledge, but only the heart knows what is gained or lost." Fan Gongming had also studied in Japan, and he was a self-proclaimed sixth-generation descendant of Fan Qin, who built the legendary Tianyi Pavilion. Only recently have scholars proved that he was not, in fact, related to Fan Qin; he was simply one of his many admirers. Even as he was offering his congratulations to Ge Cundao, the plot to eliminate Ge was germinating in his "heart."

Naturally, it wasn't Fan himself who followed Ge Cundao from Shanghai to Hangzhou, but a hired killer named Dou Niancheng. In recent years, there have been attempts to prove that he was related to Dou Sizhong, but at this point there isn't enough evidence to justify the hypothesis, so we won't go into it here. I should mention parenthetically that it is because of another case that we know that it was Dou Niancheng who murdered Ge Cundao. On March 20, 1913, Dou Niancheng took part in the assassination of Kuomintang leader Song Jiaoren at the Shanghai Railway Station. He was eventually arrested by the Nationalist government for this crime. Pull one strand of yarn, and the whole ball unravels. While being interrogated, he also admitted to the killing of Ge Cundao. This only happened in 1920, though. What follows is his confession—oddly, he seems to have been a fan of Zou Rong too!

I'm an old revolutionary. I started on the road to revolution while I was studying in Japan. At the time, the person I admired most was Perovskaya [Sophia Lvovna Perovskaya, a Russian anarchist who was hanged at the age of twenty-seven after helping to assassinate Tsar Alexander II]. But now the person I admire most is Zou Rong. He might trade in words, but he's a solid fellow. His farts are like a cannon in the woods.

In Japan, I was already part of an assassination squad hoping to kill Empress Dowager Cixi. Like Perovskaya's squad, each of us wore a pair of white gloves. You had to pull on each finger to get them off—it was quite dashing. We had a chemist from Guangzhou who taught us how to build bombs. When I got back to China, I met a man named Wu Yue. He could play Go, and during a game he'd say, Look at this piece—strike, lunge, trap, hit, charge, block, follow, tap, squash, pull, throw, grow, retreat, seal, turn, cling, stand, squeeze, stick, dig, cripple, crawl, eat! Each move was a fatal one. Sometime after that, he tried to kill some Manchu officials with a bomb. Not a single one of them was killed, but Wu Yue himself was blown to pieces. He left a note saying he wasn't targeting anyone in particular, he just wanted to express his rage at the imperial court, and enrage them so they would act with even more cruelty. Only then would the People be moved to revolt. You have to hit the ball hard to make it bounce high . . .

Encouraged by Wu Yue's example, I struck out on my own. . . . Once I broke the seal on killing, I was like a monk returning to the world. If I didn't eat meat, my stomach would be unhappy. I won't lie to you, I once went to visit Xu Xilin in Anqing. That man had two great loves: guns and his wife's bound feet. In order to ingratiate myself, I brought three-inch embroidered shoes as a gift. I thought that after this was all over, I'd be sure to touch those feet. Do you need to ask? I wasn't going to see Xu Xilin to throw my lot in with him. I'd been given some silver by someone who wanted me to kill him. I don't know who my client was; I got paid through a middleman. So in June [1907] I went to Anqing, but because I stopped off at a whorehouse, I missed my chance. Before I could try again, he'd gotten into trouble: his heart had been dug out and eaten. I hadn't done what I needed to do, and the silver had been spent. The middleman came to demand the money back, and I said, I didn't even lift a finger, and he's dead. Wasn't that what you wanted? But fuck it, he said Xu's death had nothing to do with me, and he wanted a full refund. I didn't know what to do, so I killed him.

And yes, I was the one who shot Ge Cundao. The client came to me personally. His name was Fan. I asked why he wanted to get rid of Ge Cundao. He said, Every household has its rules, and so does every profession. Ge broke the rules. He wanted it to happen far away. It would have been much more convenient to do it in Shanghai, but he wouldn't allow it. I had to strike out of town. That's the trouble with working for educated people. You think I talk a lot? He talked even more. Ge Cundao spent a lot of time in Ge Ridge in Hangzhou, taking care of his business there. The next time he went back to Hangzhou, I got there ahead of him. Fuck it, in this line of work, it's best not to be too curious, but I was young at the time, and that was my problem. I was in a Hangzhou tea house, about to do it, when suddenly I heard him mention *The Revolutionary Army* to his friend. It was written in English, and he said he could pick it up the next day. That was the book written by Zou Rong, whom I really admire. I had lots of editions, but not the English one. I paused and thought, why not wait a day, till he gets the book, and kill two birds with one stone? Then I heard him mention a French edition of Wei Yuan's *Illustrated Compendium of Overseas Territories*. That book was popular in Japan, and I had flipped through it many times. It famously exhorts us to "learn the technology of the barbarians." The great thing about these words is that they were describing me: that's exactly what I was doing when I started using the revolver.

I waited one more day, but it was suddenly impossible to find him. Still, I had accepted payment, so I had to get the job done. My only choice was to lie low in Hangzhou. You can do anything if you're determined enough. A few days later, I saw him again on Ge Ridge. There was a stand of bodhi trees there that had just started to bloom, so I climbed up into one and hid there. The leaves scratched my face, but I felt good. My index finger clung to the trigger as tightly as a silkworm, waiting for him to come out of the tea house. After a couple of hours, he finally appeared. This time I didn't give him a chance to get away. The revolver jerked in my hand, and he crashed to the ground face first. Of course, the sugar cane can't be sweet at both ends. The killing was beautifully done, but I came away with an injury. As I climbed down from the tree, a branch ripped a patch of skin off my forehead. Look, I still have the scar, it looks like a birthmark . . .

Hu An followed the instructions in Ge Cundao's will and buried him in a grove of trees by Songlu Road, right next to where the library would be. After his death, Lin Xinyi continued working to set it up. The following year, Lin Xinyi died of sorrow. And with that, the planned library vanished from everyone's mind, like an airborne flower garden blown apart and scattered by the wind.

Revolutionary Friendship

When I first got to Xinyang, they threw me a welcome party, and told me I had to be serious about reforming. After the party, I headed directly to re-education. I had heard there would be a familiar face at the tea plantation, and I wanted to see him as soon as possible. When I got there, though, it seemed he was dead. I fell into a daze, and couldn't rouse myself for half a day. Let's compare—Ge Ren traveled all that way, but all he saw at the end was a dead dad. How must he have felt? But Ge Ren really was made of special stuff. He turned sadness into strength, and soon plunged into a life of passion.

After burying his father, Ge Ren didn't go back to Qinggeng. He sat in the Hu courtyard every day, reading a book or drawing. Yes, when I said a life of passion, I meant with regard to his studies. During that time, Bingying had a teacher named Xu Yusheng who admired Ge Ren's drawings—he would praise them constantly as he looked through them. Xu had been good friends with Ge Cundao too, and had donated some money toward the library. Ge Ren spent a lot of time with Xu Yusheng, and they often went on trips together. Bingying would accompany them too. A hanger-on? Yes, you're right, that's what I was—I was always tagging along as well.

So you see, I wasn't bragging, was I? Ge Ren and I really did have a revolutionary friendship, and that was around the time it started. Apart from playing with me, he also taught me to read and write. Comrades, it's only now that feudalism has ended, and the imperialists have fled with their tails between their legs, and even Latin America, the back garden of the American imperialists, is in flames, that you can say reading isn't important. Back then, with the imperialists and feudalists still pissing and shitting on the People, it was essential to read. I wasn't very sensible back then, and I refused to learn. I said that my name would still be Ah Qing whether I could read or not. No point in adding another string to my bow—can six fingers scratch an itch any better than five? But Ge Ren said if I didn't study, there'd be no dinner for me. I asked why, and he said, You're going to shit the food out in the end, so we might as well not bother. I said I'd starve to death, and he said I was going to die eventually, so why not do it now? You see how simply he made me understand these complicated ideas—the opposite of boring ideology. So I had to study just to keep up with him. He encouraged me to keep improving, calling me the early morning sun that he was pinning all his hopes on. He really said that, I'm not bluffing. He didn't just teach me reading and writing, he also taught me English. Why did he do that? I think the reason is simple: just as Chairman Mao said, we had to overtake Britain and America in fifteen years. Comrades, this was important; we couldn't just stumble through it. If we didn't catch up, we'd be booted off the planet. No, you're right, we caught up long ago. Fuck it, the pendulum's swung back the other way, and now it's their turn to get kicked off the planet. Is it all right if I say that? Fine, then I'll continue. I'd been working so hard on my studies, even Hu An didn't think I was useless anymore. I said to him, I can't take the credit—a train goes fast because of the locomotive, and it's Ge Ren who's pulling me along. Later on, I even had westerners give me the thumbs up and say that my English was good. These were a couple of priests—a tall one named Beal and a short one named Ellis. They had beards like mountain goats, and looked like Norman Bethune from Chairman Mao's writings.

They had a girl with them. It goes without saying that as soon as she arrived, she became fast friends with Bingying. She had delicate features and short hair, and always dressed in pale colors. She was a few years older than Bingying, and would play hide and seek with her in the back garden. Mr. Xu Yusheng, who ran the private school, took quite a few pictures of them. I remember very clearly that in one of the photos, they're both dancing around a flowerbed with scarves on. I know I shouldn't have wanted to play with girls, but because of solidarity with our female comrades, I did want to. The back garden had gardenias, hibiscus flowers, and aloe vera. One time, Bingying's leg got scratched by aloe vera thorns, and the wound got infected. When the doctor came to change her dressing, the other girl knelt outside the door, hands clasped together and muttering something. She was praying to the western God for protection—that is, the Christian Lord. Yes, Marx said religion is the opium of the masses, but they were young and didn't understand that yet. I often think of this other girl. I remember she wanted to set up an orphanage in Hangzhou with the two priests, but in the end that didn't happen. She was the one who told me that foreigners don't refer to their Buddha as Buddha, but as God, and that he is a man. Comrades, he's just like you and me—he looks like a regular guy.

First Love

Ge Ren spent two years in Hangzhou, and we have his own description of his life during that time. In 1929, when Ge Ren was having a conversation with Lu Xun in Shanghai, he said:

> My first glimpse of Hangzhou was on a painted fan. A man named Xu Yusheng came to Qinggeng, and he wanted to take me to Hangzhou to see my father. He had a folding fan with a picture of West Lake on it. He

told me West Lake was heaven on earth, and he wanted to take me to this paradise. That image looked like it had been branded into the paper with hot irons, just as concubines can be beautiful whether they're plump or skinny, like pretty girls dancing in rubble.

When I got to Hangzhou, I had to sort out my father's affairs. After I decided to stay, Mr. Xu Yusheng often took me and Bingying to West Lake to cheer us up. But the more time I spent there, the more I felt like I couldn't afford to feel at home there. It's an enchanting place, but there's a kind of attraction that makes you want to run far away. It's pleasing to the eye, but never to the heart—like the sort of elegant woman you'd happily have on your arm at a banquet, but whom you could never open up to. Alas, alas, I was mesmerized by it. This place was snow in summer, blooming flowers in winter, warm winds in autumn, falling leaves in spring. It was a stanza that chimed but didn't rhyme. When the oars moved, the falling droplets were like fingers plucking a string, but the music they produced was always sorrowful.

Bingying never managed to feel at home in Hangzhou—it was always unfamiliar to her, unlike me, coming from Qinggeng. I often went with her to West Lake and Ge Ridge. She was small and dainty, in a way that made me feel protective of her. One time she gave me a flute made from a willow leaf. When Mr. Xu saw it, he recited a line from "The Quiet Maiden": "The leaves she picked from the pastures, are beauteous beyond compare. Their beauty comes not from within, but from what she bestows upon them." Bingying didn't know what he meant, and thought he was just talking to himself, but I think I must have been blushing furiously . . .

Some commentators believe that this passage demonstrates "the agony of his mind," and that this was the reason he later went to Japan. [Cf. *Journal for Ge Ren Studies*, vol. 2.] Personally, I tend to think his two years in Hangzhou were a rare time of happiness in his life. After all, what is more entrancing than first love?

Xu Yusheng, the man who brought Ge Ren to Hangzhou, was from Xikou in Zhejiang. He'd become friends with Ge Cundao during the latter's time in Japan—which is why he would personally go to Qinggeng to fetch Ge Ren back to Hangzhou, to see his father one last time. Later on, he wrote an essay titled "Snow on the Pavilion in the Center of the Lake," in which he mentioned Ge Ren, Bingying, and Ah Qing. His writing is both classical and modern, both Asian and western—a distinctive sense of period. He referred to Ge Ren as R, Ah Qing as Q, and Bingying as Y:

On a night when the snowy skies had cleared and the moon shone bright, I went with R, Q, and Y to West Lake. All three had been there previously, but it was their first time sharing a boat. R was not yet twenty, and already his intelligence and abilities were above average. Q was a straggly-haired youngster, a worker [for] Y's family.

At the appointed time, we set off on the boat to the pavilion at the center of the lake, from where we would watch the snow. The cabin windows were exquisitely carved, fitted with etched glass. At the prow were railings holding up an arched roof, from which lights dangled like autumnal fruits, or like folded buds surrounded by mist. Standing there, one could view the scenery on both shores. The hills reached up into the heavens, the clouds leaned down to touch the water, and the pier was a scar between them, the pavilion a blur within. R and Y stood at the front of the boat looking ahead, while Q was at the rear splashing in the water. I alone reclined in the cabin, entertaining myself with wine. The sound of the oars was beguiling, like slow footsteps through clouds; the drink fogged my mind, like ripples across the water.

As we passed through the circular opening of the bridge, we were suddenly assailed by music. The bridge looked like basalt, hinting at a time before antiquity. The song was like warm jade, and I wished I could give the singer something in return for it. A pleasure boat was moored beyond the bridge, its hazy silhouette all lines and angles, a soft fragrance wafting from it. After some time, the tune faded away. The boat hand spoke: This is the reincarnation of Su Xiaoxiao [a famous courtesan from the time of the Six Dynasties]. R tossed off a few lines right away: "Alas, young Miss Su of long renown, bids a loving farewell as willows sway; such beauty in the Su's frail willows, the pine before the grave still loyal." On the deck of the pleasure boat was a sloe-eyed woman. What could be better than to grow intoxicated on song? The moon was high in the sky, and all was still. I suggested that R should board the pleasure vessel and raise a glass to the girl, but he said, Su Xiaoxiao is no concubine for a common man, and it is an article of faith with me to treat beauty as no more than a street scene—besides, I can imagine her form by hearing her voice. With that, he took Y's hand and retreated into the cabin.

I remained with R, Q, and Y on our covered boat. At the lake-center pavilion, we pulled on warm clothes and lit a fire, and ordered Q to heat some wine. Drunkenly, we returned home. Recorded by Yusheng of Xikou, winter of the Jiayin Year [i.e., 1914].

Mr. Xu Yusheng will appear again many times in this book. He later went to Hong Kong, where he edited a newspaper called *Scattered Scriptures*—as previously noted, it was in this paper in early 1943 that Bingying saw Ge Ren's poem

"Broad Bean Blossoms." This passage, "Snow on the Pavilion in the Center of the Lake," comes from *Qiantang River Dream Diary*, which has a photograph of Bingying, Ge Ren, and Ah Qing as its frontispiece. I also saw my great-aunt in it—the girl who came to Hangzhou with the Reverends Beal and Ellis. In the picture, Ah Qing is kneeling in the front row, wearing a leather cap and looking a little bashfully at the camera. Bingying looks her usual alluring self in a pale gray raincoat and high leather boots, with a corner of checked scarf peeping out of the raincoat. Ge Ren is standing next to her, not looking at the camera, as if something else has caught his attention. He is gazing at a pile of rubble, and at my great-aunt standing atop it. In her arms is a baby—my great-aunt told me this was an abandoned female infant she'd found on the streets of Hangzhou, who unfortunately died soon after. Behind her, a flock of swans is emerging from a sparse grove of trees. She's in a pale-colored dress, and her hair is short, just as Ah Qing described her.

My great-aunt rushed to Hangzhou after seeing reports that Ge Cundao had been assassinated. She arrived too late, and didn't even get to see his coffin. She later told me that while idly chatting with the two priests, she happened to find out that Ge Ren was her twin brother. She ended up staying half a year in Hangzhou. During this time, she could already sense that Ge Ren and Bingying were falling for each other. They looked at each other with the glimmers of first love.

As for that first love, it would be best if we read Bingying's own description. According to Anthony Thwaite in *Beauty in a Time of Chaos*, Bingying once told him she only realized her feelings for Ge Ren on the night before his departure to Japan:

> Even Bingying could not tell when Ge Ren had fallen for her, or when she had fallen for him. She said, "Only when he was about to leave Hangzhou for Japan did I understand I couldn't leave him. I actually forgot my young girl's shyness and hugged him tightly, refusing to let go. Until then, it seemed like we had only been playmates." Ms. Ge Ren's account reminds us of a common saying: the bud does not know how it became a flower. I said to Bingying, Young love is like dewdrops on a branch. It forms out of the dampest portion of the air, and turns different colors as the light changes with time. Bingying laughed when I said the word "dewdrops," apparently agreeing with this point of view. Yet I cannot describe their first love, just as I am unable to convey the grace of dewdrops. Even the most skilled photographer could only capture some of it: some will inevitably be lost.

Bingying's words are verified in the next section of Ah Qing's narration.

Ge Ren Goes to Japan

Back then, I thought Ge Ren and I were inseparable, but very soon he wanted to leave for Japan. I should have kept him there and begged him to continue teaching me about culture, but I was trying to embody the spirit of considering others' needs over my own, so I didn't stand in his way. Why Japan? Do you need to ask? Obviously it was to find the true way to save his country and his people. What? He wanted to study medicine? No contradiction there; studying medicine was a way of saving his country and people, wasn't it?

Hu An put up the money for his trip. I went to Shanghai to see him off, along with Hu An and Bingying. Bingying had wanted to accompany him, but Hu An wouldn't let her. She threw a tantrum and said Chairman Mao had proclaimed that times had changed. Men and women were equal, and women hold up half the sky, so why couldn't she go? She kept it up until Hu An relented. He said she could go, but only after a year. His reasoning was that Ge Ren would need time to find his footing, and once he was established, she could join him. We got to Shanghai, and Bingying kicked up another fuss, wrapping her arms around Ge Ren and insisting she was a fish who couldn't leave the water, a melon that couldn't leave its vine. Comrade Ge Ren was thick-skinned, but even he blushed as red as Lord Guan.

The Ta Chang Maru

My great-aunt once told me that not long after she and the priests left Hangzhou, she heard that Ge Ren had almost died a violent death. Later on, I saw this mentioned in Huang Yan's *Dreaming Back a Hundred Years*. As I said in the first part of this book, the first person to report on the Battle of Two Li Mound, Huang Yan, had previously traveled to Japan with Ge Ren and Fan Jihuai on a ship called the *Ta Chang Maru*, which happens to also be the title of the third chapter of *Dreaming Back a Hundred Years*. Apart from sharing some vignettes of Ge Ren's life in Japan, the book also uses Ge Ren's own words to show that his initial impulse for studying in Japan was, at least in part, to get out of a difficult situation:

> It was a rainy autumn. The skies cleared as the Japanese steamer *Ta Chang Maru* pulled away from Nanjing, though the winds off the river continued to swirl cold air. At Shanghai, the ship stopped only briefly before hurriedly departing. At this time, the mainland was turbulent with war. There was anger and sadness at having to leave, but the greater part was weariness. With the pounding of waves as my pillow, I quickly fell asleep,

and dreamed once again of my father's death. The day I boarded the boat to Japan happened to be three days after the anniversary of my father's death—he was killed in the confusion of battle on September 1 a year ago, in Nanjing. One dream followed another, all of them full of dead people, their heads chopped open like melons. After a while, I started moaning in my sleep. When I woke up, I saw a neatly dressed young man standing in front of me. He looked like the bookish type, not to mention rather effete and bashful. I later found out that his name was Ge Ren. Like me, he was on his way to further studies in Japan. "Where does it hurt?" he asked quietly, bending down to me. For me, that was naturally a rare moment of comfort, although my pain was not something that could be soothed away. I didn't know what to say, but finally told him I had had a dream in which this ship had plunged to the bottom of the ocean, and every single person on board had drowned. He stood next to me, rubbing his hands nonstop, his face flushed bright red.

That was the farthest voyage I undertook in my youth. I think I had been longing for such a trip for some time, so that distance and separation could ease my unhappiness. Even so, the morning sun reflected in the specks of water splashing onto the third-class deck could not help but remind me of my father's blood. I told Ge Ren that even the candy wrappers and bottle stoppers left on deck made me think of beheadings. Get bitten by a snake once, and you will spend the next decade flinching from ropes. Although snake bites don't always kill you, ropes will hang you dead. I saw the human heads hanging from the battlements of the Nanjing city walls, covered with old wounds, eyes wide open and eyelids fluttering slightly, as if trying to figure out what sort of animal skin the ropes were braided from, to gauge how firmly they would hold their weight. One afternoon, Ge Ren swept all those wrappers and stoppers into the sea. He came up to me with a bottle of Red Daughter rice wine. It was only then that I realized there was sadness in his diffidence. But he could be expansive too, as I saw from the way he wrenched the cap off the bottle and took a swig, even as these actions were filled with the habitual swagger of youth. He told me he had boarded the ship in Shanghai. "You must have gotten on at Nanjing. When I boarded, I saw you standing against the railing, muttering to yourself, like you'd escaped from a church choir." I was confused by this, and didn't find out till many years later that he had spent time in a Christian orphanage. That night, we moved our bedrolls to be next to each other. There were two more people next to us, one short and one tall. The short guy was called Fan Jihuai, and as everyone knows, he is currently a leading lawyer in China. He did not particularly stand out from the crowd back then. It was the tall, skinny one who caught people's eye. I'm not sure why, but sometimes when he smiled, it made your hair stand on end. He had a cut on his knee that had gotten infected before he boarded. At night a thin scab would form, like the surface of a jelly—but by morning he would have scratched it off with his nails, then sat there breathing contentedly as the pus spilled out. When Ge Ren asked, he said he was from Anqing, but didn't offer anything else. So Ge Ren turned to talk to me about a young woman named Hu—she was supposed to come on board with us, but at the last minute, her father wouldn't let her. From the way he spoke about her, I knew this must be his lover. Many years later, I realized that this Miss Hu was one of China's first theater actresses, Bingying.

Now that I think about it, young romance is a lot like the scenery from a cabin: translucent night between sky and water, like oiled paper; the engines thrumming loudly or softly, the boat moving along quickly or slowly, till there is not a bit of stillness anywhere in that translucent night. I thought of my "lover" too—if she counted as a lover. She was my cousin; I guess you could call us childhood sweethearts. She had gotten married that spring. Since that time, her husband—a deputy official under the provincial military governor, whom I had met only once—kept showing up in my dreams, and he always got his comeuppance: I saw him throttled, hanged, getting his ankle caught in his stirrup and dying in agony, hacked to death by the bluntest possible knife, stabbed with the sharpest one, suffocated while cavorting grotesquely in bed, shooting himself by accident while cleaning his gun, getting dressed distractedly and garroting himself with his own sash. I had only seen him once, and I couldn't even remember his face clearly, but I dreamed about his contorted features as vividly as a dog I once had. When I left Nanjing, she came to see me, but dared not look me in the eye. Her parting gift was a pair of crocheted socks—she had heard somewhere that there were no socks in Japan because the Japanese walked around everywhere barefoot. Excellent, a pair of smelly socks to pull over that man's face. These were double-layered too; he would surely choke to death.

Ge Ren's dreams were much more poetic. He was an emotional person, and would be all his life. He told me that he and that Miss Hu used to walk in their garden, where jasmine, hibiscus, and lilies surrounded a pavilion. He said she had a scent like the lilies, which would turn in the evening to something more like peppermint, fresh with a hint of tea-like bitterness. He spoke shyly, almost mumbling to himself. I asked why he was going to Japan, when it was every man's dream to be at his books with a fragrant beauty beside him. He first said his friends had urged him to, and it was hard to turn them down, but then later he said he had no choice but to head east. There had been an attack on a tea house in Hangzhou. His friends and family were certain that he was the target, and if he hadn't been lucky, he would be in the underworld with his father now. I had no idea at the time who his father was, and only later on discovered that it was the Mr. Ge Cundao who had hoped to build China's first public library in Shanghai.

It took ten days to get to Japan from Shanghai. At the time, I felt the voyage was dragging out as long as the century. In those ten days, Ge Ren and I became the sort of friends who could say anything to each other. He enjoyed the fresh air, the vast, starry night sky, the red-beaked birds who occasionally came to rest on the *Ta Chang Maru*, the waves that roiled like a herd of beasts arching their spines. He told me that one of his many dreams for the future was to call out the names of all beautiful things, to listen to their natural music, to observe their grace, to touch their mois-ture and warmth like pearls of dew, to understand the mystery of their extraordinary wonder. If he couldn't do this, he would use all his love to nurture his children, giving them the ability to call those names out one by one.

Then something happened one evening, just as the setting sun was about to withdraw its final desolate rays. The Anqing man who slept next to us fell into the sea, like a blanket blown overboard by the wind. The *Ta Chang Maru* continued full speed ahead, and the waves bundled him into the depths. We thought he had slipped, and everyone began to weep for him. Then when we were about to dock, someone found a suicide note among his possessions. His name was Yin Jifu, and he was friends with Chen Duxiu—who at the time was studying at the Athena French School in Tokyo. When we later met Chen Duxiu, he would tell us that Yin Jifu worked at the East Asia Library in Shanghai, and had been coming to Japan to talk to him about some editorial arrangements for *Jiayi* magazine. He also told us that Yin Jifu was a poet. I remember that as the liner approached the shore, I felt as if we had been at sea for an entire century. As soon as we disembarked, we all stamped our feet, as if to make sure we really had arrived in Japan. The sorrow of being in a foreign land surrounded me like fog, and my shoulders rose up. At that moment, strangely, my eyes and Ge Ren's, as well as those of the many other students on the ship, filled with tears.

In Anthony Thwaite's *Beauty in a Time of Chaos*, I read that the tea house where Ge Ren was attacked was called Yixiang Garden. There had been a wave of assassinations across China at the time, and Bingying didn't know if that was a stray bullet or an actual attempt on his life. Still, given Ge Cundao's murder, Hu An thought it was best to be vigilant, so he sent Ge Ren to Japan.

After arriving and settling in, Ge Ren wrote Bingying a letter expressing hope that she'd soon join him in Japan. *Beauty in a Time of Chaos* contains a paragraph from this letter:

> It has been more than twenty days since we parted in Huating [part of Shanghai]. I am lodging at my Japanese friend Kawata's house, and everything is fine. The room I am in is made entirely of wood, and raised slightly off the ground. The windows open as elegantly as a butterfly's wings. If you were here, you would find it satisfactory. My heart is cut in two from missing you, and I feel like a fish on dry land. If I could be reunited with you soon in Japan, that would be true happiness.

He never could have guessed that when he saw Bingying again, she would be the mother of a small child.

Weasels Wish the Chickens Happy New Year

After Ge Ren left, I was all by myself—there was no one to keep me company. Bingying complained about my runny nose and said she didn't want to play with me. I swore by Chairman Mao that I would stop my sniffling, but she wouldn't listen. She liked watching opera back then, and knew someone called Su Mei [i.e., Mei Su]. They were always hanging out together and going to Shanghai to see an opera. On one of their trips it was raining, so they didn't come home until the next day—Zong Bu drove them back in his car. Later on, I found out that Zong Bu was Hu An's friend, and they had spent the night at his place. Yes, Zong Bu later set up a newspaper—I think it was called the *Shanghai Harbor Daily*. What Shanghai Harbor? That's the Bund. You see, he didn't call it the Bund, he called it Shanghai Harbor—surely that was meant to confuse the masses? To set himself against the People? Fuck it, such a person ought to be punished. He won't come to a good end. Pah!

I remember very clearly that Zong person stayed in Hangzhou that day. Hu An politely invited him to join us for a meal, but he spent the whole time telling us to invest in shares—he kept saying, You'll earn money quicker with shares than tea leaves. What are shares? I'll give you a little rhyme to help you remember: Grab some money in your hand, take it to the stock exchange; buy low, sell high, and you'll be grand, that's how profits you arrange. Then the People's government banned shares. That was good, no, very good. Because stocks and shares have fuck all to do with revolution—all they do is nurture a bunch of capitalists. Luckily, Hu An stood firm and refused to board his pirate ship.

All right, I'll go on. Zong Bu produced a microscope, which he liked to brag was even more powerful than the Jade Emperor's demon-revealing mirror. Bingying was floored by it. You haven't seen a microscope before? You might think your faces are clean, but put them under a microscope, and fuck it, they're full of maggots. Zong Bu said, This is called making something out of nothing. He asked Bingying if she was having fun. When she said yes, he gave it to her. She was too young to know that if you accept favors from someone, you give them power over you. Sometime later, he showed up again in his car—he had come all the way to Hangzhou to get his microscope back. But by then, Bingying had already broken it to pieces. She tried to be honorable and said she would pay him back. He said, Pay with what? I realized much later on that he had targeted Bingying from the start—this plot wasn't hatched in only a day. Letting Bingying play with his microscope was like a weasel wishing the chickens Happy New Year—done in bad faith. If only Ge Ren hadn't gone, Zong Bu wouldn't have been able to squirm into the empty place he left. What's that? Flies don't attack unbroken eggs? I'm not going to argue with you. But Bingying was so young, she hadn't had much experience with fending people off.

Later he put a bun in her oven. Seeing her stomach get bigger and bigger, I asked her what she'd been eating to get fat so quickly. She didn't answer, and almost ripped my ears off. What can I say? I was just a child, my fighting spirit wasn't strong yet. But I managed to get rid of him, or at least I made sure his evil plan wouldn't succeed. Then I swore that I would never see him again. Who'd have thought that all those years later, we would meet again on Bare Mountain?

The Microscope

Zong Bu's microscope came from Kang Youwei. In the tenth year of Guangxu's reign [1884], a missionary gave him the instrument. According to *Kang Youwei from Nanhai's Self-Compiled Autobiography* (Chunghwa, 1992 edition), that microscope gave Kang the inspiration for his theory of unity: "Beneath its magnifying gaze, a flea is the size of a wheel, an ant the size of an elephant: thus we see that great and small are alike. Because electric light rays travel ten thousand miles in a second, we see that slow and fast are alike." Kang Youwei even lent his microscope to Tan Sitong. According to *The Collected Tan Sitong* (Chunghwa, 1988 edition), Tan was less impressed by this device. He thought that the knowledge westerners gained from microscopes was like "every planet is another earth, and each one has a different length of year, and every speck of dust is a world too, and thousands of creatures inhabit each drop of water—the Buddhist scriptures speak of all these." He returned the microscope to Kang Youwei.

After the failure of the Hundred Days' Reform, Tan Sitong was killed, and Kang Youwei escaped. As we all know, Ge Cundao fled along with him—from which we can extrapolate that Zong Bu and Ge Cundao must have known each other, even if no written record has ever been found of this acquaintance. Just before departing for Japan, Kang Youwei gave his follower Zong Bu his microscope. Why give such a thing away? Zong Bu had his own understanding of its meaning. In *Half a Lifetime*, Huang Jishi records Zong Bu's words thus:

> Mr. Zong said he didn't think much of it to start with, and imagined it was no different from eyeglasses: firstly, they were both made of glass, and secondly, their only purpose was to help you see more clearly. But Mr. Nanhai [N.B. Kang Youwei's formal name] explained to him that eyeglasses show you what was already there, but the microscope makes something out of nothing. You couldn't see it before, and now you can. Mr. Zong gradually came to understand that Mr. Nanhai was using this instrument to teach him a lesson, thus fulfilling his duty as a mentor: at a time when the old was shedding its skin to become the new, and everything seemed muddled, it was important to focus on the small things to see the big picture, and spot the path ahead to future glory, when they would be vindicated and lauded.

Given what weighty significance it held, it was no wonder that Zong Bu venerated this instrument and took it with him everywhere he went. Sometime after Kang Youwei left, Zong Bu also went on the run, heading to Hong Kong and then on to France. We can imagine that the microscope was surely in his luggage too. Living in a strange country, he added another layer of meaning to this device. Mr. Huang Jishi goes on to write:

> Mr. Zong said that as he made his escape, he had the microscope with him at all times. Even though it was made in the west, it reminded him of his homeland, and served as a repository for his deeply patriotic feelings.

Interestingly, Zong Bu and Hu An happened to take the same ship to France. They didn't know each other when they boarded in Hong Kong, but an incident along the way brought them together. In *Beauty in a Time of Chaos*, Anthony Thwaite quotes a letter from Zong Bu to Huang Jishi that mentions how he became acquainted with Hu An. I wasn't able to see the original document, but here is the passage quoted by Thwaite:

As the steamer entered the South China Sea, a typhoon rose up, almost overturning the boat. Several people announced that if we went over, they would shoot themselves rather than be eaten by sharks. After the storm, one person was dead: an old man. It wasn't suicide; he'd been shaken to death by the waves. According to the custom of the sea, the dead are tossed overboard and become fish food. While attending this fellow passenger's funeral, I stood next to a young man from China. His name was Hu, and he was from Hangzhou. He told me he had watched as this man's face turned pale, and he started convulsing before he died. My heart contracted as the body spun through the air toward the ocean, and I thought about how I will die one day too. Hu said when he died, he'd be happy to become one with the waves like this. Hu had a lively curiosity about everything. He liked the desolation of Singapore, and admired the elephants, cobras, and fakirs of Ceylon [N.B. now Sri Lanka]. He even liked the monkey a Sinhalese woman kept as a pet. When it came to my microscope, he was so fascinated he couldn't keep his hands off it. In India, a female snake charmer caught my eye. He said he would buy this woman and her snake for me in exchange for my microscope. I turned down his offer, not wanting to end up with a little Zong Bu a year from now, charming snakes in some Indian coconut grove.

This letter seems to make clear one important fact: when Zong Bu produced the microscope in 1915, it was probably in order to rekindle his friendship with Hu An, rather than—as Ah Qing says—to seduce Bingying. Ah Qing was right about one thing, though: a few days later, Zong Bu did return to Hangzhou. The purpose of this trip was to reminisce with Hu An, but also to retrieve his beloved microscope. Ah Qing claims that Bingying smashed it, but according to Bingying, it was Ah Qing who did the damage. In *Beauty*, Thwaite records Bingying's memory of this episode:

When he [Zong Bu] returned to Hangzhou, the microscope he had lent me had been broken into pieces. One morning, Ah Qing and I were looking at ants when the mailman arrived with a letter from Ge Ren. I was in the back garden reading it when I heard Ah Qing sobbing. I ran over to see that he had followed the ants up a tree with the instrument, and fallen to the ground. When he [Zong Bu] came back to Hangzhou, I was terrified and hid from him, but then he wanted to go around the city with me. He could speak some French, which reminded me of my childhood, and I started to feel like I had met someone familiar in a strange place. No, he was very gentlemanly, and he never tried to get fresh with me. When he asked about the microscope, I lied that I couldn't remember where I'd left it. I didn't rat on Ah Qing, because he was already as frantic as an abandoned dog. I told him [Zong Bu] not to worry, it would surely show up someday, like a lost set of keys. He said my father must have hidden it somewhere for his own enjoyment, and when my father had had enough, he would be back to claim it. Sure enough, he was back some days later. My father offered to buy him a new microscope, but he seemed unhappy with that. He said the best microscope in the world couldn't compare with the broken one. So you see, what could I do?

I next saw him just before the Manchu restoration, when he stayed at our house. When the restoration failed, he was forced to live on the run. To avoid detection, whenever we went out together, I would pretend to be his daughter. It seemed like fun at the time, but then everything changed . . .

Zong Bu next came to Hangzhou with a duty to discharge: Kang Youwei had ordered him to make contact with the local troops in order to provide support to General Zhang Xun, restore Pu Yi to the throne, and institute a constitutional monarchy. During his time in Hangzhou, he was not only preoccupied with great affairs of state, but he also fell in love with Bingying, who was playing the part of his daughter. He wrote her quite a few love letters, in which he called her "Mengke." That word "ke" could mean a jade-like precious stone or a bridle ornament. If we take the second definition, then "ke" could also stand for the horse itself. Some believe that Zong Bu was therefore saying that Bingying was his comrade. But Anthony Thwaite points out that Mengke sounds like "mon coeur."

In July 1917, the Zhang Xun farce came to an end, and Zong Bu was now on the local militia's hit list. He and Bingying fled to Shanghai, where they went into hiding in his friend Huang Jishi's home. In *Half a Lifetime*, Huang recounts these events:

After the Braided Commander [Zhang Xun's nickname] was defeated, he took refuge in the Dutch embassy, while Mr. Nanhai [i.e., Kang Youwei] did the same in the American embassy, where he spent his time reading the Confucian classic *The Spring and Autumn Annals*. Mr. Zong Bu returned to Shanghai . . . and returned with a young woman, Hu An's daughter. She was enchanting—so beautiful she might have stepped out of a calendar picture, and when she spoke, she would tilt her head to one side, pretending to be cross. Without a doubt, they were living together. At the time, Shanghai tycoons took pride in having young maidens serve them—they saw them as delicacies among the food, like tender tea leaves or suckling pigs. As with the demons in *Journey to the West*, they believed the only human beings fit to be devoured were virgins. However, Mr. Zong was of a different breed, and Miss Hu took him at his word. Whenever she pouted, he acted as if the worst had happened, and he would do anything to win back her favor—it was hard to believe. In my humble opinion, he wasn't in love with her, but with the pain and youth he'd lost. She was a bronze mirror in which he could see his suffering and age.

Bingying's recollection differs from Huang Jishi's in several respects. According to her, Huang lived on the second floor of a building with a large hallway and a narrow staircase with a damaged railing. People often showed up there to talk about all sorts of things, particularly those who'd studied in the west. They praised the Emperor and cursed the government and the Braided Soldiers, or vice versa. They bragged, they flattered, they recited poetry, they sighed, they wept, they laughed, they vowed, and they swore. Arranged around the room were cigarettes, opium, champagne, white wine, mahjong tiles, and poker cards. Some people even showed up with their own gambling equipment and set up a Russian-style roulette game. At these times, Bingying would be holed up in her room at the top of the stairs, staring at the round mirror on her dressing table—not a bronze one, as Huang Jishi mentioned, but a looking glass—silently weeping:

Bingying said this looking glass had a crack in it. She had broken it herself. She said, "I often rest my face on the back of my hand, and don't dare to look at myself. I feel like a fallen woman. There have been many books written about bad women like me. When he [Zong Bu] comes in, I lose my temper for no reason. I drift in and out of sleep all day long, like a water lily floating in a filthy pond. I see Ge Ren in my dreams all the time. When I wake up, I wonder, was it me dreaming of Ge Ren, or him of me? Could Ge Ren, at this moment, be dreaming of me sharing a bed with a man older than my father? When I have these thoughts, I see my shame reflected in the mirror. The crack cuts my face in half, and so my shame is doubled."

These words of Bingying's inadvertently reveal how a young woman can grow infatuated with desire and her complicated inner life. She said, "What frightens me most is that at times I forget this shame. One day, Zong Bu took me to his friend's house for a dance. There were many other girls there. When I saw how shy and awkward they were in front of men, I actually thought, you see how these girls don't understand anything, not allure, not men, they're still just little kids. I was terrified that I could have such a thought, but when we got back home, I tasted such wicked pleasure on his lips."

Lying on that bed made of teak, the closer her heart got to Ge Ren, the farther her body was from him . . .

This life didn't last very long. One morning, Zong Bu woke up to find that Bingying had left him. There was a note on "that bed made of teak": from Bingying, telling him not to search for her. She went back not to Hangzhou, but to Tianjin. As I said before, at that time my great-aunt and Reverend Beal were setting up an orphanage there. Out of maidenly modesty, she didn't say a word to my great-aunt about what had happened between her and Zong Bu. After some time, my great-aunt took her back to Hangzhou, and not long after that, her father sent her to Paris, where her mother still was. Bingying was pregnant then, and the baby inside her was my mother, Broad Bean.

After Bingying's departure, it was as if Zong Bu had had his soul ripped out. I like this description, "his soul ripped out," because that shows the depth of his love for her. To be frank, I'm happy to accept that there was love between Zong Bu and Bingying. This is very important to me. As I said before, I'm a direct descendant of Zong Bu and Bingying. I tried very hard to find something in writing that spoke to their emotional life, something in exquisite prose. It seemed this was the only way my mother's and my existence in the world could feel rational. When I saw this letter from Zong Bu in *Beauty in a Time of Chaos*, it felt like I had stumbled upon something precious:

> Mengke, I found out from your father that you're in France. I spend every moment waiting for you, as a mule in the desert longs for water. Like an untutored boy, I worshipfully kiss your powder compact, because your fragrance lingers on it. I kiss the mirror you broke, because there's nothing more perfect than broken pieces reunited. I envy your shoes, for they see you every day.
>
> Write to me, Mengke. Even a line will suffice. Point out my wrongdoings. Don't forget me so soon, or at least pretend to remember me. Lie to me—even untruths would be better than silence. I love you with my whole being, and I will till I am nothing but bones.

She received this message in France. Whether she was moved by it or not, I have no way of knowing. She told Thwaite that of the letters she received around this time, one was from my great-aunt, telling her that Ge Ren had returned to China from Japan. She also mentioned that Ge Ren had mailed back a microscope from Japan, because Ah Qing had written to ask him for one.

Good Broad Bean, Be Good, Broad Bean

Can I say that? Fine, then I'll continue. At the time, I almost wrote to Ge Ren to tell him about Zong Bu seducing Bingying. But then I thought, no, I shouldn't do that. As Vice Premier Lin said, endure the small things or they'll ruin the big ones. Ge Ren was busy studying how to bring about revolution; I didn't want to distract him with these details. I thought if I told him, he might get angry and say I only cared about unimportant things, not the big picture.

Ah, so you see, I miss those days—such extraordinary times. I've totally forgotten plenty of things, but when it comes to Ge Ren, I remember all of it, clear as day. Why? Because I know that there's some life in these old bones of mine. Sooner or later, the Party will send someone to ask me about the heroic deeds of Ge Ren. Didn't I know, when I heard the magpies cawing in the branches, that someone was on their way? Give me another one [cigarette].

What should I talk about next? Same as before: point me where you like, and I'll head in that direction. In the blink of an eye, so many years passed, and I didn't see him once. After coming back from Japan, he went to Beijing. When I heard that he was there, I really wanted to go see him, and visit Tiananmen Gate while I was there, to see the spot where the red sun rose. Then I'd go see the People's Heroes memorial tablets and remember the martyrs of revolution. What? No memorial tablets? How could that be? Well, anyway, I wanted to go see him in Beijing. But then a short while later, I heard he'd gone to the Soviet Union. No, at the time we didn't yet call it the "Soviet Empire." Another blink of the eye, another few years gone, and I still hadn't managed to see him. Then I heard he was back from the Soviet Union and was teaching at Shanghai University—in fact, he'd become a professor. I jumped up and hurried straight there.

You can't say that, comrades. Teaching at a university doesn't make you a fucking intellectual. Chairman Mao himself lectured at Shanghai University, and so did Guo Moruo and Li Dazhao. Ge Ren and Li Dazhao used to visit each other all the time. Really, I'm not bluffing. Where was the school? Let me think. It was on Lingyun Road, I believe. Lingyun, like the revolutionary martyr who charged up the Jinggang Mountains. [N.B. Ah Qing remembered wrongly: it was actually on Qingyun Road, in Shanghai's Zhabei District.] Be a prof, the pounds drop off. He had lost a lot of weight, but he was still full of energy, still possessed of a strong fighting spirit. It was Russian literature he was teaching. He's the one who taught me that Tolstoy was the mirror of the Russian Revolution. Ha, don't be so quick to deny it; those weren't his own words, but— a quote from Lenin. If Lenin said Tolstoy's a mirror, then he's a mirror.

When I got to Shanghai, Ge Ren took me out for a meal, a proper meal. I was so full I started to belch. We took what we couldn't finish with us, so I had a bag of steamed buns to take back to the school. On the way back, a vagrant tried to steal the buns. I lashed out with my foot and kicked him till he was leaking piss. I walked a bit farther, and then another one came along, swaying from side to side, so hungry he couldn't walk straight. I gave him all the buns. Comrade Ge Ren noticed, and seemed pleased. He asked me if I had any plans. Plans? Just to continue studying with you. He thought about it and said, Ah Qing, you're a good person, and you're brave. You ought to be a doctor. Let me introduce you to the medical school, and then you'll have your place in society. As far as I was concerned, every word he said was holy scripture. Without another word, I agreed and said I'd start school the next day. And just like that, Ge Ren put up the money, and I started auditing classes at Shanghai Medical University. Not to blow my own horn, if I had finished the course, I'd have been a first-rate doctor. But I decided to stop because the fees were too expensive, and I didn't want to add to Ge Ren's burden.

One day, I went to look for him at Shanghai University after school. I found him with a textbook under his arm, on his way somewhere. He said he'd take me to meet someone. We took a rickshaw to Moulmein Road [N.B. now Maoming Road North], went into a small courtyard, and knocked on a door. Someone stepped out—guess who? A woman. Bingying, with a doll-like little girl standing behind her, a mini-Bingying. She babbled away, but I didn't understand a word. It turned out she was speaking some foreign language.

What's that? Whose daughter was it? Bingying's, of course. Oh, since you comrades seem to know all about it, I'll let the cat out of the bag. Yes, this was Bingying and Zong Bu's child. The problem was, this girl was born knowing the difference between friends and enemies, and she knew exactly what it was to be at odds with someone. She didn't have any time for that Zong Bu business, but treated Ge Ren as if he were her real dad. Which is why it didn't matter that he wasn't. Comrades, you've seen *The Legend of the Red Lantern*—you know Li Tiemei isn't Li Yuhe's child; nor is Li Yuhe actually Granny Li's daughter, but they're all even closer than family. It's not a question of blood relations. What's that? Like spawns like? Is that what Chairman Mao taught us? Oh, I said that? Well, then pay it no more attention than a fart.

All right, I'll keep going. Anything Li Yuhe could do, so could Ge Ren. He even chose her name, Broad Bean. He loved her so much, he was constantly worried that she'd fly from his arms, that she'd dissolve at his touch. When Broad Bean first returned, her little face was yellow as a pear. Ge Ren took action, and cooked her all sorts of tasty food. She was very close to him, and no matter where she went, she wanted Ge Ren to accompany her. Even when she went to see her grandpa in Hangzhou,

Ge Ren had to go along. He wrote her a nursery rhyme: "Broad Bean blossom, Broad Bean blossom, you give me goosebumps on my heart. All night long you howl and wail, then morning smiles your lips do part." What? I sang that wrong? You tell me, then, what's the right way? Fine, if all you comrades say I'm wrong, I will think about it some more. Oh right, I've got it, here's what it was: "Good Broad Bean, be good, Broad Bean, at eight or nine the sun comes up. Ocean liners need good sailors, one day you'll give them the thumbs up." When he sang that, Broad Bean would quiet down. After that, he could read in peace while Bingying got on with her needlework, darning the sole of a cloth shoe.

Yes, darning. I'm not bluffing. I'd forgotten about that, but a couple of days ago, I was trying to think of past sorrows to make the present sweeter, and I thought of that. The Captain told everyone to swallow their hardship, and someone said they'd just eaten some, so could we wait a few days to eat more? So he ordered us all to work on our thinking. First he said, Do you know what Chairman Mao normally eats? Do you have any idea? No one said a word. So he pointed at some guy called Zhang Yongsheng: Zhang, you study the Little Red Book more than anyone else; you have a go. Zhang's a coward, the sort who worries he might hurt himself farting. He blushed, but kept his mouth shut, as if he had a bridle in his mouth. When the Captain insisted, he said, Sir, didn't you tell us last time that Chairman Mao has two tins by his bed, one full of rock sugar, one with sesame candy? So he'd eat rock sugar or sesame candy, depending on what he felt like. The Captain said, That's right, I did say that, but the Chairman also led the way in thinking of past sorrows to make the present sweeter, and he eats plain steamed cornbread for that reason. Then he asked, Do you know how Comrade Jiang Qing normally spends her time? This time, I was the one in the crosshairs. So I said, That goes without saying—she's surely studying Mao's *Three Essays*. He asked, What does she do when she's finished the *Three Essays?* I said I didn't know. It wasn't just me; no one else knew, either. The Captain said, Fuck it, don't you even know this? When Comrade Jiang Qing finishes studying the *Three Essays*, she sits by the Chairman's side, darning his shoes. But when it comes time to think of past sorrows to make the present sweeter, she stops darning, and weaves grass slippers instead. Yes, when I heard the Captain say this, I immediately thought about Bingying doing the same thing. As Ge Ren read, she would sit by his side, darning shoes and weaving grass slippers. As for Ge Ren, he didn't just read books, he also wrote them. He'd already written a thick stack of pages, under the title *The Walking Shadow*. What does that mean? Can't you tell? Wherever you go, your shadow goes with you, and if you stand straight, then it won't bend. I was always asking him, Hey, is your *Shadow* done yet? And he'd say, There's still a long way to go. He'd write and write, then edit and edit. You could urge him to sleep, but he would refuse. He'd say, You go to sleep, don't worry about me. Not even Bingying could budge him. Sometimes Bingying would send Broad Bean in, so he would have to stop and sing her a nursery rhyme. Which one? Didn't I just sing it a minute ago? Oh, you weren't taking notes? Is it because I sang so well that you sat there listening and forgot to write anything down? All right, seeing as you comrades enjoyed it, I'll do it again. "Good Broad Bean, be good, Broad Bean, sleep until the sun comes up. The sun rises red and strong, and you'll give revolution the thumbs up." As soon as Broad Bean dozed off, he'd start writing again.

Eventually he wasn't able to write any longer. Why? Because there was important work awaiting him. He answered the call of the Party, and went to Bare Mountain. At the time, Bare Mountain was a Soviet zone. Yes, he went there twice; this was the first time. Wherever he went, I would follow. Yes, I was his shadow. If he went to the Soviet zone, then of course so did I. So you see, comrades, I went with him step by step, down the road of revolution. Later on, to serve the cause, I had to embark on my performance, and had no choice but to part ways with him. Still, the fish can't leave the water, the melon can't leave the vine, and no matter where I went, my heart remained joined with his at all times.

The Walking Shadow

As I mentioned in the first section, Bingying returned to Beijing from France after the May Fourth Movement. Ge Ren was still in prison, so they didn't meet. She went back to France, and when she hadn't heard from Ge Ren after a long time, she followed her mother to England. They settled in a picturesque village called Sawston, six miles from Cambridge. In order to write *Beauty in a Time of Chaos*, Anthony Thwaite made the trip to Sawston. According to him, the village had only one general store. To this day, the shop owner's daughter still remembers the "statuesque and striking" Chinese woman who frequently came to buy cigarettes with her little girl in tow. "She had a loosely woven shawl over her shoulders, and her face was full of sorrow." Bingying's own recollection more or less matches this:

> Bingying said that one time when she went to the general store to buy cigarettes, she saw a letter there. It was from Lin Huiyin—who later designed the National Emblem—to Xu Zhimo, and it had been sitting

there quite a while. That's how she found out that Xu Zhimo had spent time in Sawston too, and that all the mail went through the general store. She immediately sent a message to a friend in Paris, asking for all her letters to be forwarded there. Late that fall, she received the Paris mail. All of it had come from China. A woman who worked for a church [N.B. my great-aunt] had somehow found her address, and was writing to tell her that Ge Ren was back from Russia, and had been helping Reverend Beal with the orphanage in Tianjin until Yu Youren [N.B. then the president of Shanghai University] and Deng Zhongxia [then the provost] invited him to teach at their institution. She also said that he was very much alone, and still loved Bingying, as much as a deer longs for spring water.

Memory rattles the gate, and once the gate is open, the past floods into your heart. Remembrance fills the mouth with pain, and so she could not prevent her worries about Ge Ren from spilling out nonstop to her mother. She wanted to return to China immediately and be reunited with him. Every inch of her heart was filled with this passion. She said farewell to her mother and went with her daughter to Southampton Harbor. Later she wrote in her diary, "In the late autumn, England darkens early. The sky was black by the time we boarded the boat. Before us were the rough waves of the English Channel. My heart was shooting ahead like an arrow, making the steamer feel like it was standing still. Then everything went quiet, and in the distance, across the water, I could see the lights of the Isle of Wight."

After the long journey, when they finally approached Shanghai, a gale was blowing so hard they were unable to land. She languished another two days at sea. To be just across a short stretch of water and yet so far away, it felt to her as though each day lasted at least a year. A long time ago, she had said goodbye to Ge Ren at this spot. Seeing her daughter's girlish face, thinking back through all the years since their parting, tears rolled down her cheeks.

This was in the fall of 1923. At the time, Ge Ren was teaching Russian at Shanghai University, in the same department as Qu Qiubai. They lived in the same residential hall on Moulmein Road [N.B. now Maoming Road North]—in fact, Ge Ren was next door to Professor Qu and his wife, Wang Jianhong. Ding Ling, who would later become a famous writer, was a student at the university, and also lived on Moulmein Road. Ah Qing stayed with Ge Ren and Bingying after coming to Shanghai. Ge Ren would hold this post till 1927, at which time he gave up teaching in order to focus on translation. Apart from the stories of Pushkin, Chekhov, and Tolstoy, he also translated Shakespeare's *Macbeth* from the

Russian text. For many years now, he'd been wanting to devote himself to literature. Now he suddenly conceived the idea of writing a novel about his family's and his own history, to be titled *The Walking Shadow*, a quote from *Macbeth*, Act Five, Scene Five:

> Life's but a walking shadow, a poor player
> That struts and frets his hour upon the stage
> And then is heard no more: it is a tale
> Told by an idiot, full of sound and fury,
> Signifying nothing.

During this time, Reverend Beal came to Shanghai to see Ge Ren and Bingying. He recorded Ge Ren's thoughts about this work in *The Majesty of the Orient*, and even claimed to have seen a portion of the manuscript:

> His father's story was written on a stack of yellowing papers. In his eyes, Ge Ch'un-Tao was an inadequate actor, having appeared briefly on stage before quietly vanishing, like a shadow. After he had finished writing about his father, he commenced working on himself, and then his daughter, Broad Bean. He wished to spend the rest of his life on this manuscript. Inclining my ear to the parable, I opened my dark saying upon the harp, and told him this title was very appropriate, for does it not say in the Psalms that "surely every man walketh in a vain show"?

We now have evidence to show that Ge Ren died without completing this book. In 1932, the Japanese bombed Shanghai's Zhabei District. After the war, Ge Ren went to the Soviet zone on Bare Mountain, and later he took part in the Long March. Bingying said that Ge Ren made sure to take his manuscript to Bare Mountain. "He brought the book he was working on, and also me and Broad Bean. He said we could start a new life there, a life of freedom."

Yang Fengliang

When I put it like that, you comrades must understand where I'm coming from. Put yourself in my shoes, and you'll see why I was so happy when, many years later, I heard that Fan Jihuai wanted me to see Ge Ren at Bare Mountain. Fuck it, my heart was thumping so fast I thought it would leap out of my throat. Yes, as I said before, Fan told me that my main task there would be to find out for sure whether this person was or wasn't Ge Ren. If he wasn't, I should let him go. If he was, I should find out what he wanted. When he told me this, I thought the best thing would be to get to see Ge Ren one more time. When he added that I should be careful, and not harm one hair on his head, I couldn't stop laughing inside. Idiot, what a fucking idiot! You don't need to tell me that; of course I wasn't going to harm one hair on his head.

I was ready to leave right away, but Fan Jihuai caught hold of me and said, I sent an advance scout to Bare Mountain, a man named Yang Fengliang. He wanted me to make contact with Yang as soon as I got there. Fuck it, Yang Fengliang was going too? That changed everything. I thought it would be best if this person wasn't Ge Ren, because if it was, now I wouldn't be able to let him get away. If I did that, there'd be no way I could stay on in Military Intelligence, and that would destroy our underground network. I said to Fan Jihuai, General, could you send someone else, please? He asked why. I made up some nonsense: I had clashed with Yang Fengliang before, and didn't think I could work with him. There must have been something wrong with Fan Jihuai, because he immediately got all excited and said, What kind of clash? Come on, let's hear it. I wrinkled my forehead, and quickly thought up some nonsense: Yang was the sort who keeps looking in the pot even though he still has food on his plate. I had finally managed to get a woman, but after just a few days, he stole her away, leaving me with nothing. Ha, that's all I said, and he fell for it. Not only did he buy my story, he started comforting me. He said, Having nothing might seem bad, but actually it's a good thing. Poverty changes your thinking, and makes you work for revolution. A blank sheet of paper, with nothing burdening it, is where you write the most beautiful words, where you draw the most beautiful pictures. I swear to Chairman Mao, he really did say that—I'm not bluffing. He also said there are plenty of women; in fact, Yang Fengliang had a new one at Bare Mountain, the sort of beauty who makes birds fall from the sky, who shames the moon and flowers into hiding from her. Turnabout is fair play, he said, and I should go all out to compete with him, and if I worked hard enough, I'd steal her away for myself.

Is it all right if I say that? Fine, then I'll continue.

So I said, Oh, no, I wouldn't dare. And he said, Fuck it, aren't you normally the fearless sort? Why are you losing your nerve at the crucial moment? I said, General, I'm not losing my nerve—I just don't have his advantages. He's flashier than I am; he was born to please women. I can't compete with him. Fan Jihuai encouraged me, saying humility would help you get ahead, while arrogance would make you fall behind, so he was happy to hear me talking like that. Then he said, If you have advantages, you should go ahead, and if you don't have advantages, then you should find some advantages and go ahead anyway. When he said that, I found myself thinking that the dogfucker Yang Fengliang was such a bastard, if I really could steal that woman away from him, I'd be saving her from a bad situation.

You comrades mustn't think I said Yang Fengliang was a bad guy just because I was jealous of him. He was always a rotten egg. He was the one who told Fan Jihuai that Ge Ren was still alive on Bare Mountain. Yang's father had just died, and he was on his way back to Changting in Fujian for the funeral. He was passing by Bare Mountain when he remembered his old lover, so he got off the train and headed to Baibei Town. His old lover ran a tea house, and had given birth to a little revolutionary of his. He stayed there for three days. On the fourth morning, his lover and their son saw him off at the train station. That was the Shang Village stop, very close to Baibei—you could get there on horseback in the time it took to eat a bowl of noodles. It was on the way to Shang Village that his son saw Ge Ren, who was just coming from there. The little dogfucker ran over and bowed to Ge Ren. Yang Fengliang didn't recognize Ge Ren at first, though he found him a bit familiar. After Ge Ren had left, Yang turned to his lover and said, Hey, who was that guy our little bastard treated so respectfully? And that stinking bitch said, That's Mr. Mel, Melancholy. He's a hedge teacher. Yes, Melancholy was the name Ge Ren was going by. And that would have been that, except for another coincidence: that same day, someone blew up the tracks a few dozen miles north of Shang Village. Repairs would take a few days, so Yang Fengliang had no choice but to return to Baibei. That gave him time to figure out that Melancholy was Ge Ren. He was delighted, because he remembered that Chiang Kai-shek had put a price of ten thousand on Ge Ren's head. He didn't immediately shoot Ge Ren dead because of another consideration: if someone's head was worth that much, you couldn't simply chop it off, because surely the Party and Nation must be looking for this person. He thought if he went ahead on his own, not only would he miss out on the reward, he'd probably end up losing his own little life. Instead, he rushed to report this news to Chongqing, then prepared to settle in there for a while. I just want to point out here that this dogfucker Yang Fengliang spent his whole life being clever, but this was his one moment of carelessness. He didn't realize that the moment he recognized Ge Ren, he put his own neck under the blade.

When I got to Bare Mountain, I showed my face to Yang Fengliang. Then, without even stopping to eat, I went straight to see Ge Ren. It was noon, and Yang went along with me. Take a guess, where do you think that dogfucker Yang was keeping our Ge Ren? Fuck that cunt for even thinking of this—Ge Ren was locked up in Fangkou Elementary School.

Why else would he do that, except to rub salt into the wound? Why do I say that? Because the school was built with money from his father-in-law, Hu An, back in 1934. I was involved in the construction: moving stones, hefting wooden pillars, laying the foundation, building the courtyard wall. So whenever I see kids trotting along with their schoolbags on their way to assembly, I remember raising that assembly hall. It was next to White Cloud River, and there was also a small lake not far from the school. The river had a sluice gate, so Ge Ren called the school Fangkou Elementary—"fangkou" as in "sluice gate." On this trip back, he had done some maintenance on the building. His original plan had been to stay there and train up the next generation of revolutionaries, but that dogfucker Yang Fengliang turned it into his prison cell instead.

On the way to the assembly hall, I said, Yang Fengliang, the higher-ups sent me because I'm Ge Ren's old friend. I can talk freely to him, so I'll be able to persuade him to surrender, and that way he'll be able to start working again for the Party and Nation. Yang Fengliang nodded like the suck-up he was and said, Yes, yes. He added that this was exactly his thinking, and that's why he had taken such good care of Ge Ren and didn't want him to look bad. I said, That's good, he'll tell the higher-ups that you managed affairs here well. When I said that, he put a cigarette to my lips and lit it for me. No, I wasn't asking you for another smoke. I said Yang Fengliang lit my cigarette. Well, fine, then, I will have another. Is it all right if I say that? Fine, then I'll continue.

When we got to the school gate, a few soldiers in civvies were standing outside. They had no idea who I was, but seeing how Yang was wagging his tail and rolling over in front of me, they knew I must be some big shot, so they hastily bowed. I waved my hand and said, Thank you for your service, comrades. They quickly chorused, Thank you for yours, Commander. I told them, You've all discharged your sacred mission with great honor, and the Party is sure to reward you in the future. Now you can relax and accompany General Yang back to his hometown, and may I be the first to congratulate you for the promotions and riches coming your way. When that bunch of dogfuckers heard this, their butts waggled with glee. They bowed and clapped, practically kowtowing to me. I even blew some smoke up Yang's ass so he would get swept away too. I said, A strong general has no weak soldiers. One look at your men, General Yang, and I can tell you run a tight ship. His face blossomed into a flower of a smile. What kind of flower? A dogtail. To strike while the iron was hot, I announced there'd be a banquet that evening to send them on their way. At that moment, the lofty ideology of Communism blazed in my chest like a bonfire. I thought, no need to worry about anything else—I had to get rid of these dogfuckers as soon as possible, so "The Internationale" could come true sooner. It was only by remembering Vice Premier Lin's lesson—endure the small things or they'll ruin the big ones—that I was able to stop myself from striking right there and then. I thought, right now, the most important thing is to play this part well, and to the fullest.

I was about to see Ge Ren. I felt worked up; my heart wouldn't stop thumping. I didn't go in right away, in case Yang Fengliang might get suspicious. Instead I pretended to carry out an inspection, walking around the perimeter wall with my hands clasped behind my back. When I got back to the gate, I said, Even the wisest man, General Yang, will slip up on occasion. He started quivering. I said, You have to look at a problem in two ways—what went right and what could be better. He started begging me to explain. First, as if shooing away flies, I sent the other little dogfuckers off to one side. Then I said to Yang Fengliang, It's like this—you shouldn't have sent the kids home. You should have let them keep coming to class. That's how you fool everyone. Fuck it, look what you've done. Outsiders are going to guess what we're up to in this assembly hall, and that won't help at all. He started shaking all over again. I smiled and soothed him: Don't worry, I won't say a word to the higher-ups. He nodded and bowed and said he'd considered this point. The students weren't playing hooky— he had hired another teacher, and they were with him right now, having their lessons at the town temple. He added that he had put the word out that Mr. Melancholy was unwell and wouldn't be able to teach for a while. I said, All right, mending the sheep pen after the sheep are dead, maybe a little too late—hopefully this won't cause any problems.

Yang Fengliang wanted to come inside with me, but I put my hand up and told him to stay outside. Why do you comrades think I didn't want him with me? No idea? I had already thought of this when I set out from Chongqing: at our first encounter, if Ge Ren pretended not to recognize me, then it would be easy—I'd simply turn around and say, What the fuck are you doing, General Yang? You've arrested the wrong person; this isn't Ge Ren at all. No two leaves in the world are alike, and though I can see the resemblance, this is definitely the wrong guy. He might try to argue back, so I had my strategy for that planned too. I would say, Shut up. When it comes to Ge Ren, you could peel his skin off and I'd still recognize him. But in order for this duet to play out flawlessly, I would need to speak to Ge Ren in private first. So I told Yang Fengliang, General Yang, you take a break out here, don't worry about me. It's just a feeble scholar in there, not enough strength in his hands to tie up a chicken. I won't be in any danger. Well, how about it? Was that smart, or what? He bought it, anyway. Clicked his heels together, gave me a salute, and said, Take care, Commander. I said, Thank you, I can look after myself. You keep striving hard for the Revolution. I lit a cigarette and went inside.

Ge Ren was locked up in the innermost room, a fairly large one, maybe ten feet square. He was asleep when I went in. The room was so damp, there were mushrooms sprouting from the baseboards. A shutter door had been taken off its hinges, and he was lying on it. I swear to Chairman Mao, I didn't dare disturb him. Even in his dreams, he might be contemplating how to nurture the next generation of revolutionaries. I stood next to him for a while, my heart at full tide. I told myself, see, Ge Ren has exhausted himself for the sake of the Revolution. Comrade Ge Ren had already been skinny, but he'd lost even more weight now. Human bodies are the capital of revolution. Seeing him lying there like a paper doll almost brought me to tears. [N.B. The transcriber noted here that "Zhao started sobbing, as if his mother had died."] I went back outside, and Yang Fengliang rushed over to ask what I thought. I could only reply, What are you worried about? Melancholy's asleep in there, he didn't say a word. He was about to walk away, but I grabbed hold of him and said, You've worked hard too. Stay a while, let me raise a glass to you.

No, comrades, I swear on Chairman Mao, I didn't mean anything by that. I really wasn't asking for a drink of anything. I'm not bluffing. Well, all right, if you're all having one, I'll keep you company.

About Yang Fengliang

Yang Fengliang, the man Ah Qing mentioned, was actually Ge Ren's old friend. Mr. Fan Jihuai has already explained how he came to be on Bare Mountain. At this point, we should lend an ear to one of the parties involved, in order to understand Mr. Yang Fengliang a little better. That person is the currently distinguished phenomenologist Mr. Bodde Sun, well-known throughout the world of western philosophy. His birth name was Sun Guozhang, and he was part of Yang Fengliang's entourage in the early days. In the winter of 2000, he accepted an invitation from Mr. Wang Jiling, the chancellor of Straits Private University in Fujian—also a former member of Yang Fengliang's entourage—and returned to China to give a lecture. When I heard this news, I went to Fujian to meet Mr. Sun. This is a recording of the resulting interview:

Mr. Yang [Fengliang] and I came from the same county, Changting in Fujian. Changting's a great place. Our river frogs, bamboo hats, leather cushions, and tea leaves are famous all over the world. And because we were both from there, Mr. Yang trusted me completely. Even so, before we came to Bare Mountain, I had no idea what his true motives were. I thought he'd just taken the opportunity to meet up with his Baibei lover while on his way to this family funeral. On the way, he laughed at himself, using the English phrase "sweet bitterness" to describe how he felt. Only when we got to Baibei did he reveal that his real plan was to go on the run with his lover. Yes, he had loathed politics for some time now, the constant scheming and plotting, the power struggles. Then he said something I don't know if I should repeat. He said, The two filthiest things in the world you could stick your cock into are politics and a woman's cunt, and yet those are the two things men love. He was better than most men, and he could truly be loving when it came to women, but the inhumanity of politics disgusted him. He had been waiting for a long time for an opportunity to get away from Chongqing. It so happened that at this time, Lieutenant-General Fan Jihuai had a conversation with him about an important report: that Ge Ren had shown up again, on Bare Mountain. Lieutenant-General Fan wanted him to make inquiries, to ascertain whether the person active on Bare Mountain was indeed Ge Ren. Because news of Ge Ren's death had spread so widely, Mr. Yang naturally assumed this must be a false report that didn't deserve any credence. But then he thought, Bare Mountain was, as they say, as high as the sky and as distant as the Emperor. Here at last was his chance to escape the whirlpool of politics, and who knew when another one would come along.

It was a shock to hear him mention Ge Ren. Before that, I had heard the rumors that Mr. Ge had died in battle at Two Li Mound. In the few days we had spent in Baibei, I hadn't heard anything about Ge Ren being there. I said to Mr. Yang, General, we can't drag our feet. We need to report to Chongqing as quickly as possible that this whole business of Ge Ren showing up on Bare Mountain was just a wild goose chase. Mr. Yang ordered me to draft a telegram, while he prepared to set off again. That gorgeous woman of his had lived there for several years now, and she wasn't willing to go anywhere else. It took a great deal of persuasion from us before she agreed to leave. But that was the night of the incident: we had just fallen asleep when there was a dull bang, like a roll of thunder. The next day, we heard that the nearby railroad tracks had been blown up by bandits. A lot of people were dead or injured, and all travel to the north or south was suspended. We would have to stay put. Many years later, when I recall those events, I still believe they were a manifestation of the persistence of truth that Foucault talked about. In the following days, we did indeed see Ge Ren in Baibei. It turned out he was disguised as the Baibei elementary school teacher. He'd been there for some time by then, and when he wasn't teaching, he was spending his time writing. Since China's economic reforms, we have abided by Mr. Deng [Xiaoping]'s spirit of going by the facts. And so I'll go by the facts here too, and tell you that their past affection and Mr. Ge's high moral character had earned him a great deal of respect from Mr. Yang, who never once caused him any harm . . .

I will interject here to say that the "bandits" who blew up the railroad tracks were the previously mentioned gang led by Dabao [Guo Baoquan]. Although we can't speculate about history, Mr. Sun still believes that if not for that act of destruction, "Ge Ren's story might have had a happier ending."

The explosion on the tracks caused some disruption to Mr. Yang's deployment. If that hadn't happened, Ge Ren's story might have had a better ending. At the time, Mr. Yang and I were discussing how best to get a message back to Chongqing. He said he and Ge Ren were very close, so he wanted as kind a strategy as possible. Ah, genealogy, the genealogy of emotion. On this trip back to China, I've told some of the scholars here that Foucault believed we ought to combine dialectics, genealogy, and strategy and analyze them together, because those three elements determine our praxis. As I discussed these ideas from the lectern, I remembered my conversation with Mr. Yang all those years ago, when I repeatedly told him that Fan Jihuai had sent him there to see if the reports regarding Mr. Ge Ren were true or false, which put him in a perfect position to say this person wasn't Ge Ren, after which we could make our own escape.

He hesitated, then said, We shouldn't make any decisions until we've spoken to Mr. Ge. During our conversation, Mr. Yang asked about the Battle of Two Li Mound, and Ge Ren just smiled without answering, indicating there was something to hide. Mr. Yang wanted Ge Ren to leave that place with him, but Ge Ren said, "My sickness is in its final stages now. I won't survive another hard journey." Even as he spoke, Ge Ren's body seemed fine, and he probably would have been able to walk a fair distance. If we'd set off right away and gotten timely treatment in Fujian or somewhere else, Ge Ren might have been all right. But as we waited for the railroad to be fixed, the situation became more complicated. No wall keeps out all the wind. First, someone named Zong Bu showed up. I could tell from the way he talked that he wasn't, as he claimed, a teacher, but had come because of Ge Ren. And the night before I left, Zong Bu showed his true colors. . . . Afterward, the man Fan Jihuai had sent arrived too, a general named Zhao. According to him, he was also an old friend of Ge Ren's.

A few days after General Zhao arrived, I left Baibei Town. The tracks hadn't been fixed yet, so I departed on foot. I already had a bad feeling. As I had said goodbye to Mr. Yang, I'd told him, "I'll go sort out the funeral arrangements on your behalf, but you should leave as soon as possible too. The longer you stay here, the more likely something unforeseen will take place." My words were sadly prophetic, and that was my final goodbye to him. I waited at Changting, but he never came. I began to suspect that some bad fate had befallen him, and even wondered if anyone had tailed me to Changting, determined to shut my mouth. I fled immediately. Near where Shenzhen is today, I got on a small boat and crossed over to Hong Kong. From there I went abroad. I realized I was still a fundamentally useless person, so I decided to devote the rest of my life to philosophy, the most useless subject in the world.

According to Ah Qing, Yang Fengliang sent Fan Jihuai a wire to tell him that Ge Ren was on Bare Mountain. Fan Jihuai corroborates this in the third section of this book. He says the text of the wire read: "Code Zero in Baibei, producing fine words." I gingerly asked if this really happened, and Mr. Sun said, "I have no reason to lie. Mr. Yang couldn't have sent that wire. He has so much respect for Ge Ren, there's categorically no way he would have turned him in to the authorities. Remember, he didn't leave with me, but stayed behind—he must have been planning to find a chance to talk to General Zhao, who had claimed to be Ge Ren's friend, and find a way to get Ge Ren away from Bare Mountain." He went on, "The telegram I drafted was still in my hand—it was never sent." When I told him what Ah Qing and Fan Jihuai had said, he didn't reply, merely snorted disdainfully. I believe readers will be able to make their own judgment at the end of this book. I also want to point out that if Mr. Sun Guozhang's account is accurate, then Mr. Yang Fengliang's later death at the hands of Ah Qing can only be seen as the result of a gigantic misunderstanding.

Secret Telegram

I'm getting tipsy. While we were drinking earlier, I felt as if we'd already achieved full Communism. One time the Captain told us that when full Communism arrived, tasty food and strong drink of our choosing would be there. He also said that when we got there, no matter who you were, the spigot would be pouring out so much oil, even your farts would be greasy. I still dream of that day and night. You're right, the road to Communism isn't a level one. As long as you cling tightly to the Party, we'll move from victory to victory, and finally achieve full Communism.

The Party is in my heart every single moment. The very night after I saw Ge Ren, I sent the Party a secret telegram. At the time, my handler was Comrade Dou Sizhong. You know who that is? No? Then I won't say any more. I don't know much about him either. It was Comrade Tian Han who initially put us in touch. In the secret telegram, I said I had seen Ge Ren, he was locked up on Bare Mountain. Dou sent me back a secret message, saying, Refer to Ge Ren as Code Zero in future. I was taken aback. When I left Chongqing, Fan Jihuai told me he'd designated a cipher for Ge Ren: Code Zero. That was fucking weird, that they'd both picked zero. What did it mean? I thought about it, and then I realized the Party must be hearing this through another channel, and was merely using the same code words. Although later, when I saw Bai Shengtao, he told me Code Zero was the Party's own nickname—the perfect circle symbolizing fullness. Anyway, I asked the Party to send people as quickly as they could to bust Ge Ren out of there. I promised them I'd hang on till the very last minute, awaiting my comrades' arrival. I would be lying if I said I wasn't scared when I made that promise. The situation was clear, and if we messed this up, it wouldn't just mean not rescuing Ge Ren; I would lose my own life too. That's why I suggested to Dou Sizhong that it might be better to send some women over. Right, not women, female comrades. They might catch the enemy off guard. But in the end, fuck it all, it was some men who showed up. Of course, I understand this was the Party being concerned for me, and making sure my cock didn't get me into trouble.

The next day, at the first sign of light, before the magpies started cawing in the branches, I climbed out of bed and went to see Ge Ren. Yang Fengliang wanted to tag along, like the leech he is, but I wouldn't let him. When I went into the room, Ge Ren was sprawled on his makeshift bed, writing. The strange thing was, he didn't seem even slightly surprised to see me. He just smiled and said, It's been hard on you, General Zhao. I almost shed tears at those words. We grabbed each other's hand tightly. His was very hot, like the flames of revolution. He asked me if this was my second visit. I asked how he knew, and he abruptly recited a line of poetry: Most pleasant to dream within a dream, butterflies are entrancing. He said this was from Zheng Banqiao's "Xijiang River Moon: A Warning to Mortals." Then he said, I saw you in a dream. I laughed, and so many words filled my head that I didn't know where to start. He said, I'm not joking, General Zhao. I guessed a few days ago that you were coming to Bare Mountain, and I've been waiting for you a long time. Hearing this, I thought, could Yang Fengliang have told him that I was on my way? So I asked, Did you hear this from Yang Fengliang? I was thinking, fuck it, if Yang really did let this news slip, that would be perfect—I'd be able to hold that over his head, like the Monkey God's staff. I would whack him good for the crime of exposing classified secrets. But Ge Ren said no, Yang Fengliang had never said anything about it to him.

What's that? Did I get a message to Ge Ren? How could I have? There was all that distance between us. I couldn't have reached him even if I'd wanted to. I swear to Chairman Mao, everything I'm saying is true. Ge Ren's revolutionary foresight is strong, and he figured it out himself. If you don't believe me, I have another example. When I was talking to him, he also guessed that Bai Shengtao would be coming to Bare Mountain, and even specified that it would be on Tian Han's orders. At that point, I didn't know who Bai Shengtao was. He said Bai Shengtao was a friend of his. I asked, How do you know he's coming? He said Bai Shengtao wasn't just his friend, but also Tian Han's friend, and they were both doctors, which made him the best person to dispatch. He was right, completely right. A while later, Dr. Bai really did show up.

The whole time we were talking, the room was freezing cold. I went out and told those bastards to start a fire, quick. Back inside, he sat on his shutter bed and looked me up and down, then asked if I wanted a cigarette. He smoked Flying Horse brand, the one with a horse on the packet sprouting wings and galloping in the direction of Communism. I took a puff, but the tobacco had gone moldy, so I gave him one of my cigars instead. He pulled on it and immediately started coughing, until his face had turned red from it. He soon got used to it, though. I noticed there were a couple of holes in the shutter where the fastenings used to be. Why make Ge Ren sleep on something like that? I went out again and ordered those bastards to build him a wooden bed with railings and a canopy.

After that flurry of activity, I managed to calm down enough to talk with Ge Ren. I had so much to say to him, but now that we were actually face to face, I didn't know where to begin. I said, You must have had a hard time here; ask me for anything you want. Unexpectedly, Ge Ren said it hadn't been too bad—he'd been doing well, he was even happy. To be frank, comrades, at the time I didn't understand what he was saying. I paused, then thought of asking if he needed anything I could send someone to fetch. He said he needed paper, that he had some things to write. He then explained to me that he'd been wanting all along to sit down and write, but he never got the chance, so he was going to grab this opportunity, but his body wouldn't let him. I asked if this was *The Walking Shadow*, and he didn't say it was, but he also didn't say it wasn't. I told him, There's plenty of time, you don't need to rush. Bodies are capital in the Revolution, and as long as the mountain stands, it won't be short of fuel to burn. He immediately lectured me: Ah Qing, you can't think like that. Didn't Chairman Mao teach us that ten thousand years is too long, and it's better to seize the day? I'm not bluffing, that's what he said. It wasn't just talk, either; that's how he actually lived. I asked again if he was writing *The Walking Shadow*, like before. He laughed and said, You're asking very specific questions. Are you interrogating me? I hastily said, Not at all, not at all. I was just asking.

This was when I realized he was warning me, in a roundabout way, to respect Party discipline, and not ask any questions I shouldn't. As you know, we have a fine tradition of criticism and self-criticism. When he said that, I quickly self-criticized: I said I was wrong, I shouldn't have asked those questions, I would correct myself. He was overjoyed to see how quickly I'd improved, and that I had grasped my error so quickly. I'm not the one who said I improved quickly, comrades. Comrade Ge Ren did. His praise made me feel a bit self-conscious.

He had just finished complimenting me when the bastards came crashing in with the bed. They'd thought of everything, and also brought in a desk, a chair, and a dressing table. Once again, ten thousand years was too long—it was better to seize the day. Ge Ren immediately sat down, leaned over the desk, and got to work. As for me, I didn't want to disturb him, and I was anxious to get Dou Sizhong's secret telegram, so I went to the tea house. Yes, I had moved to the tea house. Yang Fengliang and the little whore had been staying there, but I had made them give me their room and move into the Bodhi Temple by White Cloud River.

Not long after I got back to the tea house, the secret telegram arrived. It said a guy named Bai Shengtao was coming to Bare Mountain to help me with my work, and also to give me a confidential order. You can imagine, comrades, how much I respected Ge Ren when I read that telegram. I could have prostrated myself before him, and that wouldn't have been too much at all. He really could see ahead, like a god. And again, I hadn't let a single word slip; he had figured it out by himself. Actually, there's nothing strange about this at all: he'd just armed his brain with the wisdom of Chairman Mao. As I was reading the telegram, the telegraph operator said, Sir, how are you going to thank me? And with that, the succubus oozed closer. My immediate thought was that this she-devil might leak the telegram to Yang Fengliang. What then? Strategy is the lifeblood of the Revolution—you need to be thinking tactics at all times. I didn't push her away, and when she draped herself over me, I decided to beat her at her own game. I hugged her, put my hands around her neck, and pressed gently. To start with, it seemed to tickle, and she giggled a little. Fuck it, she was really shameless, slipping her nipple between my lips, almost ripping my mouth apart, still giggling all the while. Laugh, go on, laugh. That's what I thought as I gripped her swan-like neck, and like thunder that comes so swiftly you can't cover your ears, an autumn wind whipping up the leaves, I squeezed. And my dear comrades, with a loud crack, the demoness went off to see the King of Hades. Just like that! In order to avoid being discovered by the enemy, I smashed the telegraph machine and pulled off her trousers. Or I tried to, but her leather belt refused to unfasten. I clawed at it, then told myself, Ah Qing, you won't fix anything by getting worked up. Take your time and calm down. At this crucial moment, it was the Party that gave me courage and wisdom and told me to rip her pants open with my knife, revealing her pearly white thighs, and right at the top of one of them, I gave her a good kick. It was beautifully done: I kicked the crap right out of her. I was sure that when they found her body, they'd think some bad guy had done this. And sure enough, no one ever suspected it was me. Of course, every debt has to be paid eventually, and blood debts are paid with blood. To make things look good for my subordinates, I pretended to spend a long time investigating this death. Later I pinned the telegraph operator's death on Yang Fengliang.

A Riddle Answered
While reading Bai Shengtao's story, I was confused about why Dou Sizhong kept being unable to contact Ah Qing. Now I finally understood: it was because Ah Qing had smashed the telegraph machine and killed its operator.

Hoping for the Stars and Moon

After disposing of the demoness, I went back outside. Standing by White Cloud River, I felt the tide of my heart rise. Inasmuch as Bai Shengtao was coming on Tian Han's orders, and moreover was Ge Ren's friend, everything should be fine once he arrived. Like hoping for the stars and moon, I wished Bai Shengtao would come quickly.

Is it all right if I say that?

Well, that goes without saying. Of course I know Tian Han is [now] the Wuji Local Party Committee secretary. Last summer, the Captain called us for a meeting, and told me to read out a newspaper report. It said the capital's Chairman Mao Artistic Thought Propaganda Performance Troupe had performed in Wuji, and Secretary Tian had presented them with a banner, and even posed for a picture with them. I was so moved when I said Secretary Tian's name, I burst into tears. The Captain kicked me and said, Fuck your crying, keep reading. So I went on: Accompanied by Secretary Tian, Comrade Little Red from the propaganda troupe, who also played the women's commander in *Chaoyang Hill*, came to the rural neighborhood to sing selections from *Chaoyang Hill* to our farmland comrades. Now the Captain said, Stop, motherfucker. I said stop. So I stopped. He said, Prick up your ears and listen, all of you, and I'll sing you a piece from *Chaoyang Hill*.

Do you know Chaoyang Hill, comrades? That's right, it's next to Two Li Mound. It's not as famous as Dazhai, but it may be as famous as Xiaojin Village. It said in the newspaper that Little Red often plunged into life on Chaoyang Hill. I didn't understand what that meant. Life is life—how do you plunge into it? Later on, I heard that Little Red would often eat and sleep with the old villagers of Chaoyang Hill, and I finally understood that plunging into life meant eating and sleeping first and singing opera later. No, the Captain didn't say that. He doesn't know shit. Of course he didn't know that, but he did know how to sing. Yes, that's the passage he sang. I know it too. Do you want to hear it? What's the hurry? I'll sing it, and then we can carry on. I've gotten so used to singing it, if a day goes by when I don't, my throat starts to tickle, and if two days go by, I get anxious.

> Chaoyang Hill, Chaoyang Hill has never been calm
> Restless in peacetime, listen for the faint sound of guns
> After land reform, the bastard landlords tried to retaliate
> All day long, they gnashed their teeth and wanted power back
> Today the Cultural Revolution raises its voice in song
> Those who long for imperialism are driven wild, like mad dogs
> The world is full of fog, the country's hearts are the same red
> Educated Youth, put down roots and bring about revolution
> Do not let class enemies destroy this great movement
> Comrades, be clear-eyed, do not let their evil plot succeed
> Even when spring comes, beware of frost and cold air
> After victory, the struggle continues
> Party, dear Party, you are like the evergreen pine and cypress
> Deep roots, full crowns, green for thousands of years
> Your words are always in our hearts
> We will stand tall and magnificent on Chaoyang Hill forever, never
>   wither away

How was that? Not good enough? I guess I'll have to keep working hard. I'm sure you comrades sing better than I do. A skinny horse has a droopy mane, and poor people's words aren't worth listening to. To be honest, the Captain wasn't great—[his singing sounded] even worse than someone sobbing, really, even worse than me. But when he sang, I obediently turned in his direction and pretended to be enchanted, although I was actually staring at Tian Han's picture the whole time. It showed him in a rural village, talking intimately with the revolutionary crowd. He was in high spirits, his face ruddy, and like me now, cross-legged with a mug in one hand and the Little Red Book in the other. Seeing how healthy Comrade Ge Ren looked, I felt a surge of joy inside.

All right, I'll continue. I'm not bragging or trying to make myself look good. The revolutionary friendship I have with Secretary Tian is higher than the sky, deeper than the ocean. I swear to Chairman Mao, this isn't some coloratura nonsense—I'm telling the truth. He and Ge Ren were from the same place, Qinggeng. Of course I'd seen him before. He knows magic. In the blink of an eye, he turned an old mother hen into a duck, his pièce de résistance. When I first laid eyes on him, he was skinnier than he is now, and crawling with fleas. He spat all over the place, like a beggar. Yet the pigeons he kept were all plump and sharp-eared. He came to Hangzhou to see Ge Ren, but Ge Ren had just come back from Japan and was teaching in Beijing, so he didn't get to see him. What? Nonsense? Who's talking nonsense? Oh, now that I think about it, pigeons don't have ears. Huh? You said it, how could pigeons not have ears? If they didn't have ears, how would they have heard where Secretary Tian was dispatching them? No matter how you slice it, they'd need ears. Those pigeons were all very obedient to Secretary Tian. He'd say, Go, catch the bugs on that tree, and they would meekly fly over there and exterminate those bugs. Or he'd say, Come here, come memorize Chairman Mao's three essays, and they'd go, coo coo, coo, and recite the whole three essays that way. Then he'd say, You must be tired now, so rest up. We'll do battle another day. Then the pigeons would tuck their heads under their wings and obediently start snoring.

Later on, Secretary Tian went to Beijing to take part in the May Fourth Movement. Before he left, he gave me some of his pigeons. Comrades, it meant a lot that he entrusted his pigeons to me. As everyone knows, doves are a symbol of peace. They could remind me at every moment to exterminate the imperialists and liberate all of humanity. After that, I didn't see him for a long time. The next time I did, he was a general in the Red Guard. I've talked about it before; this is back when I came to Bare Mountain with Ge Ren. One time I spotted a familiar face but couldn't place his name, so I asked Ge Ren, Hey, who's that? Ge Ren said, Who are you asking about? I said, Over there, the comrade who's even more handsome and dashing than Yang Zirong. Ge Ren hooked his finger around the tip of my nose and gave it a tug. How could you not recognize him, he exclaimed. That's Comrade Tian Han. Tian's memory was a lot better than mine; he immediately knew who I was, and even fondly called me "little devil." I felt warm inside, but my tears spattered the ground like a string of broken pearls.

Think about it, comrades, how emotional I would have felt knowing Bai Shengtao was coming on Secretary Tian's orders. Seeing Bai would be like seeing Secretary Tian, like being back in Yan'an. I even thought that when I'd completed my task, I would tell the Party that they should pull me back out from undercover, so I could say goodbye to this strange twilight life. Goodbye, Military Intelligence. Goodbye, John Leighton Stuart. Fuck it, I'd head straight back to Yan'an.

Brightly Colored Mountain Flowers

On page 215 of the *Annals of Wuji* (1990 edition), I found a report on Little Red Woman's visit to Wuji, which Ah Qing mentioned:

> Wind and rain see spring off, then flying snow welcomes spring back. Not long ago, the capital's Chairman Mao Artistic Thought Propaganda Performance Troupe caught a ride on the east wind of the Revolution, and came to the Wuji region. The sky was as pale as a fish belly when the troupe, accompanied by Comrade Tian Han, arrived at the terraced fields beneath the Wuji cliffs, where they performed *Chaoyang Hill* for the revolutionary masses. Little Red Woman, who plays the female commander in this show, stood on a tall rock, and as the red sun rose overhead, she sang the most famous passage for her comrades: "Chaoyang Hill has never been calm." When she arrived at the line "Educated Youth, put down roots and bring about revolution," the Educated Youth who were present raised their arms and shouted, "Long live Chairman Mao! Long live Chairman Mao!" When she finished singing, and noticed that their hands were scratched from the rocks and hammers, tears filled Comrade Little Red's eyes. She composed a poem on the spot: "Difficulties are rocks, determination is a hammer. Hammers smash rocks, and problems step aside." Comrade Tian Han also made a speech: "Ever since Pan Gu opened up heaven and earth, from the three kings and five emperors till today, this hillside beneath the Wuji cliffs has sprouted only woodlands, not crops. Brightly colored mountain flowers, chirping birds—that's the language of capitalists. And now let's embrace the spirit of capturing the moon from the highest heavens, scooping the turtles from the deepest sea. We'll chop down all these trees, clear every last one of these weeds,

and turn this into a river of rice and grain. When Comrade Little Red visits Wuji again, the comrades of the propaganda troupe will eat rice from the terraced fields. Do my comrades have confidence in this plan?" And the comrades shouted their determination so loudly, it could be heard beyond the clouds. With Comrade Little Red's encouragement and Comrade Tian Han's orders, the comrades launched into the work with a renewed spirit. Some of them refused to stop even despite suffering minor injuries. By noon, all the trees had been chopped down, and the weeds burned to nothing. Looking at this bald hillside and the red flag blowing in the wind above it, every comrade wore a smile of victory.

As Ah Qing said, "In the blink of an eye, he turned an old mother hen into a duck." Not long after the interrogation team spoke to Ah Qing, Tian Han was denounced. This had something to do with the passage above. On page 223 of the *Annals of Wuji*, the following words appear:

The local Wuji Red Guards, in the spirit of "not fearing death by a thousand cuts, toppling the Emperor from his horse," have seized the spy Tian X, who was embedded within the revolutionary army. It has been said that Tian X knows enough anti-revolutionary ideology to fill several carts, He could spout it for three days and nights and still not run out. Take a recent example. He actually dared to publicly go against the reddest red sun of our hearts, babbling some rubbish about "brightly colored mountain flowers are the language of capitalists." Surely he must have known that our great Chairman Mao once instructed us, "Wind and rain see spring off, then flying snow welcomes spring back. When brightly colored mountain flowers bloom, she smiles among them." It's there in black and white, engraved in steel. He couldn't shake off his guilt even if he tried. His ass will never be wiped clean, because his dark intentions are now laid bare. Very soon we will expose Tian X's anti-revolutionary activities to the masses. At this crucial moment in time, we must continue to have the spirit of "not fearing death by a thousand cuts, toppling the Emperor from his horse." We must denounce Tian X, then step hard on him so he can never turn over again.

I noticed that in *Tian Han: An Autobiography*, which was actually completed by Zhu Xudong, the same passage was quoted, this time to show how unfairly Tian Han was treated during the Cultural Revolution. The *Annals* called him "Tian X" instead of Tian Han because by the time they were published, Comrade Tian Han had been rehabilitated, and using his real name would have seemed treasonous.

Using All the Strength I Could Muster

I was hoping for the stars and moon, but one day passed after another, and Bai Shengtao still hadn't shown up. I was getting frantic. To make the time pass, I spent my days sitting in the tea house. Then one morning, just as the sun was slowly rising in the east, I was taking a sip of my tea when I spotted Yang Fengliang and a man in a gray robe walking toward the town temple. The man's silhouette was so familiar that, though I couldn't make out his face at that distance, I was certain I knew who it was. I even found myself thinking: Could he be Bai Shengtao? Could Bai Shengtao be a fake name?

You have to endure the small things or they'll ruin the big ones. I endured, and instead of following the two men, I grabbed hold of a tea house waitress and pulled her down next to me. Hoping to attract the newcomer's attention, I pulled out her hairpin and smacked her on the ass with it. Aiyoh! yelped the silly woman, even as she obediently perched on my lap. Her rump was so ample, my cock started to feel squashed and numb. Yang Fengliang and his companion turned and looked in our direction. Such perverts. People like that are in thrall to their base instincts, and are always on the lookout for a bit of filth. The guy was still too far away for me to be able to see who he was. Annoyed, I smacked the woman on the ass again.

All day long, my heart was filled with flames. That night, I'd just fallen asleep when one of my men suddenly knocked on the door: someone was there to see me. I thought Bai Shengtao had arrived, and not even stopping to get dressed, I ran out bare-assed. It was the man from before, still in his gray robe. He walked over to the desk and turned up the lamp. The heavens shook, the earth wept, and I saw clearly who he was and almost screamed: Zong Bu. Even a bloody idiot would have known he was there about Ge Ren. And after so many years of learning from the Party, I'm not a bloody idiot. But as for whose orders he was following and what this had to do with Yang, I couldn't have said.

He told me he was a merchant now, and often passed through Bare Mountain picking up supplies of tea leaves, mushrooms, lotus seeds, and broad beans. Dogshit! Since when do broad beans grow on Bare Mountain? Ridiculous. I said nothing, just kept watching him to see what coloratura he would throw my way next. He blithely said that tea leaves hadn't come on the market yet, so he would have to cool his heels here and do a bit of private teaching. I thought, all right, keep spewing willow branches, and when you've finished weaving your basket of lies, I'll rip them apart. He said Yang Fengliang had asked him to be a substitute teacher at the local school, and he'd agreed because it's no more effort to teach one or many. I said, You seem to get on well with Yang. Did you know him from the old days? He quickly said no, they'd never met before.

I didn't say much else to him that night. A day or two later, he showed up again and asked if I'd like to go for a walk. I said, What are you doing here? Aren't you supposed to be teaching? He said classes had ended for the day. I asked what he was teaching, and he said *The Analects*. "Is it not pleasant to practice what you have learned? Is it not delightful to have a friend visit from afar? Being slow to anger when misunderstood—is that not how a gentleman should act?" I asked him whether the young flowers of our nation could understand all this muddled nonsense. He said they talked about other stuff too, things that were easy to recite. "Ospreys squawk on the river island, gentlemen chase pretty girls." Do you hear that, comrades? What kind of rubbish is that? All the strings in my heart tightened. Pah! This old reprobate, talking about degenerate old stuff like that. Was he deliberately trying to lead the flowers of our fatherland down a bad path?

All right, I'll continue. Using every ounce of my self-control, I went for a walk with him. Comrades, the scenery around Bare Mountain is really superb—magnificent mountains and rivers, which countless heroes have bowed to. The only imperfection was that springtime hadn't fully arrived, and the bamboo groves weren't yet wearing their revolutionary raiment. We walked up a stately mound, and there below us was Phoenix Valley. The locals say that very long ago, there were many phoenixes here. Yes, I will have another cigarette, thanks. Didn't I say before? The reason I like smoking Phoenixes is because I've visited Phoenix Valley. Now I stood atop this mound, hands on my hips, and when I looked down, the tide rose in my heart, a surge of revolutionary fervor. From where I was, I could see the elementary school that Ge Ren was locked up in, its black walls and the green tiles of its roof. Deciding to be blunt, I said to Zong Bu, Tell the truth, did you come here because of Ge Ren? He insisted he'd only found out Ge Ren was there after he arrived. Fuck that, who would believe this nonsense? I asked what his plans were, and whether he would help rescue Ge Ren, for Bingying's sake. This time he was mute.

After a lengthy pause, he kicked the ball to me and asked what I was planning to do. Damn it, I couldn't tell him I was waiting to kill Bai Shengtao. So I said I was keeping my eyes and ears open, listening in all directions, waiting for favorable developments. He forced a smile and said, Good, good. Who the fuck knew what that "good" meant? He started walking back downhill. I didn't know what he had in mind, so I stuck close to him. As we passed by an enormous rock, he reached into a fissure and pulled out an azalea branch. The flowers were just budding, and he shut his eyes as he waved them beneath his nose. After sniffing at it a while, he put it back on the stone. This sort of bourgeois frippery filled me with rage. I didn't do anything, though, because I was still waiting for his answer. I thought, you've smelled your flowers, you've given yourself enough airs, how about an honest answer now? But still he said nothing, just kept heading down, until we got to a little stream, where he stopped. He cupped some water in his hand, and stared at it for a long time without speaking. Near the river were some monks from the Bodhi Temple, so poor they didn't even have prayer beads. Zong Bu watched them, his eyes narrowed in a smile. Finally, he spoke. Listen to the crap he spouted, comrades, using his small-person's mind to interpret a noble heart. He said, Ge Ren must have come to this remote place in order to bury himself. His words smelled worse than a fart, but he didn't seem to think so. In fact, he clearly found them delicious. He said as soon as he got to Bare Mountain, he had the same idea as Ge Ren, and wanted to bury himself there too. He wanted me to write a report to Military Intelligence, to make it clear that Ge Ren had no further interest in politics and was of no value to anyone, so why not just leave him here to sink or swim on his own?

I can still remember it now, how my hand moved to my rear pocket. Yes, I almost cocked my gun and shot him dead. The reason I didn't was that I remembered those words: endure the small things or they'll ruin the big ones. That's right, I didn't want to make any trouble before Bai Sheng-tao got there. With that thought in mind, I quickly swallowed my anger.

On the way back, Zong Bu suddenly asked when Yang Fengliang was leaving. He also said I should keep an eye on him—at a time like this, there's nothing Yang wouldn't do. I said, All right, I don't need you to remind me; I know that dogfucker's up to no good. He smoked one cigarette after another, not saying a word. He even asked if I wanted one. When he said that, comrades, my guard went up. When you treat someone well, that means you're about to take advantage of them. My hand was reaching out, but at this thought, I pulled it back. But then the wheels in my brain turned again, and I said to myself that there was no greater sin than waste, and the more of the enemy's money I could get him to waste, the greater my contribution to the Revolution. And so I took his cigarette and smoked it. What brand was it? White Gold Dragon, from the South Seas Tobacco Company. You're exactly right: as soon as I heard that name, I could detect the stench of luxury on him.

Just as I was busy wasting his money, he suddenly asked if I could think of a way to lure Yang Fengliang away. I laughed and said, Mr. Zong, if this

Yang were a shit in my belly, I'd happily crap him out, but he's not. He abruptly claimed that he could do Yang's job and send him home to Fujian early. I said, You make that sound easy—if you really can get rid of him, I'd be very grateful. He looked smug and said, Just wait and see, then. I guarantee that he'll be gone from Bare Mountain within three days, all the way back to Changting. You see what a rare state of affairs I'd stumbled upon. A private tutor deploying a Kuomintang general. If this worked, that would make one thing clear: that the Nationalists were finished. Only the Party has ever told me what to do. Since when did a private tutor get to do that? Fuck it, what nonsense was this?

Can I say that? All right, I'll continue. What's that? What happened when Zong Bu and Yang Fengliang talked? Ah, this will make you laugh. More bullshit than was produced by the cows in Yongyun Village [N.B. a farming settlement near the Xin Village Re-Education Tea Plantation]. The next day, he came to me and said he had spoken to Yang Fengliang, but Yang didn't care for his plan. I asked what they talked about, and he said he'd told Yang's fortune and predicted family trouble. What kind of trouble? Yang had asked. He said he couldn't tell exactly what kind of trouble, but it had something to do with a grave. In fact, I was the one who had told him there'd been a death in Yang's family, and he was just trotting that out as his own story. He urged Yang to finish up what he was doing and hurry home to have a look. Yang replied that he'd already known there was some grave trouble at home that threatened to cut off his family line, and that's why he'd had so many lovers, scattering his seed in one place and moving on, trying to change his fate through sheer volume. Besides, out of all these sons, there must surely be one who'd be military material. Zong Bu stared at him dumbfounded. After scratching his beard in silence, he said to Yang Fengliang, If you won't go back and look, your own life might be in danger. Yang asked if he was serious, and Zong Bu said he definitely wasn't bluffing, and he would quit his teaching job right away if it wasn't the truth. He even gave Yang some money and said that would cover his travel expenses. Yes, he bribed Yang Fengliang. I said to Zong Bu, So your candy-coated bullet hit the dogfucker? He said, Yes, with a single shot. He also said he knew Yang was surely going to rise through the ranks, and when that happened, he would have a part for General Yang to play, so he'd definitely be grateful that fate had brought them together that day. And just like that, he said, the dogfucker was completely taken in, and accepted the money. But comrades, Yang Fengliang was greedier than a snake trying to swallow an elephant. That bribe wasn't enough for him; now he tried to get some more. Yes, he hung around hoping there'd be a reward for his work. What? Did he [Zong Bu] give me any cash? Yes, and I took it. Didn't I say earlier that the more of your enemy's money you waste, the greater your contribution to the Revolution?

Because he hadn't managed to drive Yang Fengliang away, Zong Bu must have felt embarrassed, and he left the next day. Goodbye, John Leighton Stuart. That was the last I ever saw of him, but he's been thrown into the dustbin of history anyway, so let's not mention him again. I really haven't seen him since. I swear to Chairman Mao I'm telling the truth; none of it's a lie. I don't need you to remind me, I know I have a responsibility to history. History is written by the People, and I'm one of the People. If I'm lying, then may American imperialism be my mother, the Soviet Empire be my uncle, and my name be Inhuman Zhao. Do you believe me now?

Zong Bu's Trip to Bare Mountain

Bingying categorically denied that Zong Bu had gone to Bare Mountain at her request. In fact, when she found out he had gone, she was furious. The way she saw it, not only had he not been able to help, he had hastened Ge Ren's death. Her reasoning was that "Zong Bu's appearance would have reminded Ge Ren of the failure of his life, and added to his despair." It wouldn't take much imagination for us to see the meaning hidden in those words: Bingying regarded her marriage to Zong Bu as a source of shame, and assumed others would see it the same way, particularly Ge Ren.

After Zong Bu and Bingying separated in Shanghai on that snowy day in early 1943, Bingying went to Chongqing, while Zong Bu departed for Hong Kong. On his second day there, he went to the offices of *Scattered Scriptures*, the journal that had published "Broad Bean Blossoms," hoping the editor, Xu Yusheng, would be able to give him more information about Ge Ren. But Mr. Xu wasn't in Hong Kong at the time—I learned from his book *Qiantang River Dream Diary* that he was in Hangzhou, tending to his parents' graves—and Zong Bu wasn't able to find out what he wanted. Which is to say, all the way from Hong Kong to Bare Mountain, he had no way to be sure if Ge Ren was actually alive. All he had was a hunch that they would meet on Bare Mountain. But how did he figure that out? Mr. Huang Jishi's *Half a Lifetime* contains the following passage:

A few days ago, Mr. Zong was clutching *Scattered Scriptures*, looking dazed, occasionally even bursting into tears. I borrowed it and had a look, but nothing seemed out of the ordinary. There was a story about how Chiang Chungcheng and Soong Mei-ling were passing over the Camel's Hump [i.e., the Himalayas] on their way to Egypt when their pilot had a heart attack and almost crashed. But Mr. Zong wasn't sympathetic to Chiang's politics, so he wouldn't have shed tears over that. Besides, this was old news. The Chiangs had arrived in Cairo on November 21, and met Churchill that same day. There was another day when the sky darkened a little in the afternoon, and he became dazed again. When I pressed him, he said there was a poem titled "Broad Bean Blossoms" in *Scattered Scriptures* by a poet named Melancholy, but he recognized it as a new piece by Ge Ren, which meant Ge Ren was still alive. He believed that Ge Ren had hidden himself on Bare Mountain, where he was living with his daughter, Broad Bean. According to him, Broad Bean had gone missing on Bare Mountain in the Jiaxu Year [i.e., 1934]. This made him think the Battle of Two Li Mound had been a ruse, Ge Ren shedding his skin like a cicada. After he got away, he would have sought out his daughter on Bare Mountain. Zong Bu was pushing seventy at this point, and knowing he didn't have too much time left, he had rushed to Bare Mountain because he wanted to see his daughter too. He made his case forcefully, and when he insisted on going, no one could stop him.

I should mention here that in recent years, some overseas scholars have used this passage to claim that Ge Ren went to Bare Mountain in search of his adopted daughter. I can't say whether or not this is true. As Bai Shengtao said, any conclusion you draw about Ge Ren might be a distortion. There is one thing I can verify: Zong Bu went to Bare Mountain not to rescue Ge Ren, but to see his daughter. Unfortunately, it was not to be. In 1934, not long after the Red Guards pulled out of Bare Mountain, my great-aunt showed up, accompanied by Reverend Ellis, and took Broad Bean away. I will return to this point later.

Mr. Huang Jishi also says that when Zong Bu went to Bare Mountain, "he had a roll of banknotes in his wallet." That money was intended for Broad Bean, "and if she happened to be married, this would serve as her dowry, and also as an apology from her father." He didn't see Broad Bean, but the money was still spent. "When he got back to Hong Kong, his wallet was as empty as a beggar's." Where did the money go? Reading Ah Qing's account, I realized he had bribed Yang Fengliang and Ah Qing with it.

In the spring of 2000, when Mr. Sun Guozhang allowed me to interview him, he also mentioned that Zong Bu and Yang Fengliang had spoken to each other. Zong Bu wasn't able to see Broad Bean, and Ge Ren was back in prison, so Zong Bu changed his original plan and decided to buy Ge Ren's freedom from Yang Fengliang:

The night before I left, Zong Bu revealed his true self. In philosophy, this is known as "aletheia." He stated that he was there to rescue Mr. Ge Ren, and he asked Mr. Yang to name his price. As I recall, he once said that he and Ge Ren's father were in the same group of Kang Youwei supporters in the early days, and that's how he knew Ge Ren. At some point during that time, he'd taken responsibility for Ge Ren. Mr. Yang said he was willing to hear more. Mr. Zong explained that back in the day, he had put up the money for Ge Ren to travel to the Soviet Union. Yes, it's now the former Soviet Union. It was this experience that allowed Ge Ren to rise through the Party ranks, which is why there was now a price on his head and he was being locked up. Mr. Yang said, You must know Bingying too? That's when I found out that the man before me was the interloper I'd heard about, the Kang supporter who had come between Ge Ren and his wife. When I said that, Zong Bu was overcome with shame. He'd been guilt-stricken about this for many years. He was willing to cough up a huge sum to save Ge Ren's life, as a way of appeasing his conscience. Mr. Yang said that as soon as the trains were running again, he would take Ge Ren away from there, and that Ge Ren's life was in no danger, so not to worry. Mr. Zong didn't quite seem to believe him. He said there were already a lot of people keeping an eye on the situation there, and Mr. Yang had better not be swayed, because if he changed his mind and Ge Ren lost his life in Baibei, Yang would be seen as a villain for the ages. Mr. Yang burst out laughing and said Mr. Zong could relax. As far as I know, Mr. Yang planned to pass the money to Ge Ren that night. As for whether Ge Ren accepted it, I have no idea.

According to *Beauty in a Time of Chaos*, when Zong Bu got back to Hong Kong, he wrote Bingying a letter in which he naively informed her that Ge Ren was sure to be released, and she should wait for his good news. "He said he had redeemed himself, as if Ge Ren's capture were an opportunity that history had bestowed on him. He also mentioned Broad Bean's disappearance as the torment of his life."

At this point, I should mention that as readers will have noticed, Ah Qing's narration presents Zong Bu as a buffoon. But Ah Qing's descendants have informed me that at the time, he was merely striking the necessary pose of "beating a man while he was down." Mr. Yu Fenggao, who was part of the investigation, also mentioned to me that Ah Qing would "pivot to whoever was in power," and that he was "two-faced" and "behaved differently behind your back," "even making use of his spy skills." In that case, what did Ah Qing truly think about Zong Bu? His descendants said he had enjoyed his "scribbling," and had left some papers behind. These later fell into Yu Fenggao's hands. But by the time I finally tracked down Yu Fenggao, he was in his urn. His son, Yu Liren, told me he had the papers. Then he brought the conversation around to his multi-level marketing company, the Huawei Consumer Alliance, and how good it was. "Good," of course, meant earning lots of money. He was pushing Alaskan seal oil. In Part One, I mentioned a TV show's Two Li Mound segment, where the special prize given out by the celebrity guest was Alaskan seal oil. In order to see the papers for myself, I had to sign up with his company. Once I'd done that, Yu Liren opened a drawer in the urn and took out a notebook with a red plastic cover. From between its pages, he produced a wrinkled letter. Across the top were Chairman Mao's words: "To be wrong, and know you are wrong, but not take steps to correct yourself, instead taking a liberal attitude toward yourself—this is the eleventh type of person. ~Against Liberalism." After that was Ah Qing's handwriting:

> Today the comrades from the interrogation team came to see me, wanting to understand Ge Ren's final heroic act. They'll come again tomorrow. I had to mention Zong [Bu]. Anyway, Zong [Bu] is nothing but ashes now, and he can't answer back, so I will kick a man while he's down and give him a proper scolding. Zong Bu, if you can hear me from the underworld, you will surely understand. I've let you down, so I'll kowtow to you. Never mind, I'll see you soon enough, and then I'll apologize [to you] in person, and cut off my ears [and give them to you] as a snack. I'll explain to you that all of this was for Ge [Ren]'s sake. Enough of that, we'll talk again when I get there. I won't be scared of anything when I get there. Eat fat or eat lean, there's no fear to be seen. If you want anything, just let me know in a dream, and I'll make sure to bring it to you. But let's be clear, if what you want is a picture of Broad Bean, I don't have one. I really don't. I'm not bluffing.

Two weeks later, Zhao Yaoqing killed himself by jumping into a well.

Bai Shengtao Gets Strung Up Again

Zong Bu's bragging had come to nothing, and I was more anxious than an ant on a hot pot. I decided that before Bai Shengtao got there, if I spent my time helping Ge Ren recover his health, it could be done. I went to see him, and asked what he wanted to eat. He said some tofu would be nice. That was a problem, because they don't grow soybeans in Baibei. I asked why tofu, and he said because China has the best tofu in the world. You see how patriotic he was, even at a time like this, loving our Chinese tofu? By the way, comrades, is there any chance you could get me some stir-fried tofu for dinner? It's been quite a while since I've had any of the best tofu in the world.

I'd made sure his rations were of the highest quality. There was wine and meat at every meal, but not tofu. Now that he had mentioned it, though, I would have to make it happen. I sent someone to Ruijin City with some mushrooms and daylilies to trade for tofu. I was so happy, watching him eat that tofu. He said, General Zhao, you have some too. I blushed to hear him call me General Zhao. It took a lot of insisting before he finally switched to Ah Qing. He said, Ah Qing, I need a doctor who can dissect a human body. I didn't know what he meant, so I asked him to explain further. He said his illness was in its final stages, and after his death, he wanted the doctors to remove his lungs and donate them to a hospital for dissection, in order to help with the study of tuberculosis.

Comrades, ever since Pan Gu opened up the heavens and earth, since the time of the three kings and five emperors, who has ever willingly handed over his innards to a hospital? No one, no one at all. What a spirit. This was pure materialism. What's that? Qu Qiubai said so too? All right, I'm talking nonsense. At the time, when I heard those words, I hastily said to Ge Ren, Listen to yourself, what are you thinking? You mustn't say such inauspicious things. You'll be fine, I promise you'll be fine, I'm not bluffing. Seeing how frightened I was, Ge Ren laughed and said, All right, I take it back.

Ge Ren and I were talking in the airwell outside his room. There was a water well there, with a newly built frame over it. The winch was new too, made of unvarnished wood. It would squeak and rattle as the bucket went down. Ge Ren said he'd thought ahead to the summer, when he would lower a watermelon down to cool—children love eating chilled watermelon. I said, So do I. He smiled and said, Then it's a shame you'll never get to eat my chilled watermelon. He was in high spirits that night. I gave orders to have his rations increased, then sat with him in the airwell drinking wine and gazing at the moon. After some time, Ge Ren started urging me to go back. He said, For all you know, there's something waiting for you to deal with. I said, What could that be? Taking care of you is my most important job. But still he insisted. The moon moved past the airwell, and he said he was tired and had a bit of a headache. I said, Your body is your revolutionary capital. Promise me you'll sleep after I go; don't do any more work. This is just the first step in the long march—there's still a lot of distance to cover.

I walked back in the moonlight, and had just fallen asleep when a subordinate woke me up to report they had captured a guy, someone from outside. There was something odd about him. They had already beaten him up, and they were about to take it up a notch. A chill went through me, and I thought this might be Bai Shengtao. I remembered what Ge Ren had said earlier that evening. Had he sent me back because he'd figured out that the person sent by Tian Han and Dou Sizhong would be arriving about now? He was so clever. My men saw me smiling and thought I was going to reward them, so they started boasting about what they'd done to him. Those bastards were good at causing chaos, and nothing else. In order to keep them from getting suspicious, I actually slipped them some cash. Don't look at me like that, comrades. My thinking was that sooner or later, this reward money would find its way back into the bosom of the People, and if they'd spent any of it, we would make them shit it back out.

When I saw Bai Shengtao, they had just cut him down from the rafters. I made sure to be both stern and magnanimous, and glared at him before bending down to help him up. You can't do much with dogshit, and he didn't seem grateful at all. I remember the scene exactly. He was kneeling there, his eyes shut, dirt on the tip of his nose, still shaking as if he had malaria. I called softly into his ear, Bai Shengtao, Bai Shengtao. The motherfucker ignored me. He was almost entirely bald, which made his forehead look enormous. It was glistening with sweat, like a mantis that had just crawled out of the water. Oh yes, later on he told me that his hair had fallen out on the way to Bare Mountain. At the time, I wondered to myself, how had someone this incompetent made it all the way from Yan'an? Besides, why was he alone? Why hadn't he brought anyone with him? Fuck it, never mind where he was from; I needed to get him settled first. If this wasn't Bai Shengtao but rather some innocent businessman, then that would be easy: I'd just bleed him a little, get him to hand over some cash, and then send him on his way. Why should he have to bleed and pay up? Pah, do you need to ask? Firstly, robbing the rich to pay the poor is a revolutionary act, and secondly, I had to do something while the bastards were watching, so they'd see that when it came to the Party and Nation, I didn't do anything halfway. Comrades, Bai Shengtao would later betray the Revolution and run off with Fan Jihuai. But at the time, he hadn't revealed his true face yet. He still looked like a sturdy guy, unafraid of hardship or death. I hadn't yet figured out whether this was Bai Shengtao, so when I saw them about to string him up again, I didn't try to stop them. There was something wrong with him. He'd slumped listlessly on the ground, but as soon as they hauled him up, he became animated. As they pulled him, he said, Higher, higher. Then he said that if he could get a bowl of egg noodles every time they strung him up, he would hope it would happen more often. Now he was swinging back and forth in midair, like a fucking giant spider. His lips wouldn't stop moving.

What did he say? Stand a bit farther away, or the rope might break and I'll hit you. That sort of nonsense. It made me angry to listen. Then he said, It's best to use donkey reins—donkey reins, those are the strongest. Motherfucker, was he trying to get himself shot? His ass was on a knife's edge. At that time, there were plenty of people like this guy. I had already met another one before Bai Shengtao showed up. That one was from here. He had lost all his capital doing business, and had no choice but to come back, only to find that the poor devils around here had robbed his house of everything in it, and his family were all dead and gone. That guy just wanted to die, and the more you hit him, the more joyfully he shouted. When you see someone so committed to the capitalist road, there's really nothing you can do except take a club and beat him to death. But now I was worried that this might be Bai Shengtao, and so after he'd been hanging there a while, I signaled them to cut him down. As soon as he hit the ground, one of my men gave him a lash of the whip. His throat lengthened and a gurgle came from his mouth, as if he was about to vomit, but nothing came out.

You're right, I had to think of a strategy. I racked my brains over it. That night, I told them to give him something good to eat, then send him a couple of whores from the tea house. He devoured the food, and said at least he wouldn't end up as a hungry ghost. He turned away the whores, claiming he wasn't up to fucking at the moment—try again in a couple of days. The next day, I spoke with him alone. First I apologized, and said we'd only beaten him out of love. The lash landed on his body, but it was my heart that hurt. I even brought up how Zhou Yu had Huang Gai flogged, and said we had the same objective: one of us was willing to be beaten, and one was willing to beat. So that there was no misunderstanding, I told him plainly that I was Ah Qing, and asked if he was here about Ge Ren. Only then did he admit who he was—but he had lost the secret message from Comrade Dou Sizhong! He said as he was passing by Wuhan, he got robbed, and not only had he lost the orders, he'd almost died too. He said not to worry, it was just common bandits who only cared about money. He could swear on his head that those orders wouldn't fall into the hands of the authorities. He'd already gotten word to Comrade Dou Sizhong through the underground network about the missing letter, and Dou had replied that it was just a regular letter of introduction, because he was meeting me for the first time, and there was no other message. He added that Dou Sizhong had told him he wasn't worried, because Bai was running things, and he should just follow standard procedure. That's what I'd been waiting to hear, so I quickly asked what standard procedure was.

He said the Party had told him to take Code Zero away from Bare Mountain. But where to? That was a Party secret. He added that in order to keep this secret, Dou Sizhong had specifically instructed him that once Ge Ren left Bare Mountain, he would have no more contact with the Party.

Can I say this? Then I'll continue.

I can't say I wasn't suspicious. To make sure he wasn't bluffing, I asked him how Comrade Tian Han was doing. His answer exactly matched what I knew: that he had treated Comrade Tian Han's illness and solved a big problem for him. What problem? Shitting. After the Long March, Tian Han and many of the other leaders couldn't shit anymore. When they got to Yan'an, Comrade Tian Han continued to live simply, on a diet of black beans. When his subordinates gave him apples, he refused to eat them, and the same with pears. This meant his constipation not only failed to improve, but actually got worse. I was in Chongqing when I heard about this, and as there was nothing I could do, I merely stewed in anxiety. Later I heard that Comrade Tian Han's constipation had been cured, and I was so happy I couldn't sleep that night. I heard that someone named Dr. Bai had healed him, but I didn't know that was Bai Shengtao. What did you ask? Where did I hear that? In Military Intelligence, of course. At the time, Chiang Kai-shek was suffering from chronic diarrhea. His stools were more watery than his piss, and nothing seemed to cure him. So he sent Dai Li to ask around whether there was anyone who could help him. Not long after that, they heard of a doctor named Bai from Shanghai who'd be able to treat him, except he had run off to Yan'an to look into Tian Han's constipation. If you can treat constipation, you can surely handle diarrhea. They went to Shanghai and found a student of Dr. Bai's—I think his name was Yue—and brought him to Chongqing, where he cured old Chiang's runny stools. Now that I knew he was even aware of Tian Han's constipation, I thought he must surely be one of us. Of course, I still didn't fully understand why he was there on his own. He gave a pretty explanation, saying Dou Sizhong was worried that too many people would mean loose talk, so he'd been sent on a solo mission to keep the secret safe.

Chronic Diarrhea

There were no eyewitnesses present, so we have to take Ah Qing's word for it that this was how Bai Shengtao passed on his instructions. I should say here that the doctor Ah Qing mentioned who treated old Chiang wasn't named Yue, but Yu. He's the Mr. Yu Chengze I mentioned in "Scatology," and as I said before, he was Bai Shengtao's classmate, not his student. In the July 1993 issue of *Prominent Doctors* magazine, "Tales of the Famous" contained the following recollection from Mr. Yu:

In the spring of 1942, I was followed by several men in plain clothes. At first I thought they must be Japanese spies, but I would later discover they were Dai Li's thugs. They asked if I would "make a journey" with them. So be it; I was a little impatient with life at the time, and nothing could really scare me. They asked me about Bai Shengtao and I said, "I haven't seen him in a long while." Actually, I knew he had gone to Yan'an. The plainclothes men took me to Xi'an first, and then we flew directly to Chongqing. They behaved very politely and were never rough. I was already starting to suspect that I was being brought to treat someone, but I would never have guessed that this person would turn out to be Chiang Kai-shek himself.

Chiang had chronic diarrhea. I saw his medical records after I got to Chongqing. Naturally, his name didn't appear anywhere on them. The assistant they allocated to me said the victim was a member of the Methodist Church in his early fifties—Chiang was fifty-five at the time. The records said that this person moved his bowels only once every eight to ten days, and the stools were accompanied by mucus, pus, and [a small amount of] blood. It was easy to identify the symptoms, less so to diagnose the problem. As we know, defecation relies on the movement of the large intestine. Under normal circumstances, this takes place two to four times a day. Because I was unable to examine the patient myself, I could only instruct the relevant professionals to keep observing the motility of the large and small intestines, and also provide me with the results after they had studied and lab-tested the stools.

Two days later, after putting together the various pieces of evidence, I came to a conclusion. This Methodist was passing loose stools because his interior workings were disordered. Food was remaining in his intestines for too short a time, so his body was not able to absorb it. In addition, his autonomic nervous system was out of balance, leading to convulsions in his intestines, which was a major cause of his diarrhea. And if there was something wrong with his autonomic nervous system, there would of course be a psychological reason behind it. I told my assistant that this person must surely suffer from insomnia and an inability to focus. The Wesleyans like to say that "inner peace is true happiness," but it looked like some excrement had defeated them, because those runny stools covered in pus told me their sufferer was not happy at all.

I had said this in a humorous tone, but now my assistant started to tremble, and his face turned ashen gray. Many days later, when I found out who the patient was, I finally understood why he had been that nervous.

History can be funny at times. I had learned medicine from Kawata, a Japanese doctor, and in a certain sense, you could say that Chiang Kai-shek's nerves were shot because the Japanese had invaded China, leading to his diarrhea, and to my treating him. One more thing: during the Cultural Revolution, people would say I had met with Chiang Kai-shek, but I would never admit it. And it's true, I wasn't lying: all I ever saw of Chiang Kai-shek was his stool.

As far as a doctor is concerned, seeing Chiang Kai-shek's shit is even more significant than seeing the owner of that shit. The reason Mr. Yu Chengze became China's most famous scatologist had a lot to do with Chiang Kai-shek's shit. After he published this essay about Chiang's stools, his reputation rose even higher, and he was regarded as China's leading authority on shit. In the last few years of his life, apart from his work as a professor, he was also a consultant at a private hospital, in whose corridors I saw many patients gingerly holding their bellies, waiting in an orderly line. It wasn't Mr. Yu himself who treated them, but his disciples. One of them joked that Chiang Kai-shek's shit was the best advertisement their hospital could have hoped for. Looking at those patients, I couldn't help but wonder: if it had been Bai Shengtao and not Yu Chengze who'd "made a journey" with the plainclothes officers, would Ge Ren's story have had a different ending?

Bai Shengtao Meets Ge Ren

Bai Shengtao was in a hurry to see Ge Ren, claiming that he wanted to examine him, so I led him to the elementary school. Because he'd come from Yan'an, Ge Ren was delighted to see him. Right away he exclaimed, "Is it not delightful to have a friend visit from afar?" I noticed his clothes were soaking in a basin, and sent a sentry out to wash them. The sentry said he couldn't find any alkaline [i.e., soap], nor any honey locust, so he couldn't do laundry. I yelled at him for being a motherfucking idiot, and told him to just go grab some from town. He wanted to know who would have soap. I said I had heard there was someone called Zhou Papi in town who kept ducks, chickens, and pigeons—that's a navy, army, and air force. In order to make his farmhands get up and start work early, he would crawl into the chicken coop in the middle of the night and crow like a rooster. He surely needed to wash his hair after that, so there must be soap in his house. Please don't think I was encouraging him to rob the People, comrades. At that time, Bare Mountain was very poor. There was no oil for the lamps, no bulls to pull the plow, and young women who wanted a bit of fun were frustrated too. Why? Because the men were almost all dead, their balls gone. All right, I'll continue. Anyone with soap in their home must definitely be rich, and there's no way you could place them in any other class, which means they'd get purged sooner or later. And of course, the main reason I sent the guard for the soap was to get rid of him for a while.

Bai Shengtao asked Ge Ren about his health. What sort of questions? His weight, how he was eating and drinking, how he was sleeping. I felt a puff of anger inside me. Fuck it, wasn't he making me look bad? I was the one taking care of him, so shouldn't Ge Ren be eating and sleeping well? Then he asked if Ge Ren had coughed up blood, and if he ever woke from a nap with a fever. I interrupted to say that Ge Ren didn't have much time, and he used every moment he had for Party work, so he never napped. Next he asked Ge Ren if he had a cough. Ge Ren said no. But just as he gave his answer, he started coughing violently and brought up a gob of phlegm, which flew straight into Bai Shengtao's ear, such a direct hit that you'd have sworn the phlegm could see. It really did, I'm not bluffing. I think Ge Ren must have done that on purpose, to show he was getting impatient with Dr. Bai. But Bai's skin was so thick, a machine gun couldn't have gotten through it, and he continued as if nothing had happened. He started rapping on Ge Ren's chest. I said, Hey, what are you doing? He said this was a tapping diagnosis. Only when he was done with that did he wipe the phlegm off his ear. He said to Ge Ren, From now on, you should sleep on your side, not your back. Ge Ren said, I don't need you to tell me that. I always sleep on my side. Then he asked Bai Shengtao how his health was. Bai Shengtao said it was fine. As long as he continued to recover and took his medicine on time, he would soon be completely well again. Ge Ren abruptly said, You didn't come all this way just to examine me, did you? Bai Shengtao blushed. Fuck it, all the way up to his ears. He hemmed and hawed for some time, then finally said the higher-ups had ordered him to take Ge Ren away from there.

Is it all right if I say that?

Bai Shengtao said, If you leave Baibei, you might get better sooner. There are no doctors or medicine here; it's bad for you. Ge Ren asked, Go where? Bai Shengtao said he didn't know either. His job was just to get Ge Ren away from Bare Mountain; someone else would take over the rest of the journey. Ge Ren's next words left a deep impression on me. He said, I don't want to cause trouble for my comrades, and they shouldn't make such pointless sacrifices for me. He also thanked Bai Shengtao for traveling so far to see him. Then he asked how Comrade Tian Han was doing. Bai Shengtao said Tian Han was doing very well, and that in fact Tian Han's orders were the reason he was there. I said, Yes, and Comrade Tian Han's constipation problem has been fixed. Ge Ren was delighted to hear that. He grabbed Bai Shengtao's hand and said, Thank you for your hard work. Let me thank you on behalf of the Party and the People. Then he asked, And is your father-in-law well? Bai Shengtao said, Yes, very well. He's joined the land reform movement and is an enthusiastic participant. And your son? Bai Shengtao said his son was in the army, and was part of the struggle to liberate all of humanity. When he was done bragging about his brat, Bai Shengtao said he'd arranged for Ge Ren to have the best doctors and medical treatments. Ge Ren waved that away and said he should leave those things for the other comrades; he didn't need them. When I looked at Ge Ren's pale face, tears once again trickled down my cheeks. No, comrades, these weren't bourgeois feelings. Firstly, I was moved by Tian Han and Ge Ren's lofty revolutionary friendship, and secondly, I was stirred by Ge Ren's noble revolutionary spirit. See, even at a time like that, his first thought was for other people, not himself. He was always thinking of helping others first. What do you call that? The spirit of Communism. It's not hard to do a good deed once in your life; the difficult part is making sure you only do good deeds and not bad ones. Near the end of his life, he was still thinking about his comrades. If you had been there, you would have wept as much as I did. Of course, Bai Shengtao never shed a single tear the whole time, as if his bodily fluids were so precious he had to hang on to them.

I remember taking Bai Shengtao aside and asking him how Code Zero was actually doing. Can you comrades guess what that bastard said? His reply was smellier than a dog fart, and that's no exaggeration. He said, Code Zero's body is almost completely wrecked. If he takes his shoes off tonight, he won't be able to put them on tomorrow. We must act now, or it will be too late. What did he mean by that? Later on, I realized, fuck it, he was trying to dampen the nobility of his own side in order to strengthen the enemy's spirit.

That day, I also started talking for the first time about my own plans. I said, When the time comes, I will send people to get you two safely away from Bare Mountain. Ge Ren asked, Can those people be trusted? I said, Yes, I hand-picked them. Those bastards will go wherever I point. If I send them up a mountain, they will obediently start climbing; if I send them into a sea of fire, they will happily plunge in, without so much as a fart. Ge Ren asked, But aren't you afraid they'll say something afterward? You see, even at a time like that, Ge Ren was concerned for my safety. I could only say, You don't need to worry about that. When the car reaches the mountain, there'll be a road; when the ship reaches the harbor, it'll straighten—I'll figure something out. But still Ge Ren wasn't happy. I had to tell him, There will be no afterward. When they've finished their task, I'll dispatch them all, chop, chop, chop. As I spoke, I sliced my hand cleanly through the air. Ge Ren immediately praised me. He said, It seems that Ah Qing has grown quite a bit in the last few years. Humility pulls you forward, arrogance pushes you back. I hastily said, I just did what I ought to do. In fact I'm still far short of the Party's requirements.

But Ge Ren said he didn't want to ride any more horses, and probably couldn't anyway. I quickly said he could be carried on a stretcher.

Translucent, Graceful, Crimson

Many people have mentioned Ge Ren's illness, but my impression of it is still hazy. I have to use Reverend Ellis's words here. To this day, it's the most detailed account I can find of Ge Ren's health. While Reverend Ellis was making his rounds of Bare Mountain, he happened to learn that Ge Ren was there. For more about this, the reader may refer to the relevant section in Part Three. After accompanying my great-aunt to Bare Mountain in search of Broad Bean more than a decade ago, Reverend Ellis had never left the place. He later took up Red Cross aid work, and so he left his mark on many of the towns and villages around Bare Mountain.

Just as he says in *The Majesty of the Orient*, even if he could have "sensed the future," he could never have imagined that the next time he saw Ge Ren and Ah Qing, it would be in Baibei. I wonder whether Ah Qing didn't mention this because he'd forgotten, or because he was afraid that saying too much might get him into trouble?

The following is Ellis's account of Ge Ren's illness:

On the banks of White Cloud River, I stumbled upon Shang-Jên [i.e., Ge Ren] being kept under house arrest [sic], by which time I could barely recognize him. His hair was very long, and illness had suffused his face. At first glance, he resembled a woman in the throes of labor. And he, no doubt to protect me, pretended not to know who I was. When he had gone, I asked a nearby woodcutter, and discovered that the locals knew him as Mr. Melancholy. With that, I could be certain that this was Shang-Jên. I hurried back to my lodgings, and after dealing with some necessary matters, I returned to Paipei. The name of this town has many meanings in Chinese. "Pai" means white, but it can also connote purity, or stark-ness, or even waste. "Pei" is similarly complex, and may be pronounced pei, p'i, or p'o. It refers to a shore, or a lake, or a river bank, or a slope, or a dangerous route!

Because I knew that Shang-Jên had suffered from lung disease in his youth, I made sure to come prepared with penicillin. A colleague from the Red Cross was close to Alexander Fleming [who invented penicillin in 1928 and won the Nobel Prize in 1945], so he was able to obtain what he called this miracle drug for us. I prayed that it could cure Shang-Jên. And now I can say I was prepared for the worst. He had been away from our Lord for too long, and if he was beyond cure, I would only be able to pray for him.

Through an old acquaintance from Hangchow [N.B. evidently Ah Qing], I was finally able to see Shang-Jên and give him a full examination. His main illness was still in his lungs. In China, patients with lung disease have a slim chance of survival, but Shang-Jên was in better condition than I expected. As everyone knows, tuberculosis is also known as "consump-tion": as the blood thins, what follows is the consumption and decay of the body. Yet even though Shang-Jên was in the final, desperate stages of the illness, he refused to bow under its weight. Quite the opposite: he was more elegant, more dignified, even more spirited than ever. Consumption might have left his body as thin as a book, as weightless as a butterfly, but he remained full of life, putting one in mind of faintly veined flowers blos-soming by a spring: translucent, graceful, crimson. I believed that with careful nursing, he would make a full recovery.

I remember that not long before I left Paipei, Dr. Bai arrived. He used to sweep the courtyard of our church in Ch'ing-Kêng. Later on, he studied medicine in Peking and Russia. He agreed with my diagnosis of Shang-Jên, and reckoned that if Shang-Jên were to take Chinese medicine while also accepting western treatment, he would recover more quickly. I remember him writing out a prescription with the names of several Chinese herbs: winter asparagus, fountainplant, peony root, lily, raw foxglove, ladybell root, glutinous rice stem, almond, wolfberry bark. There were dozens of them. I don't remember the rest now, but there was one I will never for-get: fox excrement. It had to come from a male fox, and was to be burned to ash, then taken with liquor on an empty stomach . . .

This passage seems to make one thing clear: before Fan Jihuai arrived, Ge Ren was weak from his illness, but he would certainly have had no problem riding a horse.

Yang Fengliang's Death

What's your rush? I'll just have a cigarette to perk me up, then I'll continue. I brought Bai Shengtao out of the elementary school just as the guard returned with the soap, in an outrageous state: his face was streaked with blood, and one of his gold teeth was loose. He was babbling wildly, and I had to listen a long time before I was able to understand what had happened. It turned out that Yang Fengliang's men had also gone to Zhou Papi's home to help themselves to stuff, not just soap, but chickens. They happened to run into each other, and started fighting. I asked, Did they ask you what you wanted with the soap? He said, I told them everything they needed to know, but they wouldn't let go. I raised my revolutionary awareness, and asked if he had told them everything. He said he'd told them the soap was for General Zhao. They asked what General Zhao wanted with soap. He said I wanted it to give that schoolteacher, Mr. Melancholy. Then they asked, Why does Mr. Melancholy need soap? So he told the honest truth, which was that Mr. Melancholy was going on a long journey and wished to clean his clothes first. My heart went thud, and I thought, time for this idiot to die.

I said to him, They went too far. You can't beat a dog without considering who its owner is. Go back with me, point out who beat you up, and I'll take revenge for you. He immediately kowtowed to me. I told him to go ahead, and he ran as fast as a hare. As I hurried behind him, I tripped over something: a wooden pole, meant for propping the door shut. It was neither too thick nor too thin—perfect for my needs. We were almost at the spot where he'd been beaten up when I said, Hey, you need to suffer a bit more. You only lost one gold tooth—that doesn't seem like enough. You ought to bleed a little more; that way I can haul those bastards out and deal with them army-style. He thought I was going to knock out a front tooth, and obediently stood there with his mouth open and his eyes shut. He said, "Ready!" I repeated, "Ready," took aim at his skull, and brought the stick down hard. Chairman Mao teaches us that to suppress anti-revolutionaries, we have to take steady aim and beat them firmly. And that's what I did. It was perfect—without making another sound, he went off to meet his maker.

Ha, great minds really do think alike. With that done, I went to see Yang Fengliang. I wanted to tell him that his subordinates had killed someone. Bai Shengtao refused to go with me. I glared at him: What? You don't want to come? Too bad, you're coming anyway. No one gets to choose what they do for the Revolution. There was nothing he could say to that. As I said earlier, Yang Fengliang and his little whore were living in the Bodhi Temple. Even as I was causing murder and mayhem on the way there, the lovebirds were nesting together in the temple. I called him out and said, This is bad, something's happened. He said, What's happened? Has someone else come from Chongqing? I said, No, not that. One of your men killed one of my men, and my guys are now preparing to make trouble. I calmed them down, then hurried over to ask you what we should do next. He gasped and asked, Who did this? Who would be so bold as to go against General Zhao? Then he spotted Bai Shengtao standing next to me and asked, This is . . . ? I didn't want to say too much, just that this was a doctor I had asked to come there to treat the poor bastard who'd been beaten up. I told Yang Fengliang that we needed to get something clear between us: since this matter had already gotten out, we would have to sort it out as best we could, and not let it get any bigger. If word reached the higher-ups, this would end badly for all of us. And also, seeing as I worked for Military Intelligence and was connected to those in the higher echelons, I knew that the dead man was named Wu, and he was a hometown friend of Butterfly Wu, who happened to be Dai Li's former lover. Our friend Wu was just paying his dues in the lower ranks, and would surely have climbed to the top sooner or later. And now look, the Revolution hadn't succeeded yet, and he was already dead, just like that. If this were to be investigated, we would both have more on our plates than either of us could deal with.

The dogfucker got scared. He'd been fastening his belt, and now his hands relaxed so that his pants slid over his ankles. He asked what he should do. I crinkled my brow, thought a bit, and told the dogfucker, I don't have time to discuss this with you. I've already run it through my mind, and here are my three plans. One, we pin this on Ge Ren and say he tried to escape, and when one of my men tried to stop him, Ge Ren whacked him and killed him. That's a good enough explanation for Boss Dai, and maybe he'll even declare the guy a martyr, to honor his ancestors. Yang Fengliang exclaimed, That's fantastic. I said, Sure, fantastic is as fantastic does, but everyone knows Ge Ren is a born scholar, and what's more, he's so ill there's barely enough strength in his hands to restrain a chicken. He couldn't hit a man that hard. Besides, if the higher-ups were to think Ge Ren almost managed to escape, that wouldn't look good for any of us. He said, That's right, that's right. I said, Plan two, we say this guy was trying to steal something from someone's house, and when the People found him, they beat him to death. The advantage here is, we'd just need to drag that villager out and shoot him, and everyone would be happy. The problem, though, is we'd need to be thorough in our killing, plucking the weeds out roots and all, by which I mean wipe out the entire clan, just to make sure there's no repercussions. He said, Well, that's worth considering, and asked me for the third plan. I said, Number three, you bring your guy who caused this problem to me, and I'll deal with him. He looked down and thought about this a while, then asked, How will you deal with him? I said, Don't worry, General, I just want to lock him up so my guys can see that I've done something. Then I'll make sure he has a chance to escape. I emphasized that only he and I, and heaven and earth, knew about this, so he'd better not breathe a word of it to a single soul. My detailed plans seemed to boggle his mind, and just like that, he was on the hook. Hitching up his pants, he went to find his guy, saying I didn't need to worry, he'd go grab him and bring him back there.

In the time it took to smoke a cigarette, Yang Fengliang showed up with the unlucky bastard. The guy had a high forehead and sunken eyes, a total baby face. He was on a rampage, screaming, Dang it! Who's looking for me, who's disturbing my sleep? I could detect a Sichuan accent, so I used a local insult on him: Hey, son of a turtle, I'm looking for you. I grabbed his hand and said, I want to ask you about something. You can go back to sleep afterward. What's your name? He said his name was Qiu. I didn't hear it clearly, and thought he'd said something about chewing. What name did you say? He changed his answer and said he was Fan. Fuck it, Qiu one minute, Fan the next. I was losing my temper. Hey, your name! When I shouted, he went back to Qiu, as in Qiu Shaoyun [N.B. a heroic volunteer soldier who died in the Korean War; the comparison is in Ah Qing's words]. He really did say that, I'm not bluffing. He said he was called Qiu Aihua. We were walking along as we talked, and by leading him this way and that, I managed to get him to the place where it happened. When I shone my flashlight on him, it seemed the guy wasn't completely dead; his ass was still twitching. I said to Qiu Aihua, Was it you who beat this guy up? He was still worked up, thrusting his face at me and tensing his neck, bellowing, Dang it! What if I did and what if I didn't? Yang Fengliang was there too, and he said to Qiu Aihua, Take a closer look. Say yes or no, no nonsense now. I ordered Qiu Aihua to look closely. He squatted down, glanced at the guy, and crashed to the ground. Fuck it, a coward after all. The red-gray soup of brains spilling from the guy's head had been enough to make him faint.

I got Bai Shengtao to drag him over to the river. It was deserted there, with trees screening us from view. Yang Fengliang didn't know what I had in mind, and he followed us over. When we got to the water, I had Bai

Shengtao set the Sichuan guy down. Bai knelt down and squinted at him, then said, General, he's out cold. Should we try to bring him around? Yang Fengliang cursed the guy for not being able to take the heat, then bent over to have a closer look himself. What's there to look at, motherfucker, I muttered to myself, then swung into action. I hadn't planned to shoot—a quiet death would have been better—but in order to end this quickly, I put a bullet through him. Don't worry, comrades, as long as there wasn't a second shot, even if someone had heard, they'd have assumed it was a gun-cleaning accident or something like that. So I fed him that bullet, then I stuck a knife in his heart. Next I swung a club over his head, and he fell smack on the ground. Then I kicked him right in the balls. Comrades, have you ever heard a man's balls being completely flattened? It makes a sound, *bam*, like bursting a balloon. And with one final kick, I sent him flying right into White Cloud River. All in all, it was a job well done. As for the Sichuan soldier, I couldn't let him off either. Having offed Yang Fengliang, I turned to see the other guy still lying on the ground, so I stabbed him too. He gurgled in Sichuanese, Dang it, why'd you have to kill me? Then his head drooped, and he too breathed his last.

All right, I'll go on. Now that I'd gotten rid of that pair of dogfuckers, I stepped boldly over the Yalu River. Right, not the Yalu River, it was White Cloud River. As we crossed the bridge, Bai Shengtao asked where I was going. I said, To the Bodhi Temple. He said, Don't bother burning incense; we should go save Ge Ren first. Burn incense? What incense? That's just feudal superstition, I snapped, and then lectured him some more, saying it was important to use our remaining forces to go after the retreating enemy, and not be too concerned about our reputation, like a tyrant—or did he want to be like a tyrant and make the rightist mistake of opportunism? He had no response to that, and quietly followed me. Comrades, that night, when I lured Yang Fengliang's lover out of the temple and stabbed her to death, Bai Shengtao was scared witless.

Of course I didn't let the little bastard off the hook, my dear comrades. I mean the little bastard that whore had given Yang Fengliang. Why let him live? So he could counterattack in the future, and dig up the walls of socialism? The revolutionary masses disagree ten thousand times! As I said before, we should go after the fleeing enemy, and not worry too much about our reputation. Rip the weeds out by the roots. The little anti-revolutionary was tender-skinned, like tofu, like cold noodles. I flung him to the ground, then stomped on him, and soon he was a bloody mass. Leave behind evidence? What do you take me for? I tossed them all into the river to feed the fishes.

You're asking what Bai Shengtao was doing all this while? Forget it, he was worse than a fish. Even a fish knows to eat its enemy's flesh and gnaw on his tendons. But Bai couldn't tell enemy from friend. He was clutching my hand, asking if I knew what I was doing. What a stupid question! My head was on my shoulders, and my shoulders were on my body—of course I knew! This was class struggle—defeating some classes, eliminating others, and that's history, that's the history of thousands of years of civilization. When I flung that family of three into the river to feed the fishes, I was creating history. That's a good reminder, you're right: history is created by the People. Of course I acknowledge that. But no matter how you slice it, am I not one of the People? There are two good things about me: the first is that I never mess with that coloratura nonsense, and the second is that I don't rest on my laurels. Of course, if my comrades wish to praise me, and say I worked hard even if I didn't achieve anything, then I won't object. I'm not going to pretend to be humble. How could a revolutionary stand by and do nothing?

After that, I summoned all of Yang Fengliang's subordinates and had a small meeting in the Bodhi Temple. As the saying goes, the Nationalists raise taxes, and the Communists have meetings. Collecting taxes is taking something out of the People's pockets, demanding checks from them, while meetings are placing something in their brains, writing a check to them. So I say let's have more meetings, not more taxes. And during this meeting, I wrote them all a blank check. I said, General Yang is off on a special mission, and he won't be back any time soon. Before he left, he asked me to take care of you guys. So if you need any help from your humble Zhao, I'll do my best and won't let you down. One of his men didn't quite seem to believe me, and asked, Who did General Yang go off with? I had expected this, so I sat down, crossed my legs, lit a cigarette, and slowly said, That's a Party and National secret. I shouldn't say anything, but seeing as we're all on the same side, I'll tell you plainly: General Yang's gone off with Qiu Aihua. They just stared at me at first, and then—comrades, take note—their heels suddenly clicked together, at attention, and their arms shot up in a salute. Fuck it, since bullshit isn't taxable, I decided to go ahead with the blank check, and said, Brothers, you've worked hard on Bare Mountain, and when we get back to the provisional capital, I'm going to reward you all, every single one of you. You can't imagine how thrilled they were to get that blank check. They were bowing to me, clasping their hands, having an absolute field day.

Qiu Aihua

According to Mr. Bodde Sun, when he was talking to Mr. Wang Jiling, the chancellor of Straits Private University, Mr. Wang referred to Qiu Aihua's death as a wrongful one, because the man Ah Qing's subordinates had a grievance with wasn't Qiu Aihua, but Wang Jiling himself. Mr. Wang agreed to be interviewed by me, in his living room full of Ming and Qing Dynasty rosewood furniture. He had been an overseas merchant, and his humble behavior, like his antique furniture, left a deep impression on me. We had an agreement: As long as he was alive, I wouldn't publish a word about our conversation, "and you can do as you like when I'm gone." If I said anything prematurely, he would publicly "quell the rumors" by denying that our interview had ever taken place. As he passed away after a brain hemorrhage in the fall of 2000, I can now publish my interview notes here without breaking our agreement:

> I want to make it clear, first of all, that I personally know nothing about Ge Ren's case. My guiding principle in life is to always be respectful of history, and not rush anything. It's common knowledge that Ge Ren died in the Battle of Two Li Mound, so let's take that as our given circumstance and proceed from there. I don't care to speculate who it was who was imprisoned in Fangkou Elementary School. Hmm? Mr. Sun [Guozhang] says it was Ge Ren? Well, that's his freedom of speech; it has nothing to do with me. Seeing is believing, and I saw nothing, so I can't say either way.
>
> Rabbits hop, and time flies. There are many things I've completely forgotten. Qiu Aihua, though, I can say something about. He did indeed die on my behalf. The person who got into a dispute with General Zhao's subordinate over a bar of soap wasn't Qiu, but your humble servant. I still remember that the man who owned the soap was named Zhou. No, not Zhou Papi, Zhou Qingshu. He was a scholar, and a scholar wouldn't have had such a crude name. I had gone to Mr. Zhou's home to borrow some soap when I ran into General Zhao's man. We got into an argument, and then a fight, with both of us landing some blows. That night, Mr. Yang [Fengliang] asked which of us had gotten into a brawl with Zhao's men. I've never been afraid to take responsibility, so I stepped forward and said it was me. Mr. Yang grinned and said not to worry, it wasn't a big problem. Perhaps because I was young, or because we were from the same town, Mr. Yang let me off the hook, and sent Qiu Aihua to deal with Zhao instead. This Qiu was an impressive-looking specimen, and diplomatic to boot, a natural aristocrat—he was the obvious person for the job. But then we heard nothing from him after he left, which meant he was

probably dead. Later that night, General Zhao came to the Bodhi Temple, where Mr. Yang had been bivouacked, and announced that Mr. Yang and Qiu Aihua had gone away on a mission.

The atmosphere was solemn, and it felt like dark clouds were pressing down on the town. I immediately wondered if both Yang and Qiu were already in the underworld. I couldn't sleep that night, and before dawn I slipped away to Ruijin, and from there to Guangzhou. . . . I have no idea what else happened in this affair, so please don't ask me anything more.

Which version of Qiu Aihua is closer to the truth, Wang Jiling's or Ah Qing's? I can't say for certain, of course. Setting aside Qiu Aihua's appearance, what interests me is why Yang Fengliang would bring out the big guns and hand Qiu Aihua over to Ah Qing. Was it because of his "impressive" appearance and the "diplomatic" skills Wang Jiling referred to, or were there deeper considerations? And why would Ah Qing kill Qiu Aihua in cold blood, for no discernible reason? We'll have to wait for Fan Jihuai's narrative to understand what lies behind these mysteries.

But Ge Ren Didn't Leave

Bai Shengtao was still dazed. As we left the Bodhi Temple, he stumbled along right behind me, asking at every turn whether I was scared. I said, Fuck it, what's there to be scared of? Our great Chairman Mao teaches us that the true materialist has nothing to fear. Then he asked what we should do next, and I told him, Listen up: all the obstacles ahead have been swept aside now, and this is the first step in our long march. Now we can go rescue Comrade Ge Ren.

I led him to Fangkou Elementary School. As we walked into the airwell, the light in Ge Ren's room suddenly went out. No, no, he hadn't gone to sleep. He tricked you there. It was a ruse! He was pretending to be asleep! Why pretend? As if that needs to be said. Firstly, he didn't want me to worry about his health, and secondly, he wanted me to have an early night instead of tiring myself out. That's the sort of person he was, taking care of his comrades with the warmth of springtime. When I thought about this, tears speckled my face. I knew very clearly that as soon as I was gone, he would start burning the midnight oil again, working until magpies were cawing in the branches. But Bai Shengtao, that moron, misunderstood Ge Ren's meaning. He said Ge Ren must have done that to show that he didn't want to be disturbed, and we should go to bed ourselves.

Sleep? To think he could suggest that. How could we sleep at this crucial moment in the Revolution? I said to Bai Shengtao that the moon was bright, the stars were few, and the magpies were flying south, so this was the perfect night to make the transfer. There would be no more stops if we missed this one. I added, When we go in, you have to persuade him to leave with us.

As I expected, after a while, Ge Ren lit his lamp again. I went in and told him what had happened with Yang Fengliang. When I got to [throwing Yang into the river and] feeding the fishes, he laughed and said, I'm never eating fish again. You see, comrades, how he was even able to joke at a time like that. What does this tell us? It tells us that the fierce optimism of revolution was in him at all times. I said to Ge Ren, The tigers have been vanquished, and the road is clear for you and Bai Shengtao to leave. I'll send someone to make sure you get away from Bare Mountain safely. He repeated his concern that this would cause problems for me, and I said once again that he shouldn't worry—when those people came back from their task, I would eliminate them too. And if the higher-ups asked, I'd just shift all the blame onto Yang Fengliang. It's not like he was in a position to defend himself. Ge Ren turned to Bai Shengtao and asked, Where are you taking me? Bai Shengtao said, As long as we get away from Bare Mountain, anything is possible. Someone will meet us and take charge from there. Ge Ren smiled and said, I'm not going anywhere—this place suits me just fine. Then, still smiling, he said something astonishing: If you insist on my leaving, that's easy; just beat me to death, and you can carry me anywhere you like. He said to Bai Shengtao, You should go alone, as far away as you can. As soon as the words had left his mouth, Bai Shengtao fell to his knees, sobbing furiously, saying that he wanted to live or die with Ge Ren.

As I said before, I hadn't seen what Bai Shengtao was really made of—I was taken in by him. Later on, when the facade was torn away, I understood how I had been fooled by him. But you can't say I wasn't suspicious at all—that would be to underestimate me. At the time, I thought, look at you now, you think you're fit to die with Ge Ren? Comrade Ge Ren lived nobly and will die gloriously, but you, your death won't be worth a dick. After Bai Shengtao had been weeping a while, I said, Go cry somewhere else. We should let Comrade Ge Ren get some rest. I had to drag him to his feet to make him leave.

It was deep in the night by then. I wanted to talk it over with him, to see what our next move should be. We went back and forth, and before we knew it, the sky in the east was turning the color of a fish belly. I felt our chance slipping away. Why hadn't Ge Ren been willing to leave? Was he afraid it would be too tiring? But how could that be true? Revolutionaries aren't afraid to die, so why would tiredness bother him? Bai

Shengtao asked me the same question: Why wouldn't Ge Ren leave? I pondered this for some time, then counted off the reasons on my fingers. Firstly, Ge Ren was thinking of me—if I let him go, I wouldn't be able to continue in Military Intelligence, which would be a great loss to the Party. Secondly, he wanted to make the most of his remaining time to sum up his revolutionary experience in writing. Bai Shengtao seemed happy with my reasoning. I said to him, We don't have much time left. Don't worry about anything else; just get Ge Ren out of here now, as far away as you can, and I'll deal with the rest. But do you know what he said to me? He said this would need to be discussed with Ge Ren, and if Ge Ren wasn't willing to leave, there was nothing he could do.

I was so angry, I thought my lungs would explode. I said, Why did Comrade Tian Han send you here? Wasn't it to rescue Ge Ren? But at the crucial moment, you lost your nerve and pushed your responsibility onto Ge Ren. What were you trying to do? My criticism left him bloodied all over, unable to defend himself. Later, when he surrendered to Fan Jihuai, I finally understood that this dogfucker was concealing a wolf's heart, and he'd simply been buying himself more time.

Sincere Loathing

I've always suspected that Ah Qing was deliberately portraying Bai Shengtao as a clown, just as he'd done with Zong Bu. So what did he really think of Bai Shengtao? To understand this, I had to turn once again to Yu Fenggao's son, Yu Liren. Naturally, this information came at a price: for every document he showed me, I had to induce another person to join the Huawei Consumer Alliance, which meant buying a set (four boxes) of Alaskan seal oil for 1,600 yuan, plus paying another 100 yuan registration fee for a membership card. These were exquisitely designed, much nicer than a Party membership, a PhD scroll, or a bank book. Anyone you recruited then worked under you, and was known in the business as a "downline distributor." The consumer alliance used a "two-way system," by which you accumulated points through a computer ranking. How this worked in practice was, let's say you got a couple of people to be downline of you. Those two would each buy a set of Alaskan seal oil, and you would get 1,000 points. The two you recruited would then bring in more people, in the shape of a pyramid. The more people you had downline, the more points you'd get. When you hit 10,000 points, you got a 2,000 yuan bonus, and at 50,000 points there was a 11,000 yuan reward. None of my friends showed any interest in this scheme, so I had no choice but to put up the money myself, joining over and over again, using the name of a different relative each time. Let's put it this way: by the time I was done, Bingying, Zong Bu, and Hu An were all members of this multi-level marketing company. And each time I showed Yu Liren a new membership card, he'd let me read a few more of Ah Qing's words. When I had seen everything he had to say about Bai Shengtao, I realized that the truth was different than I'd imagined.

The following passage was written, as before, on notepaper, with another Chairman Mao quote printed across the top: "Army training should be a group activity, with soldiers teaching their instructors, instructors teaching their soldiers, and soldiers learning from each other."

> The investigation team didn't seem to be paying much attention to Bai [Shengtao]. I was the one who brought them to his attention. Out of all the people in the world, the person I hate most after Liu Shaoqi is Bai. Liu Shaoqi and his capitalist headquarters have been purged by Chairman Mao. An excellent purge, thoroughly deserved. So Bai's the only one left whom I hate. Chairman Mao said, Rain falls on the ancient Yan Kingdom, waves rise to the sky, and beyond Qinhuangdao is a fishing boat—the ocean stretches endlessly, and who can see the shore? True, I once placed all my hopes on Bai, hoping he would take Ge Ren away, but he was more womanly than a woman, dragging the whole business out. Of course, I have to admit that I was weak too. If I'd sent Fan [Jihuai] a telegram saying the prisoner was not Ge Ren, then he wouldn't have come, and Ge Ren wouldn't have died so terribly. But I was in a dilemma. I was following Dou [Sizhong]'s order to stay put and wait for instructions. I can't predict the future, so I didn't know that Bai would surrender. Bai Shengtao, ah, Bai Shengtao, fuck your ancestors eighteen generations back—you got me into real trouble.

It would seem that Ah Qing's loathing of Bai Shengtao couldn't have been any more sincere. I should mention here that Miss Bai Ling has also seen this passage, but it didn't anger her. Her reasoning was simple: Ah Qing wanted to "fuck" Bai Shengtao's "ancestors eighteen generations back," and not his descendants, so whether or not he did "fuck" them, it had nothing to do with her.

The Horse's Reins

I had to talk till my lips were worn thin before Bai Shengtao finally agreed to take Ge Ren away. It was dawn by then. Ge Ren had worked through the night and had now gone to bed. Bai Shengtao said, Let him sleep. We'll leave when it gets dark again. Pah, he was kicking the can as far down the road as it would go. I went to see Ge Ren in the afternoon, when he was up again. I told him about making the move. He listened till I was done, then said he wanted to go for a walk in Phoenix Valley. I thought he must want to take this opportunity to say goodbye to the hills and rivers around there. So I told a trusted subordinate, Go for a walk with Code Zero. This guy was even more loyal than a dog. If I'd said I had seen a rooster lay an egg, he'd have backed me up and said he saw it too. Next, I said to Bai Shengtao, Don't just sit around. Go pack up Ge Ren's things—you're leaving as soon as it gets dark.

Is it all right if I say that?

When all the preparations were made, I went out on horseback to Phoenix Valley. It looked like spring was on its way, and azaleas were blooming everywhere, especially in the valley. Ge Ren was sitting on a rock, smoking. When he saw me approach, his spirits rose, and he recited a little of Chairman Mao's poem "Ascending Jinggang Mountain Again." He did, I'm not bluffing. After a while, Bai Shengtao showed up too. He hypocritically told Ge Ren that he should stop smoking, that smoking was bad for him. Ge Ren spoke only to me, ignoring Bai. He said he had a request: he could do without anything else, but he needed cigarettes and wine. I smacked my chest and told him not to worry. I swore to Chairman Mao that I would keep him supplied with booze and fags.

It was almost dark when I took Ge Ren back to the elementary school. Dinner was already laid out on the table—I had arranged it beforehand. You're right, dinner included tofu, of course. Ge Ren would only drink; he didn't touch the food. I urged him to eat something, and he said alcohol was made of grain, in fact it was the essence of grain, so drinking was the same as eating. He invited me to join him for a couple of drinks and a chat. Many years ago, before he left for Japan, he and I had a drinking session like this in Shanghai, carousing with Red Daughter rice wine. This time, nothing went past my lips. I was a better drinker now, but I didn't want to encourage him, because he had a long journey ahead. In the airwell, I gave my seat to Ge Ren. It was a chair I had sent someone to seize from the nearby Xiguan Village post office, which they obediently did. Afterward, I murmured to Bai Shengtao, See you in Yan'an! How did he respond? What else could he say? He just whispered back, See you in Yan'an.

I told them to leave quickly. My aide hefted Ge Ren's luggage onto his shoulder. I handed the horse's reins to Ge Ren. He stared at them, then said he didn't want to ride; he wouldn't get anywhere like that. Then he handed the reins to Bai Shengtao. His actions were actually very Communistic, to suffer first and enjoy later. He would allow someone else to ride while he himself walked. But Bai Shengtao took those words and twisted them completely around. He said to me, Code Zero really can't ride. Could we get him a sedan chair? Fuck you, why didn't you say something earlier? You're a doctor—aren't you supposed to think of these things? Now that the shit is almost out your asshole, you want to dig a toilet. Isn't it too late? I was so angry, my nose was twisted out of shape. Then Bai Shengtao said there were clouds in the sky—what if it rained and Code Zero got a chill? How would he explain that to Comrade Tian Han? What else could I do? I took Ge Ren back inside.

I didn't sleep a wink that night. What was I doing? Watching as they built a sedan chair. I sent my guys out for a couple of carpenters, and we worked all night long. We didn't have any wood, so we were going to have to rip it out of a building—but that might have attracted attention. I was scared to death. Then I remembered there were a few trees behind the tea house, and sent someone to cut them down. The guy said to me, There are paulownia trees, locust trees, and bodhi trees. Which do you want? I was so anxious, I just screamed, Motherfucker, cut down whichever tree you like! He said, The bodhi tree, then. I asked why, and he said it was a holy tree and might bring good fortune, so the gods would protect Code Zero on his journey. What? Is this idealism? I have no idea, but it has nothing to do with me; I wasn't the one who said those words. All right, I'll continue. We finally finished the sedan just before dawn. In order to make sure no word got out, I told my men to kill the two carpenters and toss their bodies down the well in the back courtyard. Then my men carried the sedan to the elementary school. When we were almost there, we saw that the whole area was thick with guards. The earth and heavens shook, and the gods wept. I felt my brain throbbing. It's too late, I thought. Fan Jihuai is here, and now Ge Ren will never get away.

I was clear-minded in my panic, and quickly told my subordinates to go back. Along the way, I killed those two guys and threw them into the river to feed the fishes. I swear to Chairman Mao, at that moment I wasn't soft at all. After throwing those bastards into White Cloud River, I returned to the elementary school. The sun had fully risen, just like it is now. At the school gate, I saw Bai Shengtao bowing and scraping to Fan Jihuai. My eyes blazed red, and I was about to shoot him, but Ge Ren came out and stopped me. I understood what he meant: he was prepared to sacrifice himself. He would rather have given up his own life than expose my identity and destroy our underground network.

That's all I have to say, comrades. I don't wish to say any more, and there isn't anything left, anyway. For the sake of revolution, Ge Ren gloriously sacrificed himself on Bare Mountain. For many years after that, whenever I thought about it, my heart felt as if it were being sliced apart. [N.B. At this point, Comrade Yu Fenggao noted that "Ah Qing wept, as if for his dead parents."] Still, there are some things I have to mention. Before Ge Ren sacrificed himself, I didn't reveal my identity. I remember very clearly that when Fan Jihuai arrived, he wanted me and Yang Fengliang to make our reports. As you know, singing coloratura in front of a cunning enemy like this, if I'd made one slip-up, it could have brought the Party a lot of trouble. But I remained calm, didn't change my expression, and in a few sentences I had Fan Jihuai perfectly satisfied. I said to him, General, Yang Fengliang was going rogue here, making all kinds of mischief—he beat my telegraph operator to death, then my subordinate, and even his own man Qiu Aihua. I couldn't stand to see him behave like that, so I dispatched this worm on behalf of Party and Nation. And you know, Fan Jihuai really had no alternative but to believe me. You comrades are laughing, but that's a fact. And the last thing I want to say is, one person can only do so much, and even though I didn't manage to save Ge Ren, I did everything I could, and I will die with no regrets . . .

Ah Qing's Death

That's the whole of Ah Qing's narration. According to Comrade Yu Fenggao, on the morning of May 4, 1970, when the tea plantation captain summoned them to breakfast, Ah Qing tried to follow them to the canteen "to cadge one last meal out of us, but no one paid any attention to him." Comrade Yu added that two days after that, he was sent to the tea plantation again, with two tasks for the captain: to keep a strict eye on Ah Qing's movements, and to get some of the better-behaved detainees to write statements against him. Before those could be collected, though, Ah Qing was dead. According to Mr. Zhang Yongsheng, the retired professor who was undergoing labor reform alongside him, right before Ah Qing killed himself by jumping down the well, he was muttering about how "he'd let down Ge Ren, and hadn't lived up to Tian Han's sincere hopes for him."

> One day I went to see him, and he started babbling about Ge Ren and Tian Han, which startled me. He was talking as if they'd been in battle together. That's when I realized what a complicated history this guy had. He was very ill at the time, and his stomach was hugely swollen, but we were all sure he was faking. People were writing statements against him, saying he was stealing their food, as well as the pigswill. Actually, it was the people in charge of feeding the pigs who'd been stealing the swill, but all of them are now respectable PhD tutors, and I don't want to mention their names.

Before he died, his [Ah Qing's] belly swelled even more, as if he were pregnant with twins. They say this is called ascites, or fluid in the abdomen. Sufferers are normally in agony, but not Ah Qing. He seemed perfectly happy. As the CCTV commentator Bai Yansong says, this was "pain coexisting with happiness." The day before he died, I ran into him in the bathroom. He told me once again that he'd let Ge Ren down and failed to live up to Tian Han's sincere hopes for him. He also brought up someone called Fan Jihuai, though I can't remember what he said about him now. I remember the name, though, because I saw it in the papers a lot afterward. And the next day, he was dead—he jumped into a well. By the time they dredged him up, his belly was even bigger. It was a really hot day, and before they could bury him, his stomach exploded, with a bang like a car tire bursting. I won't continue; otherwise I won't be able to eat my dinner. At the time, I had the best calligraphy in the labor camp, so they got me to do all the banners and so on. After he died, the trees were full of banners, saying pretty much that Zhao Qingyao killed himself to avoid punishment, and death was too good for him. What's that? You're telling me he changed his name? It wasn't "Zhao" as in "Zhaoqing"? Well, that's hilarious. He lost his own name, and then he exploded, and he didn't even leave an intact corpse behind.

I have no way of knowing what it was that Ah Qing said to Zhang Yongsheng about Fan Jihuai the day before his death. But there's one thing we can be sure about—even at the end of his life, Ah Qing hadn't figured out what Fan Jihuai's true intentions were.

PART THREE

Okay, Okay

Time: June 28–29, 2000
Place: En route from Jincheng to Baibei City
Speaker: Mr. Fan Jihuai
Listener: Miss Bai Ling
Transcriber: Miss Bai Ling

Going to Keep a Promise

I was the one who didn't want to fly, miss. I said to our comrades in Baibei City, Save the money, put it toward Hope Elementary School. The train is exhausting, but if that buys an extra pencil for those kids, the flowers of our fatherland, it's worth it. I hope you don't mind suffering along with me, miss? I'll make it worth your while when we get back to Jingcheng. Okay, okay, what did you want to say? I might be living in a second-tier city, but I haven't stepped off the stage of history. My word still carries some weight in Jingcheng.

Train tickets cost more than the plane? The devil take you, there's no getting anything past you. Fine, I'm afraid of flying. Here's a brain teaser: which is worth more, a flatbread or an airplane? We're dialectical materialists, so let's talk dialectical materialism. Flatbread falling from the sky is a good thing, but planes falling from the sky are not. According to the authorities, in our globalized world, a plane falls out of the sky once every thirty-six hours. You can think that, but you're not allowed to say it out loud, so all you can do is pretend you're trying to save money.

Of course, taking the train also makes it easier to talk. Didn't you say you wanted to write about me? Don't think I can't tell—what you most want to know, and what you'll ask about in a roundabout way, is my time with Ge Ren [in Baibei]. Bai Shengtao too? Okay, okay, I'll talk about him. I think of him often—whenever I have trouble crapping, he pops into my mind. He ended up in Hong Kong, and I heard he died a terrible death. Nothing wrong with you young people learning a bit of history. In *Das Kapital*, Marx says that learning history can shorten or reduce the pain of childbirth. It's a shame you haven't had a baby, or you'd know that Marx was telling the truth, and that's the ideological basis of our work.

People used to come all the time, from inside the country and out, old and young, men and women, all wanting to interview me. I sent them all away. One of them said to me, Old Mr. Fan, even if you won't tell us, we all know it was you who killed Ge Ren. There was another one who claimed to be from the Ge Ren Research Center. She spent half a month running around my courtyard like a dog chasing its tail, and in the end I still refused to meet her. Dogs jump the wall when they get desperate; she finally sent me a note saying flames can't be hidden by paper, and I should just tell the truth. But I was brought up on mother's milk, not fear. I had my secretary tell her that of course I would tell the truth, just not to her. It's true that paper won't hide flames—that's an unshakable truth. But I'm sure all anyone knows is scraps of what happened. Bai Shengtao's dead, Zhao Yaoqing's dead, Bingying's dead, Tian Han's dead, everyone who had anything to do with this is dead, and there's just me left, old Mr. Fan. All I have to do is keep my mouth shut tight, and this bit of history will end up in paradise with me.

But I'm going to tell you now. As you can see, my body's sturdy enough, but any day now, an invitation from Marx might be slipped under the door. As I said to you before we set off, my purpose [on this trip] is to take part in a celebration, and to cut the ribbon for [the opening of] Hope Elementary School. But I'm actually on my way to Ge Ren. I'm going to keep a promise. Many years ago, I said to Ge Ren's grave, Goodbye, friend. I'll see you again in Phoenix Valley, I swear. And now I'm going to keep that promise. I want to see Phoenix Valley one more time, walk around, burn some incense, bow to him. Time flashed by like a white pony galloping past a crack in the door, and half a century's gone just like that. Your luck is good—if you'd missed this chance, even if you had wanted to hear it, I wouldn't have had the heart to speak. Birds chirp sadly before they die, and men speak kindly before they pass. I'm telling the truth, a great truth. I have a responsibility to history, and I want to pass it on to those who come after me.

But I want to add one thing. It's best if you don't let anyone know what I'm about to tell you. Okay, okay? You know Hu Shih? He had a famous quote: If we hadn't taken care of our own plumage, would we still be allowed to speak today? So this thing [you're writing], don't publish it until after I'm dead, okay, okay? When I'm gone, you can do what you like to me, and I won't care. The sky could fall down, and it wouldn't have anything to do with me. Is that contradictory? That's fine; everything is about unity and opposites.

A Brief Explanation

I spent many years trying to persuade old Mr. Fan to let me interview him, and though I used every tactic at my disposal, I never got my wish. His secretary always told me that Mr. Fan was China's leading legal scholar, and his time was scheduled well into the twenty-first century, so I would just have to wait. I visited his home on many occasions, but was always sent away. Now you know, the person he describes as "running around my courtyard like a dog chasing its tail" was me.

At the start of May 2000, I was visiting Baibei when I happened to find out that old Mr. Fan would soon be coming to that town. In the preceding years, Baibei had grown dramatically. In 1983 it was designated a county, and in 1997 it was upgraded again to a city. And now the local government was preparing to welcome Mr. Fan Jihuai to join them in celebrating the third-year anniversary of their city status, as well as to cut the ribbon for an elementary school. He was afraid of flying, so I was sure he would either not turn up or else come on the train. I rushed overnight to Jingcheng and arranged to meet Miss Bai Ling. She then accompanied old Mr. Fan to Baibei, and recorded their conversation. As I mentioned before, Bai Ling was Bai Shengtao's granddaughter, and she was in Jingcheng for her studies. I had shown her Bai Shengtao's narrative, and she was excited to learn what her grandfather had been up to. She got to know Fan Jihuai through his granddaughter Fan Ye, and formed an "intergenerational" friendship with him. Of course, I can't say whether her youthful good looks played any part in that. Bai Ling claiming she wanted to write an article about him was a story we'd concocted beforehand—and thank heavens he seemed to buy it.

Bai Ling phoned me when she got back from Bare Mountain and crowed, "It's done! I have what you asked for. Hand over the cash and it's yours." I had agreed that if she could get this "interview," I would pay her school fees for the next year, as well as give her a contributor's fee when the book was published. There were some unexpected problems transcribing the tapes, so I had to get Bai Ling to help me again. When we were done, we still needed a title for this section, and she said, "Let's call it 'Okay, Okay'—that was his catchphrase." I just wanted to make clear that everything here, from the title to the text, is the result of Bai Ling's hard work. I'm very grateful to her—if it weren't for her help, this piece of history might well, as old Mr. Fan said, have gone to paradise with him.

Forgetting the Past Is a Betrayal

I'm going to see Ge Ren. Hope Elementary School, where I'm due to cut the ribbon, is connected with him too. This school was built by a Japanese man named Kawai. He's the boss of a turtle-style corporation. That's like a joint stock corporation, but it's a collaboration between a Japanese and an American company. He'll be there too. The Japanese are really pig-headed. To start with, he insisted on calling it "Ge Ren Elementary School." I told him that if the words "Ge Ren" appeared, then I wouldn't be cutting any ribbons. He kept asking why, why? There's no point in trying to explain Chinese politics to an outsider, so okay, okay, I decided to make something up. I told him that Ge Ren came to me in a dream and told me so. With that answer, the devil could only retreat.

I knew what Kawai had in mind: simply a memorial to Ge Ren. Many years ago, when I was studying in Japan with Ge Ren, we lived with him for a while. This was when we'd just gotten to Tokyo, and we were taking Japanese lessons at East Asia High End Preparatory School. The school didn't have enough dorm beds, so we ended up staying with his family. Another Chinese student stayed there too, by the name of Huang Yan. Later on, he started a newspaper in Yan'an. He's settled in America now, under cover of "visiting relatives." Really, this guy was a revolutionary his whole life, and now that he's old, he's given himself to capitalism. I'm the opposite: I've spent half my life in a capitalist country, and now that I'm old, I've come back to the embrace of socialism. The two of us have been on completely different tracks.

Okay, okay, never mind that useless bastard; we won't say any more about him. Back to Kawai. Japan's a little country, but there was nothing little about his family. His brother Kawata was five or six years older than me and Ge Ren, while Kawai was five or six years younger than us. Their house had a little attic that we lived in, and when you opened the window, you could see the broad bean blossoms in the courtyard. Kawai and Kawata's mother had been a beauty in her youth, and she was still a striking woman. When she walked around the courtyard in her wooden clogs, it sounded like she was playing a percussion instrument. She liked Chinese culture, and got her children to learn our writing. Kawai's sister was named Noriko. She was only six or seven years old, as pale-skinned as a little porcelain figure. We all got along well and formed deep friendships—striking a blow for Sino-Japanese relations. Many Chinese people had been to this courtyard, none more famous than Chen Duxiu, who once asked Kawai how the broad bean harvest was in the courtyard. Kawai said this variety of broad bean wasn't for eating; it was a sort of medicine— you steeped the flowers in water to treat high blood pressure. His mother suffered from that complaint, and drinking the broad bean water had been effective. Before coming to Japan, I knew that broad beans were good for digestion and internal organs, but I had no idea the blossoms had a medicinal use too. There's knowledge to be acquired everywhere.

Speaking of which, it was because of Kawai's brother Kawata that I later switched to studying law. When I first arrived, I was a medical student— eight or nine out of every ten people who went to Japan wanted to be doctors. My father and grandfather had been traditional doctors, so for me to take up medicine was the natural thing to do. But then Kawata said to me, Being a doctor is the worst thing. All the people you see every day are defective in some way. If you became a dentist, then people would always be turning their deformed mouths in your direction. If you were a bone specialist, then you'd have to deal with missing arms and broken legs all day long. And if you were a gynecologist, that would be it for you; you'd be busy all day long between a woman's legs. Don't laugh, miss, I'm just telling it like it is. He really did say that. So you tell me, he said, what's the point of a job like that? This was a bucket of cold water over my head—I felt like I didn't know which direction was up. I went to ask Ge Ren what he thought, but he said the same as Kawata. Being born into a profession means you're three-tenths of the way there, he said. You already have quite a bit of medical knowledge, so why not learn something new? China needs legal minds, so go study law. I thought, okay, okay! I would help organize this country, and then when it opened up and liberalized, they would need lawyers for that. So I transferred to law, and as for Ge Ren, he went on with medicine, and wrote in his spare time. What did he write? Poems. He liked poetry. There was one he wrote at the time, "Broad Bean Blossoms," about the flowers in the courtyard. During the May Fourth Movement, he rewrote it and changed the title to "Who Was Once Me." You're always you, so I don't know why he was talking about someone else being him, but I suppose it's that awkwardness that makes me remember it.

Kawata had been a student of Mr. Fujino's and was now working in a hospital in Tokyo, but he was the restless sort who could never stay put, and he was always coming over to have fun with us. He was a gourmand and liked to take us to restaurants. Our favorite was a place called Ki Shiryo, in Hirakawachō in Kōjimachi, Tokyo. Chen often came along too, and so did Kawai. Kids are always eager to join a crowd; they always want to go wherever you're going. The tofu in this place was pretty good, and Ge Ren particularly enjoyed it. One time, Ge Ren, Chen Duxiu, Kawai, Kawata, and I took a picture there. Word got around after that, and quite a few Chinese students started eating there too.

Southern Chen and Northern Li

Continuing from what old Mr. Fan was saying, I should add a little about Ge Ren's life in Japan. According to A History of the East Asian Preparatory School (1957), there were more than 4,000 Chinese students in Japan at the time, 360 of them at the preparatory school alone. As a result, it was fairly common for students to seek lodging outside the school premises. In Huang Yan's Dreaming

Back a Hundred Years, he described their living conditions, and also talked about the photograph that old Mr. Fan mentioned:

> Of Kawata's household, it was his younger brother and sister who left the deepest impression on me. The sister was just a little girl then, and would run around the house barefoot, in a world of her own. We were all used to women having bound feet, and even if they didn't, they rarely went without shoes. Ge Ren said natural women's feet made him think of glutinous rice cake: fine, tender, and sweetly fragrant. I remember Ge Ren reciting to us from "Beautiful Jiangnan": "Cotton jacket, silk skirt, pale green kerchief, silver ring, jade hairpin, hair ornament aslant. And she moves like smoke." Also moving like smoke was Kawata's mother. When she walked across the stone slabs of the courtyard in her wooden clogs, the clacking sound was like the brisk ticking of a clock. Listening to that made me feel as if I'd traveled back to China's distant past. Peeping through the gaps between the broad bean blossoms trailing over the railings, I could see kanji on a nearby building that reinforced this impression. I also remember that she wore a pale blue kimono with a design on it said to be inspired by a celestial landscape.
>
> There was a period when we were obsessed with photography. One of Kawata's patients' families had a camera. This patient was devoted to Kawata, and taught him to take pictures. I remember that many of these pictures had Chen Duxiu in them. He enjoyed being photographed. We first met Chen Duxiu in Takada Village, near Tokyo, together with Li Dazhao. Sadly, I secretly burned those photographs. When I was in Yan'an, whenever anyone asked me if I'd had any contact with Chen Duxiu in Japan, I would just shake my head—I didn't dare admit it.

Takada is a small village in the suburbs of Tokyo. Ge Ren found out from his father's friend, Mr. Xu Yusheng, that his father had visited this place while on the run in Japan—so when he got there, Ge Ren found the time to make the trip himself, a sort of remembrance of his father. He once told my great-aunt what he saw there: the houses were simple and very rundown, and there was a small hill by the village with an ancient temple on the other side. From its crumbling eaves would come the occasional chirps of songbirds. Those birds flew there from the willow and black locust trees that grew by the side of the lake, which lay beyond the collapsed rear wall of the temple courtyard. The willow trees had turned green, but the branches of the locust were still black, just like the charcoal sticks I drew with as a child. A local told him that a Chinese man once lived there with a woman. He imagined this Chinese man might have been his father, and the woman Lin Xinyi. He walked around outside the village, imagining his father's life on the run, searching for some trace of him. On this day, he saw a dilapidated hut by the hill with a few Chinese words on its doorframe: Moonlight Villa. His mind rapidly wondered whether his father could have written that. But then he saw a man with an upturned mustache. This was Li Dazhao, and the person having a loud conversation with him from inside the house was Chen Duxiu, who would later have such a great influence on Chinese history. In trying to find traces of his father, Ge Ren had stumbled upon "Southern Chen and Northern Li," who would later set up the New Culture Movement.

Later, Huang Yan, Kawata, and Fan Jihuai also went to visit Moonlight Villa. When Huang Yan wrote about this, he mentioned what had happened during their trip to the Kamo River in Kyoto:

Li Dazhao had a crewcut, which made his forehead look huge, and he was always pursing his lips. Chen Duxiu looked like a poet, with a resonant voice and a habit of using his hands when he talked. Watching his hands dance through the air, you could imagine that they held an invisible knife. When Chen Duxiu asked us about Yin Jifu, we immediately thought of the man who'd drowned himself after jumping from the *Ta Chang Maru*. Ge Ren said he had kept one of Yin's candy wrappers with his poems on them. He had a good memory, and was able to recite some of these for Chen Zhongfu [Duxiu]. Chen burst into tears. As I said earlier, it was from Chen that we found out Yin Jifu had been an editor at the East Asia Library in Shanghai, and had been coming to Japan to discuss a magazine. And again I thought of Yin's suppurating wound, and how he'd touch his wound and hum, which sent a pang through my heart.

I remember Ge Ren talking about his dad. Southern Chen and Northern Li both lost their fathers at the age of two, and Li lost his mother as well when he was three. Ge Ren had a similar experience—he never saw his father as a child, and he lost his mom at an early age. All being parentless, they had many problems in common. The following weekend, Chen Duxiu followed the directions Ge Ren had left behind, and found his way to Kawata's house. Ge Ren brought out his "Broad Bean Blossoms" poem, and invited Chen to critique it. After all this time, I can't recall exactly what Chen said about it, but I do know that he started to think of Ge Ren as a literary friend, and they frequently got together to talk about poetry.

Because Ge Ren got along well with them, sometime later he, Kawata, and I accompanied Southern Chen and Northern Li on their excursion to the Kamo River. At the fork with the Takano River [N.B. The Kamo splits into the Kamo and Takano branches], it was warmhearted Ge Ren who first took to the water. Ge Ren once compared Japan to ancient Greece, a different time and place—both cultures had no prohibition against nudity, and were lands of the spirit, worth emulating. I thought he was just saying that, but now he took off his clothes in front of the crowd, like a white sturgeon. When this white sturgeon rose out of the water, I could even see the droplets of water on his genitals. Ge Ren called Kawata to join him, but Kawata couldn't be bothered. He was gathering red spider lilies from the bank, saying he wanted to take them back to the hospital and present them to a particular nurse. Chen Duxiu shoved Kawata into the water, but he quickly scrambled out. Chen plunged into the water himself, like a swooping eagle. This might be mixed with a later impression of mine, but history is made up of all kinds of impressions layered on top of each other. It may be because of all the things that happened subsequently that I saw him as not just an eagle, but also Prometheus, whose liver was eaten by an eagle . . .

I should say here that Ge Ren's interactions with Chen Duxiu took place primarily through letters. They were both concerned with the problem of romanizing the Chinese language, so when Chen finished his manuscript *A Draft Phonetic Alphabet for China* in 1929, he sent a copy to Ge Ren, asking him to correct some of the pronunciations. When Chen Duxiu died of an illness on May 27, 1942, Ge Ren was on the way to Song Village [N.B. present-day Chaoyang Hill] and was naturally unable to receive this news. As a result, we cannot be certain what thoughts Ge Ren had about Chen Duxiu's life. As for his relationship with Li Dazhao, as Ah Qing has said, they were colleagues at the university in Shanghai, and also close friends. After Li Dazhao was hanged on the orders of Zhang Zuolin on April 28, 1927, Ge Ren said in a letter to my great-aunt, "Shouchang [N.B. Li Dazhao's formal name] has passed away, and I am devastated. He was the Jesus of China, because he too died on a wooden rack. Our country was merciful, in that no nails were put through his hands and feet. I met Shouchang in Takada Village, while searching for traces of my father, and since then have treated him like a brother. I heard that when he died, his tongue was hanging out. But the spectators didn't care what he wanted to say, they were only interested in the ashes that landed on it." From these words, we can see Ge Ren's deep affection for Li Dazhao.

Forgetting the Past Is a Betrayal (continued)

Because I switched from medicine to law, I spent the longest time in Japan of my cohort. After coming back, I stayed in Shanghai representing people in court. Not long after that, I heard that Kawata was in China too, teaching at the Beijing Academy of Medicine, and Ge Ren was there as well. Around the time of May the Fourth, I went to Beijing to see them, and of course to take part in this patriotic movement. I didn't get to see Ge Ren—he'd been arrested and was locked up in Infantry High Command. I did meet Kawata, though. He enjoyed Beijing's stewed and roasted meats, and had fallen in love with Chinese stinky tofu. I said, Soon you'll turn into a housefly; you like foul-smelling things. I invited him out to moshi moshi a few times, and each time we finished eating, he'd wipe his mouth and exclaim, Yoshi yoshi. I asked about Kawai, and he told me his brother was at the Tokyo Business School, where they offered Chinese lessons, so he could now chatter away in Chinese, his accent as slurry as any Beijinger's.

Soon I heard that Kawata had quit his job. He had a pointy ass, and couldn't sit still anywhere for long. Many years passed without news from him. During the war of resistance against Japan, I heard that he was back in China. Miss, didn't you say you knew a bit about my past? Then you must know what my status was at the time. That's right, I was in Intelligence. You had to have eyes that could see a thousand miles, ears that could hear the slightest change in the wind. We learned that he was conducting research on the Greater East Asian Co-Prosperity Sphere, and he was also a translator with the rank of major. Later still, I heard he'd been shot dead by the Eighth Route Army at Chaoyang Hill [Song Village]. Two years before that, I had seen a piece of writing by someone named Zhu [Xudong], which borrowed Tian Han's words to say that Kawata had taken poison and ended his own life. No matter how it happened, he was dead. Hey, miss, you know who Tian Han is? He was from the same town as me and Ge Ren, Qinggeng. When I was abroad, I heard he got into trouble during the Cultural Revolution. Later on he managed to be rehabilitated, but he was bedridden for many years. Okay, okay, fate treats everyone fairly, and no one's guaranteed an easy ride through life. It was the same with Kawata: in his youth he roamed about as he pleased, but in the end he still died in a foreign land.

Kawata was dead, but his little brother lived on. Later, Kawai joined the army and ended up in China too. His real motive in coming here was to find his brother. Our countries were at war, so I wasn't able to meet him until a special mission came my way in 1943, but I was hard-pressed to carry it out. At this time, Kawai showed up like a ghost or a devil, and so I asked him to come with me to Baibei Town on Bare Mountain. Yes, that's where Ge Ren was at the time. He wanted to see Ge Ren, to ask him where his brother was. And now you know that's when he found out there was such a place as Baibei in China—but then I didn't have any further news of him.

Decades flashed by, just like that. A few years ago, I led a legal delegation on a visit to Japan. Our schedule was tight and we had a lot to accomplish, but I still found time to drop in on Ki Shiryo. When the restaurant owner heard we were visiting from China, he ran around making us feel welcome, and even brought out some old photographs for us to look at. As soon as I saw those, the past came flooding back. One of them was of me, Ge Ren, and Chen Duxiu, as well as Kawata, Kawai, and the boss at the time. The tour guide told us that whenever visitors arrived from China, the boss would bring these out to show off Ki Shiryo's long history and its contribution to the friendship between Japan and China. Through the boss, I learned that Kawai was still alive, and in fact he was still a regular customer. I wasn't able to get hold of him that day. When I got back home, Kawai phoned to say he wanted to visit China at least one more time while he was still alive. I thought he was only saying that, so I didn't think too much about it. But wouldn't you know it, the old devil actually showed up, and insisted on investing in Baibei Town [City]. As soon as he arrived, he got in touch with me. I was recuperating in Guangzhou at the time. He wanted to visit me there, but I vetoed that plan. Now he's finally going to see me. Miss, how can I explain this to you—I'm prepared for it, and if he tried to express remorse on behalf of the Japanese people, I'd say to him: Kawai, oh Kawai, you have to remember history, because forgetting the past is a betrayal. Don't try to stop me, miss, I have to say this. I believe, if Kawai is enlightened, he won't regard this as a slur on his character. Really, this is about the character of his country, not his personal character. You can be a little careless in your personal character, but at a national level that's not possible.

Hope Elementary School

In July 1997, Mr. Kawai, the boss of the turtle-style Japanese-American company, came to Hong Kong in the wake of the handover in search of business opportunities, and afterward continued on to Shenzhen. A week later, he arrived in Baibei, where he hadn't been for many years, in the role of both businessman and tourist. When he found out that there were plans to build a 300-million-watt electric plant on White Cloud River, he knew this was a great opportunity for him, and he hadn't made the trip in vain.

It wasn't that Kawai was ignorant of "Chinese politics," as old Mr. Fan assumed. He set his eye on the deputy mayor and threw a banquet to make his acquaintance. After that, this crucial figure sent his personal secretary, Guo Ping—the son of Guo Baoquan, the Hakka hero who, back in the day, blew up the train tracks—to see him at the hotel. Secretary Guo stated frankly that, according to normal practice, this commercial contract would have to be awarded through competitive bidding. Next, Secretary Guo casually brought up another matter: because the upkeep of Fangkou Elementary School had been neglected for many years, a few beams had fallen during a recent storm, crushing two little girls to death. "An early death isn't as good as a timely death." (I thought this sounded familiar, then suddenly realized that Tian Han had used this exact phrase in reference to the Battle of Two Li Mound.) The Hope Corporation had been looking for a site for an elementary school, and although Fangkou hadn't been on their radar, it was now a distinct possibility. Hope stepped up their efforts, and the money soon arrived at Baibei. This was also around the time the race to be promoted from county to city was reaching its white-hot phase. "If we don't spend what needs spending, and we miss this opportunity, the People will be in a rage at not getting to be city-dwellers, and they'll take it out on us." As a result, some of the money was diverted to public relations. Changing the subject, Secretary Guo added here, "We'd thought that after we became a city, we could plug the deficit, but there were some celebrations that had to take place, which further depleted our coffers, so this gap in our finances was never filled."

Kawai's no fool. He immediately proclaimed that he was willing to make a contribution to the development of Chinese education, and they wouldn't have to spend a penny of government money to build this school. Secretary Guo said, "It would be amazing if you could do that. We'll tell our residents that the building will be delayed because we wanted to build the best possible school, so the local government attracted outside investment on top of the original foundation. With such a big project, of course construction is taking longer than planned." Secretary Guo told Kawai, on behalf of the deputy mayor, that after the school was built, they would put up a stone tablet at the gates to honor Mr. Kawai for his work. But Kawai wasn't interested in that sort of memorial. He said many years ago that he came to this place for an old friend of his. In remembrance of that friend, why not call it Ge Ren Hope Elementary School? Surprisingly, Secretary Guo had no idea who Ge Ren was. Even so, he promised to pass this suggestion along to the local government. His exact words were "Everything depends on economic growth. As long as this will help our economic growth, the higher-ups will surely give the green light." What Kawai didn't expect was that old Mr. Fan would jump in there and veto his use of the name.

By the way, the full name of the school is now Fangkou Hope Elementary School. The name appears in old Mr. Fan's calligraphy—he mailed it over from Beijing.

Seasick

Okay, okay, I'll be straight with you—not counting this trip, I've visited Baibei twice, and both trips had to do with Ge Ren. For many years, all I had to do was shut my eyes, and I'd see Baibei Town on Bare Mountain. Yes, it's called Baibei City now. I knew every rock and tree in that place. All these years, I've educated my family about the tradition of revolution, with pretty good results. Let's put it this way—even the maid knows about Baibei Town. When we have guests for a game of mahjong, if the maid mentions Bare Mountain, then I'll know she's hinting she has the "bai" tile. Such a clever girl. I took her along on my last trip to Japan. Both my delegation and the Japanese commented on how smart she was. But you can't always predict the weather, and not long ago my wife chased her out with a feather duster, screaming that she's a vixen. I was so angry!

All right, back to the point. The first time I went to Baibei Town, it was the Guiyou Year, that is, 1934. As I said before, I studied law in Japan, and when I got back, I tried to find a way to serve the fatherland. I was representing westerners in court in Shanghai. Back then, the Chinese didn't go in for pressing charges. The doors of the police station were open, but you couldn't come in unless you had money or power. It was the westerners who had money and power, so of course I was working on their behalf. It's the foundation that determines the structure of the upper stories. This wasn't why I'd joined the profession, but what choice did I have? It was a frustrating time for me, and I frequently found myself on Qingyun Road, seeking Ge Ren out for a chat. He was teaching at Shanghai University at the time, and would invite me back to his lodgings on Moulmein Road for a drink. One time I found him busy packing, preparing to go on a long journey. Even if he hadn't said anything, I would have known he was heading to the Bare Mountain Soviet, something he had talked about many times. He'd been diagnosed with lung disease and should have been recuperating, but he was the sort of person who could never just do nothing. Lu Xun also tried to persuade him to be quiet and focus on recovering, but he still wouldn't listen. You know who Lu Xun is? The writer who dated a female student. Yes, that was Xu Guangping. Maggie Cheung? Okay, okay, she does look like Maggie Cheung; they both have single eyelids and puffy eyes.

Ge Ren tried to drag me down with him at his farewell dinner. He said it just so happened that the Soviet needed more manpower, and I could do a lot of good there. That night, I treated him to a movie, *Animal Kingdom*. No, not the TV program with Zhao Zhongxiang—this was a Hollywood film. At the cinema, we happened to bump into Lu Xun, who was quite a film buff. [N.B. We can work out from Lu Xun's *Diaries* that this took place on January 7, 1934, a windy Sunday: "Rain and snow tonight. . . . Saw *Ubangi* at the Shanghai Grand Cinema."] Bingying was with us, and when she saw Lu Xun, she asked why Xu Guangping hadn't come with him—had the couple had an argument? Okay, okay, I've thought of something else: you look a lot like Bingying. Your eyes, your eyebrows, your nose, and especially your smile. Bingying was a great beauty. You know how Jia Baoyu separated women into girlies and grannies? I reckon that Bingying was an eternal girlie. As we left the cinema, Ge Ren offered to treat me in return, to a coffee this time. He said, Shanghai is an animal kingdom, and we should go break new ground somewhere else. What a joke! In Shanghai I lived the life of the mind, reading books late into the night. I earned a good living, I could go to the cinema and drink coffee—a civilized life, for both body and mind. Why would I go to some godforsaken mountain?

Okay, okay, so that would have been that, but then something happened to change my mind. This was also a historic shift in my destiny. That summer, like thousands of other Shanghainese, I was mesmerized by the film star Ruan Lingyu. She was different from Butterfly Wu, who was luxurious and opulent—Ruan Lingyu had a simple, sad elegance. She was the leading starlet at the Lianhua Film Studio, and she had thousands of fans. You're being very kind, miss, but I was a nobody at the time—how could she have fallen for me? It was totally unrequited. I did manage to get on set to watch her make *New Women*, but she never looked at me, not even once. That didn't matter; she ignored plenty of people. Not long after that, I met a woman who looked just like Ruan Lingyu—sharp chin, upturned eyes, willow-leaf brows, curly hair, patterned cheongsams, smelling of Lux soap, skin as soft as water. Yes, she could have been a clone. Her stepfather was treating her badly, so she had come to press charges against him. What with one thing and another, she seduced me. Don't laugh, I'm telling the truth, no coloratura here. It really was she who seduced me. Of course, even if I had seduced her, so what? Hu Shih said it best: Which man will stay silent, which cat won't go into heat? The trouble was, my wife soon found out. Damn it! The bitch's nose was sharp. And after that, there was pandemonium at home. Experience told me it was important to stay calm, that keeping calm would win the day for me. But I tried everything I could, and nothing would stabilize the situation. Fuck! If I couldn't fix the problem, then maybe I could hide from it. So I decided to get away for a while, until she could simmer down.

You know what they say: no coincidence, no story. This was when a man named Hu An came to find me in Shanghai. He was a capitalist who had made his money in tea leaves, then later moved into property in Hangzhou and Shanghai. He was loaded. He showed up clutching a little dog, which he told me was a Shih Tzu he had brought back from France. If I remember right, his dog even had a French name: Bastille. He said it was the offspring of a French dog. This man was Bingying's father, Ge Ren's father-in-law. Ha, that should please you. You seemed unhappy when I said you looked like Bingying earlier, but now you understand—I meant you were the daughter of a wealthy couple. It was a compliment. Hu An had come from the Soviet zone. After Ge Ren left, Bingying missed him so much that she went to the Soviet zone too, and Hu An had just come from seeing off his daughter and son-in-law. He'd been enchanted with the place, and wanted to go back. I asked him, Old Mr. Hu, what on earth is so good about this place that you'd make a return trip? He said, There's struggle here every single day. It's not like Shanghai and Hangzhou, which are just stagnant water, pointless, pointless. He had come back to sell off his properties in Shanghai and Hangzhou, after which he would move to Bare Mountain. He asked if I wanted to come along; otherwise he'd have only the dog for company. I was moved, and asked how long it would take to get there and back. He said about a month, and he would cover our travel expenses. Right, that's how badly he wanted me for a travel companion. He said, Go talk it over with your wife, but don't say you're going to Bare Mountain; say you have a case in Nanjing. Okay, okay, I'd have been fine if he hadn't mentioned my wife, but that pretty much made up my mind—I'll go, I'll go! I knew Ge Ren had lung disease, so I even prepared some medicine to take to him. I thought, never mind anything else, the important thing is that I'm going to see my friends.

There was a secret route to get to Baibei Town. You set off on a ship from Shanghai, southward through the Wusong estuary, all the way to Hong Kong. I'd never been seasick before, but on this trip I vomited everywhere. In Hong Kong, a Party underground worker led us onto another boat, which took us to Shantou. From there we got a train to Chao'an, and then a third boat up White Cloud River to Baibei. Fuck! It's hard to describe everything we suffered on the way. We often had to travel through the night, then hide in the mountains and sleep during the day. At a place called Dapu, an underground messenger saw Hu An holding the dog and assumed we were bad people, so he tried to eliminate us. Luckily, he didn't shoot. In order to save bullets, he just rapped me on the back of the head with his revolver handle. Hu An? Luckily he stayed conscious. If he'd keeled over too, we'd have been hacked to pieces. I found those twilight days almost unbearable, but for Hu An they were a rare pleasure. He said he was loving this adventure, and would happily spend the rest of his days traveling this route. Fan Ye told me you're like her, you enjoy bungee jumping, what they call a "peak experience." Ha, that's what Hu An was after, peak experiences. I regretted coming along, but there's no turning back once the arrow leaves the bow. All I could do was stiffen my resolve and keep following him. And in this way, after almost a month's journey, we arrived at Baibei Town. By that point, my face was all swollen, the soles of my shoes had worn away, and my feet were covered with blisters. I must have looked like the Barefoot Immortal.

Underground

Wan Guanxi, the father of the Huawei Consumer Alliance's founder, Wan Quanshu, was at the time just an underground messenger, code name "Chef"—the one Fan Jihuai mentioned as being stationed at Dapu, the most important position in the entire underground network. Zhou Enlai, Ye Jianying, Liu Shaoqi, Xiang Ying, Ren Bishi, Bo Gu, Zhang Wentian, Otto Braun, and many others passed through there on their way to the Soviet zone. After 1949, Comrade Wan Guanxi returned to his hometown in Fujian to become a county chief, then during the Cultural Revolution he was transferred to Jiangxi, where he was put in charge of a provincial Party committee. Wan Guanxi died in 1970. At the time, his son Quanshu was sixteen years old, and had joined the rural Huangtang Commune a few dozen kilometers from Dapu. Wan Quanshu would later admit that the online marketing model used by his consumer alliance was based on the network of underground operatives back in the day: you were part of a long chain, but you only knew the persons directly above and below you, and no one else. The consumer alliance had thirty managers, which coincidentally was the same number of operatives in the Dapu underground. Of course, there were differences too: Wan Guanxi set up the network to achieve red power, while Wan Quanshu was after money. He later fled the country and used his gains to build a condominium block, but he was apprehended before the construction was complete.

I have no way of knowing whether Wan Guanxi ever mentioned Ge Ren and Fan Jihuai to his son, but there's one thing I can be sure of: this was a key node in the underground network, so Ge Ren, Hu An, Bingying, Broad Bean, and Fan Jihuai must all have passed through. I retraced their steps while doing the research for this book, following the full route from Dapu to Baibei: Dapu—Qingxi—Tongding—Raoping—Tingzhou—Gucheng—Ruijin—Yanglin—Xiaotang—Shang Village—Baibei. It's been half a century, but this road remains full of potholes, a difficult trek over an uneven dirt surface. That's not what surprised me. What I found startling was that even though the Huawei Consumer Alliance had already been disbanded, at every stop along the way, there were people encouraging me to join it, and to buy some Alaskan seal oil.

The First Night

We got to Bare Mountain after much difficulty, but I wasn't able to see Ge Ren right away—he was in Ruijin. Hu An took me to see someone else instead, a man named Tian Han, who was responsible for registering outsiders. When he heard I was Ge Ren's friend, he welcomed me warmly. Be that as it may, I still had to go through questioning. [He asked me] where I was born, where I'd come from, why I was there. I told the truth, with complete honesty. Then I asked Tian Han, What about Bingying? He said, Do you know her well? I said, Yes, we're old friends. He said, Okay, okay. Bingying was teaching at the Gorky School of Drama, and had gone on tour with the Heart-to-Heart Artistic Troupe to perform in the rural villages.

Miss, speaking of the Heart-to-Heart Artistic Troupe, I want to say something. Last year, I met Little Red Woman and her granddaughter, Little Woman Red. Do you know Little Red Woman? What's that? She looks like Teresa Teng? Ah, now that you mention it, there is a resemblance. Little Red Woman's performance group was also called Heart-to-Heart. She said it was pioneering. How was it pioneering? You can have your eyes open wide and still talk blindly. The company Bingying toured with was called Heart-to-Heart. She just stole the name. But I've always been a kind person, so I didn't expose her. Comparatively speaking, I preferred the granddaughter, Little Woman Red. Yes, she's been on quite a journey; she was the mistress of a smuggler. After the smuggler was arrested, she came to me for help, and even asked if I would mediate. I had to look stern and give her a good scolding. That's how you show affection, through scolding. Eventually she found the courage to break things off with the smuggler. Miss, if you ever want to hear her sing a cappella, I'll give her a call and get her to come over. If she dares to not show up, I'll smack her little ass.

Okay, okay, enough of that. Back to Bingying. I asked Tian Han if there was a theater there. He said, Of course, any higher ground can be a stage. Ah, he was talking about an open-air theater. Tian Han told us Bingying was in a play called *Every Possible Means of Success*. Her role was the older sister, a blind woman. I said, Bingying's eyes are so big and bright, isn't it a waste to have her play someone blind? Tian Han said, So what if she's blind; the blind are still part of the masses. That shut me up. Anyway, Hu An wasn't bothered about the blindness. As soon as he heard his daughter was in a play, he got all fired up. Ignoring me, he wanted to go straight to the theater, but Tian Han refused to tell him where the performance was, so he had to stew in his frustration. Tian Han pointed at the dog in

Hu An's arms and said, Why did you bring that? There's hardly even a few pounds of meat on it. Hu An said, I brought it for my granddaughter to play with. Then he asked, Where's my granddaughter? Tian Han said, She's always demanding meat, so Ge Ren took her along when he went for his meeting.

No, I didn't stay with Hu An. Hu An slept at Ge Ren's place that night, while Tian Han took me somewhere else—a place called Shang Village, near the train tracks. He led me to a little courtyard in the village and said, You'll have to put up with this for a night, sir, and when Ge Ren gets back, he can take over. There was a small church in the courtyard—I heard it was built by westerners, though the holy statues inside had been smashed to pieces no bigger than bricks. Tian Han called a couple of people over and told them to take good care of me, then left. One of them was called Zhao Yaoqing—I'd seen him in Shanghai, and remembered that Ge Ren called him Ah Qing. My impression of him was that no matter where Ge Ren went, he would follow, like a tail. I thought Tian Han must have brought him over to test whether or not I actually was Ge Ren's friend. Fuck. This told me that Tian Han didn't entirely trust my travel companion, Hu An. Ah Qing brought me a basin, saying it was to wash my feet in. I saw that the basin still had some flour in it, and asked if he'd brought the wrong one, but he said this was a multi-use basin: it was for washing your face, washing your feet, kneading dough, holding wine, and cooking. Hearing that it was used for cooking, I quickly pulled my feet away. Ah Qing burst out laughing and said, If you don't use it, I will. Despite that, he didn't actually put his feet in it. Okay, okay! He was a civilized man, so that was the right thing to do. The water was for me, and it would be better to pour it out than take it for himself.

The basin of water stood by my bed. The moon was particularly round that night, and its reflection in the water was like a dream. I fell asleep, but it wasn't long before I was awake again. My bladder. No, I don't need to pee now, I mean my bladder woke me up. Then I heard someone singing, getting closer and closer. The soldiers were back from the front line, singing "The Red Guard Discipline Song" and "Let's Smash the Enemy's Tortoise Shell." They were good songs, healthy and uplifting, raising our spirits—I personally had never heard them before. But I still needed to pee, so I couldn't give them any more of my attention. I tugged at the door, which clicked but wouldn't open. You're right, miss, Ah Qing had locked me in. He was standing outside, but when I yelled at him to open up, he said, Just piss in the basin. I stamped my feet and yelled that I wouldn't be able to do it in a basin. I heard his footsteps thumping as he ran off. Guess what he went to do? You'll never guess—he went to ask what he should do. By the time he got back, my bladder had almost burst. Luckily I was young and didn't have any problems in that area, or I really would have pissed myself.

Okay, okay, come with me, said Ah Qing. He led me to a wall, pointed to a nearby tree, and said, Please let go over there, sir. That's when I heard noises from the other side of the wall—people were being tortured. Someone moaned; someone else screamed for his mom and dad. Ah Qing told me they were Nationalist bandits who'd been forced into the Red Guards after being captured, but they'd barely fought for two days before trying to escape. Miss, you probably don't know this, but people's native accents slip out when they're crying. I soon noticed that one of the sobbing voices sounded very close to my hometown. That was unnerving, and I shivered for a long while, as if it were me being beaten. A few days later, Ah Qing confessed that the reason he'd taken me to the wall was precisely to teach me a lesson—striking the mountain to shock the tiger. Actually, though, I didn't hear too much screaming and weeping that day, because the Red Guards soon started singing again, which covered up all the other sounds. Officers and soldiers had lit a bonfire not far away, and they were dancing and singing around it. Heads were rolling here, and a party was going on over there. Their faces were tinted red by the fire, like molten iron, like the setting sun. Amid their chorusing, I went back into the church. My shadow went ahead of me, wobbling along with the flames. It stretched longer and longer, as if I would never get to the end of it. Finally I reached the church, and a black shape loomed out of the darkness, startling me. The figure was holding a basin as it rushed toward the bonfire. The smell of alcohol told me what the basin contained—a celebratory drink, for the Revolution.

Performance Troupe

Old Mr. Fan's memory was faulty—Bingying's performance troupe wasn't called Heart-to-Heart, it was called the Central Soviet Performance Troupe—so he wronged Little Red Woman. That said, there were some similarities between the Central Soviet Performance Troupe and Little Red Woman's group. For instance, they both did touring shows, and they both used propaganda techniques to strengthen the bond between the leadership and the masses. The play Bingying was acting in wasn't called *Every Possible Means of Success*, it was *Victory at Any Cost*. Anthony Thwaite describes its plot in *Beauty in a Time of Chaos*:

> As Bingying thinks back to life in the Soviet zone, her gaze cuts through the thick fog of time and lands in a dusty cornfield. That was the first stage

she performed on. She recalls that the show was called *Victory at Any Cost*. "At any cost" indicated that in order to succeed, foul means were permissible. This was the central tenet of revolution. The story was about a lad not yet ten and his blind older sister. They were tortured by so-called "White Soldiers" or "Nationalist Bandits," but kept their revolutionary secret and refused to reveal the whereabouts of the Red Guards. Bingying played the part of the older sister. She recalls, "The leather whips wielded by the actor playing the Nationalist never actually touched us, but I saw real fear in the young actor's eyes. He actually wet himself." In real life, the actor playing the Nationalist was an executioner, or more accurately, he was a member of the Red Guards' execution squad. His performance was extremely realistic, which elicited hatred from the audience. Many times he would slip away as the crowd screamed, "Beat the White Bandit to death!" As soon as he came off stage, he would quickly be surrounded by bodyguards. If they had been slow, there was a good chance the angry mob would have killed him—they seemed to believe he really was a Nationalist.

According to Bingying, unlike the Nationalist actor, who had to slink away in shame, the young boy playing her brother was embraced by the enthusiastic crowd. People would bring him the tiny amounts of food they had—perhaps a piece of yam or a water caltrop—and soon the little actor's parents grew wealthy. But then tragedy struck: the parents were killed, and their home was ransacked. Real life is always more exciting than what happens on stage. No one could have expected that this now-orphaned actor would, many years later, undergo a series of cosmetic procedures—the present-day version of "victory at any cost"—and become a very successful mimic, specializing in playing Mao Zedong. He often claimed to be the baby that the Chairman lost during the Long March, until someone pointed out that his age didn't match that of Mao's missing child . . .

Following a reference in Thwaite's endnotes led me to the entertainment pages of the December 26, 1996, issue of *Yellow River Evening News*, where I found that apart from cameo performances and film roles, this performer often took part in the shows put on by Little Red Woman's Heart-to-Heart Troupe. Naturally, whether he was working with Heart-to-Heart or as a freelancer, his shtick was about the same. *Yellow River* describes a performance he gave at Hulu Town, midway between Two Li Mound and Chaoyang Hill, in late 1992:

To the strains of "The East Is Red," he walked out with his hands behind his back. According to the terms of his contract, he was required to stay on stage for five minutes. As a result, he walked so slowly that it took him a whole minute just to reach center stage, and then he spent another minute acknowledging the audience's applause. Amid the cheering and clapping, he waved for silence, then greeted the People in a Shaoshan accent. This reporter noted that no matter whether he is working with Heart-to-Heart or as a freelancer—as at this performance—his lines never vary: "Hellow to the Pee-pow, Oi miss the Pee-pow. The Pee-pow are true heroes. Pee-pow, the Pee-pow, are the ones who create histowy. Long time no see. When I see village folk leading a good life, Oi feel happy in my heart. Enough of that; Oi've been here too long, Marx is about to take attendance. If Oi miss that, Oi'm in for a beating, you know." This little speech took two and a half minutes. Then he spent the last minute making a slow exit, treating the audience to the sight of his broad retreating back. As soon as he got backstage, he spent half an hour counting the vast sum he got from this appearance, then haggling with the booker about the arrangements for his next gig.

On this occasion, because some of the performers were trying to avoid paying taxes, the taxman had no choice but to detain them. When this reporter got wind of that, I rushed to the Yellow River Love Motel, where the actors were staying. In the corridor, I ran into the red-hot starlet Little Woman Red, who was taking part in the show. As everyone knows, Little Woman Red won enthusiastic applause on this occasion, with her revised version of "Chaoyang Hill." Officials confirmed that Little Woman Red was the first to pay her tax assessment in full. They expressed deep admiration for both her craft and her personal character. It was through her that this reporter was able to find the novelty performer's room. I found him screaming at an attendant because his central heating unit was making a buzzing noise. After Comrade Little Woman Red introduced us, he was happy to be interviewed. In the later part of our conversation, this reporter attempted to ask what I had heard could be a sensitive question, that is, whether or not he actually was the baby lost by Mao Zedong on the Long March. Just like the Chairman in the movies, he sat with one ankle crossed over the opposite knee, took a puff from his cigarette, and said, "Of course I am. I have ample evidence to prove it." This reporter produced a newspaper article showing that this son of Mao's was born during the Long March, but the performer had already been in *Victory at Any Cost* before the march, appearing on stage with Bingying and her father, Hu An, in response to which he snapped, "The few have to follow the many. If the majority believe that's who I am, then that's who I am. I can't go against the collective wishes of the People."

In his rush to say this, he dropped the Mao accent. This reporter wanted to continue asking if the "majority" he referred to included his clapping and cheering audiences, but before I could get the words out, he had shoved me outside. With a bang, the door slammed shut. As I left the hotel, Comrade Little Woman Red apologized for his rude behavior, and indicated that she would let her grandmother Little Red Woman know what had taken place, so that the older woman could emphasize to this performer that he needed to work on his thinking. This reporter was touched by her words. If all actors could be as dedicated to their craft and personal morality as Comrade Little Woman Red, how delightful our artistic scene would be.

On another note, the "Chaoyang Hill" mentioned in this article was indeed modified from Little Red Woman's famous "Chaoyang Hill Has Never Been Calm":

> Chaoyang Hill, Chaoyang Hill has never been calm
> Unstable amid stability, listen for the faint wind blowing
> Before liberalization, the old ways were rooted deep
> All day long, backs to the sky, facing the yellow earth
> Today the market economy raises its voice in song
> Farmers and the middle class walk hand in hand toward prosperity
> The world is full of fog, the country's hearts are the same red
> Brother farmers, improve your technological skills
> Do not let rumors destroy this great movement
> Comrades, be clear-eyed, do not let the old ways come back again
> Even when spring comes, beware of frost and cold air
> After victory, the struggle continues
> Party, dear Party, you are like the evergreen pine and cypress
> Deep roots, full crowns, green for thousands of years
> Your words are always in our hearts
> We will stand tall and magnificent on Chaoyang Hill forever, never
>   wither away

In the next section, Mr. Fan mentioned an occasion when this performer shared a stage with Hu An.

Ge Ren Told Me to Leave

I saw Ge Ren the following day. He arrived in Shang Village on a gray horse named Ashes. I was surprised at the sight—hello, was I seeing things? What was this bookworm doing on a horse? But then who else could it be? He didn't look at all like he had lung disease. The good thing about revolution is it makes you forget illness, forget yourself, forget everything. He really did look a lot better, though. It seemed I had brought along that medicine for nothing.

As soon as he saw me, Ge Ren unexpectedly told me to leave. Get out! he said. This was strange: he had told me to come, and now that I was there, he was telling me to go. My brain couldn't make sense of it, and I thought he was testing me. But then he spoke rapidly: Brother Fan, this isn't the place for you. You should get out of here quickly. I showed him the blisters on my feet and said, Surely you can let me catch my breath. He said, Fine, you can rest for two days, but then I want you out of here.

That night, Ge Ren invited me into his home to shake the dust from the journey off my feet. Once again, he encouraged me to leave the Soviet zone. Why? I asked. He said the war was getting closer and closer, and if I stayed, he wouldn't be able to guarantee my safety. Bingying was there too; she had just hurried back from a place called Xiaotang, and she was playing with her daughter as I talked to Ge Ren. She interjected as well, telling me to leave as soon as I could. Her voice was a little hoarse, from her work as an actress. There was also a well-dressed young man present, the civilized sort you could tell right away was a scholar. He didn't venture an opinion, just sat around blowing out smoke, like a chimney. I saw Ge Ren ask him for a cigarette—it seemed they got along well. Finally Ge Ren introduced us, and I learned that he had just joined the Red Guards and was one of General Cai Tingkai's subordinates. His name was Yang Fengliang. When I got to know him a bit better, he told me there was a big situation and a small situation keeping him there. The big situation was revolution, and the small situation was love. He was porking a young local woman. And she was no yokel—she could perform the tea ceremony, sing opera, play music, and she was sensuous too. My god! When she wore her red halter top, her breasts were as perky as a pair of oranges. I once snuck in to watch her sing. Her best piece was "Fresh Flower Tune." You don't know it? It's the same melody as "Jasmine Flower." Good jasmine flower, good jasmine flower, a whole garden full of fragrance can't beat her. Okay, okay. My voice isn't bad, is it?

Yes, if not for "Fresh Flower Tune," Yang Fengliang wouldn't have stayed. Art can be a special sort of ideology and superstructure, and you can see from this what an effect it has. That young woman sang so well, it made your heart itch and your bones go numb. Later, when I got to the temporary capital of Chongqing, I found that all the whores there could sing "Fresh Flower Tune." Yang Fengliang bragged that he was the one who'd brought the song to Chongqing—light from the stars can set the plains aflame. Even the people selling dumplings by the roadside could sing it. Out of everyone in Military Intelligence, Dai Li sang the best. He had a big voice that went up a full octave. One Christmas, in order to bring the cadres closer to the rest of the organization, Dai Li performed for us. He sang falsetto, sounding like a woman, and when he got to "Good rose, good rose, blooms as big as a plate / I would love to pick one to wear, but I'm afraid of your thorns," he even joined his thumb and middle finger in the traditional dance gesture. Don't laugh; he did it more elegantly than I did—maybe he learned it from Miss Butterfly Wu. As I said before, Butterfly was plush and opulent and had thousands of fans. She was also our Boss Dai's mistress. Like my dream lover, Ruan Lingyu, she often appeared in advertisements on Shanghai calendars.

Where was I? Oh yes, Yang Fengliang. When Ge Ren introduced him to me, he was thinking we could leave together, so I would have someone to take care of me along the way. I asked again why he was so eager to get rid of me—was he worried I'd get him into trouble? But he refused to say. After a few days, I found out that he really was acting out of affection for me. The government was clamping down on the Soviet zone, while the Red Guards were in the midst of purging counter-revolutionaries. Someone like me, coming from outside, wouldn't find favor with either side. Which is to say, he spoke up because we were friends. The problem was, with forces surrounding us so tightly, how would I get out? For all I knew, I might be sent off to meet Marx before I could even get away from Bare Mountain. Given the situation, it seemed best to cross the river one stepping-stone at a time. So, okay, okay, that's how it was. I decided to stay put for the time being.

Good Jasmine

As I edited this transcript, the familiar strains of "Fresh Flower Tune" kept sounding in my ear. I couldn't help thinking that if Yang Fengliang hadn't met this "young woman," or if she'd sung another song and not "Fresh Flower Tune," this book might have ended up completely different.

Before discussing this song, I should talk about some interactions between Ge Ren and Yang Fengliang. According to Bingying's recollections, Ge Ren first learned of Yang Fengliang's existence at the beginning of 1932. As everyone knows, on January 28 of that year, Cai Tingkai's 19th Route Army exchanged fire with the Japanese at Zhabei, Shanghai, in what was later called the Battle of January 28. Over more than a month, the fighting continued even as both sides negotiated. Yang Fengliang was the lead representative of the Chinese side. In order to sort out some Japanese translation difficulties, he sent someone to visit

Ge Ren on Moulmein Road. They didn't actually meet then, and after the war, Yang Fengliang followed Cai Tingkai to Fujian.

In 1933, Cai Tingkai broke with Chiang Kai-shek in opposing the Japanese, and established the "People's Revolutionary Government of the Republic of China," with Fujian as its capital. They got rid of the flag with the white sun on a blue background, and created a new one: red on top, blue below, with a five-pointed yellow star in the center. They declared it "Republic of China Year Zero." Once again, the map of China was divided into three kingdoms: the Republic of China, the People's Revolutionary Government of the Republic of China, and the Chinese Soviet Republic (or the Soviet zone). Just as Liu Bei and Sun Quan joined forces to defeat Cao Cao, the latter two factions formed a unit, attacking the Republic of China government together. After they formed this alliance, according to article 6 of the *Chinese Soviet Republic and Chinese Workers' Red Guards and Fujian People's Revolutionary Government and People's Revolutionary Army Anti-Japanese Anti-Chiang Kai-shek Draft Agreement*, each had to send the other an ambassador. The representative sent from Ruijin to Fujian was Pan Hannian, while his counterpart was Yin Shizhong. Mr. Yang Fengliang was Yin Shizhong's assistant, a position roughly equivalent to being a consular attaché today.

Attaché Yang met this "young woman" who could "perform the tea ceremony and sing opera" in Ruijin. When I was interviewing Mr. Sun Guozhang, he mentioned this occasion:

> We Fujianese like to have a drink. In his early days as a diplomat, Mr. Yang also enjoyed going to tea houses. He once told me that around this time, people in Ruijin frequented an establishment run by a family named Tao. They sold oolong tea, which we Fujianese love. When Ge Ren was in Ruijin for a meeting, he met Yang at this tea house. He was an old acquaintance of Mr. and Mrs. Tao. Not long after that, though, it was seized and converted to public property by the Soviet, and the Taos moved back to Baibei on Bare Mountain. As soon as he could, Mr. Yang looked them up there. Mr. Tao had vanished, or perhaps died, but anyway only the woman was left in the household. She was from Jiangzhe, a good talker who sang opera well. Mr. Yang was enchanted with her, and thought he'd found happiness. Many years later, he would return to Baibei under the guise of attending a funeral.

According to *A Short History of Folk Songs* (Savanna Publishing, 1979), "Fresh Flower Tune" first gained popularity in the Subei districts, including Liuhe, Yizheng, and Yangzhou, as well as in the southern region of Anhui and Tianchang. In conjunction with what Mr. Sun Guozhang said about the woman's "Jiangzhe accent," we can be almost certain that it was she who brought this song to Bare Mountain. Which is to say, she played a role of historical significance in spreading this piece of music. Below are the lyrics of "Fresh Flower Tune," as recorded in *A Short History of Folk Songs*. We can see from these words that the song is about flirtation, and thus is suitable for performance in a brothel. No wonder old Mr. Fan felt that "it made your heart itch and your bones go numb."

> Good jasmine, good jasmine, more fragrant than an entire flower garden.
>   Your servant would pick you to wear, but what if you don't grow back next year?
> Good honeysuckle, good honeysuckle, hooks reaching out as you bloom.
>   Your servant would pick you to wear, but what if flower lovers scold me?
> Good rose, good rose, blooms as big as a plate.
>   Your servant would pick you to wear, but fears your thorns.

The later song "Jasmine Flower" was refashioned from "Fresh Flower Tune." There were two main changes: "honeysuckle" and "rose" were changed to "jasmine," and "your servant" was changed to "I." In 1957, the revised "Jasmine Flower" was played on the Central People's Broadcasting Station, and became the first record to be released in China. In 1965, the tune made its first foreign appearance when it was played by the Chinese delegation at the Bandung conference. Later on, it was heard frequently in Moscow, Budapest, Tirana, Warsaw, Pyongyang, Havana, Hanoi, and Baghdad. I've personally seen it played on TV many times, in instrumental versions and with accompanying dance routines.

At midnight on June 30, 1997, I watched on TV as Hong Kong was ceremonially handed over to China, and once again I heard the Chinese Military Band playing "Jasmine Flower." That was the last time I ever heard it. Back then, I was still completely ignorant of its history.

Hu An's Death

So I stayed on, but a hero has to use his skills somewhere. So I said to Ge Ren, You have to let me do something; otherwise that would be too big a waste of talent. He said, Okay, okay. Baibei happens to lack a "national language" teacher, so why don't you take over for a couple of days? I had never considered working with kids before, but now that I thought about it, it would be in keeping with the strategy of invigorating the country through science and technology, so I didn't try to get out of it. I said, All right, I'm happy to do anything. And so, under Ge Ren's guidance, I deviated from the path of law and took up teaching. Yes, this was at what is now Hope Elementary School. It was once an earth god temple. The first time Hu An came, he donated a sum of money so that it could be expanded and turned into a school. The student body was made up of all ages—from grandfathers to boys in short pants. If anyone refused to study properly, I would lecture them in the name of revolution. Because I taught well and had a high standard of personal hygiene, one of the female students fell in love with me. She looked just like you, down to the silver hairpin. That was a gift from me—I bought it while passing through Dapu, and had planned to bring it back as a gift for my wife, but I decided it would be better used there. Don't laugh, miss. Revolution and love are twins. Since ancient times, heroes have found it hard to stay clear of beautiful women, and vice versa. Same on both sides. Where there's revolution, there will be love. Ge Ren noticed I was distracted with happiness, and asked if I was falling in love with this place. I said, Yes, I am, it's much better here than in Shanghai. In Shanghai I have to do what my wife says, but here other people do what I say. Fuck! I thought I could go on living happily there, but who knew that the war would show up just like that.

That summer, Chiang Kai-shek ordered Tang Enbo to enter the Soviet zone. Old Chiang had a sense of humor—he was bald, but the military strategy he devised was called "combing the hair." Combing Chairman Mao's hair? I hadn't thought of that, miss, but you're right—Mao had shoulder-length hair back then. At the time, though, the Soviet zone was mostly out of his hands. It was moving in a leftward direction, with Otto Braun holding the balance of the military power, and old Mao getting edged out. Of course I saw Mao. Sometimes he'd show up with Comrade Qu Qiubai in Baibei for a chat with Ge Ren. Because he was getting squeezed out, he always seemed anxious. Qu Qiubai and Ge Ren got along really well—you could say there was nothing they couldn't talk about. One day Ge Ren said to me, You know why I get along so well with Comrade Qiubai? I said I didn't know. He said Qiubai's history was very similar to his, down to their shared childhood nickname: Duo. I vividly remember a time when old Mao showed up while Ge Ren and Qiubai were talking about the question of romanizing the Chinese language. They told him their hypothesis: that Chinese pictograms were too hard to learn, and that the reason for the low level of education among the Chinese populace was the difficulty of the language. They suggested that people of the New Culture ought to use pinyin, showing the People the way forward. They would soon realize that the day we started using the Latin alphabet was the day our nation took a great stride forward. They were both scholars, and once you got them going on the subject, they could have continued forever. Old Mao said, Gentlemen, stop talking about romanization. Distant water won't do anything for present thirst, okay, okay? Let's just shoot the breeze. What does that mean, shooting the breeze? Just having a chat. He wanted to chat about the classic novels *Romance of the Three Kingdoms* and *The Water Margin*. Miss, I hate to brag, but people like me who've personally interacted with the first-generation core leadership are few and far between. I still remember when old Mao was as slender as a willow tree. He had such long hair, you could have called him a drooping willow. How can I put this? Apart from the wart on his chin, he was virtually unrecognizable as the figurehead who now appears on our hundred-yuan bills.

Yes, shoulder-length hair. Don't think it's only the young people of today who wear their hair long. Old Mao was already doing it back then. Okay, okay, the Bible has it right, there's nothing new under the moon. This sort of thing had been around for a long time. I once got into a debate with Fan Ye. She said rock and roll belonged to a new breed of humanity. New my ass, I said. Men with long hair, women with scrubbing brushes on their heads, everyone hanging out at Sanlitun, and that counts as a new breed? If you say women dressing up as men is new, then what about those ancient women Hua Mulan and Zhu Yingtai? If you want to talk about hanging out in bars, I've pissed out more alcohol in those places than you've ever drunk. So am I a new breed of humanity? Fan Ye squealed with anger. She banged the table, overturned her chair, and would happily have killed me. But even if she had, that wouldn't have made her a new breed, just a new criminal. She said her motto was: If people leave me alone, I will leave them alone—but if they provoke me, I will get them back. I was amused by that. What nonsense was this—those were Chairman Mao's words; since when had they become her motto? Don't laugh, miss, I know you're good friends with Fan Ye, you're in the same foxhole. It doesn't matter if you don't agree [with my opinion], we can still debate. Practical experience is the only way to test an ideology. I've never been afraid to debate. The truth is like a lamp wick: it gets brighter the more you pick at it.

Okay, okay, enough of that. Let's talk about old Chiang combing his hair. This combing took place from the southwest to the northeast, and it didn't go smoothly at first, but the more they tugged at the comb, the easier it got. The Soviet zone was under the command of Otto Braun at the time. Do you like watching sports? Me? Of course I love it. When I'm overseas, I often try to catch a game. In the last year or two, I've started paying attention to China's professional league too. Don't look down on those little balls; they're a scaled-down version of Chinese history and reality. You like sports too? Great, that will make my explanation clearer.

The cannons of the October Revolution brought us Marxism-Leninism. And the cannons of opening up and liberalization brought us Velibor Milutinović. That's right, our national [coach], but enough about him, let's talk about clubs. Otto Braun was the foreign-born coach. Foreign coaches don't understand the Chinese temperament. Old Mao said so in private: Otto Braun might have been a first-class graduate from the military academy, but he still wasn't as good as our eighth-roader [N.B. The term "Eighth Route Army" wasn't in use at the time] Song Jiang, who attacked the Zhu homestead three times, and every single one of his maneuvers was worthy of note. Otto Braun didn't understand the national spirit, so no matter how he tried to take control of the battlefield, he couldn't help yielding ground to the other side. The leftist route killed people. He said the Nationalists were nothing but ants—just draw a line in camphor and they wouldn't be able to cross. He refused to play defense, and would only consider a full-court press. As soon as the score got close, he went in for a Hail Mary pass. As a result, he didn't manage to either attack or defend. Many times, the front line got squashed into our little penalty box. This meant that not only did the other side manage to land many blows, but our side had a couple of own goals, smashing ourselves in the face. At the time, many of us comrades were quietly debating whether we ought to confiscate Otto Braun's camphor and give him some peppermint oil instead to wake him up.

I've heard Tian Han complain that a perfectly fine bunker could be destroyed by one cannon blast. At the time, the Nationalists were using a German-made mountain gun and 102-caliber heavy mortar. Those were powerful toys that could blast open a bunker as easily as cracking a walnut. Of the thirty-six stratagems, retreating is best. The Red Guards had already withdrawn, so we were the only ones caught unawares. One day, Ge Ren and I were out for a walk when we suddenly saw a Red Guard detachment marching west along White Cloud River. There was a cook, an honest-looking man, who came over to salute Ge Ren. Bingying asked him, Where are you going? He didn't answer her, and after he left, she complained about how rude he was. Look at that—even at a time like this, Bingying was fussing about someone's manners. Ge Ren explained to her that the higher-ups wouldn't let them reveal any information, so of course they would go mute around her. It was their iron discipline. On the same day, I noticed that my lover had blood blisters on her hand. When I asked her what happened, she said they were weaving straw slippers—everyone had to make five pairs. Because she wanted to progress, and didn't want to let me down, she'd made an extra two. Something felt wrong about this—the enemy was advancing, but instead of digging trenches, we were weaving slippers? That night in bed, I smelled something in her hair, the odor of fried noodles. I asked her, Were you frying noodles today? She said that she was. I wanted to figure out what was going on, so I quickly went to ask Ge Ren. He had just come back from Ruijin, so he ought to know. He said he had spoken to Braun about it, and had been told that this division was newly formed, and they were on the front line for their training, eagles taking wing for the first time. Many years later, I read this line in Marx's *The Eighteenth Brumaire of Louis Napoleon:* "C'est le premier vol de l'aigle" [The first flight of the eagle]. Flying? But they were clearly retreating, so what was this talk about flying? I was still uneasy, so I went to ask Tian Han—but Tian Han claimed he didn't know anything either. I told them we should prepare ourselves while there was still time; otherwise we'd be caught scrambling. They asked how I knew something was going on, and I told them about the straw slippers and fried noodles. They immediately said I shouldn't talk rubbish—didn't I know the story of Yang Xiu? Miss, do you know about Yang Xiu? Okay, okay, he was someone from the Three Kingdoms time, a very clever guy. One time, Cao Cao was leading an attack against Liu Bei when he happened to say the words "chicken rib." Yang Xiu's brain went into overdrive, and he guessed that this was a code word for retreat, so he went around everywhere spreading this rumor. What he didn't know was that he'd signed his death warrant. When Ge Ren said this to me, I felt my whole spine go numb.

I ran into Hu An on the third day after I started suspecting a retreat was imminent. I hadn't seen him since arriving in the Soviet zone—he'd been hiding away in his lair in one of the mountain gullies, leading a team of people in making counterfeit bills. These were for use in the White zone, in order to create trouble with the Nationalists' financial system. The money Hu An got from selling his family property all went into forgery supplies. He also made some fake American dollar bills, with Washington on them just like the real thing, and the words "In God We Trust." Seeing him there, I thought he must have the latest information and that he needed to discuss it with his son-in-law. Trying to probe him for news, I asked what he'd heard, but he just acted confused, saying he knew nothing and was only there to see Bastille. Finally he couldn't hold it in any longer, and admitted he was there to act. Act? Act in what? He said, Okay, okay, you'll find out when the time is right. I was about to walk away when he couldn't hold it in any longer, and said he was stifling to death in that gully. His whole life, he'd believed that money was worth no more than dirt, and now he was surrounded by piles of cash all day long—it was driving him crazy. He wanted to give up and take up acting instead, but the higher-ups wouldn't let him. Eventually they relented and gave him permission to scratch his itch: he could appear in *Every Possible Means of Success* [*Victory at Any Cost*]. He had acted in France, in *Macbeth*. When he told me this, he arched an eyebrow, then gave me a spirited rendition of Shakespeare['s words].

How was that? he asked me. I honestly thought he was quite talented. If he'd stayed in Shanghai, maybe he could have starred opposite Ruan Lingyu. He told me he hadn't had a chance to go on stage for many years, and here at last was an opportunity. I asked what role he was playing, and he said it was dull being the straitlaced hero, so he had chosen to portray the Nationalist bandit. He even showed off a bit, claiming the director was very appreciative of him. I later found out this was all made up. The only reason he got to play the bandit was that the comrade who'd originally been cast had a tantrum and walked out on the show. Hu An was very agitated, bright red in the face. I stared at him for a long time, wondering if I was worrying about nothing. If the troops really were pulling out, then the Party would hardly be in the sort of expansive mood to put on a show for our entertainment.

The performance was in Shang Village. As I said before, Bingying had already been performing there. On that day, though, she stayed away, and her part was played by another actress. This was when I found out from Ge Ren that Bingying was pregnant, and didn't want to be out in the rain. Yes, it was drizzling. She wasn't there, so Ge Ren stayed away too. Qu Qiubai had tried to find Ge Ren that day to discuss the romanization further, so he wasn't there either. Me? Of course I went, even though it was raining, for Hu An's sake. Hu An was in full makeup, and he had turned the brim of his hat to the back. Now he ostentatiously unfastened his belt and prepared to hit the actress with it, forcing her to give away the location of the Red Guards, stroking her from time to time, now the left cheek, now the right. I was highly amused by his appearance, and the person next to me couldn't stop laughing either. When I looked closer, it was Yang Fengliang. He told me smugly that he knew the actress, because she was friends with his lover and was always looking her up to learn singing and tea ceremony. We were starting to annoy the people around us, who told us to shut up. Their fists were clenched, and they were shouting, Death to the white bandits! You're right, that meant Hu An was acting well. Yang Fengliang and I were also shouting, Death to the white bandits! Death to the white bandits! Who were the white bandits? The Nationalists called the Red Guards "scarlet bandits," and the Red Guards called the Nationalists "white bandits." Yang Fengliang and I shouted ourselves hoarse so Hu An would know we were there supporting him. He looked so pleased with himself, hands on his waist, spitting on the floor, making his entrance sideways like a giant crab foaming at the mouth. When the woman "fainted dead away," he reluctantly exited. I remember the final scene: the woman climbed off the ground with difficulty, then had a big speech in which she screamed, Long live the Soviet and the Nation, long live Stalin, long live the Red Guards, beat the White Guards to death, beat Chiang Kai-shek to death, beat Tang Enbo to death! As she cried out with her arms in the air, the area in front of the stage suddenly churned like a pot of porridge boiling over, and there was a gunshot. It all happened so suddenly, I thought the actual white bandits had shown up. When I regained my senses, I realized it was someone in the audience who had fired. And the target was none other than the person who had led me into revolution, Hu An. He had just come offstage, and he hadn't even taken off his makeup. He'd been in too much of a rush to find out from the audience what they thought of his acting, but before he could ask, he took a bullet. He was lying in a puddle of rainwater, mouth wide open, eyes full of mud, and one ear torn in two like the letter V.

Okay, okay, for years now, Hu An's figure has been hovering in front of me. And ever since Kawai brought up Hope Elementary School, it's gotten even more insistent. One night I was so caught up in memories, I couldn't get to sleep. Then something clicked in my mind, and I started writing a poem. My wife thought I was writing a love letter to some young thing, and insisted on looking. I think I did a good job, and everyone who's seen it agrees. Quite a few newspapers wanted it to publish it. In the end, *Chinese Poetry* [*The Art of Chinese Poetry*] got there first, and printed it. The poem doesn't mention Hu An's name, though. It's not that I didn't want to, it's that I couldn't. The reason is very simple: he lives outside of history. To this day, I haven't seen him referenced in a single book. Who knows about him? No one. So there'd be no point in talking about him. Besides, *Chinese Poetry* favors traditional forms, and nothing rhymes with Hu An.

The Art of Chinese Poetry

I read Mr. Fan Jihuai's poem in *The Art of Chinese Poetry* in 2000, in issue number 3. It would seem from these lines that Mr. Fan was already thinking of visiting Baibei again:

Travel ten thousand miles in search of dreams, half a lifetime's light
    shines on the stage.
Soldiers and the masses both love army songs, Baibei moon reflected
    in White Cloud River.
The east calls out, the west comes together, front curtain shuts as back
    curtain opens.
Every possible means of success, you be a scarlet bandit, I'll be white.
Foreign teaching comes from the east and is met with a knife; I go to
    the west and join the Long March.
On Bare Mountain, Fangkou remains green, old tears fall sadly on the
    Soviet.

The poem doesn't mention Hu An's name, let alone his heroic exploit: creating counterfeit bills to disrupt the Nationalist government's economic order. Mr. Fan is right, though—from a poetic standpoint, including the words "Hu An" and "forgery" would probably have been disruptive to the meter. And so we see that my great-grandpa Hu An's death was not just outside history, but also outside poetry.

Great-Grandpa Hu An's counterfeiting lair was in a valley about fifteen li outside Baibei. Interestingly, it was named Back Ditch—just like Bai Shengtao's prison in Yan'an. I've visited this Back Ditch. With the passage of time, there was nothing left but a stone hut on the brink of collapse. Wildflowers I couldn't name sprouted from cracks in the stone slabs, like something in a dream. The surroundings were dense with undergrowth and trees, the branches of which were covered in bird shit. It was clear that this place had long since been abandoned to the end of time.

Shanghai's *Civil Rights Paper* and Tianjin's *Jin Gate Times* broke the news of Hu An's death, running virtually identical articles. The following is from the October 10 edition of *Jin Gate Times*, in Year 23 of the Republic [i.e., 1934]. This description of "the scarlet bandit forgery expert Mr. Hu" being shot dead by security forces of the government obviously couldn't be farther from Mr. Fan's version of events.

This reporter recently learned from XX Public Security XX Regiment that the scarlet bandit forgery expert Mr. Hu has been shot to death, a great prize for our National celebration. Since September Year Twenty [i.e., 1931], when the Kuomintang Central Command sent a letter to the Nationalist Government proclaiming a bounty for scarlet bandits, heavy losses have been inflicted on these bandits. Although Hu was not on the wanted list, he was a creator of counterfeit banknotes, through which he sought to harm the Republic, disrupting the unity and stability of our nation, and so the damage he caused should not be overlooked. According to reports, Hu was shot dead by a member of the Public Security team in disguise, while taking part in a vicious attack on the Party leadership that sought to vilify the Party and damage the image of our troops. It could be argued that death was too good for him . . .

If this article is true, then the situation was very peculiar: if my great-grandpa was indeed shot by Public Security, then the Soviet zone should have recognized him as a revolutionary martyr. But in fact, the label of martyr has never been associated with my great-grandpa. In *The Majesty of the Orient*, Reverend Beal says something that might be helpful in solving this riddle. He first states that my great-aunt saw the article in the *Jin Gate Times*, and immediately suspected that the Mr. Hu mentioned must be Ge Ren's father-in-law, Hu An—which made her worry that Ge Ren, too, had come to grief. Reverend Beal continues:

> The motto of the *Jin Gate Times* was "All the news that's fit to print," which meant that false reports did appear from time to time. By which I mean that these were quite possibly intended to mislead the populace. But I was unable to comfort her, and with the passage of time, her anxieties only increased. In the following days, I made inquiries with my friends in the Red Cross, and discovered that the deceased was indeed Mr. Hu An. Soon thereafter, the Red Cross sent word that Hu An had actually been shot by the Red Guards. Because they had been defeated in the north, they were planning to pivot to another front, and Hu An was no longer of any use to them. As for the government's assertion that the killer was a Public Security man who had infiltrated the Soviet zone in disguise, that was another attempt to cause trouble. The government's intention was plain: to induce the Red Guards to expand their counter-revolutionary operations, so that they would turn on each other, and ultimately plunge into the abyss of self-destruction, from which there would be no return.

All things considered, in looking at these various accounts, I am most drawn to believing old Mr. Fan: that my great-grandfather's death was caused by the audience being unable to draw a line between artistic representation and real life. I believe that if my theater-loving great-grandpa knew about this in the underworld, he would also repudiate the versions of events in the *Jin Gate Times* and *The Majesty of the Orient*. He might even feel that dying at the hands of an audience was an incomparable glory.

I should also mention here that I recently spotted my great-grandfather's name in the *Southern Financial Times*, on October 12, 2000. As everyone knows, we live in an era of rampant consumption, and money is king. When I saw the words "Hu An," I assumed this must be someone of the same name as my great-grandpa. The headline was "Counterfeiter Lai Zhiguo Extradited to Face Execution." The story was about the Hong Kong and American police forces who were cooperating to capture a currency-forging ring, and extraditing the leader, Lai Zhiguo, from America. The prisoner confessed that it was his grandfather who had led him down the path of crime. While he was still alive, the grandfather had revealed that he'd learned his "trade" from a man named Hu An at Bare Mountain. The following passage contains the most interesting details:

> While answering questions from journalists, the police revealed that as several other counterfeiters prior to this had mentioned the name "Hu An," they were regarding Hu as a "master criminal," and believed that several southern districts might conceal other syndicates connected to Hu An. At the reception to celebrate the arrest, the authorities stood before the fresh flowers and awards to exhort their comrades to keep a clear mind, in order to continue achieving victories for the People. Many of the comrades indicated that they would build on this experience, eschewing arrogance and impatience, in order to apprehend the "master criminal" Hu An, thus living up to the hopes the Party had for them.

So now what? It's precisely because Hu An has been excluded from history and poetry that they would make this basic error of knowledge, thus ensuring that they'd never live up to the Party's hopes for them.

Someone's Hair Turns White Every Day

The night Hu An died, Bingying cried herself into a stupor several times, until her eyes had swollen so big they looked like honey peaches. Comrade Ge Ren came to find me—he wanted me to take Bingying and her daughter away from the Soviet zone as quickly as possible. He said the leftists were beginning to get the upper hand, and if we didn't leave now, it would be too late. What on earth is the matter? I asked. He said several people knew that he and I had had dealings with Chen Duxiu in Japan, and they didn't trust us. As I said earlier, miss, when we were in Japan, Chen Duxiu came to Kawata's home many times, and we formed a deep friendship. I would never have expected this to be a problem. I was grateful to Ge Ren for the warning. Many years later, when I tried to help Ge Ren escape, it was because he had saved my life this time. Okay, okay, you're right, miss. If I hadn't left then, it's possible I would have ended up a victim of the leftist front line. Even now, when I think back, it's still the deadly leftist line that most roils me. We must be opposed to the leftists as well as to the rightists, but the leftists most of all.

Our conversation took place in Phoenix Valley, behind Fangkou Elementary School. It was very quiet, though from time to time we could hear a dog barking in the distance. I asked if they'd found out who pulled the trigger. He didn't answer the question, just kept urging me to leave as soon as possible. He hoped I would take Bingying and her daughter to Tianjin, for old times' sake. There were two missionaries there, Beal and Ellis, who would take care of the mother and child. But what about him? Ge said that even though he was named Ge Ren, which sounds like "individual," his fate wasn't in his own hands. He would send Ah Qing to escort us safely out of the Soviet zone.

By the time we got back to his lodgings, Bingying had woken up. She wanted to go to a place called Xiguan Village to fetch her daughter—she had left the girl with a villager there, because she was constantly performing and Ge Ren's lung disease might be contagious. Ge Ren said he had sent Ah Qing to get her, and he'd be back soon, so it would be best to start packing. We waited and waited, but Ah Qing didn't show up. Fuck! It was late in the night when he finally appeared, limping, his face covered in blood. He said he had seen Broad Bean in Xiguan, but he hadn't been able to bring her back. The villager had taken him for a kidnapper, and not only refused to hand her over, but even set his dog on him. Ge Ren asked why he was bleeding from his head as well, and he said he'd been attacked by starving peasants on the way back. His horse was wounded too. They only let him go when they realized he was a Red Guard. At this point, Bingying fainted again. Ge Ren kept comforting her, promising that Broad Bean would get to Tianjin. She asked Ge Ren if he could come to an arrangement with Qu Qiubai, but he said Qu's own position was precarious, and they shouldn't add to his difficulties. In the midst of our conversation, Tian Han arrived with our transit passes. Okay, okay, this seemed to indicate that he was indeed particularly good friends with Ge Ren. These passes were a lifeline—without them, we'd only be able to daydream about leaving the Soviet zone. Tian Han then told us the truth: the Red Guards were about to move out, but first there was going to be a purge. You don't know what a purge is? Okay, okay, it's a way to weed out counter-revolutionaries: everyone is put through a sieve, and anyone suspicious gets removed from the ranks of the Revolution.

We finally set off, in such a rush that I even left my lover behind. We went by the same route I'd taken with Hu An to get there, but everything seemed different. I kept thinking about Hu An's death. The gunshots kept going off in my head, like a string of firecrackers. Fate is so unpredictable. Not long before, it had been Hu An who brought me to the Soviet zone, and now here I was helping his daughter escape. If he was watching from the underworld, I had no idea what he'd think. We ran and ran, hiding by day and traveling by night, until we reached Dapu—as I said earlier, this was an important stop, but when we got there, not a single one of the underground workers could be found. There was no help for it—I handed Bingying over to a local villager. Of course, I had to give him quite a bit of money. Counterfeit bills? Ha-ha, you really are a clever devil. You're right, they were counterfeit bills. In any case, I was able to let out a sigh of relief. Ah Qing asked me what we should do next, and I said I had to go back again. He asked why, and I said I'd left my lover back in the Soviet zone. It wasn't right for a grown man like me to just leave without a word—I had to do right by her. I told them to wait for me, and when I returned with my lover, we'd continue on to Tianjin via Hong Kong. Ah Qing said he would come with me. I asked Bingying what she thought, and added that I could go fetch Broad Bean if I went back. She said, Okay, okay. She was such a good woman, reminding me again and again to be careful, saying she'd pray for me. Ah Qing and I left Dapu, and were captured by the enemy almost immediately.

I want you to know, miss, I didn't surrender right away. I held on for a few days. They said, Your side is about to get snuffed out like a candle. Weren't you in favor of violent revolution? Well, this is violent revolution—violent revolution can't be avoided, and we're about to invade the Soviet zone. Naturally, I disagreed with their point of view, and brought up Lenin's *The State and Revolution* to counter them. I said, Okay, okay, Lenin wrote that Marx and Engels's theory about violent revolution being unavoidable was in reference to capitalist countries. For a country to transform from a capitalist to a proletarian society, that could never be a natural process or one that took place within a legal framework—it was only achievable through violent revolution. By contrast, the demise of a proletarian country could only take place through self-destruction. They knew about Marx, but not Engels. I spent a long time explaining it to them, until one of them finally smacked me across the face. They said, Enough of that talk; Engels was the son of a factory owner, so he's a capitalist. That slap filled me with rage. I held out for a few days, but I ultimately couldn't keep it up—I had to surrender. Some people say I've spent my whole life surrendering, or that I can't see a woman without kowtowing to her. Did I kowtow to you, miss? No, I did not. Other people call me a natural-born traitor. What a joke! You think that bothers me? How could a little bird understand a swan? How could a dwarf make armor for a giant? To hear them talk, you'd think I had no beliefs at all. Nonsense! I had beliefs!

I believed that the country would grow strong, and soon achieve modernization. But in order to be strong and modern, it would first need to be stable, which meant squashing everything else. As you know, I have a background in law; I believe in order and running a country legally. If you don't have stability or unity, then you can't do anything. Don't you find it strange that right from the outset, these people gave me coloratura? Even so, they convinced me, and in the end I surrendered. There were major and minor circumstances leading to this point, and I can't be blamed for it. People were surrendering one after the other, just like someone's hair turns white every day. Later on, when people would squawk about something in front of me, I remembered what Lu Xun said: Walk your own path, and let other people say what they like.

Now that I'd surrendered, not to mention been appointed the deputy captain of a detachment, not just words were required of me, but also action. In order to demonstrate my commitment to stability and unity, I told them about the counterfeiting factory. The Red Guards were on the move anyway, so it's not like they had any further use for it, and now that Hu An was dead, it wouldn't matter if I spilled the beans. It wasn't just me—Ah Qing had surrendered too, and he also had ratted on the counterfeiting operation. It wasn't till 1943, when I saw Bai Shengtao on Bare Mountain, that I found out Ah Qing had been one of Tian Han's men all along. A while ago, my secretary showed me a document written by someone named Zhu [i.e., Zhu Xudong] that said Ah Qing's surrender was arranged by Tian Han. When I thought back to that time, I couldn't help wondering about something: Was it Ah Qing who leaked the information that led to my capture? Of course, that's just a guess—I don't have any evidence. What? Inform on Bingying? No, no, I never did, and neither did Ah Qing. That I can guarantee.

A Little More about Ah Qing

The document Mr. Fan mentioned was part of *Shooting the Breeze with Tian Han*, which Zhu Xudong edited and distributed:

> Whenever I mentioned Zhao Yaoqing, General Tian would say he had no clear recollection of him. But there was one occasion when Tian himself brought up the subject. He said, "I sent someone to take Bingying away, and that person was named Ah Qing." To tease him, I asked if he meant the Ah Qing from the Peking opera *Sha Jia Bang*. He said, "No, a different Ah Qing." Then he started talking. "One night, I was washing my feet when that guy came running over to ask for some time off. Ge Ren wanted

him to escort Bingying out of the Soviet zone, so he had to do it. Ge Ren had already talked to me about it. The problems with the leftist route were serious then, and if Bingying didn't get out of there, not only would she be in danger, but she might drag Ge Ren down too. I told Ah Qing not to say anything about where they were going, and to just do as Ge Ren said. He was worried that they would be captured by white dogs [i.e., white bandits] along the way. I said he could continue working for the Party even as a prisoner. He looked at me, confused, and I said it would be like getting allocated to a different position. He had to learn from Comrade Lei Feng [N.B. Zhu Xudong added a note here to say that Comrade Tian Han must have been confused, because the case of Lei Feng wasn't yet known at this time] and love whatever job he found himself doing, eternally pleased to be a nail of the Revolution. I told him that if he were to be captured, he should tell the enemy about the gully where the currency counterfeiting was taking place. The actual place, the honest truth. This way, the enemy would start to trust him and treat him more like a guest, so he'd be able to infiltrate them successfully. He dropped to his knees, and said again and again that he didn't dare. I stroked the back of his head and said, You look ridiculous. Get up! The counterfeiting operation has been abandoned—it's just sitting there, so we might as well leave it to the white dogs. If they decide to make false banknotes too, that's great. They'll disrupt their own economic order—that's more damage than a knife through the heart. The kid heard me out, then burst out laughing. He was cleverer than a monkey, and he managed the whole business without a single mistake. Of course, this had to do with Dai Li too. They were from the same hometown. The Nationalist insurgency was always very parochial—they thought whenever two people from the same town met, their eyes would fill with tears and they'd forget their principles. Later on, many of our situation reports were brought to us by Ah Qing, until he suddenly disappeared. Some time after that, we heard he'd ended up in Henan, and suffered quite a bit during the Cultural Revolution. But that's nothing; the sugar cane can't be sweet at both ends. In the beginning, we were fighting on the front line while he was enjoying life in Chongqing. So he had a good time, and then went through a bad patch. It evened out. I heard he had mental problems. Can you imagine that, trying to haggle with the People over your worth? I heard he eventually jumped down a well. Die if you have to, but why ruin a well too? Terrible."

When I asked if Ge Ren knew that Ah Qing's surrender was part of a plot, General Tian waved the question aside. "You'd have to ask him that. I'm not his tapeworm; I wouldn't know." Easy for him to say, but where would I find him to ask? Everyone knows Ge Ren died decades ago, at Two Li Mound.

Bingying was left at Dapu, waiting for Fan Jihuai and Ah Qing. She later told Anthony Thwaite that there was a hill outside Dapu called Mount Jingxian. She'd heard that the valley on the other side led to Phoenix Valley, and she would often stand there, wishing she could see through the hills, waiting for her daughter to appear. As the days passed, her despair grew. She started to think she would never see her daughter again. And in fact, it wasn't just Broad Bean whom she'd lost, but also the baby growing inside her. In *Beauty in a Time of Chaos*, Thwaite recorded Bingying's own words:

> In the blink of an eye, my father had been dead for three weeks. In China we call this "three sevens," and it's a day when we remember the deceased, so I went up Mount Jingxian to light some incense. Through the fog, I thought I heard my daughter crying, and imagined I saw Ge Ren not knowing what to do with her. I was so scared I would never see Ge Ren again, I started to weep. Then a villager came up behind me, saying that someone was looking for me. I thought this must be Fan Jihuai and Ah Qing, and asked if they had a child with them. He said no. The visitor was someone from our theater troupe who'd played a white bandit in *Victory at Any Cost*. He told me that Fan Jihuai and Ah Qing had been offered amnesty by the government. I asked how he knew, and he said the pair of them had led enemy troops into the Soviet zone. They were riding tall horses, wearing white gloves, with handguns at their waists. I asked about Broad Bean, but he said he didn't know anything about her. I tried to think of the best-case scenario, and imagined that Ge Ren had brought her to safety. Even so, terror and sadness took hold of my heart. Two or three days later, I had a miscarriage. Ge Ren liked little girls, and I thought that must have been a little girl baby. After that, I felt so guilty, like I'd never be able to make it up to Ge Ren. But the world wasn't done tormenting me yet. A year later, I heard from a friend who'd arrived from Shaanbei that he'd seen Ge Ren, but there was no sign of Broad Bean. Everything went black before my eyes . . .

A Dog's Philosophy

I waited till I figured that Ge Ren and the rest would have moved on before leading my detachment to Back Ditch. The counterfeiting factory was undamaged, so I hustled to have my troops remove the equipment, which we then handed over to a Public Security platoon garrisoned nearby.

Probably in order to make me serve the Nationalists wholeheartedly, when the higher-ups heard about this, they sent someone over to give me an award. In addition, they put Ah Qing back under my command. They also arranged for several talks to be given in my honor, all of which emphasized the importance of stability and unity in fighting the Japanese. After we were done with all that, I managed to extricate myself and took my forces back into the Soviet zone.

Did I return in glory? Forget it. I was worried about meeting anyone I knew—that would have been embarrassing. I put on a pair of glasses, hoping that would make me unrecognizable. At first I tried some gold-rimmed ones, but my subordinates said they made me look like a gangster on the Bund, so I switched to another pair. They said those were less gangster, more accountant. Back then, anyone who looked like they had money was in danger. So I hardened my heart and smashed out one of the lenses. Then I looked like I was wearing a mask.

As it turned out, I had worried for nothing. I didn't see a single person I knew, all the way to Ruijin. After several battles between the Red Guards and the Nationalists, everyone had left, and only corpses remained. I was curious about all these [dead] people with no faces or skin, until I found out that dogs had been gnawing at them. No, miss, I'm not trying to frighten you. Don't be scared, there's no such thing as ghosts. As a materialist, I've never believed in ghosts. If you're really afraid, come lie down next to me; then the ghosts won't dare do anything to you. Okay, okay? Not enough room? If you can't squeeze in, we'll think of something else. We need to be good at identifying problems, as well as solving them. Now look, you interrupted me, and I can't remember what I was saying.

Oh right, the dead people. There was no skin or flesh on them, just bones—skeletons. Their mouths were open wide, like they were laughing; their eye sockets were black and empty, and at first glance it looked like they were wearing dark glasses. All right, all right, I won't frighten you any more, let's talk about something else. I don't know where they came from, but some pastors showed up and, without a word, buried the bodies in the fields. I went over and tried to talk to them, but they ignored me. Their faces were completely blank, like roaming spirits. Quite a few were foreigners, so I couldn't give them a hard time. I continued on into Baibei, where I saw more dead people under White Cloud Bridge. One of them had a silver clip in her long hair. My heart jumped right through my throat—was this my lover? I told my aide to pull her out of the water right away. Then a pack of dogs showed up, their doggy eyes staring as they inched closer. Honestly, I didn't know what they wanted. One of my subordinates flung a rock at them, trying to scare them away, but that didn't stop them. They went around me onto White Cloud Bridge, toward Ah Qing, who was strolling by the river with his hands behind his back. Then I noticed that whenever Ah Qing had his hands behind him, the dogs would advance, but when he showed his hands, they'd freeze. Fuck! This was like something from a cartoon.

Later I realized they were waiting to eat Ah Qing. Dogs are connected to humans, so dog philosophy is the same as human philosophy. After living through so many battles, dogs have learned to see the world through a split lens, dividing humankind into two groups: hands behind backs and no weapons means criminals or prisoners of war who are about to be shot dead, and therefore may be eaten; the second group have rifles slung across their chests and are about to shoot the first group dead—they're not for eating. As I said, dogs are connected to humans. We humans enjoy dog meat, and dogs like eating humans too. Okay, okay, same, same. Now I realized why I'd seen so few female corpses. Their faces and breasts had been eaten away, turning them sexless. Many years later, when I was trying to persuade Ge Ren to surrender, I told him about those dogs. When he heard what I had to say, tears flowed down his cheeks. I had thought that if I could get him to weep, I would get my own way—but that turned out not to be the case.

The woman [was] dragged ashore. It was the same hairpin, but a different person. I had been mistaken. There was a hole in her cheekbone. Of course it was a bullet hole; do you even need to ask? It had grown larger from being in the river, and now it looked like it had been made with a poker. Suddenly, a crab crawled from that hole. What did you say? A surreal image? I don't know about surrealism, but I knew this was real. I also remember mentioning that crab to Ge Ren. He vomited in response, then after a while, started spitting blood like a cuckoo.

I told Ge Ren that I had once searched for his body in Baibei. I was telling the truth. At the time, I thought he'd been disposed of as a counter-revolutionary, so whenever I saw a body, I got off my horse to have a closer look. Ge Ren joked that I only did this so that I could take all the credit, plus any rewards they might be offering. Okay, okay, I don't deny that. But still, at the time, I really was anxious about where he might be. By coincidence, in Xiguan Village not far from Baibei, I saw Broad Bean. She was lighting a fire outside her front door, filthy as a mudskipper, playing with an animal bone. An old man sat next to her, staring at her through narrowed eyes. Seeing us walk over, the old man hastily shoved the girl behind a wall. I hesitated, wondering if I should take her away. After an intense mental struggle, I finally persuaded myself not to do anything rash. Here's what I thought: if Ge Ren was still alive, what if he came to get his daughter but she was gone? He might die from worry.

Okay, okay, I stayed the night at Baibei Elementary School. I had no idea that many years later, Ge Ren would come back and we'd face each other there. I couldn't get to sleep that night, so I went for a walk in Phoenix Valley. It was dark all around, except for where the light from the lanterns reached. All of a sudden, I heard someone moaning in the undergrowth of goji bushes and brambles. The soldiers heard it too, and immediately ducked down, as if the enemy had arrived. Cowards, all of them. I ordered them to go search. They bent over and moved toward the sound, gradually shrinking the circle until they'd closed in on the person, whom they dragged out. He was badly injured, and couldn't even stand upright. I couldn't see his face, which he'd pressed into his arm, like a chicken tucking its head under a wing. I told a soldier to make him show himself, at which he squealed and howled. Seeing him suffer like that, I wondered if I ought to show some revolutionary humanitarianism, and send him to heaven with a gunshot. As I hesitated, I spotted many tiny points of light appearing in the darkness, blinking like will-o'-the-wisp. Ha-ha, see how frightened you look. Didn't I just say I'm a materialist, and I don't believe in ghosts? Those weren't spirits, they were dogs. Stray dogs, circling around now, waiting to eat him.

When he heard the dogs bark, he pulled his head out from under his wing [i.e., his arm]. The lanterns shone on his face, which was crusted with blood. He cried out, Old Mr. Fan, old Mr. Fan [N.B. Back then, wouldn't it have been plain "Fan"?], save me. Hearing him call out my name, I realized who he was. God damn it, it was Yang Fengliang. He later told me he'd taken his "Fresh Flower Tune" lover to safety in another town, but when he got back, he saw corpses everywhere, and heard that Ge Ren might be dead too. Okay, okay, when I heard this, I hurried to Xiguan Village, but I couldn't find Broad Bean.

From then on, I made covert inquiries about Ge Ren's whereabouts and kept an eye on the newspaper reports, but there was never anything about him. I started to think he must really be dead, and I wondered again about the child. The night before we were due to leave Bare Mountain, I had another dream about her: her skinny face, oval as a melon seed, her large eyes, her long lashes, how her eyes would darken when she got angry, like dusk arriving on a clear day. The child stared at me in my dream. And again I remembered my friendship with Ge Ren, and felt I'd let him down. I finally brought a few of my trusted followers to Xiguan Village.

After a lot of searching, I finally found the old man who'd been taking care of Broad Bean. He told me someone had taken her away. I asked who it was, and he said it was a woman. Gesturing in the air, he tried to tell me what she looked like. The strange thing was, she sounded a lot like Bingying. Fuck! This was nonsense. As far as I knew, Bingying hadn't been back there since her departure. I gave him a lecture about politics, impressing upon him how important this matter was, and that he had to tell me the truth. If I found out he was lying to me, I said, I would make sure he paid for it. But although he twisted back and forth, that was all he would say. I was in a rage. Just as I was about to put some fear into him, one of my subordinates suddenly shot him dead. Please remember, I wasn't the one who pulled the trigger—it was a reactionary Nationalist. I've never shot anyone dead, I swear. My hands are clean. Just before he died, the old man pointed up at the pitiless sky, as if to say only heaven knows where Broad Bean is. Because he had once taken care of Ge Ren's daughter, I disposed of his body properly. No, I didn't toss him into the river to feed the fish, I dug a pit and buried him. Is that enough? No matter what, the dogs weren't going to gnaw on him.

Bastille Virus

The name of the old man who protected my mother, Broad Bean, is now lost to history. As I said before, Broad Bean had been taken away by my great-aunt. The man was probably pointing at the sky to tell Fan Jihuai that he wasn't lying, and heaven would bear witness.

My great-aunt set off for Bare Mountain in October 1934. Because "the counterfeiter Hu" had been shot dead, she fretted the whole way there that something would happen to Ge Ren and Bingying too, leaving Broad Bean an orphan. She went by boat to Quanzhou in Fujian, then continued on to Baibei. As I mentioned earlier, Reverend Ellis was with her. When she got to Baibei, she found the same scene Fan Jihuai described: not a soul in sight, just stray dogs roaming around. Of course, like Fan Jihuai, she also saw the silent clergy. According to Reverend Ellis's *The Majesty of the Orient*, those individuals were on a mission from the International Red Cross, and had come from Jiujiang in Jiangxi to gather the corpses. It was from them that my great-aunt and Reverend Ellis learned that a little girl with a foreign accent was staying with an old man at Xiguan Village. They had pleaded with him to get the child away from there, but he had insisted on staying put. They also told her that a little dog had been seen following the old man and girl around. My great-aunt thought this might well be a descendant of Bastille, the dog Hu An brought back from Paris. And from that single clue, she and Ellis found the old man and Broad Bean in Xiguan Village.

That dog from the street outside the Bastille had indeed had puppies, and one of them had been named Bastille—but my great-aunt never got to meet him. A few days before she and Ellis arrived at Bare Mountain, Bastille was bitten to death by the stray dogs. The old man was starving and couldn't bring himself to get rid of the corpse, so he cooked it. They found Broad Bean playing with a new toy: Bastille's thigh bone, as small and shiny as an opium pipe. The next day, my great-aunt departed for Tianjin with Broad Bean, while Reverend Ellis stayed behind. He started out collecting dead bodies, then moved on to disease prevention. Many years later, he met Ge Ren again.

My great-aunt said Broad Bean fell ill after they got back to Tianjin, running a "persistent low fever," "crying out in the night," and "refusing to have the lights turned off." Her condition got progressively worse, until she was completely bedridden. My great-aunt thought she might not have much longer to live. According to a doctor named Gordon Thompson at Tianjin Church Hospital, Broad Bean had been infected with a strange new virus. His gaze landed on the opium-pipe-like toy in her hand, which he was shocked to discover was a dog bone. When he found out that this little girl had recently eaten dog meat—my great-aunt said he looked like he wanted to vomit—he was certain her illness must have come from Bastille the dog, and so he named it Bastille virus. He probably didn't expect that the news of this case would spread far and wide, finally earning an entry in the *Encyclopædia Britannica*'s medical supplement, and becoming his great contribution to modern medicine.

Dr. Thompson's careful treatment saved my mother, Broad Bean's, life, but Bastille virus left her prone to anxiety and mood swings, which became a torment to my great-aunt. Many years later, my father—a person who left me with no memories whatsoever—decided he could no longer stand this torture, and walked out on us. Broad Bean died in the spring of 1965, when I was two years old. It was my great-aunt who brought me up. She liked to say that we were a cow and calf, separated by a generation. According to her, my mother died after becoming paralyzed. A few days before she passed, her eyes couldn't focus, her throat kept convulsing, and she drooled nonstop, filling half a spittoon each day with saliva wrung from her pillowcase.

While interviewing the scatologist I mentioned before, Dr. Yu Chengze, I met a virologist at his home, and I took the opportunity to ask him about Bastille virus, out of fear I had inherited it from my mother. In the course of compiling this book, I have often felt anxious, and I've experienced short-term loss of concentration. I was worried that I would leave this world before finishing this manuscript. The virologist told me that the fastest you would die with Bastille virus was two weeks, but the disease often lay dormant inside you, turning your entire body into its incubator, until many years later, when it would slowly kill you. I asked if it was hereditary, but he didn't answer directly, and said instead that he encountered Bastille virus carriers almost every day. As we were talking, one of Mr. Yu Chengze's professors walked in and joined the conversation. He told us that the Friday before, a new computer virus had surfaced—also called Bastille virus, with the same characteristics as the medical version: impossible to eradicate, liable to flare up at unpredictable intervals. According to him, even the newest antivirus programs were helpless against this new scourge, and in fact they could become infected themselves and turn into vectors too.

What he said inevitably reminded me of Dr. Thompson's fate: in 1954, he died of Bastille virus. I have no way of knowing whether it was my mother or another patient who infected him. Thompson's death saddened many of his students, including the future winner of the Nobel Prize in Medicine, Fernando Galbiati. In his book *The Broken Wave*, Mr. Galbiati mentions Thompson treating Broad Bean:

> My teacher Mr. Thompson's destiny was changed because of a Chinese girl. She was the descendant of an anti-Japanese hero named Ge Ren. Mr. Thompson diagnosed her with Bastille virus. Bastille was the name of a dog that Ge Ren [*sic*] brought back with him after finding it outside the famous Bastille prison. Yet strangely, this virus didn't show up in Paris until the 1970s. According to the *World Health Organization Annual Report*, Bastille virus has been spreading rapidly in recent years through Africa, Russia, western China, and the Persian Gulf countries. Each time I read this, my fears deepen, and I miss Dr. Thompson a little more . . .

Tonsillitis

Two years later, I found out by chance that Ge Ren was still alive when I saw his condolences for Lu Xun's death printed in a newspaper. I had also sent a contribution, and I'd been checking to see if it would be published. Mine never appeared, but Ge Ren's did. As I said before, Ge Ren had many dealings with Lu Xun. They were both literary figures, and they had a lot in common—they swam in the same waters. Now Ge Ren spoke in lofty terms about how he'd lost his other half and had been weeping floods of tears—his contemporary, the rock he'd leaned on.

It was only when I saw this that I realized that Ge Ren hadn't died, and that he'd not only taken part in the Long March, but had successfully reached Shaanbei. Still, it was many years before I had more concrete news from him. At the time, I had joined KMT Military Intelligence, and my sources in Shaanbei informed me that Ge Ren was in Yan'an, translating Tolstoy. You know who Tolstoy was? No, not a fashion designer, he was a writer. Lenin called him a mirror of the Russian Revolution.

After the Nationalists and the Communists formed a united front against the Japanese, people would come to Yan'an from time to time. On one occasion, a group of American journalists traveled from Shanghai to Chongqing and wanted to visit Yan'an. One of them was named Goodman—I knew him a little, because he'd been to Chongqing before. I bought him a meal and asked him to help me find out about Ge Ren. He misunderstood that I was asking him to gather intelligence, and protested that he was a reporter and didn't want to get involved in politics. I hastily reassured him that I'd been good friends with Ge Ren, and having heard that he was translating Tolstoy, I wanted to publish his books in Chongqing—I had no other motive. Goodman told me that when he left Shanghai, a theater actress named Bingying also asked him to bring back news of Ge Ren, particularly how his lung disease was doing. Okay, okay, that's when I remembered that Ge Ren would indeed still be suffering from lung disease.

I happened to be away from Chongqing when Goodman passed through again on his way from Yan'an, so I didn't find out about Ge Ren['s situation]. A short while after that, I heard that he'd died in battle with the Japanese—a bad death; his entire regiment was wiped out. This was huge, yet that sack of straw we sent to Yan'an actually didn't know anything about it! You know why I call him a sack of straw, miss? He literally was a sack of straw, because his surname was Xiao, with the radical on top that means "grass." Believe it or not, I called him that to his face! Of course, he's dead now, so I can call him a sack of straw all I want and he won't hear me. He didn't pass this intelligence to me, so I had to wait to read it in the papers, but it never appeared there either. I got so anxious, my gums swelled, and my tonsils got inflamed too, filling with pus. Come closer and see, miss. You see? I don't have tonsils, they were cut out. They had to be; they kept getting infected. All in all, it was of no use for me to get anxious—the only thing to do for it was to chop them out. I remember at the time, the *Xinhua Daily* was at Chongqing's Tiger Mouth—it was the Communist newspaper. I sent people there to ask around, but they didn't know anything either.

Huh? Crying? No, I'm not crying. You're still young, miss; maybe you don't understand how marvelous that was. When I heard the news, I felt a mix of sorrow and joy. Okay, okay! The *Poetry Classic* put it best: brothers may squabble, but they unite against a threat from outside. To die in a war of resistance and become a hero of the People would surely be a stroke of good luck in a time of misfortune. I wanted to find out how Ge Ren died and help spread the word, so that I could bask in his reflected glory.

I even made the effort to read *Hochi Shimbun*, a Japanese newspaper, and sure enough, there was a report about Ge Ren's death, proclaiming with great fanfare that the Battle of Two Li Mound had been yet another major victory.

A week or so later, I got another secret message from Xiao, the sack of straw, also saying that Ge Ren had sacrificed his life in the Battle of Two Li Mound, and that a wake had already been held. As an old friend, I thought I should send a condolence telegram to Yan'an. We were part of the United Front, after all. But it was all over, and sending condolences at that point would have been like shutting the stable door after the horse had bolted. People might even have thought I was deliberately rubbing salt into the wound. I spent a lot of time thinking it over, and finally decided not to.

No Better Than a Straw Dog

The person old Mr. Fan was referring to as a "sack of straw" was Xiao Bangqi, though in fact he was nothing of the kind. According to the *Biographical Dictionary of Republican China* (White Crow Press, USA, 1989), Xiao Bangqi graduated from the Moscow Medical Academy and became a surgeon. One of his classmates was Zhang Zhankun, who was mentioned in the first part of this book. In 1948 he went to Hong Kong, and then to teach at a university in San Francisco. In his book *Re-creating an Individual Identity*, written late in his life, Mr. Xiao described his encounters with Ge Ren at Yan'an. He also mentioned Zhang Zhankun getting killed. The following passage is titled "No Better Than a Straw Dog." It first appeared in Hong Kong's *Eastern Ocean* before being anthologized in the third issue of the *Journal for Ge Ren Studies:*

> As Zhuangzi said, "The useless tree does not fear the axe, and does no harm, so it may stand untroubled." It was because I had studied medicine that I was sent to Shaanbei and became a performer. After the Long March, there were as many officers and soldiers with lung disease as there were hairs on an ox. Mr. and Mrs. Zhou Enlai had lung disease [*sic*], and so did Ge Ren, not to mention many more in the lower ranks. There was a great deal of resentment because we were short of medicine and bandages. As far as I know, the two most common complaints that we saw were constipation and tuberculosis. Kuomintang Military Intelligence thought that by sending me there, I would be able to give them inside information about the scarlet bandits. As the ancient saying goes, it is better to walk a thousand days south than a single day north. To be honest, I should not have accepted this mission. Fan Jihuai came to talk to me. He said he had

once heard Mr. Hu Shizhi say that Cao Yin (Cao Xueqin's grandfather), who oversaw weaving in Jiangning, had been named a purchasing official of the imperial household. He actually served as a spy for Emperor Kang Xi and fought in the United Front in Jiangnan, but he was still loved and respected by his descendants . . . I started out at Bao'an, the end point of the Long March. I once heard my former classmate Zhang Zhankun say that on May 28, 1869 (the seventeenth day of the fourth month in the lunar calendar, or the eleventh day of the fourth month of Jisi Year 19), the Nian Army, the remnants of the Taiping Forces, first arrived in Bao'an and were defeated by the Qing forces. That was the conclusion of the most recent Long March in history before this one. Going by the historical example, I thought the Red Guards would be defeated by the government within the next few days, and I would be able to get away from this godforsaken place to head back home. Laozi said, "Heaven and earth see all things equally, no better than a straw dog." With battles all around me, my life was naturally no more than a piece of straw [N.B. or stalk of grass], no more than a dog. With peace on earth hanging in the balance, what was the point of worrying about my existence?

My first sight of Ge Ren was during the first snow of that year. I was walking by the river with Bai Shengtao and Zhang Zhankun. The water had not yet frozen, and a boat was sailing past as the snow drifted down, a striking image—and on that boat were Tian Han and Ge Ren. Because Fan Jihuai had asked me to find out about Ge Ren's illness, I turned to Bai Shengtao and deliberately said that I had heard that Ge Ren was in the final stages of his disease and was not responding to treatment, but now that I had seen him in person, I knew that those were merely rumors. Bai replied that Ge Ren did have lung disease, and it was indeed getting worse, and asked if I would see him and try to find a cure. About a week later, Bai Shengtao took me to meet Ge Ren, saying he was coughing due to an obstruction in his chest, and that his condition was not good—did I know anything that might help? I saw Ge Ren in a cave house. It was dark in there, but once we lit a candle, I could see the whole place: there was a wooden table against the wall with a copper pen holder on it, containing two brushes, a red-and-blue pencil, and a liquid [fountain] pen. There was also a trade edition of Tolstoy's short stories, translated by Qu Qiubai. I had once read through that book, and ended up making plenty of marks with my own red-and-blue pencil, covering it in notes and corrections. Ge Ren said he wanted to retranslate this Tolstoy book and write a new foreword. He also mentioned having heard from Bai Shengtao that I had spent time in Russia. His voice was low, like a piano when you step on the pedal. I urged him to take care of himself. He said he felt time pressing on him, and that he would never be able to finish everything he was meant to do, so those tasks kept accumulating. For instance, he wanted to raise money to publish Lu Xun's work in Yan'an, but he had not yet managed to do anything about it. It felt as though he was not interested in my medical expertise, and only wanted an idle chat. He asked what the origin was of the Russian name Astapovo, and I frankly said I had no idea. He said he had been to Tula and knew that name meant "intercept," but he had no idea about the definition of Astapovo, only that it was a small train station. Zhang Zhankun later reminded me that Astapovo is where Tolstoy died—as far as Ge Ren was concerned, his Astapovo was Two Li Mound.

I heard about the Two Li Mound affair through Ge Ren's good friend Huang Yan when he came to the hospital to seek treatment. Since hearing that Ge Ren had died in battle, he had frequently had trouble sleeping, eventually growing dizzy and experiencing trouble breathing. He said he wanted to write about Ge Ren's heroic exploits to raise everyone's spirits and encourage those who would come after. For some reason, I never saw that manuscript appear. . . . Not long thereafter, the dung-collecting campaign began. My former classmate Zhang Zhankun was taken in for questioning. Someone came to investigate my dealings with him, and hinted that if I gave him up, I might be able to save myself. I spent a long time thinking about it—if I kept my mouth shut, I would be signing my own death warrant and could forget about seeing my wife again. After much consideration, I revealed that he had once talked about the Nian Army's Long March to point out that the Red Guards' Long March had a precedent in history. The investigator exclaimed that this alone would be enough to send him to hell. Mao himself had told us that the Long March was a proclamation, a propaganda campaign, a seeding machine, that ever since Pan Gu opened up heaven and earth, from the three kings and five emperors till today, there had never been anything like this Long March. Before the campaign was over, Zhang Zhankun had been beheaded. The word was that he had confessed to being a spy sent to Yan'an by the government. And it was I, the actual spy, who had sent Mr. Zhang Zhankun to the guillotine. After that, I blamed myself constantly, and found it impossible to stop wallowing in guilt. On March 12, 1947, the government forces invaded Yan'an. I was hit by shrapnel, and concealed myself in a cave house to lick my wounds like a dog. It was spring, but the air remained thick with snow. On the evening of March 18, government soldiers entered Yan'an, and I was captured as a Red Guard. Fortunately, it was my leg that had been hit. If it had been my chest, and I had not been able to speak up, I would surely have been shot. When they found out my actual identity, they seemed much less enthusiastic. They would have preferred it if I really had been a Red Guard, so they could have claimed their reward . . .

When I got to Xi'an, Fan Jihuai sent a telegram asking me to return to Chongqing. I told him that until my leg healed, I would not be able to go gallivanting anywhere. I hoped he understood. . . . For many years after that, I did not return to the Party, but neither did I throw my lot in with Chiang. I found a small house and became one with the People, only wanting to survive this turbulent time, living as peacefully as someone in the Land of Peach Blossoms . . .

The reader might remember that in the first part of this book, Bai Shengtao said it was his disclosure that led to Zhang Zhankun's death. Now it seemed Mr. Xiao Bangqi was to blame too. I told Bai Ling that her grandfather wasn't the only one responsible for Zhang Zhankun's beheading, thinking she'd be pleased, but she merely shrugged and said it was the same, nothing but dog-eat-dog.

Talk Poetry

Okay, okay, let's go on. After a few months, General Dai Li summoned me to Yat-sen Road in Chongqing, where Shulu, the Military Intelligence headquarters, was. What, you've never heard of Shulu? How about this—I'll take you there sometime for a couple of days. I promise you'll be more comfortable than in any five-star hotel. Ay! If I tell you Dai Li once had his office there, you'll understand how plush it was. Of course, history is all about progress, and both hardware and software are constantly improving, so it's even more comfortable these days.

Dai Li looked like some sort of feline creature, and smiled like a tiger. He was a learned individual—you can tell by his name, which means "to wear a bamboo hat" and comes from the *Poetry Classic*. "He rides in a carriage, I wear a bamboo hat, but when we meet, he steps out to greet me." Of course, his name is also intended to remind you to greet him with proper deference. And so each time I saw him, I not only bowed, but also clasped my hands. I've done my share of such greetings in my life. But at the end of the day, a clasped-hand bow is one of our traditional Chinese virtues. In this globalized world, because of the spread of AIDS, I've spoken up in all sorts of places, big and small, to say that we ought to bow more instead of shaking hands or kissing, in order to prevent infection.

Okay, okay, let's not get sidetracked. Dai Li laughed and said, No need, no need. Miss, I have a universally applicable theory that I should share with you: if you're knowledgeable and talented, you'll receive respect and adoration wherever you go. Dai Li showed me a lot of respect. Without my asking, he gave up his seat, poured me some tea, and offered me a cigarette. Next he said he had a question for me. I said, Sure, ask away. I even gave him a bit of praise to make him happy: I said this was a way of getting in touch with the masses. He said he'd seen a poem that he liked well enough but didn't really understand. That gave me a secret thrill. Okay, okay! This was exactly my area of expertise; now I could show him what I knew. He handed me a copy of *Scattered Scriptures*, a newspaper edited by someone in Hong Kong called Xu Yusheng. I glanced at it—the poem was "Broad Bean Blossoms." I didn't immediately recognize it, though it seemed familiar. I said, It's just about broad bean flowers? Lots of pretty language, but that's just pointless nonsense from some poet. Dai Li said he'd heard that Chen Duxiu was fond of broad bean flowers—could this have been written by him? I said definitely not; I had read Chen Duxiu's writing, and he used classical forms. Then could it have been written *for* Chen Duxiu? he asked. That's when I thought, ah, he's a smiling tiger. The drunkard isn't interested in the wine—but in Chen Duxiu. So I said, Isn't Chen Duxiu dead? So forget about him! What the hell! As I was saying this, I started to remember—the poem was by Ge Ren. He wrote it in Japan. After the May Fourth Movement, as I think I already told you, he published it again in a magazine called something like *New Century*, and it caused quite a stir. The name of the author of this poem was just a string of English letters. I had to stare quite a while before I made out what it said: Melancholy. That confirmed it. This had to be by Ge Ren. His Russian name was Melancholsky.

I wondered why the smiling tiger was showing me this. Did he suspect me of being mixed up with the Communists? I wasn't too worried, though, because Ge Ren had died at Two Li Mound, and surely Dai Li didn't suspect me of using necromancy to communicate with the dead! I just said, Whatever you want me to do, just say it. Dai Li said he'd managed to find a bit of free time in the midst of everything else, and he wanted to talk poetry with a friend to balance his life. Naturally he'd thought of me. Then he asked if I still read poetry. I said yes, I did—poetry was a special form of ideology, and it would not be acceptable to stop reading it. Next he wanted to know which contemporary poets I liked. I wondered what he was trying to get at—and decided that nothing I said should get any poet into trouble. So I said Xu Zhimo's work was pretty good, although he was dead now. And Tagore was great too, although he was in India. Poets are known to be malcontents, but those two never complained about anything. They only wrote about twilight clouds and flying birds, and cared about nothing but lyricism. All poets should learn from their example. Okay, okay, as soon as the words were out of my mouth, he said that hearing a scholar say one line was better than a decade's worth of reading. I hadn't even shown what I was truly capable of, and he was already praising me. He raised a glass to me. You probably don't know, miss, that when it comes to drinking, I've always stuck to the three-cup rule: just three cups of anything, and not a single drop more. But I had to make an exception that day, because it was someone from the leadership raising a glass to me, so I ended up downing quite a bit more than usual.

The fox showed his tail when he asked about Ge Ren's poetry. He said, Doesn't Cui Yongyuan [N.B. a CCTV presenter—from Mr. Fan's own words] believe in speaking the truth directly? There's no one else here, so just speak the truth directly. So I had to say I hadn't read much of Ge Ren's work, and hadn't looked recently at the earlier stuff. He replied, I guess you haven't, because the piece I just showed you was by Ge Ren. I didn't think I could get away with pretending ignorance, so I smacked my head as if I'd just realized: Now that you mention it, I've suddenly remembered that this is by Ge Ren. I think he wrote it in Japan. Dai Li said that around "May the Fourth," he was a hot-blooded youth who liked reading new poetry, and he saw this one, though back then it was called "Who Was Once Me." If that son of a bitch already knew all this, what was he asking me for? I said nothing, but anger was filling my belly. That's when he clapped his hands, and his secretary brought in that long-preserved copy of New Century. She was gorgeous, that secretary, and smelled lovely, like a second Butterfly Wu. She handed me the magazine and walked away, her hips swaying. Dai Li had done his homework meticulously—every line that had changed from the original was outlined in scarlet ink. Just as I was wondering where this was leading, he abruptly asked, Mr. Fan, can Xiao Bangqi be trusted? I said, He's had so many years of Party education, and I've never heard about any problems. Then he wanted to know if Xiao had been the one to report Ge Ren's death. I said yes, and hadn't I already passed on that information? And that's when the smiling tiger told me Ge Ren was still alive. I had considered all kinds of things he might possibly say to me, but not that. I won't lie to you, miss, the news filled my head with confusion, and I even wondered if there was something wrong with Dai Li. After a while, I said, Are you joking, sir? He said soldiers never joke, and this poem made it clear that not only was Ge Ren alive, but he was probably on Bare Mountain.

Suddenly I was completely sober. Bare Mountain? What would he be doing there? I asked. He said he'd been pondering that too, but the reports they had managed to intercept suggested that Ge Ren wrote "Broad Bean Blossom" on Bare Mountain. He'd sent someone to find out more, and they reported that a stranger had indeed been spotted in Baibei Town. His spy didn't know Ge Ren, but judging by the physical description he sent back, it was probably him. I insisted this couldn't be—it was clear from the intelligence that Ge Ren was dead. Dai Li banged his glass on the table twice and said, Let's not jump to conclusions. We have to finish our analysis first. Then he said he had told the old man [i.e., Chiang Kai-shek] everything, and gotten his permission to dispatch me to Bare Mountain to find out what was going on. If that was indeed Ge Ren, I was to find out what he was doing there, and then persuade him to surrender and join the Nationalists. Fuck! So that's why I'd been summoned to Shulu.

It looked like he had already thought this through, because he now produced a plan. It consisted of many points, but they all fell under the same three headings: principles (that is, the good of Party and Nation above all), effectiveness (that is, tactics), and discipline (that is, the need to keep it all a secret). He said as long as I took care of those big items, the little things would take care of themselves. The smiling tiger's parting words were that I had to move him with emotion and persuade him with reason. Mr. Ge Ren had to understand the simple truth: that fish can't leave the water, and melons can't leave the vine. There could be no revolution without the Three Principles of the People.

You see, miss, Dai Li understood well the principle of being loose on the outside and tight within, of hiding the knife in his smile. If you were trying to make a living under him, you'd have to remember not to annoy him in any way—that would never end well for you. After he finished giving me my orders, he pretended to show some understanding, and added that if I really felt uncomfortable about this, he could consider sending someone else. I was well aware that at this crucial moment in history, if I dared to say the word "no," he would dare to take me out and have me shot. I wasn't about to die at his hands, so without even blinking, I said, Okay, okay, I'll go. Dai Li was delighted at that. He said, Just put in whatever requests you have, and the Party will find a way to make them happen.

Xu Yusheng and Scattered Scriptures

As we already know, after Mr. Ge Cundao was assassinated, Hu An sent Mr. Xu Yusheng to Qinggeng to fetch Ge Ren back to Hangzhou. In the two years after that, Xu Yusheng and Ge Ren formed a deep friendship. When Ge Ren departed for Japan, Xu Yusheng left Hangzhou too, for Hong Kong. According to Xu's *Qiantang River Dream Diary*, Ge Ren wrote him many letters from Japan. When he heard that Xu had founded *Scattered Scriptures* in Hong Kong, he had the following suggestion:

> *Scattered Scriptures* ought to publish the great works of Zhongfu [i.e., Chen Duxiu] and Shouchang [i.e., Li Dazhao]. He sent me Shouchang's "Youth," and I was deeply moved by the lines "Spring days bring the sun, the east wind ends the frost. From distant ocean islands, a return to ancestral lands. The desolate wastes transform in an instant to clear brightness; the frozen days are once more filled with a hundred plants in bloom. Every change of the seasons fills my heart with thoughts."

This essay did indeed appear in *Scattered Scriptures*. According to Mr. Xu Yusheng, many people got the impression that *Scattered Scriptures* was "close to the Bolsheviks" entirely because of this one piece. In the following years, Ge Ren rarely communicated with Xu Yusheng. Then in 1929 he received a letter from Ge Ren, which said he was now teaching at Shanghai University and was working on a book titled *The Walking Shadow*. Xu wrote back immediately to say he would like to serialize it in *Scattered Scriptures*, and also that "I know a little about the circumstances in which your father died far from home. If you have time to visit Hong Kong, we can speak further about it, and perhaps that will be of benefit to you." After that, they once again stopped communicating for several years, though he "was constantly hearing" about Ge Ren's movements and his exploits with Bingying in the Soviet zone, as well as his participation in the Long March. Later, he applied to the People's government for permission to travel to Yan'an. His aim, apart from visiting the place, was to see Ge Ren. Because he had the reputation of being "close to the Bolsheviks," his request was turned down. It wasn't till 1941 that he heard from a Hong Kong reporter who had passed through Yan'an that Ge Ren was working as a translator. Thinking that Ge Ren's own book might be finished by now, he sent him another letter asking the same question: whether he could serialize it in his paper. In the winter of 1942, he heard from a friend who'd fled to Hong Kong that Ge Ren had died at the hands of the Japanese, in the Battle of Two Li Mound. A short while thereafter, he was still deep in pain and regret when he received a poem titled "Broad Bean Blossoms":

> Because this letter had passed through many hands, the envelope was so grubby it was impossible to make out the postmark. The letter wasn't signed, but the handwriting was clear, and I knew this poem had come from Ge Ren. The author's name was listed as the English word "Melancholy." I thought he must have mailed it before his death—in a way, these were his last words.

As for when this letter was actually mailed, that subject comes up during Ge Ren's meeting with Fan Jihuai, so we won't discuss it any further here. As we know, Xu Yusheng soon published the poem in *Scattered Scriptures*, "in order to show my deep remembrance of Ge Ren, as well as my respect for a warrior who was martyred for the cause of Chinese Communism." The full text of "Broad Bean Blossoms," as it appeared in the January 6, 1943, issue of *Scattered Scriptures*, is as follows:

> Who was once me,
> Who was the daytime in my mirror,
> The rippling brook through Mount Qinggeng
> Or the broad bean blossoms flourishing by White Cloud River?
>
> Who was once me,
> Who was the springtime in my mirror,
> The bees on the Arbat
> Or the lovers singing amid broad bean blossoms?
>
> Who was once me,
> Who was the lifetime in my mirror,
> The red flame flickering in the cave house
> Or the shadow of fluttering broad bean blossom petals?
>
> Who warns me in the darkness,
> Who walks toward me from the crowd,
> Who breaks my mirror into tiny shards
> So that I turn into countless selves?

Compared to "Who Was Once Me" as it appeared in *New Century*, the urgent and brave inquiry into the truth about himself is still present, and it's only individual words that have changed: Mount Qinggeng, White Cloud River, the Arbat, and cave house, for example. Like the string through a pearl necklace, these words draw a thread through Ge Ren's life. Dai Li, whose sense of smell was sharper than any dog's, naturally wouldn't miss a single one of them.

Mr. Xu Yusheng could never have expected that publishing "Broad Bean Blossoms" not only would lead to Ge Ren's death, but also would change the fates of many people connected to Ge Ren, including himself: on June 9, 1944, Xu Yusheng was assassinated by a Kuomintang Military Intelligence spy along Sha Shek Lane, on his way to Hong Kong's Repulse Bay Hotel.

Forming a Team

I required one simple thing: that an assistant of my choosing would go ahead to find out what was going on before I arrived in person. Dai Li agreed, and said he would give the green light no matter who I picked.

Okay, okay, now that I had carte blanche, it was time to start forming a team.

How would I do this? Well, when I tell you, you'll understand how much effort I put into it. The first person I picked was Yang Fengliang, whom I mentioned before. There were several considerations at work here. Firstly, Ge Ren had never treated him badly. He had joined Kuomintang Military Intelligence, but when I brought up Ge Ren privately, he still spoke about him respectfully. So I thought if that person really was Ge Ren, Yang Fengliang wouldn't give him a hard time. Secondly, Yang Fengliang was a diplomat by training, and he had the gift of the gab. He could convince you that a piece of straw was a gold bar, and vice versa. I would need an expert like him if I was to persuade Ge Ren to surrender. Thirdly, I got along well with him. During our time in the Soviet zone, we were both outsiders. What are outsiders? That's what you'd call anyone out of the ordinary. We were on the same wavelength, and when we got to Chongqing, we continued to see each other often. You've surely noticed that I'm the sort of person who likes to be part of the crowd all the time, and although I have a higher position, I never put on airs. Whenever he visited, I would receive him with good food and wine—everything he could want but a woman. Not that he wanted one. As a romantic, he thought only about his "Fresh Flower Tune." She was still on Bare Mountain and had given birth to his child. He'd been longing to be reunited with them for some time now. A gentleman makes good things happen for others—that's a traditional Chinese virtue, so why wouldn't I go along with it?

That reminds me: A few years ago, I accepted an invitation to a tourism festival at Mount Heng. While I was there, I met a monk with ordination scars the size of date pits. He told me he'd come there from the Bodhi Temple. That gave me a shock—did he mean the one in Baibei Town? After the event, the monk came to find me at my hotel. Seeing how nice and polite he was, I asked him to have a seat. You'll never guess what, miss—this little monk turned out to be Yang Fengliang's nephew.

When he said that, I immediately noticed his resemblance to Yang Fengliang. They looked a lot alike—it was uncanny, especially those big flappy ears. They might have come out of the same mold. His eyes were a lot like "Fresh Flower Tune's." Even though he was a monk, they were full of longing and brightness, as if they could speak. He said he'd heard someone say my name at the ceremony, and he wanted to ask me something. The person who had mentioned me was Sun Guozhang—who was he? I thought about it for quite a while before recalling that this was Yang

Fengliang's aide in Chongqing. So I asked, Hey, little monk, what did that Sun guy say to you? He answered that Sun Guozhang had told him Fan Jihuai knew how his grandfather had died. I told him he was a monk now, so he ought to let go of the bad ways of thinking, and give his whole heart to Buddha. He clasped his fingers together and muttered something about me being a benefactor, but still he didn't leave. I asked what was wrong, and he said he also wanted to find out whether I knew Liu Faqing. Do you know who that is, miss? Liu Shaoqi's grandson. He's now a Taoist priest on Mount Heng. I told the little monk I was there for the tourism festival and couldn't get involved in anything else. Fuck! It took a lot of effort to get him to leave. Before he went, he said, Get some rest, sir, and when you've gotten in touch with the Taoist priest Liu, I will come find you again. Fuck! I didn't want this guy to keep bothering me, so I left Mount Heng that very night. But you don't need to worry, miss. I've phoned ahead to the Baibei authorities, and told them not to let any monks take part in the ceremony. I'd be annoyed if I saw them there.

Yang Fengliang's Descendants

Yang Fengliang's grandson that Mr. Fan mentioned was called Yang Min—Min as in Minnan, a very Hokkien name. His grandmother wasn't "Fresh Flower Tune"—she and her son died at Ah Qing's hands—but rather Yang Fengliang's first wife. When Yang Min arrived in Baibei in 1996 to pay homage to his ancestors, he ended up remaining there and becoming a monk at the Bodhi Temple, changing his name to Minghai.

The Bodhi Temple is now located at 63 Shanbei Road, Guancheng District, Baibei City. Diagonally across the road, at number 60, is where "Fresh Flower Tune's" tea house once stood. That plot is now occupied by a three-star hotel called Jade Flower Garden, a jewelry tycoon's investment property. I stayed at this hotel during my various trips to Baibei. Jade Flower Garden is a tranquil place, with everything you need for a comfortable stay. The only inconvenience is that it had too many prostitutes, who rang at all hours offering their services and disturbing my sleep. I often slipped out for a walk around the Bodhi Temple, which now occupies fifty mu of land in the form of a U-shaped courtyard, with urns at every corner. The first time I visited, they were in the middle of a calligraphy competition, which was won by Mr. Guo Ping, whom I mentioned earlier. Secretary Guo said he'd been practicing his craft for many years, so it was a well-deserved victory. I had several conversations with Secretary Guo in that U-shaped courtyard, but he never mentioned Minghai.

After I finished editing Mr. Fan's transcript, I made another trip to Baibei. This time I reached out to Secretary Guo specially, to ask about Minghai. He dismissed my question with a single sentence: "Alas, due to karma, Minghai has left us." Dead, at such a young age? What of? But he refused to say another word. I had a chat with a monk at a tea house not far from the temple. He was called Minghui, though I should refer to him as "former monk Minghui," because he has since returned to the secular world. He had a round face with stubble like a potato sprouting after winter. He was from Ruijin, and after he left the temple, he returned there to set up a tea house, which he named Minghui Tea House, on the grounds that customers would find a monk's name reassuring. His establishment had an alcove in which hung a painting of oil lamps and scrolls, the tea house's brand. In front of it was the cashier's desk, on which was a figure of a red-faced Lord Guan—representing not loyalty, but the God of Fortune in another guise.

Minghui had been very close to Minghai—they had made the trip to Mount Heng together. According to Minghui, it was he who told Minghai the story of Liu [Faqing] the Taoist priest. With that, he walked over to the cashier's desk, while calling for the waitress to top up my tea. He returned a moment later with an old newspaper, the August 6, 1995, edition of *East China Information Daily*, which he said he had bought at a subway station in Shanghai while on pilgrimage. It contained an article about Liu Faqing:

> Liu Shaoqi's grandson Liu Faqing, 30, has become a Taoist priest on Mount Heng. Shortly after Liu was born, his parents were detained in the "bullpen." Not long after that, his father, Liu Yunbin, was tortured to death by the rebels. Later, his mother took him back to her old home on the plains of Qinghai. The nomadic herders gave him food, and the living Buddha at the Lama Temple taught him to read and write and to recite scripture. He joined the army and fought in the war of defense against Vietnam. After his demobilization, he returned to Qinghai, where he became a village chief. Six years ago, he joined the Taoist priesthood at Dragon Gate Cave in Baoji, a place he had often passed with his nanny as a child. While he was in the priesthood, his pilgrimages took him to many places. Last spring, he settled in a temple on Mount Heng. This grandson of the Chinese Republic's president wore two bands of cloth around his head, a cotton cassock, a braided silk sash around his waist, and a seven-star sword.

Former monk Minghui said they never once saw Liu during their time on Mount Heng. After his return, Minghai would frequently reread this article. Minghai believed that, apart from the name, the religion, and a few other details, he was like the person being discussed. His grandfather wasn't the president of the Republic, but he had been a diplomat; his father was tortured to death; and his mother once fled with him to Wuyi Hill, where they lived on wild fruits and plants. As for himself, not only had he fought in the Vietnam War, but he'd lost part of his fibula and several toes in a bomb blast, which had left him with a duck-like gait to this day. He had never been a village headman, but that wasn't too far from his experience. His voice trembling with tears (which somewhat injured the dignity of Buddhism), he recalled that because of a dispute over ancestral graves, he had gotten into an argument with the local headman. As a result, he was tied up and taken to the police station, where a flashlight was aimed directly into his eyes as long as he refused to admit his guilt. Former priest Minghui told me he had no idea if Minghai was telling the truth or not, because the Śūraṅgama Sūtra says, "Every kind of dharma arises from the mind, and every kind of mind arises from the dharmas," and the Mahayana Sūtra says, "If you can see the cause, you can see the dharma." I had no idea what this meant, so Minghai explained that thought affects matter, and matter affects thought. Afraid that he hadn't been clear enough, he elaborated, "For instance, I want to earn money to get married, so I opened this tea house. Now that I have money, women come flocking to me, so I don't want to get married anymore. Why buy a cow when I can get the milk by leaning across the fence? That's what it means when we say 'Every kind of dharma arises from the mind' or 'If you can see the cause, you can see the dharma.'"

Minghai believed that their life stories were very similar, so if Liu Qingfa could become a Taoist priest, then he should be able to find some position at the Bodhi Temple. Apart from chanting scriptures, there was nothing he liked better than organizing cultural activities. He was the one who had made the calligraphy competition happen, by offering up his savings of many years. He had made an arrangement with Secretary Guo beforehand: after Guo's victory, he would get to work with the higher-ups to have Minghai appointed as head abbot. To make sure that Guo didn't change his mind, Minghai even presented him with some of the temple's urns. Guo told him not to worry—from the point of view of promoting young cadres, the abbotship was his for the taking. Sure enough, Guo got his first prize, but the "job of abbot" (in Minghai's words) went to another monk. Minghai went to see Guo, and the two of them had an argument—though actually it was the three of them, because the new abbot joined in too. According to former monk Minghui, Secretary Guo said something inappropriate: "Baibei is about to become a city. How could we have a cripple as head abbot? That would be bad for our image." Minghui said this enraged Minghai. "Was that why he died?" I asked.

"Died? Who died?" Minghui's eyes grew rounder and shinier than ball bearings. When I told him what Secretary Guo had said, Minghui slapped his thigh and burst out laughing. Minghai hadn't died, he said, but like the Bodhidharma, he had "crossed the river on a reed, and returned to the west." I didn't get the allusion, so Minghui explained that the Bodhidharma was debating the scriptures with Emperor Wu of Liang, and when they got into an argument, he folded a single reed into a boat and sailed across the river. Similarly, Minghai had gone off with an American tourist. As Minghui put it, he'd had enough of being a monk, and switched to being an American missionary. He took the English name Walter See. Minghui said he found this a little odd, but as he turned it over in his mind, it suddenly dawned on him as he was sipping his tea: this was meant to sound like "wait and see." I didn't understand. Wait and see what? Former monk Minghui explained that in Buddhist teaching, this was called "seeming to move but remaining still, seeming to go but staying. The spirit understands, the material world is weak."

Bai Ling had told me that when Mr. Fan was in Baibei, he also visited Minghui Tea House. I asked former monk Minghui what he thought of Mr. Fan, but while Minghui had no trouble remembering Baibei and the Japanese man Kawai, he had no recollection of Fan Jihuai. I tried to remind him, and he realized, "My god, that guy. Secretary Guo brought him here. He was too much: too much talking, too much phlegm, too much pee." In the time it took Fan Jihuai to go for a piss, Secretary Guo had added Minghui to his organization. I asked, What organization? It turned out to be the Huawei Consumer Alliance. Although the company had been abolished, Secretary Guo insisted that he join, and he had no choice but to comply. He said to me, "Comrade, you don't have to pay your bill afterward, but I must insist that you buy a box of Alaskan seal oil from me."

Two Birds with One Stone

A crescent moon hung in the sky as Yang Fengliang left. I remember that moon distinctly—a thin sliver, okay, okay, like the sickle blades our farmer comrades hang on their walls. I saw him off at the airport, and repeated Dai Li's instructions to him. Then I said, in a meaningful voice, Fengliang, listen, Fengliang, the first thing is to find out for sure whether that person is Ge Ren. If it is, then wait for me to deal with him. If it isn't, then quietly come back home, and don't cause a disturbance. We would make our Party look bad if anyone found out, and people would laugh at us in Military Intelligence.

I even gave Ge Ren the code name Zero. You can tell from this, miss, how painstaking I was. Zero means there's nothing there. As long as you weren't an idiot, you'd know what I was really saying—and he was cleverer than a monkey. Yes, my meaning was that if he thought it wasn't Ge Ren, then he should let him go. He was a smart guy, so he should have known what to do. When we got to the stairway leading up to his plane,

I asked him to say hi to "Fresh Flower Tune" for me. I reminded him that his body was his revolutionary capital, and he should take loving care of it. What's so funny? What are you laughing at? I didn't mean anything by that; I was just showing concern for a subordinate.

Yang Fengliang had seven or eight people with him. As it says in the *Commentary of Zuo*, no matter how long your whip is, you won't hit the horse's belly. In order to be certain that the information I got was accurate, and to prevent Yang Fengliang from getting into mischief behind my back, I made sure that my godson was part of his team. He had delicate features and a name like a girl's: Qiu Aihua. He was an orphan. At the start of June 1941, the Japanese bombed Chongqing. Many people took refuge in a tunnel but ended up dying there, his parents included. Okay, okay, that's actually quite funny. The war of resistance lasted eight years. About a thousand Chongqing residents died thanks to Japanese bombing—that's only a few more than a hundred every year. But on this occasion, more than ten thousand were trampled or suffocated. I was ordered to help clear the bodies, and we filled truck after truck. As we were burying them in the countryside, I suddenly heard someone sobbing in the pile of corpses. Yes, it was Qiu Aihua, aged fourteen or fifteen. He was bare-assed, and his little cock hadn't even sprouted hair yet. Oh, beg your pardon, miss, I'm just telling it like it is. At the time, the government was running a campaign to get us to show loving kindness, so I responded by adopting the kid. He was very loyal to me. I could have asked him to sit his naked ass on a block of ice, and he'd have done it without a word. I sent him to the army so he'd have basic training, then turned him into an important chess piece by inserting him into Yang Fengliang's entourage. Yang didn't know how Qiu Aihua was related to me. One time I went over to Yang's unit for an inspection, and when I noticed Aihua's gear wasn't in order, I slapped him a couple of times and said to Yang, Where did this kid come from? Make sure you teach him a lesson. Yang kicked Aihua and made him write a self-criticism. How about that? If he'd known that was my godson, would he have dared?

Okay, okay, let's go on. After Yang Fengliang left, I started counting the days till a telegram would arrive. After a few days, I thought he must surely have gotten there by now, and I started staying in every night, waiting for him to send word. Damn it, I waited and waited, but it never came. I got anxious and thought Qiu Aihua would phone, at least, but that didn't happen either. This was strange. Was he up to something? Had he guessed my secret plan? Ah, that's clever of you, miss. If you'd been around in '43, you would have been spy material for sure. Sending Yang Fengliang was indeed hitting two birds with one stone. The best-case scenario would be if Yang quietly let Ge Ren go, and no one ever found out. Still, you have to be prepared for anything. What if word got out and Dai Li started doling out blame? Okay, okay, well then I'd have no choice but to bring the knife down on him. What? Me take the blame for him? That wasn't going to happen; I still had a lot of things to do. Sacrifice myself for pathetic Yang Fengliang? That would hardly be worth it. Besides, a real man takes responsibility for his own actions. If he was still a man, then he ought to step forward and bravely take on this duty.

More Information about Qiu Aihua's Death

Mr. Fan was a little too clever for his own good. According to Mr. Sun Guozhang, Yang Fengliang was aware quite early on that Qiu Aihua was Fan Jihuai's adopted son:

> On the way from Chongqing to Baibei, Mr. Yang gave me special instructions to treat Qiu Aihua well. Qiu had a baby face and was pleasantly plump—just like Shirley Temple. I only had one can of food left, but I let him eat it. He had a record player, probably obtained by Fan Jihuai. Mr. Yang treated him kindly. I once watched with my own eyes as Yang Fengliang opened a can and put it in Qiu Aihua's hands, as if he were Qiu's subordinate and not the other way round. When I asked about it, Mr. Yang said Qiu had neither a father nor a mother, so he was treating him like his own flesh and blood. After we got to Baibei Town, he [Qiu Aihua] often had nightmares. One night, he even wet the bed. Yes, wet the bed. Later on, I often thought about this boy and his dreams. He always dreamed about his own death. I guess that's because he'd experienced it once. As you know, I later studied philosophy, which from a certain perspective is the study of bad dreams. The Greeks call nightmares "efiáltes," which is the name of the demon who brings bad dreams. The Latin word "incubus" is also the name of a demon. The German word "Alp" refers to nightmares, but also to spirits, as well as demons. Mr. Wang Jiling told me that Qiu died not long after I left. Had he really been snatched away by demons?

The mention of Qiu having experienced death is a reference to the tunnel tragedy Mr. Fan spoke about. According to the historical record, there were two major Japanese attacks on Chongqing. The first was from May 3 to 4, 1939, when the Japanese Navy Air Force took off from their base in Wuhan and, after breaking through the Nationalist government's air defenses, carpeted Chongqing with bombs. At the time, Kawai was in the First Air Raid Unit. During their conversation at Minghui Tea House, Kawai described the situation to Secretary-General Guo Ping and Bai Ling:

> This happened in the early summer of Year 14 in the Shōwa era [i.e., 1939]. Flying medium-sized bombers, we reached Chongqing around 1 P.M. Okabe, my co-pilot, said our target was the wealthy district between Chaotian Gate and Central Park. He quoted Zen Master Ikkyū: "If you encounter a Buddha, kill a Buddha; if you encounter an ancestor, kill an ancestor." You know Zen Master Ikkyū?
>
> Okabe is still alive today. Don't the Chinese say that short people are clever? He was only five shaku [N.B. A Japanese shaku is about 30.3 centimeters], and truly brilliant. Like that gentleman [pointing at the tea house owner, Minghui], he became a monk after the war, and took the name Nikkyū. That day, we dropped a hundred bombs and seventy incendiaries. The following afternoon, we launched our second wave. The first consisted of twenty-six [aircraft], the second of twenty-seven. We didn't drop too many bombs that time, but the results were extraordinary. In the words of the Eighth Route Army, we concentrated our military force to eliminate the power of life. We destroyed some churches and embassies, though I have no idea how many people died.

According to The Great Japanese Bombing (Chongqing City Publishing, 1989), these two days of bombing left 3,391 dead and 2,323 wounded, and destroyed 847 buildings. The religious institutions that were leveled included the Holy Congregation Church, the Eternal Peace Church, the Catholic Assembly, and the Chinese Christian Assembly. The Seven Stars Cathedral burned down, leaving only its thirty-meter-high clock tower and the bell, which had been imported from France. A photograph in the book shows how an exploded pipe organ was flung into a neighboring pile of rubble, like a tiny bier. The book also notes that the printing plant, editorial offices, and management of the Xinhua Daily, which were then located on Cangping Street, were blasted to rubble. The Cathay Cinema collapsed, killing two hundred audience members. All of this makes it clear that when Mr. Fan said, "About a thousand Chongqing residents died thanks to Japanese bombing—that's only a few more than a hundred every year," he was quite far from the truth.

Two years later, on June 5, 1941, Japanese forces attacked Chongqing again. This was the occasion of the tunnel tragedy Mr. Fan spoke about. According to records, around 6 P.M. that day, as the ear-splitting air raid sirens blasted, huge numbers of Chongqing residents surged into a tunnel. As it grew more crowded, they started to run out of fresh air, and the temperature rose. People inside started struggling to get out, but others were still pouring in, and it soon grew chaotic. The enemy planes reached Chongqing around seven, by which time many in the tunnel had already died or passed out from lack of oxygen or crushing. Between eight and ten, there were two "waves of attack" (in Kawai's words), and by eleven, almost everyone in the tunnel was dead. We can be certain that Qiu Aihua's parents were killed in this tragedy. Kawai didn't participate in the attack, but he was familiar with the circumstances:

> I didn't take part in the Shōwa Year 16 [i.e., 1941] bombing—that was another detachment and had nothing to do with us. You have to understand that the Navy Air Force didn't think much of the attack on June 6. More than ten thousand people suffocated or were crushed to death in that tunnel, or you could say they died of fear, but that had nothing to do with our battle skills. There's a haiku that goes "Bananas ripen / the southern wind blows softly / spring brings azaleas." The bananas are already ripe by the time the south wind arrives, and one has nothing to do with the other.

Qiu Aihua, who was rescued by Fan Jihuai from the pile of corpses, could never have expected that he would die on Bare Mountain—or did this scenario feature among his many nightmares? Let's return to that crucial moment, as described by Ah Qing. Ah Qing got into a dispute with one of Yang Fengliang's subordinates over a piece of soap. He ended up killing this man and pushing the blame onto another member of Yang Fengliang's entourage, which allowed him to barge into the Bodhi Temple to demand the culprit. So Yang Fengliang handed Qiu Aihua over. As we know, it wasn't Qiu Aihua who stole the soap from the home of Zhou Qingshu [or Zhou Papi, as Ah Qing insisted on calling him], but Wang Jiling, who later became the chancellor of Straits Private University. We can now hypothesize that the reason Yang Fengliang handed Qiu Aihua over was precisely so that Ah Qing would kill him, thus preventing him from passing any more intelligence on to Fan Jihuai. Yang didn't anticipate that Ah Qing would kill not only Qiu, but also Yang's beloved "Fresh Flower Tune" and her son, and then toss all three of them into the river to feed the fish.

If this hypothesis were valid, then we could also be certain that, firstly, Yang Fengliang did indeed plan to let Ge Ren escape; secondly, Yang Fengliang would never try to contact Fan Jihuai; and thirdly, Fan Jihuai must be straying quite far from the truth in the following section when he claims to have received a telegram from Yang Fengliang.

Bingying in the Fog

Damn it! Two days later, the secret telegram from Yang Fengliang finally arrived. Fuck! He really did go in for poking his fingers where they shouldn't be. The thing I'd been most worried about had now happened:

the telegram contained only the line "Code Zero in Baibei, producing fine words." Damn it! Was he trying to make my life difficult? I was so angry, I saw stars. Was Yang Fengliang tired of living? Such a bastard—he hadn't spared a single thought for his commander.

Just as my anger was simmering, one of my subordinates suddenly told me that Bingying had arrived in Chongqing. This guy was friends with a pianist, and when he took his kid over to practice, he happened to hear the pianist and his wife arguing. Apparently the pianist had run into Bingying at Chongqing's Jiulongpo Airport. When he got home, he began showing less interest in his wife, until she realized what was going on, twisted his ear, and asked if there was someone else. Can you guess what this comrade said? He said, You're a broken-down old instrument. You're so out of tune that no good music will ever come out of you. The wife grabbed his other ear and demanded to know what piano *wasn't* out of tune. He refused to answer her, but privately told my guy that there was only one piano in the world in perfect tune, and that was Bingying—which led to the whole story about the airport encounter. He said he'd met her once before while studying at Shanghai University, and even after all those years, she was still as beautiful as ever.

This was just casual chat, but the listener was vigilant, and came straight to me with his report. I wondered what she was doing there at this crucial moment in history. Did it have something to do with Ge Ren? That sent a shiver through my heart. I worried that the pianist might have gotten it wrong, so I made a trip to Jiulongpo myself. You know the place I mean? That's right, it's Jiulongpo Train Station these days. Back then, when Mao Zedong and Zhou Enlai arrived in Chongqing for their negotiation, it was Jiulongpo Airport that they landed at.

It was no sweat to find out where she was—this was my territory. In no time at all, I knew that this woman was indeed Bingying, and she was staying at Joyful Song Hill. I put someone on her tail, but she must have noticed that she was being watched, because she soon moved to Confucius Lake, a place where people gathered in honor of the great sage. So what if she'd moved—she wouldn't get away from me that easily. The comrade I'd sent to keep an eye on her told me that only one person had visited her. I asked who that was, and he said Zhao Yaoqing. Okay, okay, I told him to keep up the surveillance, while I tried to think up a way to find out what they'd talked about. The guy said it didn't seem like it was anything urgent; he'd only seen them burning incense at the temple, and then releasing some turtles into Confucius Lake. That was something people did back then, to accumulate merit. I rushed right over and saw the two of them through a window. Sure enough, they were buying turtles to release. Chongqing was full of fog, as usual. It was particularly bad then, so I couldn't see Bingying's face clearly, but her silhouette showed that she still had the same grace and elegance. She wore a broad-brimmed hat, blown aslant by the wind, which only emphasized her poise. As the saying goes, if your hat goes on crooked, don't stick flowers in it straight.

Which reminds me of something else. At the 5th Plenary of the 8th National People's Congress, when Chongqing became self-governing, I decided to visit again, and found myself back at Confucius Lake. The lake had been filled in and the temple leveled; a high school stood in their place. The comrade who had accompanied me told me that during the Cultural Revolution, the revolutionary masses split into two factions, which descended into armed combat on this spot. Just as they were getting into the swing of battle, something bizarre happened: a huge number of turtles crawled out of a toilet bowl, like little dinosaurs from a Hollywood film, taking in the sights as they waddled down the road. Okay, okay, so everyone quit fighting, dropped their weapons, and fled. Later on, people said the turtles were responsible for stopping this unprecedented fight. The local leader comrades told me they'd investigated, and found that these were the same turtles that had been released into Confucius Lake back in the day. How had they survived? Chongqing is built on a hill, and they must have stayed alive in rock fissures below the city. When the gunshots startled them, they came out to see what was going on. I got distracted as they were explaining all this, and started wondering whether the turtles Bingying released had been among them. It was quite something that those turtles were still alive today. Ma Junren, the track coach, should have boiled them up as a tonic for his athletes; then maybe we'd have won a few more gold medals at the Olympics.

Where was I? Oh yes, Bingying and Ah Qing. That guy is normally all kinds of arrogant, but in front of Bingying he was polite and respectful. Seeing him like that lit up a thought in my brain: why not send him to Bare Mountain? You probably don't know that Ah Qing was once a servant in Bingying's house, and later traveled around with Ge Ren. What's that? I've already told you? You see how it is—when current affairs become ancient history, I forget all about them. Am I really old? It's your fault, calling me old Mr. Fan this, old Mr. Fan that. Recently I've even heard "old man Fan." Just call me Mr. Fan from now on; forget about the "old." There's something you have to understand, miss: everyone wants to live a long life, but no one wants to be old, especially in front of a gorgeous young woman.

The more I thought about it, the more I became convinced that Ah Qing was the right person to send. I saw him say goodbye to Bingying and leave; then, after standing by the lake for a while, Bingying left too. I let her get ahead, and had my driver follow her. What? Was I tailing her? No, my eye wasn't on her tail. For me to personally tail her would have been a waste of my talent, and would have gone against our hierarchy. An officer has to behave according to his rank. The reason I was following Bingying was to relive my friendship with her and Ge Ren. The fog grew thicker, and there was Bingying in the fog, looking lost and lonely. Where was she going? Once again, I wondered if she was there because of Ge Ren. Had she found out that he was still alive? I remembered the smiling tiger's [Dai Li's] words, saying that I should persuade Ge Ren to come to Chongqing and work for the Nationalists. And I thought that if Ge Ren came to Chongqing, he'd be able to see Bingying. As a friend, shouldn't I try to make their reunion happen?

I followed Bingying to a restaurant. Okay, okay, I remember the name: it was Yihe Garden. No, not like the Summer Palace—"yi" as in "pleasant." Bingying went inside, and so did I—I could hardly hang around outside. I went straight up to the second floor, from where I could watch Bingying below me. Someone was kissing her hand. Thud! My heart thumped violently. Who was this punk? His back was to me, and I couldn't see his face. You can imagine how little of my food I managed to eat! He put some food on Bingying's plate, and she did the same for him. She raised a glass to him, and he returned the favor. Their glasses clinked, and then a moment later clinked again. Damn it! Who was this? How did he get Bingying to look at him like that? When he stood up to pay the bill, I finally got a good look at him. Damn it! It was Kong Fantai. You probably haven't heard of him—he did jail time with Ge Ren after May the Fourth. I had seen him in Shanghai, where he was teaching at the university after returning from France. I remember Ge Ren telling me he was a seventy-fourth-generation descendant of Confucius. I took him out to dinner back then, so you could say we were old friends.

After they parted ways, I put someone on Bingying's tail, while I followed Kong Fantai myself. He got in a sedan chair and enjoyed a leisurely ramble around downtown. Chongqing is so hilly that I gave up driving and, leaving a subordinate to take my car home, got in a sedan myself. Kong Fantai made a round of the city, then went back to Confucius Lake. The guy I had left there was still waiting, and as soon as he saw me, he began stammering that Ah Qing had just been back there too. At that moment, Kong Fantai suddenly noticed me, but I turned in a hero's performance at this critical juncture, and strolled over to him as if I'd only just set eyes on him. Give me your hand, miss. This is how I shook his hand, and then embraced him. He was so moved by this warm reception that he was speechless. I exclaimed, What a small world! I was just passing by and saw you from behind. I thought you looked familiar, and it really was you! I called him Confucius, and he called me Lawyer Fan. I took him out for a drink, then back to my humble abode. He stayed there that night. I asked what he was doing in Chongqing. He said he wanted to pay his respects to his ancestor at Confucius Lake. Ha-ha, who did he think he was kidding? He'd come all the way to Chongqing to light a few sticks of incense by the side of a lake? Trying to figure out whether this had anything to do with Ge Ren, I deliberately brought up our last meeting in Shanghai. No sooner had I said Ge Ren's name than he began weeping and wailing, as if his own mother had died. He told me that he was in France when he heard about Ge Ren's death in battle, and that was a good death for a man, to spill his blood on the field of war. His tears were real, and so was his snot, so it's not like I didn't believe him. But I wanted to get at the truth, so I had to bring up Bingying. If he admitted to having met her, then I would believe every word he said; if not, then I would know this was just so much coloratura. So I said, This has been hard on Bingying. The perfect couple, torn apart just like that. Bye-bye. They'll have to wait for their next lives to see each other again. I added that if either of us saw Bingying, we would have to be sure to comfort her, and urge her to turn sorrow into strength, continuing comrade Ge Ren's legacy and making her own contribution to our country. Mr. Kong Fantai simply said, Okay, okay, then muttered something about Bingying looking good and not looking like she was particularly suffering. I asked, How do you know whether she's suffering, Confucius? He sighed and said he had just seen Bingying. They had talked about French theater, and she hadn't mentioned Ge Ren once.

Bingying's here? In Chongqing? I pretended to be shocked and jumped to my feet, spilling my cup of tea. Confucius said, Yes, she's in Chongqing, but she doesn't want to see anyone. Now I finally believed that her visit had nothing to do with Ge Ren. I asked Kong Fantai who else he'd seen in Chongqing, and he mentioned Ah Qing. Every time he saw Ah Qing, he said, he thought about the Lu Xun character Ah Q, except that Ah Q wore a torn felt hat and traveled in a river boat, while Ah Qing preferred a flat straw hat and drove a jeep. I said, That's right, that's right, our comrade Ah Q is doing well. He said, You're doing well too. I waved that away and told him that no matter how important my title might seem, I would always remain a servant of the People.

Ferrand's Record

In the first part of this book, I mentioned that Ge Ren's jail buddy Kong Fantai traveled to France with the help of the French journalist Jacques Ferrand, and later became a disciple of Rousseau. He and Ferrand remained lifelong friends. In the spring of 1943, Kong fell ill and died, not long after returning to France. In his memory, Ferrand wrote an essay titled "L'Entretien infini" [The Infinite Conversation; also the title of his subsequent collection], which mentioned Kong's visit to his hometown. It was from this essay that I learned Kong Fantai wasn't in Chongqing to burn incense for his ancestors, but in order to make contact with the Chinese League for Civil Rights, which had been set up by Lu Xun and a few others. The following passage speaks about Ge Ren, Bingying, and Fan Jihuai:

> It was not until 1942 that Kong [Fantai] found out, through a report about George Bernard Shaw's visit to China [in February 1933], that Lu Xun, Cai Yuanpei, Yang Quan, et al. had established the Chinese League for Civil Rights, which fought for the release of political prisoners, providing them with legal support, as well as the civil rights of publication, association, speech, and assembly. This aligned with his own belief in innate human rights, and so he made his way back to China, hoping to meet the members of the League. Thinking of all the old friends he would soon see, he was unable to sleep. . . . He also talked about Ge Ren, a poet with whom he had shared a prison cell, a flower of secrecy existing in isolation. I remember the night Kong recited one of Ge Ren's poems to me: "Who was once me, who was the lifetime in my mirror, the blue flame flickering in the breeze, or the wild rose unfurling in the dark?" Mr. Kong himself was both the blue flame and the wild rose releasing its fragrance in the dark. I recalled that the first time I met him, many years ago, he had recited this poem to me too. At the time, he had just been released from incarceration in the Infantry High Command stables, and he still smelled of horse manure.
>
> He flew over the Hump [i.e., the Himalayas] and returned to China, only to discover that the League had disbanded in June 1933. This trip had been for nothing. Nor was he able to meet Yang Quan, the secretary of the League, who had made the arrangements for Shaw's visit. He returned to France and told me that in June 1933, Yang Quan was assassinated by the Nationalists in Shanghai, the so-called "Paris of the East." I remember Kong pointing out, with some sarcasm, that the Shanghainese loved to compare their city to Paris, New York, and London, but perhaps they should be thinking of Kuala Lumpur, Saigon [N.B. now Ho Chi Minh City], and Manila instead. At least Paris and New York have never been colonies. In Shanghai, secret agents were slaughtering people in broad daylight. Yang Quan was

shot dead on a Sunday morning, along with his son. I have a very clear recollection of him referring to those murderous agents as "thugs."

In Chongqing he met Ge Ren's widow, Bingying, and a servant of theirs named Zhao [i.e., Ah Qing], as well as a lawyer he had known many years earlier in Shanghai, Fan Jihuai. He tried to persuade Bingying to return to France with him, but she said she was too ill to travel. Interestingly, both the servant and the lawyer held positions of command within their spy organizations. When Fan asked Kong why he was back in the country, he said he was paying his respects to his ancestor, which seemed to earn the lawyer's trust. As we know, Kong Fantai was a descendant of the sage Confucius, who was born in the sixth century B.C. After Confucius's birthplace of Qufu in Shandong Province fell to the Japanese, Confucius Lake in Chongqing became his main shrine. Kong said that the morning after their conversation, Fan personally escorted him to the temple to pay his respects. Like a flower bud, their previous friendship suddenly blossomed again, but alas, no friendship could bridge the political gulf between them. When Kong attempted to explain to Fan how unhappy he was with the state of affairs in China, the lawyer made use of *Cat Country*, a novel by Lao She, a Chinese writer who had spent time in England. This book introduced the concept of "sharekyism," which Fan now insisted was necessary in war. Kong had to remind me that sharekyism is defined by Lao She as "everyone works, everyone is happy, everyone shares everything." Fan's reference to Lao She was meaningful: on the one hand, he showed that he was aware of the political activities of the expatriate Chinese; and on the other hand, he made it clear that he was against Kong Fantai's ideology of innate human rights, captured in the book as an idea of the irresponsible cat people. Kong told me that as they parted, Fan said to him in a mocking tone, "As a Chinese person, I have always been a believer in Confucius; you are a descendant of Confucius, but you are turning your back to his morality."

Fan was not wrong. In China, the long-lasting Confucian value system is not underpinned by human rights. Confucius believed in a binary world: workers and thinkers, little people and the elite, slaves and aristocrats. From a certain perspective, Confucius and Rousseau were like fire and ice, and could not possibly coexist. And Mr. Kong Fantai, this eastern gentleman and follower of Rousseau, was treading a path between fire and ice all the way up to heaven . . .

This passage shows that even as acute a China observer as Ferrand believed that Ge Ren was dead. At the time, and for many years afterward, it was common knowledge in the west.

Remember to Wipe Your Ass

Okay, okay, as soon as Confucius left, I summoned Ah Qing and told him everything I had told Yang Fengliang. Of course, the new situation had created new problems that I had to consider. I hinted to him that when he got there, he was free to bump off Yang Fengliang.

How did I hint? That was easy. I just said, Ah Qing, when you get there, work with Yang Fengliang if you can, but if you can't, then take over his command. When Ah Qing heard this, he was so overjoyed, you'd have thought I'd given him a wife. He said he'd be sure to gloriously fulfill the task given to him by the Party and Nation. Strictly speaking, I should have written an order for Ah Qing to take with him, to ensure that Yang Fengliang would obediently hand over his command—but I didn't. I left that out on purpose. Ah Qing was sharp enough to ask about it, and I lied by saying that I'd already spoken to Yang Fengliang about this, and he knew that anyone I sent was representing me, so he should do whatever they told him to. It's like that saying: to kill three warriors, make them share two peaches. Okay, okay, now Yang Fengliang and Ah Qing would start plotting against each other. I knew very well that there was no way Yang Fengliang could ever beat Ah Qing, because Yang Fengliang was a diplomat and liked to talk his way out of problems, but when a scholar meets a fighter, his theories have no effect. Ah Qing was cultured too, but nothing like Yang. He might not even wait for Yang to finish talking before plunging his blade into him. Of course, dialectics tells us that we have to look at every question from both sides, so I considered the other possibility, which was that Yang Fengliang would finish off Ah Qing. Even if that happened, the sky wouldn't fall down. As soon as Yang Fengliang realized that I'd lost my trust in him, he would flee Bare Mountain with Ge Ren. As far as I was concerned, that would also be an acceptable outcome.

Ah Qing set off from Jiulongpo Airport too. When I went to see him off, he asked if I had any more instructions for him. I said only one thing: Remember to wipe your ass. As he climbed the stairs to the plane, I yelled meaningfully after him, "Ass!" He knew what I meant, of course. I believe that from that time on, every single time he wiped his ass, he thought about my order.

After Ah Qing left, I was back to playing the waiting game. Damn it, for some weird reason, it was exactly the same as the previous time—I waited and waited, but I heard nothing from Ah Qing. Around this time, the Commander [i.e., Dai Li] phoned for an update, and I had to tell him, We'll have to wait and see—we're in the information age now, and information is everything, so we're sure to go wrong if we act without accurate intel. I urged him to be patient. Policies come from above, but counter-policies meet them from below. I was afraid he'd get suspicious, so I fed him some soothing medicine. I said, Ah Qing is completely loyal to you, to me, to the Party, to the Nation, and there's no way he'd betray us—as soon as there's any news, I'll be on my way. Somehow or other, I convinced him. But then a day or two later, Dai Li phoned again and asked me to meet him at Shulu. When I got there, he told me to make a trip to Wuhan, where the Japanese had captured an American pilot. He wanted me to negotiate with the Japanese, then go from Wuhan straight to Bare Mountain. It looked like I would have no choice but to make this trip in person. I said, Okay, okay, just let me go pack. I'll set off right away. He said he had already asked old Chiang for permission, and once I got to Bare Mountain, if that was indeed Ge Ren, I was to say yes to anything he asked for, no matter what. And if he agreed to surrender to the government, then the government would be magnanimous and allow him to form a new party, which would be allocated six seats on the National Defense Advisory Council. I asked, Can we count on the Generalissimo's word? Dai Li replied, We can talk about that later, but anyway, if it turns out to be five seats instead of six, that's fine too; four instead of five, still all right. And I thought to myself, if we really could get four, that actually wouldn't be too bad.

Next we talked about the captured American. I said little Japan was being far too bold, starting a feud with the Americans. Fuck! Weren't they just asking for trouble? Of course, you have to look at every situation from both sides. The Americans were being arrogant too, pushing their hegemony everywhere and interfering in other countries' governments. It would do them good for little Japan to get the upper hand for once, and besides, that gave us an opportunity to make nice with them. Dai Li appreciated my point of view. He said, Our relationship with America is never unimportant, so we'll have to make this next move carefully. Without hesitation, I accepted his order. I set off, accompanied by a Japanese man—a spy named Junichi Inamoto. This guy spoke not just fluent Mandarin, but Cantonese too—he pronounced "you" as "thou," "miss" as "muss," and "comrade" as "cum rag." Ha-ha, we were going to hand this Japanese "cum rag" over in exchange for that American guy.

As the saying goes, your luck goes back and forth. On the boat from Chongqing to Hankou, I kept thinking how history always repeats itself, with minor variations. Okay, okay, see if you agree with this: the first time I went to Bare Mountain, it was at Ge Ren's invitation, and I was the one who ended up a prisoner; this time, it would be Ge Ren's turn to be captured. I thought some more: we took the same boat to Japan for our studies, and here I was on another boat, on my way to demand his surrender. I remember very clearly that while boarding the boat, I bumped into another member [of the National Defense Advisory Council] named Zhang—Zhang Xiruo. You know him? He was a well-known maverick—a born contrarian, he even dared to butt heads with old Chiang. As soon as he saw me, he grabbed me and asked, Is it true that Bingying's in Chongqing? I said I didn't know. He said, I can't trust a word you people say. Zhang Xiruo had spent time in France too. Damn it! If he found out my trip had something to do with Ge Ren, there'd be trouble! He'd make sure everyone knew about it. I'll tell you the truth, miss. If he hadn't been a well-known figure, I'd have sent someone to get rid of him. Instead, I told one of my guys, Keep an eye on him! Try to find out what he's heard, and report back to me right away.

Zhang Xiruo

Like Miss Bai Ling, I hadn't known anything about Zhang Xiruo. It was only after Mr. Fan mentioned him that I looked him up.

Mr. Fan Xiruo was born in 1889, making him ten years older than Ge Ren. He was from Chaoyi in Shaanxi. Like many of the other people in this book, he studied medicine early on before going into political research instead. He was a foundational figure in contemporary Chinese political studies, and served as the dean of politics at Tsinghua University and at Southwestern Associated University. In the *Morning Post Supplement* on October 5, 1925, Xu Zhimo described Zhang Xiruo as "a hard man" and "a straight arrow," with a natural, unshakable dignity "and a peculiar charm amid all this rigidity, like Zhang Fei or Niu Gao."

During the war of resistance, Zhang Xiruo joined the National Defense Advisory Council as a representative of cultural organizations. Old Mr. Fan was right—he did indeed "butt heads with" Chiang Kai-shek. In 1941, he complained bitterly about government corruption and Chiang's authoritarian tendencies in front of the man himself, a great insult to Chiang, who had to remind him, "Your opinions are welcome, but not your mean-spiritedness." Still in a temper, Zhang Xiruo flounced out. In 1946, on the eve of the former Chinese People's Political Consultative Conference, Zhang accepted an invitation from the Southwestern Associated University's Student Union to make a speech, where he proclaimed, "If I had the chance to see Mr. Chiang [Kai-shek] again, I'd be sure to tell him he should be put out to pasture. That's a polite way to put it. If I were to be more direct, I'd say he should get lost." Mr. Fan seems to have been right—Zhang Xiruo was indeed a "maverick."

According to the introduction to *Zhang Xiruo's Writings*, Mr. Zhang Xiruo was selected to join the National Committee of the Chinese People's Political Consultative Conference in September 1949, as a non-aligned patriot. At the first plenary, when the name of the country was being discussed, with options such as "Chinese People's Democratic Republic" and "Chinese People's Democratic Nation," he thought they were all too long-winded, and pushed for "the People's Republic of China" instead. His reasoning was that the words "People's Republic" already "express the idea of a people's democracy, and there's no need to repeat that with the word 'democracy.'" His luck was good on this occasion, and the plenary voted to adopt his wording. Damn it! (To quote Mr. Fan.) If Fan Jihuai had murdered Zhang Xiruo at Chongqing Harbor back in the day, our country would have a different name today.

In May 1957, the Party turned to outsiders to help rectify its ideology. When Mao asked for his opinion, Zhang blurted out, "You want to achieve too much, so you rush to short-term gains. You despise the past, and look superstitiously to the future." Honestly, it's a miracle he even managed to stay alive until 1957. On page 498 of *Zhang Xiruo's Writings*, he says, "Saying 'long live' anyone will be the downfall of human civilization."

In 1973, as everyone in the blessed land was shouting "Long live Chairman Mao, long live Chairman Mao," Mr. Zhang Xiruo died.

Kawai Looks for His Brother

I worked hard to correct Junichi Inamoto's thinking on the boat. I told him that China and Japan were cut from the same cloth, with just a bit of water separating us, and we ought to be good friends and neighbors. As an intellectual, he should be leading the charge to end this unjust war. He gave me his full attention and listened in silence. I told him I had many friends in Japan. He asked who, and I told him how close I was to Kawata and his family: Kawata, Kawai, Noriko. I said that after the war, I was definitely going to look up my old friends in Japan, and do my part to improve China-Japan relations. Damn it! He still thought I was lying. I said, You have to believe me, Chinese people are very trustworthy. As you know, miss, I really did visit Japan later on. Oh yes! Aren't we doing our bit for China-Japan relations right now, by going to Bare Mountain to meet Kawai?

I stopped in Hankou for two days, and with the covert help of the local underground organization [i.e., the local branch of Kuomintang Military Intelligence], I was soon able to exchange the Japanese guy for the American pilot, whom I had someone escort back to Chongqing. For those two days, the whole of the Jianghan Plains seemed to be embroiled in war.

Bullets don't have eyes, so they might land on anyone's head. Which was why, as soon as the American left, I couldn't wait to get out of there. On the night I was preparing to leave, a Japanese man suddenly appeared like some sort of ghost. I didn't recognize him at first. He was leaning against the door, holding a bunch of dried flowers—Japanese cherry blossoms. I bet you can guess who it was, miss. Ha-ha, it was Kawai, whom I'm on my way to meet now! Speak of the devil. I had just mentioned him to Junichi Inamoto, and now here he was in person—spooky. He wanted to ask me where his brother was, and said his mother had picked those flowers from his father's grave for him to take to his big brother—apparently Kawata would know what his mother meant by that. I asked what she meant, and he said it was to tell him he ought to take over the family business. You probably don't know, miss, that Japanese family businesses are always inherited by the elder brother, and younger sons only get a shot after their big brothers have had first pick. I was certain that Kawai had found out where I was staying from Junichi Inamoto. Baka-yarō! How could such a thing happen at a crucial moment like this?

Kawai said that when his mother handed over the cherry blossoms, she told him that as long as he could find Ge Ren, Huang Yan, or Fan Jihuai, any one of them would be able to tell him Kawata's whereabouts. But now Ge Ren was dead, and Huang Yan was alive but far off in Yan'an—so that only left me. It all sounded very nice, but let's get real: he wasn't asking for his brother's whereabouts, he was asking me to hand him over. But come on, his brother was dead. What was I supposed to hand over? He was being aggressive enough that I could tell that if I didn't produce Kawata, I could forget about sneaking out of Hankou. Damn it! Foreigners are fine and all, but there's one problem with them—they take everything too seriously. The guy was dead, so what did he want with him? Besides, he had died in China, as a Japanese folk hero of sorts, so he should have been proud. Wouldn't Kawata have been ashamed to see his little brother sulking like this? Of course, I didn't say any of that out loud. As I was thinking all this, miss, it was like the sun was coming out from behind the clouds. Folk hero! A hero of the People! Okay, okay, you're right, that's exactly what I said when I found out Ge Ren had died in the Battle of Two Li Mound. But now, in front of this Japanese man, I felt even more strongly. Diving into the deep end, I thought, if I was left with no choice but to put Ge Ren to death, then why not use Kawai as my weapon, so that Ge Ren could be a hero of the People once more?

What's that? Killing with a borrowed sword? My dear girl, if I may be frank, that's utter nonsense! I was thinking only about Ge Ren. If it had been anyone else, do you think I'd have spent this much time and energy? Okay, okay, if you insist on thinking that, there's nothing I can do. But as an older person, I have to tell you, the world has always been this way. As long as you're aiming for the right target, it doesn't matter if your methods are ugly. It's just like a lawyer defending someone in court. Don't forget, miss, in all the history of the world, no lawyer has ever been able to mount a defense without feeling at least a little bit guilty about it. Even an innocent person has toxins in his spittle. Don't stick your tongue out at me, miss. You're just a girl, you still don't understand: every young person believes that what he sees is the truth, so he lives according to his eyes; but when you become an adult, a fully fledged citizen, you get shaped by how other people see you, so you live according to their eyes. You understand? That's all right, then. This is a fundamental truth, like one over two is point five. Think about it. Ge Ren was so intelligent, he was sure to understand that I was doing this for his own good. This might sound ridiculous, but in order to make him immortal in our ridiculous world, I had to make that brave decision. So I hardened my heart and took him with me when I left. We would go to Bare Mountain, and he would make his demand from Ge Ren in person. Of course, I couldn't say so directly; I had to put a beautiful spin on it. I said I was heading south to visit a friend, and that friend might know where his big brother was, so I'd be sure to ask, and let him know the answer. No, I didn't say that the friend was Ge Ren. If I had, he'd surely have thought I was trying to trick him, because he'd heard the news of Ge Ren's death. After I'd said my piece, he broke off a stalk of flowers and gave them to me, saying, Mr. Fan, you truly are the seven gods of fortune we Japanese believe in. You're among friends, I said. No need to be so polite. No need for seven gods of fortune or whatever compliments you have; this is just a traditional virtue of us Chinese people. Your family was kind to me, and droplets of goodness must be repaid with a fountain. When I'm back, I will find a way to get word to you. He grabbed me and said, Once you leave, I'm afraid I will never see you again. I said, You still don't trust me? Well, if you're not afraid of hardship and maybe death, then why not come with me?

This Japanese guy had always been the hot-blooded sort. He believed in doing things quickly, so he wanted to leave that very night. You probably don't know that the Japanese call trains "cars," and cars "automatic vehicles." He said he wanted to take an automatic vehicle out of Wuhan, then change to a car. Baka-yarō, I'd been away from Japan for so long, I got confused at this. My aide thought an automatic vehicle was a trishaw, so he went out to hail a couple. I had to make him send them away. No,

I have nothing against trishaws. But didn't I just say that the whole of the Jianghan Plains was caught up in war? Wuhan was a dogfucking courthouse, easy to enter but impossible to leave. I'm sorry, I wasn't going to swear, but I have to tell it like it is, and it just came out. Damn it! We had to disguise ourselves by smearing our faces with soot from the bottom of a wok and coloring our hair with plant ash. We looked like beggars from a Jin Yong novel. So tell me, how could a couple of beggars afford to take trishaws?

We promptly fled to somewhere called Wulong Springs, where we caught our breath and washed our faces. When I saw my reflection in the water, I looked uglier than a ghost. What sort of life was this? No one could understand my pain. Kawai kept saying we should leave. He was driving me mad. You, Yang Fengliang, and you, Ah Qing, this was your doing. If Ah Qing sent a telegram this minute to tell me the man in Baibei wasn't Ge Ren, I'd turn right around and not have to suffer anymore. The problem was, all the way to Bare Mountain, I didn't hear a single word from Ah Qing.

The Seven Gods of Fortune and the Magpie Banquet

On the day of the ribbon-cutting ceremony for Hope Elementary School, Fan Jihuai and Kawai had a historic meeting at the aforementioned Jade Flower Garden hotel. By the way, those three words, "Jade Flower Garden," were in Secretary Guo's hand. Mr. Fan's room was on the third floor, Kawai's on the second. According to Miss Bai Ling, just as old Mr. Fan was "putting on airs" and waiting for Kawai to seek him out, Secretary Guo showed up and asked if he had rested. Mr. Fan said he'd no sooner arrived than a young lady phoned and offered him her services. He thought this meant cleaning the room, so he let her in, but as soon as she was through the door, she started undoing his belt. Secretary Guo immediately said that Mr. Fan needn't worry, they were going to have a sweep to eliminate these unwholesome elements. Mr. Fan sighed, "Mary Magdalene did the same thing, trading her body for cash." Secretary Guo didn't know who Mary Magdalene was, but it sounded like a western name, so he thought Mr. Fan was hinting that he wanted a white woman. He leaned over and murmured, "We have a few Russian girls, gorgeous and talented, straight from Moscow's Arbat. Shall I get one of them to wait on you?" Mr. Fan batted away the offer. "I appreciate the thought, but I have work to do."

Bai Ling said that this was when Kawai appeared. He bowed deeply, then he and old Mr. Fan hugged. "My god, they looked like a couple of bears." Then they had a "friendly talk," during which Kawai once again called Mr. Fan his "seven gods of fortune." I had to look through quite a few books before I figured out who those seven gods were: Ebisu, Daikoku, Hotei, Fukuroku, Bishamon, Benten, and Jurōjin. I'm not sure exactly what they stand for, but from their names, I'd guess it has something to do with happiness and good fortune. The following is a transcript of Secretary Guo's recording of their conversation:

KAWAI: Mr. Fan is my seven gods of fortune. Do you [N.B. Bai Ling and Guo Ping were also present] know what that means? You have the gods of Prosperity, Success, and Long Life, but we have seven of them. I was happy to hear that Chi Na has recently added one more god: Joy. I wasn't sure which character that was, but then I realized it was the same one as in "magpie." Mr. Fan, I wish you peace and plenty; prosperity, success, long life, and joy.

FAN: Ha-ha, same, same. Guo, go find a musician who can play "Magpie Bridge Fairy" for Mr. Kawai. That song is a little like a haiku; you're sure to find it familiar.

KAWAI: Fate threw me together with Mr. Fan. In Shōwa Year 18 [i.e., 1943], if Mr. Fan hadn't brought me to Baibei, I'd have been sent back to Nagasaki. Several of my friends were deployed there, and all of them ended up in Kamikaze missions. In Shōwa Year 19, they flew from Nagasaki to Luzon [in the Philippines], and afterward there was nothing left of them but dust.

FAN: Was this the Yamato Unit of the Kamikaze?

KAWAI: Yes. Even if they hadn't been sent to Luzon, they still would have died in Shōwa Year 21, when the Americans dropped the atom bombs on Hiroshima and Nagasaki. I went to Nagasaki after the war. It was so ugly. There was a waka poem about the dead of Nagasaki that went: "Our ancestral country has become so hideous, it makes one feel sorry for those who gave their lives." Then in Heisei Year 2 [i.e., 1990], I went back to Nagasaki and saw the cherry blossoms at the harbor, and I thought about Mr. Fan's kindness.

FAN: That was nothing. We have a saying in China: It's better to save one life than to build a seven-story pagoda. I remember you were holding a stalk of cherry blossoms when you came to see me in Hankou.

KAWAI: I brought those flowers to Bare Mountain. Though I didn't understand at the time that Mr. Fan wanted me to kill someone. He wanted me to kill Ge Ren.

FAN: We have a saying in China: Let bygones be bygones. Don't go raking up the past. How's your health?

KAWAI: Everything's fine, except my digestion's getting worse as I age. It's a little . . . a little blocked, that's all.

FAN: Many years ago, a doctor [N.B. He means Bai Shengtao] told me that eating magpie flesh was good for the digestion, though you have to make sure you get a male bird.

Mr. Fan was clearly trying to cut Kawai off, but Kawai "didn't understand" and continued talking about how he'd gone AWOL from the Japanese Navy Air Force, firstly because he was afraid of death, and secondly in order to search for his brother. This meant he had the Japanese Army after him. He didn't return to Wuhan, but fled to Hong Kong. There he had to avoid the numerous Japanese agents who were out to kill him. Then he managed to get in contact with the British, to whom he announced that he was a "pacifist." With their help, he took RMS *Empress of China* to America. Being a "pacifist" meant he was allowed to stay in America, but as time passed and life went on, he began to miss his mother and sister back home. At this point he quoted a haiku by Yosa Buson [N.B. Japanese poet, 1716–1783]: "Late one autumn night, I miss nobody, except Mother and Father." In Shōwa Year 48 [i.e., 1973], he found out through a chance encounter that a new torii [i.e., a memorial archway] was going to be built at Japan's Yasukuni Shrine, and he immediately made a decision that contradicted the "pacifist" status he'd clung to all these years: he would donate funds for the construction of this torii, then move his brother Kawata's memorial tablet to the shrine. It turns out that there was only a single step between a "pacifist" and a democrat. He said this was his little sister's wish. After their mother died, she was going through her belongings when she found an envelope from their big brother. In his letter, Kawata told their mother why he'd come to China. Noriko passed the letter on to Kawai.

> After reading this letter, I understood what my brother was saying. He was telling me in this letter that he felt proud and honored to have lived through the era. Before the war, his life had been sluggish, directionless, vulgar, and meaningless. He had finally found a life of value and broken free of the emptiness that had engulfed him at every moment. He persuaded my mother to let me come to Chi Na too, so I could live the same sort of life as him. Only then did I understand why my mother had let me make this trip.

He believed that if he moved his brother's memorial tablet to the Yasukuni Shrine, Kawata's spirit would surely receive the protection of the seven gods of fortune. And so he went back to Japan with a wad of cash.

KAWAI: I arranged to meet my sister at Kudanshita [N.B. a subway station opposite the Yasukuni Shrine]. She showed up with our brother's picture in one hand and a little navy flag in the other. It was the photo with you in it, do you remember? The one we took at Ki Shiryo [Restaurant]. We talked about China, Ge Ren, and Huang Yan.

FAN: And me? That [photograph] is truly precious—a symbol of friendship between China and Japan. Is your sister well? Back then, she was a true broad bean blossom.

KAWAI: She's gotten old too. She had a small bag with her that I thought contained our mom's things, but when she opened it, it was a navy uniform, exactly like the one I had back then. The epaulets and buttons were bright and shiny.

FAN: Hey, [Secretary] Guo, have this photo copied and hang it up in the reference room at Hope Elementary. China-Japan friendships should be passed down from generation to generation. We mustn't forget history. Remember, forgetting history is a betrayal.

At this point, an attendant showed up to take them downstairs for dinner. As they walked down the flower-lined corridor, Secretary Guo whispered a message to Bai Ling, who relayed it to old Mr. Fan, who in turn reminded Kawai not to refer to China as "Chi Na." "It sounds terrible, and our mayor won't like it. But I don't want to be the one to tell him; it might affect our China-Japan friendship." Bai Ling told me that after she passed this on to Mr. Fan, he squeezed her hand hard to show he'd understood.

There was one dish at the banquet that couldn't be ignored: braised magpie. Clearly the local government had paid attention to the conversation between old Mr. Fan and Kawai about remedies for constipation. As a result, this evening became known as the magpie banquet. Incidentally, after this, braised magpie became a specialty of Jade Flower Garden, and the local magpie population shrank dramatically. Soon, only honored guests from far away were allowed to taste this special dish. When the mayor came over to toast old Mr. Fan, he said, "Let's raise a glass together to Baibei bettering itself and becoming prosperous." The mayor wanted to toast three times, but old Mr. Fan said he never had more than three cups, in observance of the three-cup rule. Next, somewhat tipsy, Mr. Fan made a speech. I watched a video of it on my second trip to Baibei. He remained seated through the whole thing, and although it didn't make a lot of sense, and he frequently said the wrong word—constantly referring to Kawai as Kawata, for instance—it was full of emotion, and very persuasive:

Even an old horse in his stable dreams of galloping a thousand miles. And in his twilight years, a martyr's heart still beats strongly. In the past, our rousing songs turned to the east. Why was that? Because we faced the wall for ten years in order to break through it, deep in scientific study to fix the world's problems. Huh? "Facing the wall for ten years" is a saying from India, and "Chi Na" comes from India too. In the fifth century, China's Buddhist scholars referred to themselves as "Chi Na." When Tripitaka went to the west to seek the scriptures, his favorite thing to say was "our great Chi Na," spoken proudly. From there, Buddhism was passed on to Japan, and they started calling us "Chi Na" too. Some comrades say that during the Edo period [N.B. 1603–1867], the English word "China" came to Japan, and *that's* when the Japanese started calling us "Chi Na." That's irresponsible nonsense! The law is all about relying on evidence to get at the truth, so we law experts care about the facts. I have a question: Doesn't this deliberately shrink the history of cultural exchange between China and Japan? We can ask Mr. Kawai. When the hell did the Japanese start calling us "Chi Na"? Okay, okay, you see, Mr. Kawai agrees with my version. After the Japanese were defeated, the Republican government reached out to Japan's Ministry of Foreign Affairs and asked that they stop referring to us as "Chi Na," because it was a dismissive name for us, a slur. They should call us the Chinese Republic. I had already moved overseas by then, but when I heard this news, I knew that Chiang Kai-shek was finished. There was no pride there. No pride. As long as you have hair, you aren't afraid that someone will turn the light on. Of course, old Chiang was a baldy. Not a blade of grass up there. Fuck! Can't you tell when someone's honoring you by saying you have a long history, a solid foundation? But no, you think they're cursing at you. No backbone at all. A government like that could never win hearts and minds, so of course they would collapse. Comrades, when I was talking to Mr. Kawata earlier, I was very happy to hear that Mr. Kawata still respectfully referred to us as "Chi Na." Comrades, doesn't that make it clear? It's obvious that Mr. Kawata respects our history. He loves our history. That's the basis of our friendship. Let's raise a glass to friendship and cooperation between China and Japan. Cheers!

The erudite Mr. Fan left everyone stunned. According to Bai Ling, after the magpie banquet ended, Mr. Kawai accompanied Mr. Fan up to his room. When Mr. Fan said, "Cigarette," Kawai hastily grabbed him one. When Fan said, "Water," Kawai took a cup from the waitress and passed it to Fan with both hands. Fan said, "Light," and Kawai lit his cigarette. Mr. Fan sucked on it, muttered, "Good cigarette," and stubbed it out. Then he said, "At least I wiped your ass clean for you. Remember, after leaving Baibei City, you're not to say Chi Na people anymore. Haven't you lived in America? So just call us Chinamen. When people ask you why, tell them it's because there are Chinatowns in America, and you've gotten used to it. Hey, you know what? Huang Yan's in Chinatown now. I don't know if he's dead yet."

Investigating and Analyzing

Damn it! I'm not going to talk about how much I suffered along the way, all the pain I endured, because I was just doing what I had to do. Is it worth talking about? No, it isn't. I hate those people who do one little thing and then go around crowing about it, as if they're afraid no one will notice. Still, my dear young lady, in order to be responsible to your readers and the next generation, when you write this story, be sure to include all of that [i.e., his suffering during the journey]. Okay, okay? For example, you could say we had to keep hiding from enemy airplanes, or mention that we were starving. You can use your imagination here. How about this—whatever bad things you can think of, I've experienced. Did Kawai suffer too? Yes, I'll admit he did. But he was doing this for himself, and I was doing it for Ge Ren. There's a fundamental difference there; you can't mix up these two things.

When I got to Bare Mountain, I didn't head straight to Baibei, but went to Shang Village, very close to Baibei. I had stayed at the little chapel there on my first visit, and now here I was again. The chapel had been swept clean and was clearly occupied, but when I sent my men to search the area, they didn't find a single soul. I sat there, soaking in reminiscences, recalling the circumstances that had brought me there before. I still remember Ah Qing bringing me a basin of water to wash my feet. It sat by the bed, and the moon was reflected in it, like a dream. My aide seemed to understand what was going through my mind, and brought me a basin of water. I washed my feet and got to work. I couldn't have a point of view until I carried out my investigation. You can't devise the right strategy without sufficient information. No matter how you sliced it, my first job was to investigate and analyze, until I knew enough about what was going on. I said to my aide, Hey, kid, you can go. I'll pour the water out myself. Go walk around Baibei [Town] and see what the devil Yang Fengliang and Zhao Yaoqing are up to. Oh, and bring "Fresh Flower Tune" back with you. He asked if I wanted to hear her sing. I scolded him for that. Fuck! Listen to music at a time like this? Work comes first, songs can wait. Now, scram! But he insisted on pouring out the water before he went. He was a good comrade. They don't make them like that anymore.

After he left, I sent for Kawai. Before we could start talking, my aide came back in, running and screaming. When he saw Kawai standing there, he hesitated. I said, Spit it out, what's happened? You look like you're scared out of your wits. He said, I saw a foreigner headed this way. A foreigner? Here? Was it the local priest? I looked out the window, and sure enough, there was an old foreign guy. He really was a priest, and also part of the International Red Cross. Later on, I found out that this was Reverend Ellis, whom Ge Ren had mentioned earlier. He was the one who'd swept the chapel.

I sent my aide out to fetch Ellis. He came in, paused for a second, then called me Mr. Fan. Well, now, how did he know my name? Had the secret mission been compromised? I asked how he knew my name was Fan. I'll never forget his reply: Ge Shangren. I thought his pronunciation wasn't very good, to mangle Ge Ren's name like that. Ge Ren must have heard from Yang Fengliang and Ah Qing that I might be on my way to Baibei. Okay, okay, leaking military secrets was enough of a reason to have those two shot dead.

In any case, I had my answer—the boss's [Dai Li's] intelligence had been right. Ge Ren had been there, and he might still be around. How can I put this, miss? It may have been what I'd expected, but I still felt like I had a fish bone caught in my throat and couldn't get a word out. It took a while before I recovered my senses and asked him for more information. He didn't call himself a priest, but rather a doctor who was there to treat Ge Shangren. He'd wanted to take Ge Shangren away from there, but Ge had said another doctor would be coming to treat him, someone named Fan—Fan Jihuai. Isn't that you? Didn't you study medicine in Japan? Kawai, who'd been standing to one side, suddenly opened his mouth. That was good—I'd been pondering how to broach the subject of Ge Ren with him, and now there was no need. I pulled him into a chair and said, Hey, little Japan, the person I'm taking you to see is our mutual friend Ge Ren. He's still alive, and he's the only one who knows where your brother is. Kawai's mouth gaped open, and he didn't seem able to close it. He made for the door, wanting to see Ge Ren right away, but I grabbed hold of him. Hang on! If anyone finds out you're Japanese, they'll turn you into honeycomb. He gaped, not knowing what I meant by that. I pulled out my revolver and mimed shooting him full of holes. Now that he knew I wasn't joking, he just stood there, docile as a dog.

Reverend Ellis stayed with me that night. I sent one of my men to lock up Kawai so he wouldn't do or say anything stupid. Striking a thoughtful pose, I said to Ellis, Tell me, how is Comrade Ge Ren's health? Ellis said, Ge Ren has tuberculosis. Sure, even I knew that! But I stayed calm and didn't say anything. He said he'd given Ge Ren a shot of penicillin, and his condition was improving. I said, Okay, okay, then you should keep doing that. He seemed to take me for a doctor, and wanted to discuss various treatments for tuberculosis. I had no idea what to say to this naive foreigner. When I lied that I was a Christian too, his eyes lit up, and he began stroking his beard with delight. Like Marx? Yes, Marx had a big beard too. He did look a little like Marx, but just a little. How should I put it—if Marx were a fine stallion, then Reverend Ellis would be a donkey. Ha-ha, he really did look like a donkey. He asked if I would stay there with him, treating illnesses and spreading the Word. I said, That was wonderfully put, healing the sicknesses of the body as well as of the spirit. The body is the foundation, and the spirit is the edifice built on top of it. You have to grasp it with both hands, grasp it firmly. He was frantic with joy, clutching his beard even more wildly. And so, without too much effort, I had gained his trust. He started jabbering nonstop, and I soon found out that Ge Ren was in Fangkou Elementary School. That's right, that's now Hope Elementary School, where we're headed now.

Didn't you ask me about Bai Shengtao, miss? Okay, okay, I'm going to talk about him now, because this bearded foreigner brought him up. He said, Dr. Bai can stay here too and work with us. I was confused. Dr. Bai? Who's Dr. Bai? He said Dr. Bai practiced traditional Chinese medicine, and Mr. Zhao Yaoqing had brought him there to treat Ge Ren. Dr. Bai's prescriptions were odd, he said, with ingredients like fox dung. From the way he was talking, I assumed that Bai Shengtao was a local folk doctor. It was only later that I discovered he was an intestinal expert from Yan'an. Don't worry, miss, I'll come back to Bai Shengtao later. Didn't I tell you I often think about him? Through the mists of history, whenever I've had constipation, I've thought about him. And not only then, but also when I eat bananas. Why? Don't you even know that? Then I'll tell you. If you eat bananas when you're constipated, your turds become as mushy as the bananas, and line up single file to march victoriously out.

Okay, okay, let's get back on point. That investigation lasted late into the night. The next morning, I went to see Reverend Ellis again, but he had already gone, leaving a note that said he was going out of town to buy medicine for Ge Ren. He didn't say where, so I couldn't go looking for him. Such a slippery customer—you really can't trust foreigners. What's that? You think I wanted to kill him? Ha, that's clever of you. I won't lie, the thought did cross my mind. As the saying goes, there's no greatness without poison. But he didn't wait around for me to poison him, that donkey; he just slipped out from under my nose.

It was also that morning that my aide told me Yang Fengliang wasn't in Baibei. That sent a thud through my brain—so Ah Qing had disposed of Yang. I asked if "Fresh Flower Tune" was around, but he said she'd disappeared too. Fuck! Had he killed her as well? When I imagined Ah Qing putting a bullet through that frisky woman, I felt as if a cat had dragged its claws across my heart. This was a classic slaughter of the innocents, not to mention a breach of protocol and discipline! This was nothing but anarchy! Later on, when I saw Dr. Bai, I learned a new word from him: liberalism. When theory meets practice, something clicks into place. This was right—Ah Qing had committed the error of liberalism. What's that? I told him to do it? Where did you get that from? Oh, wait, now that you mention it, I did order him to wipe his ass clean. I'll own up to everything I said. The past is over, and I'm not going to deny it. But listen carefully—what I meant was that if necessary, he should send Yang Fengliang to heaven. I never said to send "Fresh Flower Tune" to hell! Damn it! There was nothing wrong with the scripture, just the priest chanting it out of a crooked mouth. He deserved death by a thousand cuts. Sure, he had wiped the ass clean, but he'd left the asshole raw and bleeding.

I said to my aide, Hey, kid, go back there and fetch Qiu Aihua. He didn't say anything for a long while, and then he finally told me that Qiu Aihua had disappeared along with Yang Fengliang. But surely, for the sake of the Buddha if not the monk, Ah Qing wouldn't have bumped him off as well?

The Beginning of Me Becoming Myself

After Reverend Ellis left Baibei, he wrote to Reverend Beal, describing his conversations with Ge Ren and Fan Jihuai. This letter was published in *The Majesty of the Orient*; here is a portion of it:

> With Ah Ch'ing's permission, I spoke with Shang-Jên in the airwell. He sat cross-legged on a wooden stool and kept his voice low. Beyond the doors, the mountains leaped like rams, and the foothills like little lambs; the lake rippled like wind chimes, and the river burbled melodiously. He said, "If that man Fan comes to Bare Mountain, he'll stay at Shang Village." I was startled by this prediction. He chuckled, but his laughter soon turned into a coughing fit. I asked how he knew, and he said he'd had a dream the night before about Fan and himself on the deck of a steamer. "The bed shook," he said, "like a ship at sea." He kept laughing the whole time. I said, "Shang-Jên, if this is true, it's nothing short of a miracle. God is revealing to you that you will leave Paipei, just as he told Moses he would lead the Israelites out of Egypt. The name of the Lord is holy and to be feared. It is right to be in awe of Him, and those who follow His commandments are wise. God is eternal, and eternally to be praised." He said he hadn't dreamed about Moses or his staff. As you [i.e., Reverend Beal] know, time may be well-intentioned, but it becomes the accomplice of

evil. Therefore, when I urged him to leave, I did so through the Chinese interpretation of dreams: "The ship is an omen of departure—you should listen to the augury of your dream." He replied, "I have a destination in mind, but not a pathway to get there. So the road is a worry." At the end of our conversation, I advised him to worship God. He said, "To this day, I cherish life, but I have never been able to place my faith in any religion. My only goal is to write a memoir. It will be more thrilling than any novel. It's about how I became a person like this. Maybe this is the beginning of me becoming myself, although I know I'll never finish writing it." He stood up and showed me a sheet of paper the color of yellow mud, on which was written "The Walking Shadow." It seemed he was destined to remain there. He wept as I prayed for him. That was the first time I had seen him shed tears since coming to Paipei. He seemed ashamed to be seen crying, and a red cloud spread across his cheeks, like the morning sun reflected in water. He said, "It's hard to forget what happened to you as a child, but no one wants to return to their childhood." Then he told me to leave Paipei immediately. "This isn't a place where you should stay. I feel deeply uneasy for you."

The fact that Shang-Jên predicted Fan's arrival showed that he'd been thinking about his fate. I thought his friendship with Fan might save his life. Poetry tells us that friendship can turn barren rock into a lake, a desert into a spring. As Shang-Jên foresaw, I met Fan in Shang Village. He was very thin and exceedingly polite, and evidently he was serious, like a friar at a midcentury monastery. My heart filled with hope as I spoke with him through the night. I called him Dr. Fan, because Shang-Jên once told me he used to be a doctor. Just as silver is shaped in a crucible and gold in a forge, praise can mold a fellow human being. I complimented his morality. For the sake of Shang-Jên's fate, I didn't ask what his purpose was in coming there. I didn't want to provoke him. Earth is heavy and rock heavier, but nothing weighs as much as the rage of an ignorant person. I told him that this place had flowing rivers, fresh shoots in the spring, herds of goats, a chapel, women pounding their mortars. He could enjoy the peaceful surroundings while treating the illnesses of the indigent. He said my words made sense, and he would consider them. After a while, I noticed how sleepy he was, and advised him to get some rest. Still, it was almost dawn before he went to bed. While he slept, I hurried to Shang-Jên's quarters to tell him that a miracle had taken place—Fan was at Shang Village—but the guards wouldn't let me in. They said Ge Ren had been up all night, and had not lain down until just before dawn. I didn't return to Shang Village, but set off for Canton to buy more medicine for

Shang-Jên. The sun had fully risen by the time I left Paipei. I thought Fan must have seen the letter I'd left him by now, with the advice "He does not snap the broken reed, nor blow out the guttering lamp. At his hands, universal truth is victorious, and all people venerate his name." I thought that if he valued his reputation, he wouldn't let Shang-Jên be killed.

There is a note after this letter adding that two weeks later, when Reverend Ellis returned to Baibei, he found Fangkou Elementary School standing empty, with not a soul to be seen.

Ah Qing's Report

Ah Qing's nose was sharper than a dog's, and not just any dog, a police dog. That morning, just as I was about to go see Ge Ren, he appeared at my door. Okay, okay, he stepped inside, and right away, bam! He kowtowed loudly in front of me. Then he held his rifle over his head and told me to make an example of him. I could smell alcohol on him—he reeked of it—and also onions. I hate people who eat onions. Do you like onions, miss? No? Excellent, that's excellent. That means we can live together. You might as well move into my courtyard home when we get back to Jingcheng.

Okay, okay, enough of that, let's talk about Ah Qing. My first thought was that this bastard hadn't followed the spirit of stopping at nine cups. In our line of work, the worst sin was getting drunk. You know what they say, in vino veritas—and what's more dangerous than the truth? I frowned and shouted, Get up! You're a military man, but I don't see a scrap of army discipline in you. How dare you. Stand up! He obediently climbed to his feet. He told me he hadn't been able to fulfill his duties, and felt he had let the leadership down. Sit down, I said. Sit down and tell me what's going on. He didn't dare to sit, but remained standing, rubbing his knees as he spoke. This isn't good, he said. Yang Fengliang's gotten us into real trouble. Miss, you just have to ask my secretary and she'll tell you, my biggest virtue is that I care a lot about the People, and about my subordinates. I asked what on earth had happened, and he said that right from his arrival in Baibei, Yang Fengliang had been giving him attitude and refusing to work with him, not to mention giving him grief in every way possible. When Ah Qing got there, he wanted to see Ge Ren, but not only did Yang Fengliang say no, he wouldn't even tell him where Ge Ren was staying. And yet Yang hadn't bothered to follow my three orders, but had spread the news far and wide that Ge Ren was in Baibei. Really? I said. So who knows? He said, Think about it: wasn't telling Zong Bu leaking the secret? Zong Bu is a newspaperman, he's even more powerful than Chongqing Radio. If he knows, then everyone else knows. Damn it! I hadn't expected to run into anything like this. It felt like someone had stuck a bamboo skewer right into my heart.

Go on, what then? I asked. He said that when he found out Ge Ren was locked up in Fangkou Elementary School, he got up early to go see what was going on, but got detained by Yang Fengliang's guys. Ah Qing stuck his hands behind his back and knelt down again, to show me how the guards had tortured him. And that's when he saw Ge Ren, flanked by a couple of guards, on his way back from a walk in Phoenix Valley. Ah Qing wanted to call out a greeting, but Yang Fengliang's soldiers stuffed a towel in his mouth, almost suffocating him. In his entire life, he grumbled resentfully, he'd only been gagged twice, including this time. Curious, I asked what the other time was. He said it was in Hangzhou, when he mentioned to someone that Ge Ren's dad was killed with a revolver. Ge Ren's father-in-law told him not to talk nonsense and stuffed a towel in his mouth. That little bastard. Why was he bringing that incident up at a time like this? Was he trying to remind me that he was close to the Ge family, or to indicate he wasn't happy with them? You're wrong, miss, this isn't a dialectical question. As I understand it, this was the message he was sending: Ge Ren treated me well in the past, but I also have a problem with him; and so, okay, okay, you've finally put in an appearance, you can decide what to do, and no matter how you end up dealing with Ge Ren, it has nothing to do with me, Ah Qing. Damn it! What a little devil.

I wanted to hear what crap he had to say, so I told him to speak freely. He said that when he got back to Baibei City [actually, Town], he looked for Yang Fengliang, who apologized to him and said it was all a misunderstanding. In order to keep the peace, he didn't argue. Next, Yang Fengliang started asking questions, trying to find out who told Ah Qing that Ge Ren was in Hope [actually, Fangkou] Elementary School. After going back and forth, Yang pinned it on someone named Qiu Aihua. Qiu Aihua? Who's that? Why does that name sound so familiar? I pretended ignorance. Ah Qing said, Qiu Aihua's one of Yang Fengliang's subordinates. He's from Chongqing, very capable, a straight shooter. He didn't like how Yang Fengliang was openly conducting his affair with "Fresh Flower Tune," which went against Council Chairman Chiang's New Life Movement. This made him a thorn in Yang's flesh, so Yang took the opportunity to get rid of him. And then? I asked. Ah Qing replied that one of his subordinates had been coming back from patrol that night when he heard someone sobbing and howling by the side of White Cloud River.

Idiot—did he want to die? Then a few gunshots—bang, bang, bang! That's how his subordinate reported it. He quickly grabbed some men and went to investigate. Ah Qing started weeping—he'd gotten there too late, and Qiu Aihua's corpse was gone, leaving nothing but a puddle of blood on the ground.

Why didn't you report it to me? I asked. He said he'd wanted to send me a report as soon as he got to Bare Mountain, but Yang Fengliang had smashed the telegraph machine. Then he got on his knees again and said, I wasn't able to fulfill my duties with honor, Commander. Please punish me. I asked where Yang Fengliang was. He jumped to his feet and said proudly that he'd thought I might end up having to come to Baibei, so for my safety, and to avenge his dead comrade, he had gotten rid of Yang Fengliang. And "Fresh Flower Tune"? I asked. He said if the bitch didn't lift her tail out of the way, the male dog wouldn't be able to mount her. Yang Fengliang was so corrupt, she must be implicated too. He got rid of her.

I didn't entirely believe everything he was telling me, but he looked drunk enough for me to trust him. In vino veritas. Besides, what choice did I have? Even if I had shot Ah Qing dead on the spot, that wouldn't have solved anything. And so I had to go against my conscience and praise him for doing well, saying I would mention his heroic deeds to Dai Li and make sure he was rewarded. He bowed to me and said, Thank you, Commander, for your guidance. Two days later, I would find out from Dr. Bai who Ah Qing really was, and the actual circumstances of Yang Fengliang's death, but by that time Ah Qing had fled. No, he never returned to Chongqing. I don't know where the hell he went. Still, at the time, I couldn't help but admire his performance, even if I suspected he'd deliberately had a few drinks to help with the deception. You can see the sun's radiance in just a drop of water, miss. At that moment, I believed more fervently than ever that if even the likes of Ah Qing could achieve heroic results, then Chiang Kai-shek was surely done for, and the Communist Party would be victorious. How about it, was I right? Of course, it's easy to say this in hindsight.

After Ah Qing finished speaking, he stood at the doorway gesturing for me to go ahead. He wanted to ceremonially escort me to Ge Ren. The way he was talking about it, you'd have thought it was because of him that I'd stayed alive long enough for this encounter. There was a horse standing outside, and as I walked toward it, I started peeling off my white gloves—but it was as if they had fused with my hands: they simply would not come off. Damn it! That's when I realized my palms were sweating badly, and the gloves were soaked through. How was I going to meet my old friend? All of a sudden, I understood that I might have been wrong to blame Yang Fengliang and Ah Qing. If Ge Ren had been willing to leave, either of them would have been glad to let him go. I was the reason he was still there. He'd waited because of our long friendship. This brought tears to my eyes. Tears of emotion, miss. I told Ah Qing to go ahead on the horse and give Ge Ren a heads-up, to say I'd soon be there. But Ah Qing, still pretending to be drunk, was unable to mount the horse, so I told my aide to give him a leg up. Ha-ha, Ah Qing looked ridiculous. We hefted him up onto the horse's back, but he just fell off on the other side. The last time we tried it, he hit a rock and cut his leg open, bleeding everywhere.

Truth Is an Illusion?

Comparing Ah Qing and Mr. Fan's accounts, we see that on many occasions Ah Qing describes certain situations one way, while Mr. Fan has quite a different recollection. For instance, Ah Qing says that he and Fan first encountered each other at the school gate, as he was walking back to Fangkou with the sedan chair he'd made to carry Ge Ren to a safe place. "When we were almost there, we saw that the whole area was thick with guards. The earth and heavens shook, and the gods wept. My [i.e., Ah Qing's] brain seemed to expand. Right away I thought, it's too late, Fan Jihuai is here, and now Ge Ren will never get away." Yet Mr. Fan says he met Ah Qing at Shang Village, and it was Ah Qing who "appeared at [his] door."

Like many avid readers, I often suffer from a misapprehension: that when you hear a repeated story, the last version you hear is the one closest to the truth. That is to say, while listening to Mr. Fan's tape, I often felt that Ah Qing must have been lying, while Mr. Fan's account was closer to how events actually unfolded. A psychologist once told me this indicated that I was a subconscious believer in "human progress," and that I had the conviction that as time passed, humanity got more and more trustworthy.

In fact, "truth" is a completely illusory idea. If we take the onions Mr. Fan mentioned as an example, then "truth" is the core of the onion. You peel away layer after layer, only to discover nothing at all. While we're on the subject, I should add that we should look askance at Mr. Fan's statement that Ah Qing had been eating onions, because they didn't start growing onions in Baibei until 1968.

It was through talking with Miss Bai Ling that I came across the concept that truth is an illusion. I'd said to her beforehand, "If you can get Mr. Fan to tell you the truth about how Ge Ren died, I'll make sure you're rewarded." She answered right away, "It's his tongue, in his mouth. How would I know whether he's telling the truth or not?" Besides, she added, Mr. Fan himself might not be certain if he was lying. "He wanted to show me how good his teeth were, so he chewed his way through a dozen bags of ice on the train. I heard them crunching away, but they were all false. Still, you can't say that false teeth aren't teeth." She sounded so convincing, I had nothing to say. Then she snapped, "Don't try to bluff me—everything is fake. Only the American dollar is real." Which is why, when we discussed her compensation, she insisted on being paid in American dollars, not yuan. I would get her cassette tapes when I handed her a pile of greenbacks. "American dollars can be fake too," I teased. "My great-grandfather was a forger, you know. His American banknotes looked like the real thing." She hadn't realized that my great-grandfather was the late Hu An, and now that she knew, she lowered her voice and asked if I could explain something to her. The bank near her school had a scanner for counterfeit notes, but it was so inaccurate it was clearly just for show. Fake notes got through all the time, "but sometimes it starts beeping, and when you look closely at the bill, it's a real one." I said this clearly showed that the scanner itself was fake. As I answered, I had the sudden thought that the "truth" was like Mr. Fan's description of Ah Qing mounting the horse—boosted up one side only to come crashing down on the other. Bai Ling cut through my musing and said, looking completely serious, "Don't try to trick me. I'll get them appraised by an expert."

She really did do that—her boyfriend told me. Her boyfriend—the "expert"—is named Mick Jagger, just like the guy from the Rolling Stones. I had always suspected this wasn't his actual name, and then I got my proof: in order to turn himself into Mick, he'd grown out his hair and had surgery to make his lips puffy. If you find ape lips sexy, then you'll have to admit that Mick Jagger the Second's mouth is sexy indeed. Sadly, sexy Mick Jagger the Second wasn't able to distinguish real American dollars from fake either. When he revealed over dinner that he'd taken Bai Ling to have the banknotes checked, she looked a little embarrassed. I told her that I didn't see this as an insult. The most beautiful way to interpret it was as a longing for the truth: even if everything in the world were fake, this longing would always be real.

I was talking about Bai Ling there, but I could have equally directed those words at myself. If not for my longing for the truth, I wouldn't have combed through three different transcripts, racking my brains to deal with the many obvious errors, omissions, and lapses of logic, correcting, supplementing, and editing them as needed. I've been wandering in a fog for a long time. Even as I despaired over the many parts of the narrative where it was impossible to tell true from false, I slowly grew to understand one fact: the story of every person in this book is an echo of history. Back to Mr. Fan's onions: even if the onion has nothing at its core, that doesn't affect its taste. Those tightly wrapped layers are still as sharp and bitter as always.

Bai Shengtao

In the end, Ah Qing didn't manage to get on the horse; he hobbled down the road ahead of me instead. When we got to White Cloud Bridge, we saw someone coming toward us. Guess who it was, miss. No, not Zong Bu—he had already left by the time I got to Bare Mountain. Weren't you asking about Bai Shengtao earlier? Well, there he was. I remember very clearly, he had a bridle in his hands, as if he were searching for a missing horse. Ah Qing's limping got his attention. Seeing him standing there, Ah Qing said, That's Dr. Bai over there. He's an expert in all four main methods of diagnosis. I shook his hand and said, Thank you for coming to Baibei. He said, I'm just doing my duty. I said, Look, Ah Qing's hurt his leg, and I don't have any medicine on me—could you deal with it? Dr. Bai said, No problem. And with that, he dashed behind the horse, scooped up some dung with his bridle, and said, This will fix it.

Okay, okay, sure, horse shit—what a bargain. I asked how he'd learned this remedy, and he said it was from the Bible. I asked if he was a Christian, and he neither admitted nor denied it, but said he used to work at a church hospital. When Ah Qing saw him walking over with steaming manure, he sobered up immediately and screamed, Isn't that shit? How can you use it as medicine? Bai Shengtao said, Of course it's medicine. Even if the anti-counterfeiting hero Wang Hai [N.B. Mr. Fan's actual words] were here, he wouldn't dare say this wasn't medicine. But Ah Qing held his nose and kept backing away. I knew the dung would just be applied to the skin, but still said to Ah Qing, Loyal words are hard to hear, and good medicine is bitter—but go ahead and eat it. Ah Qing ducked behind me, as if it were a time bomb. I said, The Revolution isn't over yet, so we comrades must keep fighting—get better, and keep working for the Revolution. Dr. Bai protested that it [the dung] wasn't for eating, but for external use. Ah Qing had no choice but to roll up his trousers, and Dr. Bai spread it on his leg. He did this very carefully, like someone smearing lime on a fruit tree trunk.

After he'd finished applying the horse dung, we continued on in the direction of [Fangkou] Elementary School. I was really worked up—this was the place where I used to fight, live, and study. Ah Qing said he smelled bad now, and didn't think it would be right to see Ge Ren like this. I ignored him and said to Dr. Bai, Comrade Doctor, you've spent a lot of time with the patient recently. What do you think about his state of mind? That's right, I didn't say Ge Ren's name, I just called him "the patient." Bai Shengtao said, Do you mean Code Zero? I said yes, and asked how he knew. He said he had heard General Zhao say it, and it was such a strange thing to call someone that he'd remembered. I ordered him not to tell anyone else, and he said that as a church doctor, he only cared about treating patients, and otherwise ignored the material world. When I asked about Ge Ren again, he amened before telling me that Code Zero had tuberculosis and needed to recuperate in peace. I asked how much longer he thought Code Zero could hold on. He amened again, and said the Lord might take him away at any time. I told him to use whatever medicine he thought needed to be used, whether it was penicillin or something else, and not to worry about the expense. He said, I knew you were a medical expert as soon as you opened your mouth, General—it saves a lot of trouble, having an expert in charge. I could see, miss, that he was speaking from the heart. That's how it is: once you set the level, everyone has to stick to it. He asked me to tell Code Zero when I saw him to take his medicine on time.

We were still talking when we got to the school gate. I might look old, miss, but when I think back to that moment, I remember every detail. When Ge Ren saw me, we hugged, and he said he was sorry I'd had a hard time getting there. That was too much, frankly—I felt a little embarrassed. I told him I'd seen his poem in *Scattered Scriptures* and realized he was still alive, so I had come to visit him. He was so sensitive that he immediately started explaining that this had nothing to do with *Scattered Scriptures*, and would I please not give Xu Yusheng a hard time? I laughed and said, I won't—when the Premier [i.e., Sun Yat-sen] was alive, didn't he say the world belonged to everyone? Okay, okay, then your friend is my friend, so relax—I'm not going to do anything to Xu Yusheng. He still seemed uneasy, and said that Xu Yusheng must surely think he was dead, and that the poem was mailed before the Battle of Two Li Mound. He'd gotten a letter from Xu Yusheng asking if he'd finished writing his memoir. Even after all these years, he had never found the time to settle down and write, so he amended an old poem and sent it to Xu instead. When I think about that, even now I feel bad. I mean, miss, what the hell—he published a poem, and for that I had to end his life? It was too much.

He said that while he was writing the [amended] poem, he felt a great longing to visit Bare Mountain again, to see White Cloud River, and to search for his daughter who'd gone missing there. If he hadn't been discovered, he would have stayed in this school that Hu An put up the funds to build, and worked on his manuscript again, fulfilling the dream he'd had since he was a boy of becoming a literary figure! Okay, okay, don't laugh; those were the exact words he used: becoming a literary figure. He didn't anticipate that after mailing the letter, he would go to Two Li Mound, where his men were badly outnumbered and fled in all directions. Ge Ren was wounded, but he managed to get out alive. And so he went to Baibei, where he lived under a false name. The people who'd been there before were all dead, so no one recognized him. At least he managed to eke out a few days there in peace. At that point, he emphasized once again that Xu Yusheng must surely think he was dead, just like everyone else, and that he was now a hero of the People—otherwise he would never have printed that poem. As further proof, he made sure to point out that Baibei City [Town] didn't have a post office, so he couldn't have mailed it from there. In his eagerness to convince me, he had unnecessarily invented a false detail. I sent someone to investigate, and guess what? Xiguan Village had a post office—built by the Red Cross. Ge Ren was dead by the time I found that out, though, so I couldn't confront him with the truth. I still remember that the post office employee in Xiguan Village was a cripple. He said it was from a dog bite. My subordinate did the right thing—he was extremely dedicated to his work. In order to prevent any leaks, and to ensure stability and unity, and of course to wipe his ass clean, he slaughtered the cripple. What? My subordinate's name? Ah, I'm too old. It's on the tip of my tongue, but I can't quite seem to remember.

In any case, during my conversation with Ge Ren, he was very insistent that he'd mailed the poem before coming to Bare Mountain. I could see he was getting agitated and starting to cough, so I patted him on the chest and said, Okay, okay, never mind whether Xu Yusheng knew you were alive or not. I won't take it out on Mr. Xu. I'm a legal expert, miss, so my word is worth its weight in gold. And after all this, I let Xu Yusheng off the hook. Of course, he was killed anyway—took nine bullets in the torso. That wasn't me, though. It didn't have a damned thing to do with me.

The Xiguan Village Post Office

According to *The History of Local Post Offices in China* (Southern Publishing, 1998), the Xiguan Village branch, established in October 1935, was the first post office on Bare Mountain. Mr. Fan's recollection was correct—it was indeed set up by missionaries from the Red Cross. All the letters Reverend Ellis wrote to Reverend Beal were mailed from there, by the way. We can even see what it looked like, from the photograph printed in *Local Post Offices*: a gray building with a tiled roof, and a honey locust tree by the front door. That tree is still alive, and its crown has grown enormously, casting a huge shadow—during the summer, this must be a perfect spot to cool off. As I was leaving, I noticed a board hanging from the tree. Written on it in red paint were the words "Harden your heart and cut those tubes." It was signed "Soc Spi Off." I asked the locals, and they told me that the "tubes" were the vas deferens and the fallopian tubes, and that "Soc Spi Off" stood for the Xiguan Village Socialist Spiritual Enlightenment Office. As I stood before that slogan, I couldn't help thinking that perhaps this was the very spot where Ge Ren had mailed his poem "Broad Bean Blossoms" to Xu Yusheng.

Of course, there is no way to know now when he actually mailed this letter. Mr. Fan said he swore that he did it before coming to Bare Mountain, but I'm certain he was just saying that to protect Xu. As I said before, I lean toward believing it was sent from Bare Mountain. My reasoning is very simple: firstly, if Ge Ren was searching for Broad Bean, then he must have been to Xiguan Village. And perhaps Fan Jihuai (or his subordinate) killed the "cripple" in the post office because he was afraid he would recognize Ge Ren. Secondly, Xu Yusheng says in *Qiantang River Dream Diary* that he received "Broad Bean Blossoms" at the end of 1942. If Ge Ren had mailed it from Yan'an, then the latest it could have arrived would be May 1942, before he went to Song Village [Chaoyang Hill]. It was a chaotic time, but no letter took half a year getting to its destination—that seems far too long to be plausible.

If my hypothesis is correct, then the next question to ask is, Why did Ge Ren mail this poem to Mr. Xu Yusheng? Was he trying to let his loved ones know that he hadn't actually become a hero of the People at the Battle of Two Li Mound? Or to give notice to the world that he wanted to be a real person, and that his real life had only just begun? As Reverend Ellis said, he saw it as "the beginning of me becoming myself." I'm unable to answer any of these questions, but I imagine that everyone who finishes reading this book will arrive at conclusions of their own.

Step by Step

As we spoke, I noticed that Ge Ren's cheeks were ruddy, though he was a little thin. He was neatly shaved, and he still looked like the professor he'd been back at Shanghai University. When he wasn't coughing and bringing up blood, he didn't look like a sick person at all. The problem was, he *was* coughing up blood, and I had to show some concern. I asked how his health was doing, and he said he'd dreamed about his lungs looking like chunks of fermented bean curd, but Dr. Bai and the reverend both said they weren't so much bean curd as cheese—the tuberculosis was like lumps of cheese. I told him to concentrate on getting better, so he could continue with the Revolution. After all, your body is your revolutionary capital. I remember clearly how he lit a cigarette and slowly said that Dr. Bai was against him smoking, but seeing as how he was dead anyway, he might as well continue. He asked the doctor to brew him a cup of tea, adding that Ah Qing had brought him the tea leaves—they were good. Ah Qing was quick-witted enough to jump in there and say that I was the one who had told him to bring them. Damn it! For once, he was actually doing what his Commander required.

So you see, our meeting that day progressed step by step, from shallow to deep. That's how things work in diplomacy. I remember Ge Ren once said that when old friends get together, they shouldn't talk about national matters. I said, Fine, anyone who messes up will have to drink three cups of wine as punishment. It was like now, miss—at first Ge Ren and I were just making small talk. We spoke about the *Ta Chang Maru*, Kawata, Kawai, Huang Yan, Hu An—covering everything under the sun. I said if he had any requests, to please pass them on to the leadership. He said he was comfortable there, and satisfied with everything. Then he said, Didn't you say at the beginning that this place was even more comfortable than Shanghai? You see how good his brain was, remembering those words from so many years ago. Even so, I said to Ah Qing and Dr. Bai, Remember, you have to do a good job—get the hardware and software up to date. Then I asked Ge Ren if he had seen Broad Bean. He said he'd looked everywhere for her, but all the current residents had moved there recently and didn't know about anything that had happened earlier. He hadn't been able to find her. I tried to comfort him by saying, Girls become women at the age of eighteen, and they get more and more beautiful. It's been so many years. For all you know, maybe Broad Bean's gotten married. She could walk right past you and you wouldn't recognize her. He said, How could that be? Ever since she was little, Broad Bean has looked exactly like Bingying. If I set eyes on her, I'd know it was her right away. I said, Perhaps someone brought Broad Bean out of the Soviet zone. You know the slogan "When the car gets to the mountain, there'll surely be a road, and where there's a road there's Toyota." I'm sure she's well, wherever she is, and you shouldn't worry. He sighed, but said nothing more. I told him that if you lose the skin, the fur goes too, so he should take care of his health. There'd be time in the future to be reunited with his daughter.

What I actually wanted to say to him was: Broad Bean isn't even yours, damn it, so what's the point of spending all this energy? But I held back, because that wouldn't have changed anything. Even at the moment of death, he was such a scholarly gentleman, unable to leave his tender feelings behind. So I said, Nothing's impossible in this world—you simply have to climb higher. When I'm done with all this, I will put the resources of Kuomintang Military Intelligence into the search, and we're sure to find Broad Bean. But he said he didn't have much time left, and he wanted to see his daughter once before he died, firstly to make up for his failings, and secondly because he owed it to Bingying. So that's where he was, unable to write his book, unable to find his daughter. Okay, okay, it's just as well he mentioned Bingying. That suited me—I'd been planning to use her name to get him to surrender, and now I didn't even need to bring it up. My granddaughter Fan Ye is always hiding in the bathroom and singing some song about "you're the eternal ache in my chest." I don't know who the ache in her chest is, but I'm sure the ache in Ge Ren's chest was Bingying. It's always the same story, those tender feelings. It would have been undiplomatic of me to drag Bingying into the conversation, but now he'd said it first, so he couldn't blame me. I quickly mentioned that I'd seen Bingying in the provisional capital. He seemed shocked, and asked what she was doing there—was she performing in something? I lied that she wasn't in a show, but had gone to Chongqing to find out about him. Then I lit a cigarette for him and said, Ge Ren, my dear Ge Ren, you lucky fellow, she still seems very much in love with you.

My eyes are sharp, and I could see how moved he was. Striking while the iron was hot, I said, Ge Ren, my brother, why not come back to Chongqing with me, and you can be reunited with Bingying. A light bulb went off in my head, and I abruptly understood why Ge Ren had come back to his old haunt—to wallow in his long-ago love. Didn't I mention earlier that he'd spent some happy days with Bingying on Bare Mountain? Now he laughed and said, Ah, old Mr. Fan [probably just Mr. Fan?], now you've shown your hand—you're here to persuade me to surrender, aren't you?

My Great-Aunt's Misgivings

We've now seen various explanations for why Ge Ren was on Bare Mountain: He was "a literary man down to his bones, and perhaps he was on Bare Mountain because he wanted a peaceful place to write." Or else he "might be there to recuperate. He had lung disease, and needed the moist air and sunlight of the south" (Bai Shengtao). Or he was there to sum up his revolutionary experience and "provid[e] an ideological basis for the Revolution" (Zhao Yaoqing). And here, Mr. Fan is using Ge Ren as a mouthpiece to claim he was there to write his book, search for Broad Bean, and "wallow in his long-ago love." Naturally, I find it hard to tell whose explanation is closest to the truth, but there's one thing we can be sure of: Ge Ren had no idea before he got there that someone had taken Broad Bean away. When my great-aunt talked about this, she said:

> In the winter of 1936, I saw Shangren's message of condolence for Lu Xun, and knew he was still alive. I wondered if I ought to tell him about Broad

Bean. It wouldn't have been difficult—the Red Cross often sent people to Shaanbei, and I could have gotten one of them to deliver a message. But I didn't. So much time had passed, he might have already forgotten about the whole affair. If he found out how seriously ill Broad Bean was, he would surely blame himself, and I couldn't bear to add to Shangren's pain. I didn't tell Bingying either, for the same reason. Besides, I also had to think about Broad Bean's safety. There were Judases everywhere, and if anyone had found out she was the Communist Ge Ren's daughter, she'd have been ostracized and smeared, or even hauled into court. And if that happened, there'd only be death left for her. So for years after that, I kept my mouth tightly shut. No one knew she was Shangren and Bingying's daughter. During the Cultural Revolution, someone mentioned Shangren in an essay criticizing Chen Duxiu. My god, if anyone had known then that Broad Bean was Shangren's child, I can't imagine what would have happened next.

As I said before, it wasn't just my great-aunt who came to Bare Mountain in search of Broad Bean—Reverend Ellis did too. In the spring of 1943, Ellis had already seen Ge Ren before the arrival of Fan Jihuai. Which is to say, when Ellis spoke to Ge Ren, he might have brought up Broad Bean being rescued—Ellis wouldn't have had my great-aunt's misgivings because he didn't know Broad Bean had fallen ill in Tianjin. Unfortunately, I haven't found a single written record confirming that Reverend Ellis spoke to Ge Ren about my mother. My great-aunt's guess is that even if Ge Ren had found out from Ellis about Broad Bean's whereabouts, it wasn't possible for him to get to Tianjin. Just as he seemed to have a premonition that someone would seek him out on Bare Mountain, he might also have sensed that even if he had gone to Tianjin, they'd still have come knocking at his door. And if that had happened, he wouldn't have been the only one who got killed, but Broad Bean and my great-aunt would have been caught in the crossfire too.

Persuading You to Surrender

I'm sure you've noticed, miss, that there's one good thing about me—I don't beat around the bush. Okay, okay, so now that he'd brought it out into the open, I wasn't going to deny it. I said, All right, so let's say that's why I'm here, I'm persuading you to surrender. I poured him a drink, lit him a cigarette, and told him what Dai Li had said as I was leaving Chongqing, about setting up a new party. I said, Old Chiang's agreed to it—as long as you're willing to come back to Chongqing, they'll let you have this new party with six seats on the National Defense Advisory Council—that's a huge honor. He laughed at that: Six seats? Isn't that one more than Mr. Chen Duxiu himself? He was right—before Chen Duxiu's death, the Kuomintang had promised to let him establish a new party, with five seats on the council. Can old Chiang be trusted? he asked. He seemed interested, so I clinked my glass to his and said, Do you even need to ask? Orders from up top are like imperial edicts: one word of his is worth ten thousand of anyone else's.

Let me show you what Ge Ren did next, miss—give me your hand. My, what a soft hand you have, even softer than Ruan Lingyu's. Don't misunderstand; I'm not in the habit of holding girls' hands—I just want to give you a demonstration. When I told Ge Ren he could have six seats on the council, he pinched his own fingertips one by one, like this, and said, Lawyer Fan, six is too many. I can't count them on the fingers of one hand—let's forget it. Fuck! At first I thought he was just being humble, but soon I realized he genuinely wasn't interested. He said, I know exactly what you're trying to do—you want the People to find out that Ge Ren is still alive, and that the Battle of Two Li Mound was a false report from Yan'an. That way you'd be in for a reward from the Central Government.

I had to admit that Ge Ren was clever—very clever indeed. He had seen right through the government's plan. Yes, this was exactly what Dai Li had said to me before I set off. This was the main reason we wanted him to surrender. But we were at the negotiating table, so I had to bite off the words and deny everything. I said, Ge Ren, you're thinking too much. The government greatly respects your scholarship, and that's why they sent me to bring you back to Chongqing. It's all for your future. You know what he said to me? He said, The anti-Japanese war of resistance will be over soon, and then we'll be back to the civil war. And when that happens, old Chiang will be completely defeated by the Communists. To be honest, I didn't think much of that idea at the time—I assumed he had a high fever and was just talking nonsense, because the territory occupied by the Communists at that point wasn't worth a fart. Adopting the reactionary stance that was in vogue, I said, Ge Ren, oh, Ge Ren, you need to be more realistic. The country's in a tough spot now, and everyone recognizes old Chiang as the leader of the resistance. Even Zhang Xiruo is doing his bit for the government, so why can't you let go of your beliefs? Will your beliefs keep your belly full? Surely not. You don't have to worry that old Chiang won't accept you. Look at Zhang Xiruo—he set himself against old Chiang, but now old Chiang treats him with respect and dignity.

Ge Ren interrupted here to say that it wasn't like his beliefs were leading him by the nose—his words had nothing to do with his beliefs. Then he used the fact that his name sounded like "individual," insisting that he was speaking as an individual, and this had nothing to do with the inter-party conflict. I said, My brother, there's no one here but us. You don't need to be humble. Don't you think I know your bottom line? You believe in Communism, like many other people. I respect all of you down to my marrow, but life passes like a dream, so why hang yourself like that? This wasn't just coloratura, miss, I was speaking from the bottom of my heart. And yet he wasn't moved at all.

So I didn't manage to persuade him, and in the end he was the one who convinced me. That was unexpected, really unexpected. I had thought this would be as easy as catching a fish, but now I was the one on the hook. He advised me not to go back to the provisional capital; otherwise I'd surely end up like the First Emperor's terracotta warriors, buried in old Chiang's tomb. What do you mean there were no terracotta warriors back then? It looks like you really do have to move in with me, young lady, so I can give you remedial lessons. There were terracotta warriors during the Qin Dynasty. They were the first of the eight world wonders. Two years ago, I took some foreign visitors to see them, and they were so impressed. Absolutely in awe of Chinese intelligence and skill. What? Oh, you mean they weren't uncovered during Ge Ren's lifetime? Well, I'll admit that's true, but let's not quibble over minor details. Anyway, Ge Ren told me I shouldn't go back to Chongqing. I said, That's cute of you. I suppose you think I ought to surrender to Yan'an? Ge Ren laughed and said, I'm not trying to get you to surrender—I have no power. I'm just telling you this as a friend. Then he said he appreciated the pains I'd taken, sending Ah Qing and Yang Fengliang, which was surely because I wanted them to let him go. How well Ge Ren understood me! I hugged him again. He asked me not to blame Ah Qing and Yang Fengliang—he was the one who'd refused to leave, and it wasn't their fault. I could tell from his tone that he had no idea Yang Fengliang was currently fish food. I told him to relax. The ocean is wide enough to absorb a hundred rivers, and I was old friends with those two bastards. I wasn't going to give them a hard time.

Without our even noticing, the sun had risen. It was Bai Shengtao who told us it was day. He'd been following my order to sit in a corner and keep an eye on Ge Ren as we talked. Now he said the cocks had already crowed three times. He told Ge Ren to get some rest, and grumbled that he would wreck his body if he went on like this. Then he turned off [blew out] the lantern, but Ge Ren turned it on [lit it] again. He asked if Ge Ren wanted to write some more, but Ge Ren said, Write what? I've burned my manuscript. I just want to have a cigarette before bed. Then I heard Ge Ren say, In life there's a little rest and a big rest. The little rest is sleep, the big rest is death—and I'm looking forward to my big rest. That sounded familiar. After I'd walked out of [Fangkou] Elementary School, it came to me: Qu Qiubai had said something similar early on.

Little Rest, Big Rest

Probably due to his age, Mr. Fan sometimes contradicts himself. Here's one example: he previously said there was no one else present when he spoke to Ge Ren, but now it seems that Dr. Bai was sitting in a corner and keeping an eye on Ge Ren. Unless Dr. Bai doesn't count as a person? I'm not going to debate his humanity here, of course. Besides, in addition to Bai Shengtao, Fan's aide Ding Kui was also present.

In the spring of 1996, having read Bai Shengtao's account, I finally managed, after some maneuvering, to interview the man who'd transcribed and edited this narrative: Mr. Ding Kui. Before this, my sole impression of him had come from a photograph in the *Journal for Ge Ren Studies* that showed Mr. Ding already ravaged by age: double chin, puffy eyes, unfocused gaze, slackened flesh on his face. During our conversation, he revealed that he burned the manuscript of *The Walking Shadow* on Fan Jihuai's orders!

> [Taking part in the conversation] were ala [us] three. You don't understand Shanghainese? Fine, I'll switch to Mandarin. There were three people: Fan, Ge, and me. Oh, and Dr. Bai. We were eating tofu as we talked. Ge wasn't going to surrender. Fan said Chiang Kai-shek would give 'im [him] a few seats on the council, but 'e [he] didn't seem to care about that. I've forgotten how many. 'e said, You see, 'e only wanted to rest, and a doze [sleep] was a little rest, but death was a big rest. 'e wanted a big rest. I'm hoping for a big rest now. My liver's completely wrecked, and so's my heart. Death can't be far away.
>
> When someone's close to death, their words turn to good. At a light [time] like this, everything I'm saying is true. Don't tell anyone else, though, at least not until I'm dead. I was the one who burned Ge's book. I didn't read any of it, not a single page. You have to obey your commander at all times, and Fan gave the order. Mud-yellow pages, a thick stack of them, like the Xinhua Dictionary. Fan said, Burn that to protect 'is [his] reputation. There'll be trouble if we don't. What kind of trouble? Many people will find out that Ge Ren didn't die [N.B. He probably means he didn't die in the Battle of Two Li Mound], then scratch [fuck] 'im. If that happened, what ala [we] did will be exposed.

"When someone's close to death, their words turn to good," and so I tend to believe Mr. Ding Kui's version. Sure enough, not long after our meeting, he passed away. To be honest, I've always had a great deal of respect for Mr. Ding. If he hadn't offered up his transcript of Bai Shengtao's words, I would never have known how my grandfather Ge Ren died. Of course, I later learned from his granddaughter that those materials hadn't been offered freely, but were sold to the Ge Ren Research Center.

After Mr. Ding's death, I got a letter from his granddaughter, saying she had something she wanted to talk to me about. She said:

> About a week after meeting you, Grandpa was reading a poem in bed one day. Yeah, it was that "Broad Bean Blossoms" one you talked about. He was reading out loud, swaying his head back and forth. We found the noise annoying, so we ducked out. Just before noon, we came back to make lunch and found him in bed, completely silent. I went over for a closer look. His head was tilted over to one side, and there was blood at the corners of his mouth. The eye facing the door was wide open—I guess he was waiting for someone to come in. He was holding a wooden box that was covered in dust. He must have collapsed after going to get it. It was too late to try and save him; he was long gone. His face was stark white, though his body was still warm.

I thought whatever was in that box must surely have something to do with Ge Ren, so I asked if I could see it. First she said she didn't know where her family had put it, and then she started talking in a roundabout way about how they'd spent a lot of money on her grandfather's funeral, and how we now had a socialist market economy, so if I wanted what was in the wooden box, then shouldn't I behave according to the laws of economics? This wasn't an unfamiliar request. As I said before, Yu Fenggao's son Yu Liren did something similar. She also wanted something Yu Liren hadn't mentioned: could I keep this from her parents? "If they find out, they're sure to try to squeeze more cash out of you. I'll tell you the truth—they already got quite a bit out of the Ge Ren Research Center. Scratch [fuck] them, they gave all that money to my brother." She got the box out from her dressing table and smacked it. "This will blow your mind. I promise it's worth this much!" She held up one finger, and I thought she meant a thousand, but it turned out to be ten thousand.

After a bout of haggling, she agreed to accept two boxes of Alaskan seal oil—which I had no use for anyway—in exchange for the wooden box. I opened it and found some old newspapers inside, now shredded. The rat droppings told me who was responsible for that. I managed to make out that there were two copies with "border" and "report" in their titles: one was probably the *Border War Report* from October 11, 1942, which I mentioned in the first part of this book. This was the issue that Huang Yan's essay "A River of Iron behind Enemy

Lines" appeared in. I only worked out the date of the other one later. There was also a *People's Daily*, and a something *Harbor Daily*—I guessed that this was the *Shanghai Harbor Daily*. Finally, there was a something *Scriptures*. From Fan Jihuai's narrative, I realized this must be the journal published by Xu Yusheng in Hong Kong, *Scattered Scriptures*.

History Is Written by the Winners

That's right, it was Qu Qiubai who talked about the little rest and the big rest. You have to listen to the words beyond the words, the rhythm beyond the music. So I thought, was Ge Ren hinting that he'd lived long enough, and I ought to take a lesson from Song Xilian and bump him off? You don't know who Song Xilian was? He was the commander of the Kuomintang 34th Division. Graduated from Huangpu Military Academy. Some people say that all crows are equally black, and there's not a single decent person in Hongdong County. Damn it, that's far too one-sided. Pure metaphysics. Song Xilian was a good person. Otherwise, how would he have become a representative of all the people in the country? [N.B. He was a member of the Chinese People's Political Consultative Conference.] I'm a good person too. I didn't save Ge Ren, but I'm still a good person. If not, why would all the newspapers call me a person of integrity? It says so in print!

Let me say this, miss. Even at this point, I was still hoping to preserve Ge Ren's life. I wondered what to do—should I talk to Dai Li? I wasn't sure how that would go, but you cross the river one stepping-stone at a time, and you're always struggling for the next one. And so, after my conversation with Ge Ren, I called Dai Li's cell [N.B. He means "phone"]. I told him I'd gotten to the bottom of the matter, and it was indeed Ge Ren who was here, but he was refusing to surrender. I also said how serious his illness was. Then I asked Dai Li, What's my next step? I'm waiting for an order. He asked me to call again in a while. You're smart, miss. He couldn't make a decision, either—he had to ask old Chiang. I called again after a while. Dai Li, the smiling tiger, was completely ruthless, and now he said, Since he'll be dead soon anyway, just shoot him. I said, Why don't we bring him back to Chongqing? He said, What for? If he's not going to surrender, then that's a waste of money, and it'll be a lot of trouble. Not worth it. No, I didn't mention Kawai. It would have been too hard to explain over the phone, and if he were to learn that I'd had dealings with a Japanese, he'd be sure to get suspicious. That's right! This sort of thing should only be discussed in person, when you can take your time. Heh, after this trip with me, miss, you'll have learned quite a bit about fighting tactics.

I'd be lying if I said I wasn't in pain after I put down the phone, but what could I do? Everything's decided by the big climate and the little climate. And to be frank, I wasn't hurting *that* much. First of all, I was psychologically prepared for this, because someone like Dai Li wasn't going to suddenly turn kind. Secondly, I'd already done everything I could for Ge Ren, and if I shot him now, I'd just be doing what he wanted. If he really believed the Kuomintang was going to collapse and the Communists would definitely be victorious, then by killing him, wasn't I enabling him to become a martyr? As Hu Shih said, history is like a young woman: you can dress her up any way you like. Remember, whoever wins is automatically right, and history is written by the winners.

It was now clear what was going to happen, and the only question was how to do it. Would I have to pull the trigger myself? No, I couldn't do it. Worried that people would find out and my reputation would be ruined? I knew that's what you'd think. Not just you—Little Red Woman said so too. Last year, she quietly asked me if I'd had to wrestle with this decision, and I answered, No, honestly, no. She laughed at me and said, Look, your face is all flushed. Nonsense, it's not like this was anything to be ashamed of, so why would I be blushing? I was about to explain to her, then I thought forget it, no point lowering myself to her level. She's just a performer; it's not like she'd have the brain capacity to understand. You're different from her, miss, so I don't mind explaining it to you in a bit more detail. Now, you can write what you like in your article, I won't interfere, but let me just warn you that it might be better if you didn't include what I'm going to say next. I will tell you this: the reason I didn't pull the trigger myself was that I was starting to think there might be something to Ge Ren's prediction that the Communists were sure to win, and the Kuomintang would definitely be defeated. Zhuge Liang was cautious his whole life, and Lu Duan was never careless when it mattered. These are the characteristics I've cultivated in myself, over a long period of conflict. No need to be scared of everything, but be prepared for anything. If the Eighth Route Army was defeated, then wouldn't Ge Ren have died for nothing? Okay, okay, I thought, best to let Kawai deal with this. That way, no matter who won or who lost, and who got to write history, Ge Ren would still be a hero of the People. My dear young lady, this is how it goes: those who know me understand my pain, but it's a mystery to those who don't. My conscience is clear—I did what I did out of love for Ge Ren. At the time, I thought it would be best that no one ever found out about this, but if word did get out, then I'd be able to say, That's right, Ge Ren died on Bare Mountain, but it was a Japanese man who did it. I got there too late to save him. Yes, you're right—I had already considered this in Wuhan, and that's why I took Kawai with me. Still, I was improvising a solution to a new problem, because I hadn't expected that Ge Ren would actually stay on Bare Mountain and not try to leave.

I said to my subordinates, Go get Little Japan. Kawai had been locked in an abandoned hut, so when he appeared, he was covered in dust, and his hair was full of cobwebs. He stared at me and asked, Mr. Fan, have you found out where my brother is? I told him to have a seat, and poured him a cup of tea. Then I said in a sorrowful voice, My friend, I've asked Ge Ren, and your brother's dead. I'm sorry. Tears came to his eyes, and he was silent for a long time. Fuck! It was like his brain had gone. I scolded him for that—if you can't weather the storm, how will you ever see the rainbow? By the way, miss, I'm pretty certain that in this globalized economy, the reason Kawai's done so well has a lot to do with my little lecture back then. If you pour wisdom over someone's head, some of it has to seep in. He slowly recovered and asked how his brother died. I gathered my courage and said the words I'd run through my mind many times. Listen, Kawai, do you know who the commander at the Battle of Two Li Mound was? He said, Yes, Ge Ren. I said, Your brother died at Two Li Mound. But you shouldn't hate Ge Ren—your brother died for the Emperor, which to you Japanese means he lived a noble life and died a glorious death; you should be grateful to Ge Ren. Grateful? He yelled as he jumped to his feet. I grabbed him and said, Don't get so worked up—you should be grateful to him, and you should help him. Ge Ren's seriously ill, and I want to give you the chance to help him: you should kill him. That way, Ge Ren will become a hero of our People, and you can go back to Wuhan and tell your commander that you ended Ge Ren's life, so you'll get to be a hero of the Yamato people. As soon as I'd said all that, his face turned pale with fright, paler than his ass. What a useless guy! He started backing away in little crooked steps, until he was pressed against the wall. Then he squatted down and started weeping, his hands over his face. It seemed that my lecture hadn't been as immediately effective as I'd hoped. I said, You can say whatever you like, but what's the point of crying? No crying! He wiped his tears and asked in a ragged voice if I was going to have him killed next.

I burst out chuckling at how silly he was being, but he misunderstood. He thought this was murderous laughter, and I really was going to chop off his head. Fuck! What would I want with his head? But then, miss, he made a dash for the exit. My men were standing in the doorway, so he made it only a few steps before he knelt down and called me his seven gods of fortune again, begging for mercy in the name of his brother and mother. I kicked him in the ass and yelled out, Attention! Form up! At ease! To make sure he focused on his work, I tried to calm him down by telling him I would let him go, I truly would—and we Chinese have always been trustworthy.

And so it was set. That night, Ge Ren became a hero of the People. It must have been around Jingzhe [i.e., March 6], because thunder was rumbling nonstop, and people had already started planting water bamboo in White Cloud River. I wasn't there—it had been raining all day, and I couldn't be bothered to go outside. Of course, I wasn't just sitting around. I had set up a makeshift secure telegraph apparatus in the little Shang Village chapel, and I was sending a message to Dai Li. Not to brag, miss, but the stories that ran in every rag, from the *People's Daily* on the Mainland to *Scattered Scriptures* in Hong Kong, were all based on this telegram. In this secret message, I suggested that the Central Government should designate Ge Ren as a hero of the People and a role model for the masses. It was almost dawn by the time I finished. After all that work, I thought I should grab some shut-eye—but no sooner had I dropped off than I had a dream. What, a daydream? You could put it that way, because the sun had already risen. I dreamed of Ge Ren with a blissful smile on his face. What did that mean? Need you ask? He was thanking me for everything I'd done for him. I'm the sort of person who hates to hear a compliment, so I quickly said, No need, no need. I just did what I should have. Damn it! At that very moment, my aide woke me to say that Ah Qing and Dr. Bai had been fighting, and if he hadn't stumbled upon them and forced them apart, Dr. Bai would have been killed. I was furious—how dare Ah Qing be so disrespectful to an intellectual? I ordered my aide to investigate and find out exactly why they had come to blows, then get Ah Qing to write a self-criticism. I would deal with him later.

After my aide left, I couldn't get back to sleep. I thought they must have been fighting over horse shit again. Oh, I forgot to tell you: one day Ah Qing fell off his horse and cut his leg open, and Bai Shengtao treated the wound with horse dung. What, I already told that story? It's this brain of mine; it keeps turning recent history into ancient history. I imagine Ah Qing must have thought I was making fun of him, but one chooses the softest persimmons to bite into, so rather than lose his temper at me, he took it out on Dr. Bai instead. My aide came back a while later and said he'd gotten to the bottom of it: Ah Qing had struck the first blow. I asked if it was because of the horse shit. He said, No, it was Kawai. Bai Shengtao told Ah Qing that he'd seen Ge Ren and Kawai talking in the middle of the night. In the small hours, he noticed the light was still on in Ge Ren's room, and went in to tell him to get some sleep. But when he got there, he found Ge Ren lying in bed, the eye closest to the door staring toward it. His body was cold. Bai Shengtao told Ah Qing that Kawai must have been the killer, but Ah Qing wasn't having any of it. He lunged at Bai and grabbed his rifle butt. I said, Go fetch Ah Qing, kid. We need to have a meeting to discuss the new problems of this new situation. But my aide told me that Ah Qing had run away. Run away? Where to? He said he'd gone after Kawai. Fuck! Ah Qing really couldn't get anything right. This was no way to treat his commander. After all, I had deliberately let him [Kawai] get away. I said, The rain's going to come, sure as a bride needs a groom. Let him [Ah Qing] do what he likes, and go fetch Bai Shengtao.

Yes, my plan was to take Bai Shengtao back to Chongqing with me. I thought if the Commander [Dai Li] asked any questions, I would need him as a witness, to testify that every word in my secret telegram was the truth. Then I got worried that he'd say too much and let something slip that he shouldn't, so I let him go while we were passing through Hong Kong. Of course, I also did that for my own reasons. Yes, I was already preparing a way out. If Dai Li started to get suspicious, I would take discretion as the better part of valor, and if my escape route took me through Hong Kong, it might be useful to know someone there.

In any case, Dr. Bai was grateful for everything I did, right up to his death. You know, miss, I still remember what he looked like when they arrested him. Ha-ha, his nose was broken, and blood kept blowing from his nostrils, like a couple of geysers. I told my aide to wipe his face clean, then asked where he wanted to go. Luckily, he was quick enough to say that he wanted to come with me because the country needed people, and perhaps he could be of service. I won't lie to you, miss—if there'd been the slightest hesitation, I'd have put a bullet through him right away, and sent him up to heaven . . .

Epilogue

Mr. Fan's narration continues, but this is the end of the portion that pertains to Ge Ren. After tidying up the passage above, I managed to find duplicate copies of the newspapers Ding Kui had kept hold of, from Year 32: 1) June's *Scattered Scriptures*, 2) June's *People's Daily*, 3) June's *Shanghai Harbor Daily*, and 4) June's *Border War Report*. They all contained articles about Ge Ren's death, but about three months after the event [around March 6].

Out of these, the report in *Scattered Scriptures* was the most comprehensive. This issue also contained stories about prices going up and a burglar going down; the city walls being breached while Japanese soldiers breached women's defenses; a driver taking a mistress while a brothel offered 20 percent discounts; the Japanese entering Burma while Burma Road was closed down; a young kid going missing and a young miss going against her parents. The report about Ge Ren was sandwiched between advertisements for Morishita Jintan medicine and Sacred Skincare cheese facial cream:

> In recent days, my colleagues at the newspaper have been reminiscing about Mr. Ge Ren. He was from Qinggeng, a descendant of Ge Hong. His father, Ge Cundao, was a follower of Mr. Kang Youwei in his early days. Ge Ren studied in Japan, and took part in the May Fourth Movement after returning to China. He later spent time in the Soviet Union, examining the structure of society after the October Revolution. Thanks to his experiences there, he quickly rose through China's Bolshevist ranks after moving to the Bare Mountain Soviet zone. Mr. Ge Ren wrote about those years in his memoir *The Walking Shadow*, and it is a great pity that this manuscript has since disappeared without a trace. One year ago today, he departed to enter into battle against the Japanese, and sacrificed his life in the Battle of Two Li Mound. To this day, his body has not been found. Some time ago, when rumors began circulating that Ge Ren was still alive, there was not one journalist who did not rejoice. Recently we have discovered that these referred only to Mr. Ge Ren's spirit, which is indeed immortal. He is truly to be elevated above all others. And now he has placed the full circle of a period at the end of his life, a model for all literary figures.

That last sentence evidently caused some unease for the Central Government of the time. Perhaps they believed that "the full circle of a period" was a reference to Code Zero, a hint that Ge Ren hadn't actually died at Two Li Mound. As a result, the *People's Daily* carried this report the following day:

> Your reporter has just received information that the Central Government is considering a campaign to learn from the achievements of the anti-Japanese resistance heroes. Regardless of party or nationality, as long as they died in the war of resistance, they are worthy role models for our populace. Ten heroes have been selected, including Zhang Zizhong, who died in the Battle of Taierzhuang; the American Frank Schiel, who was killed in Hengyang; Ge Ren, who lost his life in the Battle of Two Li Mound; and the Canadian Norman Bethune, who passed away in Huangshikou Village.

A day after that, Zong Bu's *Shanghai Harbor Daily* reprinted this article without changing a single word, adding only this editorial note: "On May 10, 1943, the American journalist Pearl Buck pointed out in an article for *Life* magazine titled 'A Warning about China' that "oppressive elements in the government are becoming more oppressive," and "the Chinese people are asking that the American government somehow safeguard its loans to the Chinese people, to be used by the people and for the people, and not to establish any political group, either Right or Left." From Huang Jishi's *Half a Lifetime*, I learned that this editorial was written by Zong Bu himself. I should add here that I searched through all the newspapers of the period and after, but found no evidence that the Nationalist government ever organized such a campaign.

In the June 4 issue of *Border War Report*, I came upon an article by Huang Yan titled "The Year of Battle," which recalled how, on June 4 the year before, Wang Shiwei, the leader of the Trotskyites, was hauled before the Party Assembly for a struggle session. At the end of this essay, Ge Ren appears as a positive example:

> The last year has been a year of war, and a year of victory. One year ago today, we exposed the evil machinations of Wang Shiwei in a struggle session before the Assembly. And today, we have completely rooted out the Trotskyites who'd lain hidden within our revolutionary ranks. Our program of rectification is now complete. . . . Events have shown that Wang Shiwei knows no shame, and believes himself to be far superior than he is, when in reality, his only ability is deception and false arguments. A few days ago, I met Comrade Tian Han by the banks of the Yan River. He told me something that gave me some insight into Wang Shiwei. Comrade Tian Han said that before he was martyred, Comrade Ge Ren told him that Wang Shiwei's Russian was atrocious, yet he tried to pass himself off as an expert, ignoring the criticisms of his comrades. When someone said one thing to him, he would say ten things back. But now he has finally been forced to shut his mouth. . . . The more we miss our good Comrade Ge Ren, the more we loathe people like Wang Shiwei. . . . Comrades, we may have gained a great victory, but we must continue to be ever more vigilant and study hard. Only in this way can we clear all obstacles from the path of revolution and forge boldly ahead.

I also tracked down the June 6, Shōwa Year 18 [i.e., 1943], issue of *Asahi Shimbun*. Ge Ren's name appears there too, in an article titled "The Cherry Blossoms of My Homeland":

> June 1, International Children's Day, found your reporter in a Kyoto kindergarten, watching the children sing "The Cherry Blossoms of My Homeland" to the visiting imperial troops. The sight brought tears to my eyes. In Year 17 [i.e., 1942], imperial forces eliminated Eighth Route Army Commander Ge Ren at Two Li Mound, an important incident in our Greater

East Asian War. Eighth Route soldiers prefer guerrilla activity. But as we go to press, we have received reports that the Mount Gui Division of the Japanese Imperial Army has surrounded the "donkey detachment" of the Eighth Route Army, led by Shen Furu, at Shijiazhuang in Northern China. It is my hope that these children's voices will drift across the ocean and encourage the warriors of the Mount Gui Division to win another victory after Two Li Mound.

I took pains to find this article because its author was Kawai's sister, Noriko. We can see from this that Kawai didn't tell a single person about his trip to Bare Mountain. Bai Ling told me that after the ribbon-cutting ceremony at Hope Elementary School, in the car on the way to tour the construction site of the White Cloud River hydroelectric power station, she quietly asked Mr. Kawai why he hadn't spread the news that Ge Ren was killed at Bare Mountain. Kawai didn't say a word in response, and Mr. Fan jumped in to answer for him: "Do you need to ask, miss? He did it for the same reason as the rest of us—out of love." This might sound nice, but it's a little vague. To this day, I still have no idea exactly who Mr. Fan meant by "us," nor who the recipient of this "love" was.

END.